KINN PORSCHE

KINN PORSCHE

NOVEL
02

WRITTEN BY
Daemi

TRANSLATION BY
Frigga, Onyx, Linarii

INTERIOR
ILLUSTRATIONS BY
Avaritia

Seven Seas

Seven Seas Entertainment

Seven Seas press and purchase enquiries can be sent
to Marketing Manager Lauren Hill at press@gomanga.com.
Information regarding the distribution and purchase of digital editions is available
from Digital Manager CK Russell at digital@gomanga.com.

Follow Seven Seas Entertainment online at
sevenseasentertainment.com.

TRANSLATION: Frigga, Onyx, Linarii
ADAPTATION: Abigail Clark
COVER DESIGN: M. A. Lewife
INTERIOR DESIGN & LAYOUT: Clay Gardner
COPY EDITOR: Imogen Vale
PROOFREADER: Ami Leh, Adrian Mayall
EDITOR: Hardleigh Hewmann
PREPRESS TECHNICIAN: Salvador Chan Jr., April Malig, Jules Valera
MANAGING EDITOR: Alyssa Scavetta
EDITOR-IN-CHIEF: Julie Davis
PUBLISHER: Lianne Sentar
VICE PRESIDENT: Adam Arnold
PRESIDENT: Jason DeAngelis

ISBN: 979-8-89160-078-2
Printed in Canada
First Printing: December 2024
10 9 8 7 6 5 4 3 2 1

CONTENTS

16

Scars

PORSCHE

THE SOUND OF MOANING continued to echo through the hotel room. Panting hard from exertion, I felt like my body might burst open. Kinn kept relentlessly thrusting his cock into me; I lost count of how many times. I was unable to hold any thought in my head, my brain short-circuiting. My gut told me I should resist Kinn—I wouldn't be able to stand the pain or the embarrassment tomorrow. Still, my body betrayed me by responding eagerly to everything Kinn did.

"Oh, fuck," Kinn swore, "why do you keep clenching so hard around me?"

I shook my head frantically, incredibly embarrassed by Kinn's filthy mouth. I was on my back as Kinn hooked his arms under my knees to lift my ass off the mattress, slowly pushing his dick back into me. It didn't hurt as much as the first time, but I was sore and numb.

"Ah, Kinn... It hurts..." How many times had I told Kinn that it was painful? It didn't seem to do anything to stop him. Kinn kept going until he was buried inside me completely. Then, he bent down to kiss me passionately. I kissed him back, my tongue feverishly swirling and probing against his. Kinn's warm breath and his unique scent seemed to help me relax and forget about the pain for a moment.

We kept groaning and grunting until Kinn started to move his hips, slowly pulling out of me and pushing back inside. I hated to admit it, but being fucked by him felt way too good. Sex with Kinn was unlike anything I had ever experienced, even though it was agonizing.

Bit by bit, I started to come to my senses, and I became truly aware of what we were doing. I felt disgusted with myself for having sex with a guy, especially when I was the one allowing Kinn to do disgraceful things to me again and again. I should have suppressed my urges and prevented things from escalating to this point.

"E-easy... I'm sore." My voice stuttered as I told Kinn to slow down, but he didn't hold back. His rough thrusts made my body sway violently with each motion, my back rubbing against the sheets. His lips barely left my body, biting and nibbling on my skin.

Kinn seemed able to tirelessly fuck all night. Maybe he'd been holding himself back for too long—he was acting very sexually frustrated. I flinched, reaching back to hold onto the headboard to stop my head from bashing into it. My other hand grabbed Kinn's shoulder, digging my fingernails into his skin every time he hit my prostate. Instead of stopping, Kinn kept hitting it harder and faster.

I tried to stop myself from making embarrassing noises, but it was getting more and more difficult to stay quiet. Kinn turned to lick at my arm, the one holding his shoulder, like he was fascinated by my tattoo.

"N-not so hard. I'm gonna hit my head," I told him. My eyes squeezed shut as my body shivered from the pleasure coursing through me.

Kinn chuckled slightly before slowing down. He lifted me off the bed while still buried deep inside me. I didn't have any strength left to resist him, so I let him flip me around until I ended up strad-dling him. Kinn stretched out his legs, his hands going to my hips to support me.

I squinted at Kinn. His eyes were glazed over with lust as he stared back. He smiled slightly before burying his face in my bruise-covered neck, squeezing my ass so hard that it hurt.

He started urging me to move. The friction startled me, and I quickly braced my arms around his neck to steady myself.

"Mmm," Kinn moaned, "move..."

He lifted me up and down on his dick. I rested my forehead on his shoulder and bit him hard to alleviate some of the pain.

"*Fuck*, that feels good," I whined, not knowing when I'd started to ride Kinn myself. His hands moved from my ass to gently cradle my back. I arched up at the sensation, biting my lips hard and enjoying being able to control the pace.

Kinn let out a long moan. "Shit...you're so tight. It's almost pain-ful for me, too..."

I was pissed at him, but my body seemed to like it, quickening the pace against my will.

"Yeah, faster...just like that," Kinn ordered, and my body eagerly complied. I wasn't used to this feeling—like my world was full of bliss. My mind shattered in ecstasy every time Kinn hit my prostate. It felt better than any sex I'd ever had.

"Are you sure it's your first time? You keep clenching me," Kinn chuckled, making me pound my fist hard on his back. He retaliated by bending down to bite at my chest with equal force.

"Damn it! You're gonna make me come again," Kinn hissed, grip-ping my waist more tightly before snapping his hips up in a forceful thrust.

"Ah, don't bite me," I whined, "I can't hold back..."

I grasped his neck more firmly. As Kinn quickened his pace, he alternated between biting my nipples and grazing them with his teeth. I swore at him under my breath. This bastard just kept tormenting me. I did not know what I should yell at him for: ruthlessly pounding into me, or biting me like a damn dog.

"Shit, I'm gonna..." Kinn let out a low groan before laying me flat on my back again. I didn't have a chance to curse at him as he frantically drove his hips into mine. My body moved violently with the strength of his thrusts, constantly making my head hit the headboard until waves of dizziness returned. *Bastard!*

My stomach tensed as I got closer to the edge. Kinn kept roughly fucking me—it was too much to bear. My mind went blank as I came, my whole body shaking with the force of my orgasm. Kinn snapped his hips a few more times until he spilled inside me, fucking me through it before he finally pulled out.

I felt my eyelids grow heavy, and I was unable to maintain consciousness. The pain started to overwhelm me. I cursed at myself over and over for allowing this to happen.

I began to drift asleep from exhaustion. I didn't know how ashamed of myself I would be when tomorrow came, but right now, I was too fatigued and entirely unprepared to face anything.

"Shit... That was really something. I guess it's a good thing I'm out of condoms. I wouldn't let you sleep otherwise."

I heard Kinn mutter something before I felt his warm breath on my forehead. I turned away and quickly pulled the blanket over myself so I could curl up in peace.

I desperately hoped that this night was just a bad dream. I couldn't wait to wake up and forget about everything...

⚜

[NOON]

"Have you brought the car around, Pete? Mm-hm...he's fine. Yes, it's good that Father isn't mad. Yes, I want you to keep looking into this."

A faint conversation stirred me from my slumber. When I tried to stretch my body, pain shot through me from head to toe. My face scrunched up as my headache intensified. Before I could recall what happened last night, my eyes met a familiar face.

I stared wide-eyed as the memory of last night rushed back, like someone had hit a replay button. I couldn't believe it. I was in shock, unable to accept what had happened.

"Why are you looking at me like that? Want another round?" Kinn teased me before getting off the bed to smoke on the balcony. He was dressed only in the white bathrobe provided by the hotel. I could see glimpses of bruises here and there on his skin, a stark reminder of what we had done. My body was more bruised than his.

"That's my cigarette," I said hoarsely as I saw Kinn take a pack of my cigarettes from my pants pocket without asking. I pushed myself up so I could sit against the headboard.

"Just lend me a couple. I didn't bring mine," Kinn replied, gazing out of the room.

This was the first time I'd seen Kinn smoke. My eyes lingered on him as he took a drag, a strange feeling stirring inside of me. I quickly looked away.

A long sigh escaped me as I finally took in the state of my body. I felt both angry and ashamed, unsure whether to blame Kinn for doing this to me or myself for allowing him to do it. Kinn didn't waste his opportunity to abuse me. However, the person I should be most furious with was the one who drugged me in the first place. *Don't let me know who you are, asshole! I'll kill you and your entire family!*

"What do you remember?" Kinn asked, matter of fact.

My gaze shifted downward nervously, unsure of what he meant. If he was referring to what happened last night between him and me, then yes—I remembered all the gruesome details.

"I mean, do you remember who drugged you?" Kinn quickly clarified when he noticed me go quiet and tightly grip the bedsheet.

"No..." I rasped, feeling absolutely parched.

Kinn went to grab a bottle of water from the fridge, poured it into a glass, and handed it to me.

I accepted the glass of water from him and quickly took a sip without looking at him. It reminded me of the incident last night.

"Pfft! I thought you would go on a full rampage after you woke up," Kinn said with a smile.

I didn't reply. I still didn't know how I should feel about us. Kinn was not really in the wrong for doing that to me—I let him do it.

"Can you tell me what happened? Anything at all?" Kinn asked, sitting down next to me on the bed. I tried to shift away from him, even though my entire body ached.

I recounted as much as I could remember. "Someone told the waiter to bring me two glasses of whiskey. I drank them, went to the bathroom, and the last thing I remembered was someone trying to...rape me...but I-I don't know."

The assailant had been more brutal than Kinn. He kept hurting me, using brute force to make me do things against my will. Although my body had responded to his touch, I only felt disgusted and horrified. It wasn't the same when Kinn was touching me.

"What did he look like?" Kinn asked in a serious tone.

I shook my head at him. Suddenly, my headache returned, more intense this time. I kneaded my temples.

"Are you all right?" Kinn asked softly. He lifted his hand as if to touch me, but I quickly brushed him off and tried to get off the bed from the other side.

Thunk!

"Porsche!"

As soon as I tried to stand up and my feet touched the cold tile, I dropped to the floor. My legs shook uncontrollably; I didn't have the strength to get up. The impact also made me feel a stinging pain in my backside.

Kinn tried to assist me. I swatted his hands away.

"Don't…"

"Why are you bleeding so much?" Kinn suddenly sounded very concerned as he looked down at where I had been sitting on the bed. My gaze followed his.

I bit my lip hard at the horrendous sight: the once-white bedsheets were now covered in trails of blood. I quickly looked at the back of my bathrobe to find it equally bloodied.

"You didn't bleed much last night—why is there so much blood now?" Kinn asked.

I glared at him before attempting to get up from the floor again. Kinn hurried to help, but I pushed him away.

"So tough," Kinn muttered in amusement, placing his hands on his hips as he watched me hold on to various items in the room, struggling to get to the bathroom.

I felt blood ooze out of me, the metallic smell intensifying with every step I took. I finally reached the bathroom as Kinn followed not far behind. I immediately shut the door in his face and locked it behind me.

A wave of nausea overwhelmed me, almost making me lose my balance. I'd never thought my body could feel this weak. As I sank down to the floor, tugging my hair in frustration, something in the trashcan caught my eye.

There were several condoms in the trash, obviously used and covered with blood. I didn't want to count how many were in there; I knew we didn't stop after one round. I remembered eagerly riding Kinn during our last round, too. The thought of what happened disturbed me, and I loathed Kinn even more. However, I hated myself the most. I hated myself for giving in to my desire, for allowing Kinn to do whatever he pleased, and for always ending up in shitty situations.

Why was this my life? Both my parents were dead. I had to struggle to provide for both my younger brother and myself. Now, I'd been sexually assaulted... If there was nothing good in my life, what was the point of living? How long should I endure these hardships when fate was never on my side?!

There was a knock on the bathroom door. "Hey...don't stay in there for too long. I'm going to take you to a doctor," Kinn said. I quickly covered my ears, not wanting to hear his voice right now. It made me even more depressed. I abhorred my body so much—I wished I could cut myself open, stab myself to death. There were only two people to blame: me and the bastard who dared to drug me.

I finally forced myself to peel off the bathrobe, revealing my bruised body. I turned on the water and stepped into the shower, hoping it could wash away all these disgusting feelings. I nearly rubbed my skin raw, trying to scrub away the bruises—blatant reminders of what had happened.

I reached between my ass cheeks, and a painful burning sensation shot through me as soon as my finger touched my hole. I quickly braced myself against the wall before my knees could give out on me again. Taking a deep breath, I washed off the gunk between my legs.

I didn't know what to do next. I'd never had sex with a guy until last night. I had never felt attracted to men at all, not even once. My dignity had been completely stripped away. I wondered if I could ever take a dominant role in bed again when the vivid memory of what happened last night lingered in my mind.

"Porsche, it's been a long time. Are you all right in there?" Kinn asked just as I opened the door, still in the same bathrobe. I averted my eyes.

"Where are my clothes?" I demanded.

"Are you okay? I'm taking you to a doctor," Kinn said before handing me a neatly folded pile of clothes. I quickly closed the bathroom door and took a deep breath. What should I do? I wanted to run away. However, I was forced to confront the problem I'd created. *I should just bite the bullet, right?*

I walked down the stairs with Kinn, even though it was the most challenging walk of my life. I could barely move my lower body, but I had to force myself to keep on walking. Kinn attempted to help hold me up several times, but I brushed his hands away.

Kinn told me to wait for him in the lobby. I had already told him that I'd head back on my own; I did not want to go to the hospital. Despite this, Kinn dragged me to wait in the lobby with him standing close by. I wanted to run away, but my body would not cooperate.

"I'm so sorry," Kinn said as he paid a fine to the hotel concierge. It must have been for all the blood on the bed. The employee took the credit card and smiled at me. I scowled and looked away.

Every time I tried to move away from Kinn, he would reach out and grab my arm. *Ugh!* If only I had the strength, I swore I'd confront the bastards who put me in this situation, starting with Kinn!

Kinn successfully dragged me into his fancy sedan. I resisted a little bit, telling him that I would go home by myself, but he pushed me into the passenger seat and closed the door.

"I'm fine," I said, staring out the window as Kinn slowly drove.

"Damn it, you don't look fine at all. Don't be so stubborn. You were such a good boy last night," Kinn said, laughing, but I didn't find it funny at all. I did not want to endure the ridicule, the loss of dignity.

"Stop! I'm getting out!" I barked at him.

"I was just kidding," Kinn teased, his eyes still on the road. I was sick and tired of his bullshit. The more I looked at him, the more disgusted with myself I became.

I unlocked the door on my side, ready to get out of the car while it was still moving.

"Porsche, what the hell are you doing?!" Kinn slammed on the brakes so suddenly that the car lurched forward. We jerked forward and Kinn grabbed my arm.

"Let me go! I don't want to go with you!" I yelled, pushing his hand away. I couldn't take it anymore, so I'd made a rash and stupid decision to jump out with the car still in motion. Before I could, Kinn grasped my arm tightly and closed the car door on my side.

Screech! With my unpredictable actions making us stop in the middle of the road, traffic piled up behind us. Kinn let out a small grunt before quickly maneuvering the car out of the jam.

"Are you crazy?" Kinn growled. "Do you *want* to die?!"

I remained silent and sat still, my eyes still looking out the window.

"I know it's hard to accept, but it happened. What do you want me to do?" Kinn sighed, his gaze shifting forward.

"Why didn't you *stop*?" I blurted out without thinking, fully aware of how tense the situation was.

"I was just trying to help you," Kinn said with a small smile. I turned to glare daggers at him before turning my gaze back outside the car window.

Eventually, we arrived at the hospital. Ever since I got in the car, I'd been shivering—like I was coming down with a fever. My head periodically throbbed. Kinn helped me open the car door and took me to the examination room in a wheelchair. I sighed. I was in an absolutely terrible state.

Kinn put his hand on my forehead. "You're running a fever, too..."

I quickly shook him off and shot him an annoyed glance. I kept telling him to leave me alone, but he wouldn't listen; I didn't have the energy to yell at him.

"Mr. Pachara? Examination room two, please."

A male nurse pushed my wheelchair into the exam room when my name was called. Kinn followed along behind me. I had no idea what I was going to tell the doctor.

"You can just leave," I told him.

Kinn ignored me, walking to sit in front of the doctor and politely greeting him with a wai gesture.

It seemed like the doctor knew him. As soon as they saw each other, they exchanged pleasantries. So, the doctor was an acquaintance of Kinn's? I wanted the ground to open up and swallow me whole.

"What's the matter, Kinn? Who do we have here?"

"He is a friend. How are you, Uncle? Are you busy?"

"Of course I'm busy. People are getting sick more and more every day."

The doctor—who was also Kinn's uncle, apparently—examined me and exchanged glances with Kinn. Then, he instructed the male nurse to take me into the inner room.

"Hmm... Pachara, you appear to have a fever. Go into that room. Lie down and wait."

"Don't follow," I quickly told Kinn, and he smiled in acknowledgment.

"What brings you here?" the middle-aged doctor asked, smiling at me. At this point, I was lying on the exam table, absolutely mortified.

"Uh... I... Wh-when I woke up this morning, I was bleeding from..." I stammered, unable to speak clearly. I wanted to ask the doctor if there was an injection that could just put me out of my misery. I just wanted to fucking die.

"I see... Take off your pants, then."

"Huh?!" I jerked my head up in shock. The doctor just chuckled and smiled gently. He then instructed the male nurse to pull down my pants and lift my legs. Damn it! If I died now, how could I muster the courage to face my parents in the afterlife?

This was the most embarrassed I'd ever been. When the doctor bent down between my legs, I couldn't bear to watch; I felt the urge to cover my face and bite my lip to suppress the insurmountable shame. *Damn you, Kinn!* I wanted to grab a scalpel and cut his dick off. *How dare you make me feel this embarrassed?!* I wanted to disappear!

"Whoa!" the doctor exclaimed, managing to crush my spirit for a moment. Was it that bad?

The doctor sighed. "Oh, Kinn..." he muttered to himself before instructing the nurse to pull my pants back up.

"I'll prescribe medication for you. In the meantime, take care of yourself. Maintain good hygiene and take your medication on time," the doctor said. Then, both the doctor and the nurse led me back to the examination room, where Kinn sat smiling.

"How is he, Uncle?" Kinn asked.

"Kinn... You need to be gentle next time," the doctor replied with a sigh. "The tissues there are delicate."

My face went rigid. I didn't know who I wanted to punch first: the doctor or Kinn. The doctor shook his head slightly while Kinn just sat there cheerfully smiling. If I wasn't so weak right now, I would have lifted my wheelchair and smashed him with it.

"I'm giving you antibiotics, anti-inflammatory medication, an electrolyte solution, and something to reduce the fever," the doctor told me. "The bleeding should stop soon. Get some rest and drink plenty of fluids."

I sighed deeply. I don't think I could ever accept what had happened last night.

I took the medicine. Kinn paid for all my medical expenses, then grabbed me and put me in his car again to take me home.

Inside the car, I felt both feverish and cold. My headache grew more intense, and my breathing became so hot that it irritated my nose. I leaned back in the seat and closed my eyes as Kinn started driving.

I was startled when Kinn suddenly spoke: "Don't be so quiet." He briefly shifted his gaze away from the road to look at me. "I'm not used to this. Usually, you'd have yelled at me by now... Being silent is just not like you."

I was indeed not my usual self. I didn't know how to cope with what I was going through. I wanted to blame myself—I wanted to *kill* myself. I felt such a potent mix of hatred and fury that I did not dare to express my feelings outwardly.

"You can't go back and change the past, Porsche. All you can do is accept it," Kinn said, but I disagreed. I couldn't bring myself to accept the major mistakes of my life. *You're not me, so of course you can say that, you bastard!*

"Do *you* want to get fucked next time?!" I yelled at him without thinking.

"So...there's going to be a next time?" Kinn chuckled, but I didn't find it amusing at all.

"No! There will be no next time!" *I'll fight you to the death before that happens, you son of a bitch!* I would not allow Kinn and his smug face to get away with this.

I shifted in the seat, turning my back to Kinn. My gaze wandered outside the window until I drifted off to sleep.

"This is your place," Kinn said, waking me up.

My heavy eyelids struggled to open. I saw Kinn opening the car door on my side and leaning in close. His hand held the bag of medicine the doctor had prescribed me. I quickly pushed him out of the way; he smiled in response.

"Are you okay?" he asked, reaching out to help me, but I stared him down.

"You can go now," I said bluntly, then snatched the bag of medication from his hand.

"Do you want me to order something for you to eat?"

I forced myself to walk into the house as quickly as possible, slamming the door in Kinn's face with a loud bang before he could say anything more.

I struggled up the stairs to my bedroom, feeling a sharp, stinging pain in my ass. Every time the pain coursed through my body, I felt miserable and ashamed...

Once I was in my bedroom, I quickly searched for a bottle of water. I took the medicine the doctor prescribed, not caring to check if I needed to take it with food or not. Then I collapsed on my bed. The image of Kinn's face still lingered in my mind, hurting me even more.

If the situation was different and Kinn had forced himself on me, I would have killed him myself. I would've made sure of it. However, putting the blame solely on Kinn wasn't fair. I vividly remembered everything he said—I was the one who instigated everything.

I was so ashamed of myself for begging Kinn like that. I hated myself to the point of madness. If I had to yell at or slap anyone, it would have to be myself. I'd submitted to him, cried out for his touch...

But even so, I still hated Kinn. If I'd hated him before, now I abhorred him even more. I didn't want to look at him, stand close to him, or have anything to do with him. I didn't even want to *think* about him. I shook my head a little to chase away the memories, but the more I tried to forget, the more I remembered. Both his body and his gaze from last night were burned into my mind.

"Hia, are you okay?" a familiar voice woke me up.

Even in the dream I'd just woken from, Kinn's face still haunted me. In that dream, I'd punched and kicked him without any mercy, and I'd started searching for a gun to shoot him with.

"Ugh," I groaned. "You're back?" I grabbed my phone where it was plugged into the wall and looked at the time. It was five in the evening. I didn't even know when I fell asleep.

"Hia, what did you do? Why are you covered in...?" Chay eyed me in suspicion before I pulled the blanket up over my body to hide the marks.

"I had a little problem, but I'm okay," I told my younger brother in a hoarse voice. I grimaced in pain when I swallowed.

Chay tapped my forehead. "You're running a fever... I'll heat up some porridge for you," he said, then walked downstairs.

I took a deep breath, looked at the closed door, and then glanced down at my body once again. *Why, why, why? Why did I have to go through this?* What would Chay do if he knew? Would he be able to accept me after what I had been through?

After sleeping for a while, my urge to know more about the person who brought me into this terrible situation intensified. Who was behind all this? Why did he drug me? What did he want from me? What was his motive? I had to investigate and find out who was behind this. I swore that I would not let him go unpunished.

"Here you go. Finish your food first, then take some medicine," Chay said, placing a tray of porridge beside the bed. "Oh, you have medicine already?" He went to grab the bag of medicine. "It's from that expensive hospital, too. Good! You'll recover quickly," he said, flashing me a smile. He handed me the bowl of rice porridge.

"Where did you get it? That was quick," I said before propping myself up against the headboard and taking the bowl of steaming porridge. Its fragrant aroma spread throughout the room.

"I didn't. I saw it hanging on the doorknob in front of the house. I thought you ordered it and forgot, so I heated it up," Chay replied. I paused for a moment and glanced at him.

"It was just hanging there?" I asked.

"Yeah, it was in front of the house. If you didn't order it, who did?" he said, looking puzzled. I put down my spoon and pushed the bowl toward him.

"Go buy a new one. I don't know whose it is," I said. I figured Kinn had put it there. Besides him, no one else knew that I was sick at home.

"Hey, I'm too lazy to walk to the street where the food stalls are. Just eat it. If it's at our house, it must be ours," Chay said, stirring the bowl of porridge. He scooped up a spoonful and blew on it slightly before holding it up to my lips.

"No, I don't want it. If you're too lazy to go out, then go to the kitchen and make me some yourself," I said. I didn't want to take anything from Kinn. I hated him. I didn't want to be involved with him in any way.

"Are you crazy?" Chay laughed. "You know we've never cooked for ourselves. Every time we cook, it's a disaster. We're lucky we know how to make instant noodles."

"Then make instant noodles for me," I said, pushing his hand away from my mouth.

"You're being so stubborn. Just eat what we have. Nom, nom!"

"Ugggghhh!"

Chay pushed the spoon into my mouth. It took significant effort to chew and swallow it down. My taste buds no longer worked; all I could sense was warmth and bitterness sliding down my throat.

"Hurry up! Open your mouth," Chay ordered. I opened my mouth slightly and forced myself to chew and swallow another spoonful. Before he could scoop up more, I raised my hand and signaled him to stop.

"Enough! I'm full," I said, picking up a glass of water to drink.

"You've only had two bites! Just one more! Down the hatch!" Chay shoved a mouthful of rice and a large shrimp into my mouth. I had to chew for a long time before I could swallow it all down.

"Enough! Do you want me to puke in your face?!" I snapped. Chay finally put down the bowl and handed me my medication.

"Anti-inflammatory, antibiotics, electrolytes..." He read the label on the side of the packet. His eyebrows furrowed. "What's wrong with you, hia? Why are you taking all of this?" he asked, holding up the various containers of medicine. I bit my lip slightly before I answered him.

"I got beaten up by a whole gang of guys. I stepped on someone's foot in the bar and it set them off. Just hand those over," I said, grabbing the medications from his hand. I took them out from their packets one by one, swallowing them with a sip of water.

"Ugh, you could have died, hia... Well, I'll go make you some of that electrolyte drink."

I knew Chay wouldn't believe my lie, but it seemed like he was going to let it go. That was a relief. Soon, Chay returned with a glass of the electrolyte solution and placed it next to my bed.

"Thanks," I said before taking a sip.

"I don't know what you went through, but if you're okay with making me worry myself sick over you, then go ahead and continue with your job," he said before sullenly walking out of the room.

I took a long, deep breath. I doubted I could figure out how to tell Chay about what happened to me.

Rrrring!

I answered the phone when I saw it was Tem. "Hello?"

"Why weren't you in class?" Tem asked. "I texted and called you a bunch of times but you never answered."

"I'm sick... I might be out this whole week. Please write down what assignments we have," I replied with a hoarse voice.

"Oh... Is it serious?" Tem asked, sounding concerned.

"No, no. I'm good..." I answered before I remembered something. "Tem, could you tell P'Beam to find someone to replace me? I don't think I can be in the competition."

In my current state, I would lose if I entered the competition next week. I was not at all prepared to be kicked or punched right now.

"Are you that sick? Okay, I'll talk to P'Beam. Where are you, by the way?"

"Home. I'm gonna get some rest now."

"Okay. Rest up. Don't worry, I'll take care of it," Tem said before hanging up.

I tossed the phone next to my pillow and slowly lay back down. When I closed my eyes, all I could see was Kinn. Even when I told myself to think of something else, I kept flashing back to the image of his face. I tried to open my eyes, but the medicine was making me drowsy; I soon fell back asleep.

[MORNING]

Rrrrrring!

I slowly woke up and fished for my phone under the pillow. Who was calling me this early in the morning? I looked at the unsaved phone number, and my eyes widened in shock when I recognized whose it was... Kinn's!

I quickly rejected the call and turned my phone off. I was shocked to see his number because I'd dreamed of Kinn again last night. In my dream, I was pointing a gun at his head, ready to fire. However, my dream self suddenly broke into tears. I wanted to go back to sleep so I could blow his head to pieces—that would be incredibly satisfying.

I saw a bowl of porridge and my medicine on a tray sitting atop the bedside table. Chay must have prepared it before he went to school today.

I got out of bed, feeling better than yesterday. I could still feel a painful burning in my rear, and I was a little chilly, but it wasn't as severe as before.

I grabbed a cigarette and headed toward the balcony. Lighting it up, I took a drag and blew out the smoke to vent my anger. My body felt better than yesterday, but my heart felt even worse.

I leaned onto the banister, looking at the tattoo on my upper arm. I remembered Kinn's particular fascination with this part of me. The thought of him touching me made me squeeze the banister in agony. What would I do when I saw him in person? He haunted me, even in my dreams. How could I stand following him around at work? How could I bear having those images appear in my head over and over again? Would I hate myself even more?

My whole day revolved around having a few bites to eat, taking my medicine, and falling asleep. Around dusk, I walked up to the rooftop. Chay and I kept it locked because there were no guardrails, only an old satellite receiver and overgrown moss. I sat down and kept lighting one cigarette after another, feeling the cold air on my face.

I absentmindedly looked up at the sky, missing my mom and dad. If they were still here, my life wouldn't have turned out like this, right? I wouldn't be in disgrace. I wouldn't hate myself. My heart sank as I reflected on the chaos of these past few days. How could I find a way out of this? How could I face anyone?

I felt vulnerable in a way I never had before. I was tired, weak, and outright drained. The pain in my body reminded me every second of what had happened, and the pain in my heart made me feel like I had nothing left to live for. I grew up without anyone to lean on. I felt alone. I had always been the one to lift myself up and move forward, but today, I couldn't heal the pain in my heart. I felt discouraged and hopeless. I didn't know where to turn.

I looked down from the roof, my heart quivering. Would I be able to live with this hideous body? It was black and blue, covered with marks that would forever be drilled into my mind. My heart wanted someone to protect and support me—could it be Mom and Dad? *Please be here with me. I'm so tired.* All the sorrows I'd been through made it more absurd. I was a man with nothing, not even my dignity. Did I not belong in this world...?

A part of me wanted to see my mom and dad right this instant. I wanted to be in their arms. But before I could do anything, someone pulled me out of the abyss of dangerous thoughts and brought me to my senses.

"What the hell are you doing?!" Chay shouted, wrapping his arms around my waist and pulling me away from the building's edge.

It was dreadful, going down into the abyss of my mind...

"Chay..." I lifted my head to see my little brother sitting down and panting next to me. He frowned in anger and softly pushed my chest.

"What the hell were you doing? Did you even stop to think about me?" he protested, hitting my shoulder. It ached.

"Nothing, I was just smoking," I said, pushing down my dark thoughts.

"Why the hell are you smoking up here? What if you fell?" my brother implored me.

I stared at Chay. I forgot who I should be living for. I had to stay alive for him! Why was I thinking about dying? I pulled him close and hugged him, sighing in relief. The only person who pulled me up from the depths of despair was him. Though I had nothing left, he was the one person I had to take care of for the rest of my life.

"Sorry," I whispered.

"Go quit your job. I don't know if it's because of your job or not, but I can't stand it anymore. You're never happy. Every time you're home, you're either injured or you're sad. Go quit—right now!" Chay lightly smacked my back. His voice was sharp, like he

was giving me an ultimatum. I didn't reply, but I kept hugging him for a while, reminding myself that I should always keep him at the forefront of my mind.

⌒◦⌒

The next day, Chay treated me the same as always, but he locked the door to the rooftop and kept all the keys to himself. No matter how much I told him I was not going to kill myself, he said it was a matter of safety. He was afraid I might do something impulsive because I was so stressed out. He was right. So, I tried to play games and watch TV to get all those images out of my head.

In the evening, Tem and Jom came to visit. They noticed how bruised I was, even though I was wearing a long-sleeved shirt and pants.

"Did you get in a fight with a dog?"

"There was a minor altercation. I'm fine," I murmured.

"Do you still have a fever?" Jom asked, putting the back of his hand on my forehead.

I lightly shook my head. "I'm okay."

"Damn! You've been getting into trouble recently. Did you take your medication?" Tem asked. I nodded.

"The bandages on your neck seem to get bigger every time I see you. I wonder where that starving vampire is," Jom said, squinting his eyes at me. I shifted in my seat, pretending to pay attention to the TV.

"Huh? Very well, keep your secrets. But don't come crying to me for help." Tem crossed his arms.

"I've never cried to you!" I huffed, flipping through the channels and stopping at my favorite cartoon.

"Pfft! Whatever you say. And since you've gotten better, we came to get you to go out for a drink with us. There's a new place with good music and gorgeous chicks. Let's flush out your fever," Jom said leisurely. I could tell Jom didn't really care about my health; he just wanted someone to drink with. *Jackass!*

"Would that be all right? Porsche looks pretty tired," Tem commented.

"Maannnn, he just needs a drink to wash the fever out! With all the lights and music, I guarantee you'll feel better in no time!" Jom said.

I hesitated for a second. Well, it sounded like it might be a good idea. Keeping myself busy would help take my mind off of those thoughts. Although I couldn't really walk properly yet and my body still ached, if I succumbed to my sorrow, I could end up drowning in it. It would be better if I went outside and interacted with the world.

"Okay, let's go."

I took a shower and changed, remembering to put on something with long sleeves. I decided to wear a turtleneck just to avoid any prying questions, and it should fit with the vibe of the place. Tem and Jom told me that it was "luxury on a budget." Both of them looked perplexed when they saw me walk downstairs, though.

"Aren't you hot wearing that shit?"

I said nothing and followed them to the car. We drove straight into the city. This new club was not that far from our university. It looked fancy from the outside, like a high-class bar, but there was live music, and good deals on booze were listed on the wall.

"This place is new, so I needed you to come check it out," Jom said, and turned to order a drink from a waitress. A bunch of chicks followed Tem and me with their eyes. This place was excellent, just as Jom had said.

"Twelve o'clock. You have a deal," Jom said and winked, signaling me to look at a scantily clothed chick. I smiled, and she smiled back.

"Cheers to Porsche, who has recovered," Tem chuckled and lifted his glass in the air. We toasted each other and downed our drinks in one go.

We chatted as we drank until the place started to get crowded, groups of people flocking together. It was a good thing we'd come early enough to get a table to ourselves.

I checked how popular I was by smiling and lifting my glass for a toast at random people. Finally, the same girl who had eyed me when I first walked into this place came and led me by my hand to the dance floor. I wasn't a good dancer and I still couldn't really walk right, so I just placed my hands on her hips and swayed with her.

Not long after, she led me to the bathroom and locked the door. I hesitated—would she freak out if she saw all the marks on my body? But I had no more time to think, as she pulled my neck down and fiercely kissed me. I kissed her back, sliding my tongue into her mouth. I couldn't keep my hands to myself, caressing the curve of her hips until I could reach inside her dress.

Suddenly, an image of Kinn fucking me flashed in my head. I jerked away a little, and she looked up at me in confusion.

"It's nothing," I said, starting over. I closed my eyes and tilted my head to receive her kiss. This time, I quickly moved my hands to her breasts. As I grabbed them, an image surfaced in my mind of me stroking Kinn's body. My eyes snapped open, but I didn't push her supple body away. I let her suck and kiss my lips as much as she wanted.

Maybe if I had sex with her tonight, I could erase some of these thoughts of Kinn. So I nuzzled her neck, trying to turn her on.

"Mmm," she moaned, unhooking my pants before shoving her petite hand inside. I fondled her breast with one hand while the other started to slide under her dress.

"Huh? You don't wanna do it?" she exclaimed. She broke the kiss and pulled my flaccid dick out of my jeans. I went a little pale— I wasn't turned on at all.

"Umm...let's try again," I told her, and I leaned down to kiss her lips. This time, I reached down to stroke myself at the same time. *That'll get it up!*

I rubbed my finger around the tip until I started to feel some dampness—and then I was shoved hard.

"Let's stop it right here... Goodbye," she huffed, looking between my legs in disappointment.

I sighed heavily and watched as she left, feeling pathetic that I couldn't get hard. I locked the stall door and sat down on the toilet, trying to think of a reason why my dick didn't work. That woman was *exactly* my type. How could it be possible that I didn't feel anything when she touched me there?

Suddenly, images of Kinn reappeared—the touching, the kissing, and when we...

A rush of pleasure raced through me. It was a satisfying feeling that I'd never felt before. I let my mind wander until...

"Shit!" I exclaimed when I saw that my dick—which still hung outside my unzipped pants—was hard.

"Damn it!" I pressed my lips together tightly and controlled my breath, trying to will away my erection. What the hell?! Hooking up with a chick couldn't get me hard, but Kinn could? That bastard!

I finally managed to get my dick soft again by thinking about horror movies. I zipped my pants back up, unlocked the door, and left the stall. As I looked toward the sink, my entire body froze. The man in my thoughts had come to life...

"Kinn..." I whispered. He was washing his hands, but he stared back at me through the reflection in the mirror. As our eyes met, he slowly cracked a smile.

SPECIAL: PORCHAY

"**G**O QUIT YOUR JOB. I don't know if it's because of your job or not, but I can't stand it anymore. You're never happy. Every time you're home, you're either injured or you're sad. Go quit—right now!"

I'd spoken those words from the heart. Porsche was never happy. It was really bad the most recent time he came home. My brother was never afraid of anything, always confident in himself, and was always the coolest one of us two—however, the Porsche I knew seemed to have disappeared the day he started working at that damned house...

"Stop here, please." I told the cab driver to stop in front of a massive, impressive-looking door. *Wow! Amazing!* I thought. But then again, my brother worked for the mafia, right? I mean, if they had to hire bodyguards, it made sense that their house would be really over the top.

I'd seen a guy named Kinn barge into my house, and he looked powerful. My brother probably worked under a lot of stress. He really wasn't acting like himself anymore...

I paid the taxi driver, got out of the car, and glanced at the opulent door. I took a deep breath. I could not stand to see my brother like this anymore. Whatever happened—if I got out of here alive or not—I would not be afraid. For the sake of my brother, I feared nothing, not even the mafia. I was just going to talk to them and make them understand...

Because I was not going to lose my brother.

"Listen! We are all we have. What will I do if something happens to you?"

I wasn't going to just sit there and wait for that day to come!

I rang the doorbell furiously, standing with my foot tapping and my arms crossed. It was a very cool pose, if I do say so myself. *Hmph!* Just because these guys were the mafia, it didn't mean they had all the power around here. I could even call the police to come arrest them. It was taking a while for someone to come and open the door, so I kept indignantly ringing the bell.

If you asked me how I knew the way here, well, it was because I'd been secretly following my brother. At first, I didn't want to act like an idiot and interfere with his work—I didn't want to look like a dumb kid. I was far more mature than my brother thought I was.

And today, I'm going to stand up for my brother. Watch out, mafia! You're gonna get to know me today. This is Porchay Pitchaya, Porsche's younger brother! I don't even study, I get by on hopes and prayers, he he.

"Dang!"

I'd been pressing the doorbell for so long that my hands were starting to cramp. Was no one wondering who was out here ringing the doorbell? If I were inside, I would have come out and scolded me by now.

While I stood there frowning, a luxury car switched on its turn signal and prepared to enter the mansion. The gate slowly began to open. I looked between the vehicle and the gate before deciding to do something.

"Stop!" I yelled, throwing my arms out with all my strength. Then, I jumped in front of the moving car with my eyes squeezed shut.

Beeeeeeep!

The car's horn blared for a long time, so loudly that I had to cover my ears. What the hell was the point of all that noise?

Thud! Woosh!

I heard movement in front of me and behind me. I instinctually raised both my hands above my head with a dazed look on my face. Everything happened so quickly.

"What the hell is going on?" said one of twenty men in black suits, who emerged from both the car and the house pointing guns at me... *Guns! Right, they have guns!* Even though I said I wouldn't be scared, my legs shook so much that I almost collapsed. *Hiaaaa! Help meeeeeee!*

My mind went blank, my ears went deaf, and I felt like I was going to faint. Then, a deep and imposing voice shouted from the car.

"Are you all out of your minds?!"

Everything fell silent. Those words clearly carried the power to send shivers down everyone's spines, because each gun was swiftly lowered.

"That's a high school student. Use your brain."

A chill swept over me as the door of the car opened, making my hair stand on end. Trying to get my bearings, I grabbed at my school uniform, spinning around to check that I was still alive.

"Kid, running in front of a car like that... Have you got a death wish or what?"

I looked up at the tall figure, who was imposing and intimidating—and somehow, kind.

"I..."

He was a middle-aged man, tall and elegant. He had a handsome face and slightly intimidating eyes. When he stood in front of me, my legs and mouth shivered so violently I thought I was at the North Pole.

"What's the matter, kid?"

"You are..." I said, trying to suppress my fear. Judging from his demeanor, it seemed like he might be the leader of this house, but I was not entirely sure—out of everyone in the mafia, I had only met Kinn and some guy named Kan or something.

"This brat has been ringing the doorbell at the front of the house for fun for a while, sir," a man in a black suit reported.

What the hell?! I was not here for fun! I was here for real business, damn it! He saw and heard me but didn't open the door? Should I punch him in the face?

I immediately turned to glare at the man who spoke, but when I saw that he was holding a gun, I kept my fighting spirit inside.

"What's up, kid? Do you have some business here?" the intimidating man asked in a comforting tone, gradually assuaging my fears.

"I..."

The man must have seen my hesitation, so he quickly intervened, casually putting his hands in his pockets. "I'm the owner of this house. Who are you looking for?"

"My brother...um...Porsche," I said boldly, though I still felt afraid.

The man immediately fell silent, looking like he had just heard something shocking. However, after a moment, he smiled slightly.

"You're Porsche's brother, huh? No wonder you look so much like him."

"Do you know my brother?" I asked.

"Of course, I know him. I hired Porsche myself."

Hearing that, I felt like I was no longer in a dangerous situation, and I became furious again.

"So, it was you..." I said with a sigh. This old man could be the one putting so much pressure on my brother, almost to the point of coercion. He did have an imposing demeanor, after all. *Argh... I will get revenge for you, hia!*

"Yes. Let's go inside first. I'm not sure if Porsche is here yet," he said, gesturing toward the car behind him as if to invite me to get in.

"Wait!" I commanded. My hands seemed to have a mind of their own, settling on my hips as I looked up at him defiantly. I wanted to make it clear that I wasn't here as a friend, but as an adversary! *Hah!*

"Hmm..." He turned to look at my stance and smiled. I did not know what he thought was so funny. Had he never been challenged by someone younger, or what?

"I'm here to negotiate," I said, and the old man raised his eyebrows. "I don't want my brother to work here anymore," I continued in a firm tone—but the old man kept smiling!

"Like two peas in a pod," he remarked with a shake of his head, but his face showed no sign of distress.

"What?"

"Why don't you want Porsche to work here?" he asked.

"I don't want my brother to be so stressed out. I guess you're some kinda power-crazy person, because every time my brother comes home, he's depressed," I said, pacing around with my hands on my hips, circling the old man. I was not afraid of his henchmen, who stood around with angry expressions.

"Watch your manners! Do you know who you're talking to?" one of his lackeys piped up. He looked just as intimidating as the old man, but even more hostile. *Do they think they can scare little Porchay? Nope, I'm not scared at all!*

"So what? Where did you come from to be so high and mighty?" I told the henchman. "Let me ask you this honestly. If you have children or grandchildren, would you want to send them to work in a dangerous place like this?"

As Porsche's younger brother, I was not afraid of anyone. Even though my heart was pounding fast, it was still strong, pumping out warrior's blood.

"What's wrong with Porsche? I saw him recently; he was just fine."

If I was not mistaken, the old man was looking at me with compassion. There was no sign of anger, which was weird. If I were in his place, I would have shot me in the face already for daring to insult a mafia leader. But hey—he must have been afraid of my power, which gave me the strength to fight for my brother with everything I had. The love I had for my brother was so potent that they could sense the fearsome potential in me, Mr. Porchay! *Heh. Let them know who they are messing with!*

"Fine, my ass!" I shouted.

"You little brat!" another old man—who looked like Mr. Number Two—acted like he was going to slap me, so I quickly shut my mouth.

"Calm down, Chan," Mr. Number One said, holding him back. He sighed. "Is something bothering Porsche?"

"I'm the one who should ask that, old man! What did you do to my brother?!"

"Your brother is too stubborn. I don't dare to even say anything to him," the old man said with a faint laugh.

"Liar! My brother has to take medicine right now. He's badly sick, and he's really stressed out. He's acting like someone suicidal! I can't bear to see him like that," I said. "It looks like you already have a ton of bodyguards. Sparing my brother and letting him go won't do you any harm, right?"

"Hmm...if he's not comfortable with anything, let him come and talk to me... But I can assure you that I take care of Porsche like one of my own children," the old man said as he walked over to the hood of the car and leaned against it, arms crossed. I thought he seemed tired because of his age, but a mafia boss shouldn't get tired so easily, right? It was confusing!

"You can say whatever you want, you power-hungry mobster!" I yelled.

"Let's go inside, sir. We've wasted enough time here," Mr. Number Two said, probably eager to taste my powerful punches.

"Wasting time?" I said. "I want you to promise that you won't let Porsche work here anymore. I know that my brother is talented and cool as hell. We, the Kittisawat family, are of undeniable prestige: we're full of courage and we're super intimidating. I know how much you want him on your side. But I'm sorry, I'm not sharing him with you!"

The old man shook his head lightly as if he had just been told a funny story.

"Well...let me talk to Porsche myself," he said.

"You have to promise that you won't let him work here again!" I demanded.

"...What's your name, kid?" the old man asked, ignoring what I'd said.

"Why bother learning it?"

I pressured him to agree to my demands, but the old man kept trying to change the subject.

Suddenly, another fancy car pulled up and parked behind the first one.

Beeeeeeeeeeeeep!

Argh! Why the hell is that car honking so loudly? Are they deaf? I cursed internally.

"Want to go inside the house first?" the old man continued.

"Why would I? Neither I nor my brother will step foot in this house again!"

"Father! Is something wrong?" a mysterious voice made the whole group turn to look. When I saw the newcomer walking in gracefully, I...

"Kim, my son. You're back?"

Son? Son? *Son?* I looked back and forth between the magnificent mansion and the guy named Kim. Only one thing came to my mind: *I am screwed!*

"What's going on, Father? Oh!" Kim turned to look at me in curiosity.

Oh shit, shit, shit! That's right! I knew this guy. We'd had a bit of a disagreement, and it did not end well. I never thought I would see him here...

I stood stock-still, like my entire body was frozen solid. My inner badass smacked my head, trying to wake me up. In my thoughts, my alter ego and I were beating each other up like crazy.

"Excuse me! What did you just ask?" I tried to divert my focus to the old man, not Kim, because I hated his guts. He had caused a lot of trouble for me. *Ugh!*

Now I knew why my brother got sick and stressed out. Working at a house belonging to Kim's father must be nerve-racking. I bet the old man was no different from his son! *Ugh!* The more I thought about it, the more resentful I became! Wouldn't it be great if I could just eliminate all of them for good?

"I've asked many questions. What's your name? Do you want to go inside?" the old man asked.

"Uh... No!" I took a deep breath, straightened my back, and lifted my head, displaying strength for everyone to witness. "Promise me that you won't let my brother work here anymore, old man."

"Who are you calling an old man?" Kim scowled, looking back and forth between me and his father. "Dad! Do you know this kid?" Kim pointed at me. *This kid, this kid, this kid?! Kim, you bastard!*

"I don't know him yet. He hasn't told me his name," the old man said, smiling.

"Well...should *I* tell you, then?" Kim smiled wickedly as he slowly stepped toward me. My body automatically moved backward. "His name is Porchay..."

"Back off, damn it!" I barked. With every sentence Kim said, he stepped closer to me and I stepped back.

"Studying in an international school," Kim continued.

"I'll tell my brother!" *Damn you, Kim! You asked for it!*

"He's seventeen years old."

I turned and looked around, searching for a stick I could use to whack him in the face.

"I'll hit you!" I warned.

"Eleventh grade, class two," Kim pressed on.

I swallowed hard, fear creeping in as my back pressed against the fence of the palatial house. Everyone here stared straight at Kim and me—especially the old man. He still stood there smiling with his arms crossed, looking smug. *Don't you think you should stop your son?! Do you know you can go to prison for harming a minor?*

"That's enough, Kim. This is Porsche's little brother," the old man said. "Chan, don't tell Porsche about this. He'll go on a rampage again, and I don't want to deal with the headache. I'm tired."

My ears went numb for a moment. It was like I couldn't hear anything around me except Kim's stupid voice. He kept sending murderous glares my way.

"By the way—!"

By the way, what? What the hell are you going to say, Kim? I broke out in a nervous sweat, feeling strangely restless.

"Stop that!" I shouted at him.

"He has—*ow*!"

I closed my eyes tightly and raised my leg, kicking Kim forcefully between the legs.

"What the hell are you doing?"

Kim collapsed to the ground, clutching his crotch. Five or six bodyguards rushed in and grabbed me, pinning me down with lightning speed. At the same time, several other bodyguards ran over to help Kim up, looking shocked beyond belief.

"How dare you kick my boss!" one of his henchmen cried as he reeled his fist back, prepping to punch me in the face. I quickly turned my face to duck.

"Stop it, Nont! Don't hurt him. Let him go!"

The fist froze in midair, accompanied by the sound of rapid breathing. This Nont guy was seriously pissed off.

"Let's take Mr. Kim inside, sir... The rest of you, take the kid to the street entrance. Do as you were ordered—don't hurt him!" Mr. Number Two commanded. His lackeys all bowed their heads in acknowledgment. When I saw this, my fear was replaced by confidence once again.

"Huh?! I thought you'd be tougher than that... If you think you're tough, come at me! Come at me right now!" I glared at Kim and Nont, who were trying to calm themselves down. I was dragged out by my arms, my feet kicking the air.

I cursed and shouted, not caring who overheard me. "Damn it! You think you're so tough, you bunch of wannabe gangsters?! You haven't faced me yet! My name is Porchay! Remember that, you bastards!"

However, as I was threatening them, I felt a strange emptiness in my chest. It was like my heart was telling me to stop, but my brain was telling me to be fearless and keep yelling. It was so confusing that some words of wisdom popped into my head: *Porchay, if you're gonna be a coward, then don't be such a smartass!*

I love you, hia, but that was all I could do today, I thought. *I'll leave it for now and settle things later!*

KINN
PORSCHE

17

Emphasize

I STOOD STILL FOR ALMOST a full minute before I was able to pull myself together. I quickly looked away. I tried to force my petrified legs to move, to get the hell out of here, but then a big hand grabbed me. It wasn't forceful, but it was enough to hurt my muscles as the momentum turned me around.

"Not going to say hello?" Kinn asked.

I quickly shook his hand off, refusing to face him. "What do you want?" I asked curtly.

"Am I seeing a ghost? Because you look pale as hell," Kinn said with a laugh. He was smiling, which was unusual.

"I have to find my friends," I said, trying to walk away, but Kinn blocked me with his arm. I gave him a dirty look and took a step backward so I didn't have to stand too close to him.

"How are you?" he asked.

I stayed silent and put my hands in my pockets, trying to look anywhere other than at him.

"Seems like you've recovered," he observed. "I saw a girl come out of your stall."

Kinn crept closer and closer as I stepped back further and further. When had that happened? I wasn't sure. My body was on autopilot. Every time I heard his damned voice, I got goosebumps.

"Wh-what? What do you want?" I stuttered, paranoia starting to surface in my mind. I wanted to shove him, to punch him hard in the face for once, but I couldn't control my body at all. All I could do was let him follow me, even as my back hit the wall.

"Nothing... Just saw that girl's face when she left. What did you do to her?" Kinn asked, clearly amused.

Suddenly, there were voices outside the restroom. I recognized them as Tem and Jom's. They were having a colorful conversation as they approached.

"How about we try cockblocking Porsche? I saw him go in there with that girl! Heh."

I hadn't managed to squeeze myself past Kinn. His hand then snatched me and guided me back into a stall—the same one I'd just left—and locked the door.

"What are you doing?!" I yelled, wanting to get out of this cramped stall.

"Shhhh!" Kinn pressed a finger against his lips, then held both of his arms over me to keep me from escaping. My back and my head hit the wall. I pressed firmly against it, sinking all the way back and trying to get as far away from Kinn as I could.

"Move," I whispered, hearing the restroom door open and Tem and Jom's footsteps stop right in front of my stall.

"Hey, Pooorsche!" Jom's annoying voice hollered. "Aha! Must be this one. You got yourself a quick snack, huh?"

I didn't know how to handle this situation. Should I cry for their help? But if I cried for help, wouldn't they question why the hell I was in here alone with Kinn? Shit!

"Hey, let me hear your voice!"

The shadows under the door gap belonged to Tem and Jom. It sounded like they were pressing their ears against the stall.

Kinn giggled.

"What's so funny? Let me go!" I said, my voice barely more than a whisper as I pushed his chest with my palms.

"You didn't finish, did you?" Kinn whispered back. His face inched closer, as if to help me hear him better.

"How would you know?" I scrunched my face in annoyance, keeping my voice as quiet as possible. This stall was claustrophobic as hell, and my idiot friends were right outside the door. Ugh! I couldn't leave now. Why did this bastard have to shove me in here?!

"A guy like you would last longer than that... Let me guess, you couldn't get it up for her?" Kinn murmured in my ear. He was right. I shut my eyes, trying to turn away from him. As our bodies drew closer and closer together, Kinn's cologne and his musky scent underneath hit my nose. My heart pounded so fast that it skipped a beat. I found myself excited and unsettled at the same time.

"Get out," I said, my voice trembling.

"What are you doing in there, meditating? Why are you so quiet, Porsche? Make some noise! Woooooo!" Jom hadn't given up on trying to be a nuisance.

"What if that's not Porsche?" said Tem.

"Of course it's him! I saw him go in!" Jom argued.

Damn it! Help me, please! But no matter how much I wanted to scream and get out of there, I'd be too ashamed to give my friends an explanation.

"What are you afraid of?" Kinn's husky voice whispered in my ear, sending a shiver down my spine. The hard tip of his nose softly nudged the crook of my neck. Once again, my body froze, powerless. I was disgusted with myself—right now, I should be kicking Kinn, shoving his face down the toilet and flushing it. But it was only a fantasy; all I could really do right now was turn away from his touch.

Kinn's hot breath brushing my neck sparked memories from that night at the hotel, the images flashing right behind my eyes.

"You want my help? I can give you some release," Kinn breathed. I lifted up my trembling hands, trying to push him back by the stomach, but I was too late. His hand got to my pants first, undoing the button and unzipping my fly.

"I'm gonna be in the next stall taking a shit, okay? I won't ruin your good time—pinky promise. Tem is chilling by the sink. Don't go anywhere!" I heard Jom say.

My mind clouded over. Everything happened so fast. In the blink of an eye, Kinn slid my pants and boxers down my thighs and wrapped his hand around my cock. I shoved him as hard as I could, but it just wasn't enough to get him off me. Just one touch from him was enough to make my body writhe in confusion, denial, and pleasure. I was in a daze.

"Hah... At this point, you're still gonna say no?" Kinn purred, his eyes glancing down to where my dick was betraying me. It stood hard and aching, completely unlike a moment ago.

"L-let me go. I... No. No more," I said, my voice hitching. Both my hands tried to bat his away. But every time I resisted, he squeezed me harder.

"Shh, don't worry... I'm not gonna fuck you. I'm just helping you come..." Kinn pinned one of my arms to the wall as I shook my head. Once again, my heart was too weak to resist him, and this time, I wasn't under the influence of any drugs. My body refused to fight back. It responded readily to Kinn's touch, just like that fateful night.

"Mmph!" I quickly covered my mouth with my free hand, afraid my voice would escape. Kinn's hand began slowly stroking me. His face nuzzled my jawline as he smelled my neck. I kept my eyes tightly shut, refusing to look at him. I was completely cornered, unable to dodge left or right. My body tingled, and the wound in my heart was ripped back open.

"I promise I won't do anything else..." Kinn murmured in my ear. Maybe he noticed that my body was trembling.

His nibbled at my ear and dragged his tongue all over the side of my face. His hand continued to jerk me off, his pace growing faster and faster. My body contorted in pleasure; after three drinks, the alcohol in my veins seemed to heighten the sensation. Why did this feel so different from how it had with that girl?

"Ah," I moaned when Kinn's thumb glided over my cockhead, circling it. His hand gripped me tighter. I didn't know when he'd unpinned my hand from the wall, but I found myself bracing it on his shoulder. As I got carried away in the rhythm of his strokes, he took advantage of my pleasure-hazed state and pulled my hand away from my mouth. He guided it under his shirt, making me feel his well-muscled abdomen. I vividly remembered this feeling of rock-hard muscle and smooth skin beneath my fingertips, the way it had made me lose control. I ran my hand all over him.

"Um...hey, Porsche," Kinn panted heavily as I let out a soft moan. When he pressed and rubbed his thumb over the head of my dick again, I could barely stand it. My head snapped up as I bit down hard on my lip, trying to suppress the feeling.

"I can't take this anymore," Kinn said before using his free hand to unbuckle his pants. He pulled out his cock and lined it up against mine so he could stroke both of us at the same time. New sensations coursed through my body, a tingling thrill that was pleasurable in a way that I couldn't describe.

Kinn's hand slid under my shirt to caress my abdomen before moving up to my chest. He squeezed and kneaded my pecs and played with my nipples, sending shivers down my body.

Kinn moaned, tilting his head to kiss me. He sucked and nibbled at my lips, pressing our mouths so tightly together that I had to gasp for air. He took advantage of my open mouth and invaded me with his hot tongue, curling it against mine. I tried to push his tongue out, but it ended up an invitation for him to suck on it, resulting in an even deeper kiss.

"*Ah!*"

Kinn increased his pace. A loud moan tumbled from my throat, unbidden.

Bang! Bang! Bang!

"Hey, keep it down in there!" Jom snickered from the next stall over.

The banging made me flinch, snapping me out of it. I opened my eyes, watching in dismay as Kinn jerked us both off. I bit down on Kinn's tongue—hard.

"Ow!" Kinn yelped loudly, pulling his head away from mine. He gave me a threatening look before moving his hand even faster, so fast that my head snapped up to look at him once again.

"Porsche? Is everything all right in there?!" Jom called. I didn't get a chance to answer him before Kinn bent down to press his lips against mine again. He didn't invade me with his tongue this time, only nibbling on my lower lip. Then, he bit down harshly.

"That hurt!" I snapped my head and yelped at him before his face moved in closer to my ear.

"If you bite me again, I'll alert your friends," Kinn growled before rejoining our lips. This time, he grabbed my hand that had left his torso and guided it to wrap around his cock. I shook my head slightly, but he forced my hand to stroke along to the rhythm.

"*Mmm,*" Kinn groaned, letting me know how close he was to coming. He guided my hand to stroke his cock as he stroked mine.

He increased the pace yet again, making me gasp for breath. His fingers stimulated me, sliding up and down my shaft so fast that I couldn't take it any longer. I didn't know how to stay quiet, so I buried my face in his shoulder to muffle my cries as my hand involuntarily twisted in his hair.

Kinn nuzzled the side of my face before I finally reached my peak. My brain went blank, and I shuddered as I came, shooting my load all over Kinn's hand.

"I'm close," Kinn whispered in my ear with a moan, forcing my hand to stroke his cock. His body spasmed with the strength of his orgasm.

"Ngh... *Ah*..."

I barely had any energy left. It felt like my fever was coming back. Coupled with the muscle aches and the shame, I didn't dare lift my face from his shoulder.

"Hey, we're heading out. Hurry up. Your bosses just turned up," Jom said. I heard his footsteps leaving the restroom—that was a relief.

I immediately pulled myself away from Kinn as my brain started to come back online. Kinn stared at me and smirked. He grabbed some toilet paper to clean himself, then handed some to me. Taking it from his hand, I quickly turned around and took care of myself. As soon as I pulled my pants back up, I snapped my head toward him, full of anger, and shoved his chest as hard as I could.

"What the fuck was that?!" I shouted. Earlier, it was like all my principles had evaporated entirely. But now, regret flooded through me nonstop. I had failed to keep control, letting my deep desires take over.

"Shh! Don't be like that," Kinn smirked, leaning against the wall I'd pushed him into.

"Kinn, you son of a bitch! This has gone too far!"

I knew I was being unreasonable. Had I screamed when he came in here and immediately left the bathroom, I might have made it. But things happened so fast—too fast for me to even think.

I grabbed him by the collar and yanked him forward. I swore after that night that if this happened again, I would crush him. And now it had happened again. I wouldn't let him walk away so easily.

"I'm warning you—if you hurt me, it won't end there," Kinn said, tearing my hand away from his collar. He pointed at me threateningly, his brows furrowed. "If you think I won't kick your ass here, think again."

I gritted my teeth in anger. My blood boiled, heat flowing through my body as my head throbbed. If Kinn started a fight right now, I was afraid I wouldn't be able to fight back. I simply shoved him hard, sending him tumbling back into the wall again. I left the stall, washed my hands quickly, and immediately walked back to my friends.

"Damn it!" I cursed.

I approached my table and was surprised to find some extra faces gathered around it.

"What's up, man? Did you have a good time?" Tem greeted me with a grin. I shot him a dirty look, which surprised him.

"Hey man, are you okay? I was so worried," Pete said, coming over to me with a troubled expression on his face. There were a bunch more people at our table: Time, Tay, Pete, and a few bodyguards that I recognized.

"I'm fine," I answered brusquely. "How did you get here?"

"Well, one of Mr. Kinn's associates owns this place. The boss ordered us to come, so we had to bring him," Pete said, then tipped his head toward a spot in front of the stage where Tankhun was busy dancing. Now it made sense that I had run into that bastard Kinn in the bathroom. I placed my hands on my hips loosely before heaving out a sigh.

"I'm leaving," I said. I pushed past people to reach the table and grab my wallet and phone. Tem and Jom looked at me, a bit confused.

"What the hell, Porsche? We only just got here. Why are you leaving already?" Tay, one of Kinn's friends, cried out. I gave him an annoyed glance. *Why are you joining us like this, huh? Were there no other tables? Damn!*

"Dude, don't leave now. The fun's just started," Tem said, standing up and grabbing my arm. He took my phone and wallet from my hands.

"I have a fever. I'm leaving," I told him. I wasn't staying in this bar, no matter what.

"Aaaaaah! Porsche! It's so good to see you! Come here, come here, come here. Drink, drink!" Tankhun sauntered over, slinging his arm around my shoulder. He picked up a glass and forced it into my hand. I glared daggers at him, but he smiled from ear to ear and forced me to take a drink.

"Boss, I'm not feeling well. I'm leaving," I hissed. Tankhun didn't listen. A guy like him, listen? Hah! He made me hold the drink in my hand and forced it into my mouth; I had no other choice but to swallow it down.

"Chug! Chug! Chug! Yay!" Tankhun cheered. I drank the whole glass, hoping he would leave me alone if I finished it, but he didn't let go of me. Instead, he wrestled me into a headlock, dragging me toward the stage. Then, he shouted along with the singer:

"When my shitty life gives me shitty lemons
When it's not me that she wants

What can I do?
Guess it's time to let go of you!"

I let out a long sigh. Tankhun yelled, waving his glass along to the music.

"If we're gonna get screwed, just let it be.
Curling up in pain won't help anything!"

The lyrics spewing from the singer felt like a punch in the gut. At the same time, Kinn emerged from the restroom. He spared me a quick glance before going to join his friends.

"All this pain, let's celebrate it.
Cheers to love because it's shitty.
Cheers to life, 'cause life's a pity.
Let's drink to all the shit for once,
Drink to the disappointments!"

That singer and Khun kept yelling into my ears. *Yeah, keep it coming. Thanks for reminding me that my life is shitty. Fuck!*

The song hit too close to home. I reached back for a drink from the table and chugged it down, hoping it would wash away some of my fucked-up feelings.

I inched closer to Khun and yelled in his ear, "Mr. Tankhun, I'm leaving!"

Tankhun turned to me, annoyed and bratty. "No! If you try to leave, I'll trash this place!"

On the outside, I looked at him calmly, but inside, I hated his guts. I wanted to kill his entire fucking family. Make them go extinct. Both of these brothers were the bane of my existence!

"Boss, I'm sick," I insisted.

"No, no, no, no, no!" Tankhun yelled, turning to mix me another drink and shoving it into my hand. I held the glass, completely fed up with him. *Watch it, Tankhun, or one day I'll feed you rat poison.* I was gonna kill this entire family. The younger brother just violated me in the bathroom, and now the older one was forcing me to get wasted. My heart was going to burst from all the rage I was suppressing.

I heard a new voice over the loud music. "Hello, P'Kinn. Oh, P'Khun, you're here too? What a coincidence!"

Everyone at the desk turned around to see Vegas standing there with a drink in his hand. He was smiling at his cousin Kinn, who smiled back.

"Oh, Vegas, are you here with someone?" Kinn asked.

"I'm here with my friends over there," he gestured. "P'Khun is drunk already?" He shifted his gaze toward Tankhun, who looked furious as he glared at Vegas aggressively. Vegas looked past Khun and broke into an even bigger smile when he saw me. I nodded at him to say hi.

"Vegas! What the fuck are you doing here?!" Tankhun screamed loudly.

"Well, it's a bar. I think I'm here to do laundry, maybe?" Vegas smirked. This just made Tankhun angrier. He readied himself to lunge at Vegas, who stood there smiling calmly. I quickly held Tankhun back by his arms.

"Why are you stopping me, huh?! I'll make you fucking bleed, Vegas!" Tankhun yapped like a mad dog, his arms flapping in an attempt to shake me off. I managed to hold my grip on him until Pete and the other bodyguards got up to stop their boss.

"Oh, P'Khun, still good with your fists, I see. Why don't you try using your brain for once? Maybe things will work out better," Vegas said playfully. He seemed harmless, but that mouth was a piece of work.

"Vegas, you little shit! You're a dead man!" Khun went berserk, forcing his arms and legs free from our hold. He picked up an ice bucket, preparing to dump it on Vegas.

"Khun! Don't!" Kinn yelled for his brother to stop, but it was too late...

Slam! Crash!

Khun dumped the ice bucket on Vegas. Luckily, Vegas dodged it and only a little of the water splashed his clothes. The music stopped abruptly, every pair of eyes in the bar moving to glare at us. The owner ran out to check on the situation.

"What's going on, Kinn?" the owner asked.

"It's all right, P'Nueng. Just an accident," Kinn said. Nueng didn't seem convinced.

Kinn ordered us bodyguards to separate Tankhun and Vegas. Actually, it was more like prying Tankhun away from Vegas, because Khun wasn't done throwing his temper tantrum. He was acting like a madman.

Once I saw that Vegas and Khun had gone their separate ways and everything was back to normal, I escaped the chaotic bar and went to have a smoke outside. What a fucking day this was. I pushed my hand through my hair in frustration.

"Fuck, could this get any worse?!" I cursed.

"Are you all right?" came a friendly voice. Vegas walked up to me with a pack of cigarettes in hand. He picked one out and lit it up, joining me for a smoke.

"Oh...yeah," I said. Holding the cigarette between my fingers, I took a drag and blew out the smoke. I glanced at him out of the corner of my eyes before asking, "Are *you* all right?"

"Oh, got some water on me, but it's fine," Vegas said with no discernable trace of anger. He was so chill about it—he couldn't be more different from Tankhun, who likely wasn't done throwing a fit.

"You're here to guard my cousins today?" Vegas said with a smile.

"No, I just ran into them," I said truthfully.

"You like to go out drinking?" he asked. I nodded in reply.

"And are you drunk yet?" Vegas continued.

"Nah, I haven't had that much," I answered.

"Hey, Porsche! I thought you left. Here you are!" Tem said as he walked up to me. I offered him a cigarette, which he took from me and lit.

"Hi, Tem."

"Hi, Vegas... How was your shower?" Tem joked, looking Vegas up and down.

"Not too bad."

"What's the deal with you guys?" Tem asked, curious. "You almost traded punches."

"Traded? That was all him. I didn't do anything," Vegas said with an amused smile. Tem nodded in agreement.

"Tem, I'm leaving," I told my friend.

Tem hesitated. "You don't want to stay a little longer? I don't think Jom will leave so easily."

"You can stay here with Jom. I'll take a cab," I said. I didn't want to ruin my friends' night out. I'd gotten here in Tem's car, so I figured he thought it was his responsibility to drive me home.

"How about this. I'll give you a ride home first, then I'll come back for Jom."

"It's fine. I'll make it home by myself," I said, serious. I didn't want to be anyone's burden, and Tem seemed like he wanted to stay.

"Porsche, where do you live?" Vegas asked.

"Oh, down that way," I replied politely.

"That's in the direction I'm heading. Let me drop you off, so it's not a hassle for Tem," Vegas said with a smile. I didn't know why Vegas was always so happy. Ever since I'd met him, all he did was smile, smile, and smile some more. Did he feel anything aside from happiness?

"It's okay, Vegas. Please, stay and have fun. I'll be fine," I politely declined. Even though we'd met several times now, I didn't feel close enough to him to ask for a ride.

"I'm leaving anyway. My clothes are wet, so I don't think I'll be having any fun if I stay," Vegas said, gesturing at his outfit.

I gave it some thought. "Well, if you don't mind me being a nuisance," I said. It may have been my imagination, but I think I saw a strange glint in his eyes. It surprised me, but I tried not to think too much about it. He probably just wanted to make friends.

"Then we should go get our things," Vegas said before going back into the bar. I threw my cigarette butt away and followed him inside.

When I got back to the table this time, I decided not to tell anyone that I was leaving. I tried to be inconspicuous as I grabbed my stuff. I saw Tankhun in front of the stage, jumping up and down with one of Kinn's friends, so I felt he was distracted enough that I could easily leave. I grabbed my phone and my wallet and left the club, ignoring Kinn's piercing gaze. I didn't want to look at him— I pretended he wasn't even there.

I marched out of the bar once I'd retrieved my things. Tem followed me outside one more time to see me off. Meanwhile, Jom was absolutely plastered, rolling around on a sofa.

I walked up to Vegas, who was waiting for me in front of the bar. He smiled as soon as he saw me. I returned the gesture, just to be polite.

"Tell me when you're home," Tem insisted, then gave Vegas a nod goodbye. Vegas started to lead me over to the parking lot when we were stopped by a familiar voice.

"Where are you going?"

"Porsche is leaving," Tem answered for me.

Kinn walked up to grab my arm, forcing me to look at him. "And he's leaving with…?" he asked coldly, sending a shiver down my spine. I shook off his hand and turned away.

"With me, P'Kinn. Porsche's place is on the way, anyway," Vegas chirped.

"Who said you could go?" Kinn growled. He glared at me, deathly serious.

"I'm not working today! I can leave whenever I want!" I protested. I had a profound urge to run away.

"I'm not letting you go," Kinn vowed, emphasizing each word. He stared straight at me. I started to get uncomfortable and tried to shift away from him a few times, but he always pulled me back.

"What right do you have?!" I retorted, frustrated.

"Do you want a list?" Kinn crept closer, his voice dropping so low that only I could hear him.

I shoved at his chest weakly. He had my wrist in an iron grip; I couldn't shake it off. I was too weak, due to so many things—injury, for one, but my mental state as well.

"I told you not to get too close to Vegas. I told you to stay away from the Minor Clan," he hissed, pulling me closer.

I didn't give a damn that Tem and Vegas were watching. Kinn's voice wasn't loud enough for them to hear what we were talking about, anyway.

"That's my business!" I snarled, trying to twist my wrist out of his grip.

"P'Kinn? What's the matter?" Vegas asked, walking closer to us.

"Nothing. I'll drive him myself. Go home, Vegas," Kinn commanded without even looking at his cousin. His gaze was fixed only on me, with no intention of backing down.

"But...it's no trouble. Let me give him a ride," Vegas said.

As soon as I managed to get my wrist free from Kinn's hand, Vegas nodded at me to come with him. I took a quick glance at Kinn. He let out a sigh and put his hands in his pockets, looking like he was trying to hide some emotion.

Vegas smiled at his cousin, but Kinn didn't seem to return the gesture one bit. "Go back and have fun, P'Kinn," Vegas said. "Don't worry. I will..."

"Vegas, I think you'd better stay out of this. Porsche is my man. I can handle him," Kinn cut Vegas off before he could finish. Vegas's smile slowly faltered. His eyes went blank for a moment before he forced a smile back.

"Fine," Vegas said, complying easily with Kinn's command.

Kinn's hands gripped my arm again and pushed me toward the parking lot.

"Porsche," Tem called, watching everything unfold. I could see the questions written on his face. He'd called out quietly when he saw Kinn gripping my arm and dragging me like that.

"If you don't want to freak your friend out, walk nicely. Be good," Kinn whispered in my ear. So I took a deep breath and turned to Tem.

"It's nothing. You can go," I told him.

"Call me when you're home," Tem said. I nodded at him. Then, Kinn's hand resumed pulling me along with him.

Once we reached his car, he forced me into the passenger seat. I had to admit that I felt paranoid at this point. I was starting to get scared of Kinn. Whenever I was with him, it felt like all my strength got sucked right out of me. There was only Porsche, a scared little boy with no way to fight back.

As soon as Kinn's swanky car rolled out of the parking lot, he yelled at me. "How many times have I told you to stay away from Vegas?!"

"What's it to you? I can talk to anybody I want. Don't stick your nose into my business," I said angrily, pointedly looking out the car window. I didn't want to see his face. I didn't want to be near him, either—his mere presence reminded me of those horrible moments, made them replay in my head over and over.

"Why not? I've already stuck more than my nose into you."

I wanted to kick him in the face. I tried to block out his words, purposefully ignoring the innuendo.

"I'm warning you. If you go near Vegas, you won't hear the end of it," Kinn snarled, his face twisted in rage. He stepped on the gas, making me jerk back in my seat. It wasn't the speed that scared me—it was him. I was scared something was going to happen to me after this. Sitting here alone with him was already unbearable.

My resolve was so weak; I couldn't believe that this was what I had become. The pain in my heart hung over me like a shadow. I tried to forget everything that happened between Kinn and me, but I couldn't. I just loathed myself even more. I hated and hated and hated, and it still wasn't enough. I didn't know what to do, especially after my body had betrayed me. I didn't know how to cope with how disgusted I was.

Kinn and I drove the rest of the way to my house in total silence. He strictly followed my directions, which made me feel a little better. I was worried he was planning to take me somewhere else and touch me again. But he didn't, to my huge relief.

I could feel my fever flaring. My eyelids were heavy, and my brain felt muddled and cloudy. My symptoms were much worse than back at the bar.

Kinn's car finally slowed down in front of my home.

As soon as the car stopped, Kinn attempted to feel my forehead. "Do you still have a fever?"

I pushed his hand away.

"Let me check your temperature!" Kinn said, sneaking one hand behind me to hold my neck in place and trying to place the other on my forehead.

"Let me go!" I batted his arms away, using all my strength to resist him.

"I'm just checking on you. You don't like me being gentle, huh?" Kinn spoke up before inching his face closer to mine. He held my neck and invaded me with another kiss, but I'd never give in to him again. I used my arms and legs to shove and kick him away.

"Let me go, Kinn! Stop being such a scumbag! I'm so disgusted with myself, you bastard!" I screamed and pushed him so hard that his back hit the car door. I quickly opened the door on my side and stormed out of the car as fast as I could. I half walked, half jogged, immediately retreating into my house.

I quickly walked to my room and flopped on the bed, feeling like I was going to pass out. My vision was starting to go black. Maybe I'd just spent too much energy on dealing with everyone's bullshit today.

My body hadn't fully recovered, and my fever hadn't gone down completely. My head throbbed in pain, but I couldn't even bring myself to go pick up my medication. I lay completely still with my eyes closed as horrible feelings continuously flowed through me. Why had I let myself do that with Kinn in the bathroom? It made me sick. A strong wave of nausea crawled up my throat.

I jerked my head to the side, held it over next to my bed and puked out everything I had bottled up onto my bedroom floor. I'd been holding so many things inside of me, and my body was completely overwhelmed. It had to come out.

"Hia!" Chay called out, opening my bedroom door. I didn't know what kind of face he made or how surprised he was, because

I was barely conscious. I could vaguely sense the damp clothes on my body and my sweaty face. I might have swallowed some pills and water; I wasn't sure. After that, I drifted off to sleep, unaware of anything else.

I woke up, checked the clock, and found it was already noon the next day. The ache in my head and my body had subsided. I looked around, noticed that the air conditioner had been turned on, and that there was a tray of food and medicine left out for me like yesterday. Chay must have cleaned up after me last night—my room looked spotless.

I poured myself a glass of water. As I took a sip, I saw a yellow sticky note on the rim of my plate. It was a short message from my brother:

Don't forget your food and meds, hia. I'm worried.

His messy chicken-scratch made me smile. I was hit by the realization that I needed to stop myself from sinking deeper into this nightmare—I didn't want my brother to worry about me like this ever again.

I called Tem.

"Is class over?" I asked.

"Jom and I didn't go. We're glued to the bed, man," Tem said. His sluggish voice told me just how hammered they must have gotten after I left.

"Are you free around six?" I asked. "Pick me up at my place, please."

"Where are you going?"

"Can you take me to *that* house? I've got some unfinished business..."

"Uh-huh," Tem affirmed. "I'll be there around five thirty."

Once I finished my meal and took my medication, I showered and got dressed, then waited around for Tem to come pick me up. I'd thought everything through, and I couldn't stand it anymore.

Tem came to pick me up and Jom tagged along. I guided them to the house where I worked. Tem didn't ask me much, just let me sit with my thoughts. Jom didn't bother me either—he was so hungover that he passed out in the backseat.

Once the car pulled up to the fence, I told Tem to stand by—this wouldn't take long. Tem nodded and told me to call him right away if anything happened.

I walked straight toward the familiar front door. The bodyguards who recognized me said hello along the way. I acknowledged them with a nod, then headed toward a certain room with haste.

[IN MR. KORN'S ROOM]

Knock. Knock.

I took a deep breath and waited for an answer. By this time, he must be home...

"Come in," P'Chan's voice answered, so I turned the doorknob and stepped in.

"Oh, Porsche? What is it?"

I greeted both P'Chan and Mr. Korn with a wai gesture. They looked busy with a bunch of paperwork piled up on the desk.

I approached them with a solemn expression on my face.

"Have a seat," Mr. Korn said. I sat down in the chair in front of his desk, pressing my lips into a thin line.

"What is it?"

I filled my lungs with another deep breath, closed my eyes for a second, then spoke firmly: "I'd like to quit, sir."

As soon as I said it, both P'Chan and Mr. Korn looked up at me, completely abandoning their paperwork.

"What happened?" P'Chan asked in a stern voice.

"Uh... I just want to quit, sir," I said, addressing Mr. Korn. "I don't think I belong here." I couldn't look him in the eye. The entire time I'd worked here, he'd been so kind to me—I respected him.

"Did Kinn do something?" he asked.

I flinched a bit when I heard the name, then shook my head slowly.

"No... I just...don't want to do this anymore," I said calmly.

"Why? If there's a problem, you can tell me." Mr. Korn put down his pen and folded his hands on the desk, his eyes still serenely focused on me.

"I really don't want to stay here. As for the termination fee, I promise to pay it back," I said. I let out a sigh, relieved to get the words out, but I felt uncomfortable from the eyes staring at me.

Mr. Korn sighed wearily. "If anything is bothering you, you can tell me. If you're stressed out or exhausted, then go get some rest. I'll let you take a leave of absence, but I'm not terminating your employment right now," he said.

"I've thought it through... I really don't want to do this anymore," I stubbornly insisted.

"You know, I care for you like one of my own sons. If you need to, go get some rest. Think about it carefully... Try separating work from personal matters. Give your mind a break. After that, you can properly think it through."

"Why...?" I asked weakly.

"I've seen a lot of things. Just one look at you and I can tell. If something is bothering you, take some time off to rest. Let's say seven days," Mr. Korn said. "After that, if your answer is still the same, I won't hold you back. I don't want to force anyone to stay against their will." Mr. Korn took a sip from his coffee mug.

I became even more tense. Today or seven days from now, my decision would be the same. I'd thought it over thoroughly, and I knew I wanted to quit.

"But I..."

"In seven days, come meet me. I'll be waiting for your answer," Mr. Korn said, standing up from his chair.

"Seven days won't—"

"Get some rest. I don't want to hear anything else right now. And I really do hope that in seven days, your answer will be different," Mr. Korn said, ignoring my protests. He disappeared into a smaller room in the back.

P'Chan gestured to the door. I watched Mr. Korn leave, then bade P'Chan farewell with a wai gesture before exiting the room.

"Hey, Porsche! Let's grab dinner," Arm called out to me. I really wasn't in a good mood, so I just made a beeline to the front door and got in Tem's waiting car.

I didn't get it. Why couldn't Mr. Korn just let me leave? It was clear that I couldn't work here anymore. I even promised to pay them for terminating the contract. Why did nothing in my life ever go how I hoped? I should have left today, to save myself all this trouble—for my sake and my brother's. But nothing went my way at all. Mr. Korn refused to listen to me, saying I had to come back in a week. I wanted to cut them out of my life right now, so I wouldn't have to be reminded of all the trauma I'd been through. I wanted to forget it all.

Tem drove me home. He did ask me what happened, but I refused to answer, and thankfully, he didn't press any further.

"If you're in trouble, you know you can always call me," Tem said with concern in his voice. I nodded, then waved him goodbye until his car took off.

I walked into my house in a miserable mood. I noticed Chay on the couch playing on his phone. He looked up at me in surprise.

"Eh? I thought you were at work, hia... Hia, I'll go around the corner. What do you wanna eat?"

I ignored him and went straight to my room upstairs. I needed to lie down. I was so pissed off that my head was throbbing again.

Chay came up and shook me awake. "Hia, please come eat."

I blearily awoke. After I lay down last night, I had passed out cold. Now it was already past eight. Both the fever and the side effects of my medications had completely jumbled my head. I was exhausted.

I washed my face, then followed my brother downstairs. I found out that he had already set the table and prepared my food.

Chay stared at me expectantly as he ate, but I was too tired to explain anything to him. *Let's just wait seven days. When I quit for real, I'll tell him.* I didn't know if Mr. Korn was trying to come up with some convincing speech right now, but there was nothing he could say that would make me stay.

Bam! Bam! Bam!

Someone was pounding at the door. Chay and I both looked up in confusion. It was such a violent knocking, like someone was trying to break down the door. Whoever was doing it better cut it out, or I'd kick their ass. They could have been gentle—we'd still have heard it. Damn!

"I'll get it," Chay said, running out of the kitchen to open the door. I was worried for him, so I followed close behind.

"Hia! It's your friend!" Chay hollered before I left the kitchen. I walked up to see who had decided to visit us this late at night.

As soon as I recognized the broad figure in front of me, my heart skipped a beat. Kinn was standing at the entrance, his face a picture of rage.

"Porsche!" he exclaimed when he saw me. I took a few steps back and looked at him, stunned. I didn't know what to do.

"Who said you could quit, huh?!"

18

Feeling

KINN

"WHO SAID YOU could quit, huh?!" I shouted, my voice echoing through Porsche's townhouse.

Porsche froze like a deer in headlights the moment he saw me. I strode forward furiously, forcing him to take a step back. There wasn't a trace of his usual confidence in his fearful eyes. His cocksure bravado had morphed into paranoia—he looked like an entirely different man.

"Kinn," Porsche said weakly.

I was taken aback to see his eyes shimmering with emotion. I hadn't thought he'd change *this* much. Developing a fever after having rough anal sex for the first time wasn't uncommon, but the shock and terror on Porsche's face was profound.

His expression made me feel a bit guilty, but it didn't quell my anger at all. "I'm talking to you, Porsche!" I shouted. "Who told you to quit?!"

When I got back from the university earlier the same evening, Father had called me over. He asked if I had done something to Porsche recently that prompted him to leave us. I darted out of the room immediately without waiting for him to finish speaking, and drove straight to Porsche's house in a rage.

Before I could get to Porsche, Porchay moved in front of me, shielding his older brother.

"Leave my brother alone!" he shouted.

"Did that shithead Vegas say something to you? Tell me, Porsche!" I demanded. I stood still, angrily glaring at him. I didn't care about the dirty looks his little brother was throwing at me.

"Go upstairs, Chay," Porsche said, seeming to get a handle on his emotions. He shifted his gaze from me to his brother, nudging him toward the stairs.

But Porchay was stubborn. He held Porsche's hand tightly, refusing to go upstairs. "Hia! Who the hell is this crazy fucker? Why is he yelling at you?"

"Come on, it's nothing. Go upstairs!" Porsche told him sternly. "And don't come down."

"But..."

"Go!" Porsche's voice got a bit aggressive. Porchay glanced between his older brother and me, then obediently walked up the stairs.

As soon as Porchay's door clicked shut, Porsche walked past me, bumping my shoulder as he went. He was headed for the front gate.

"Where are you going?!" I demanded, following him outside.

The moment he reached the front gate, he turned to confront me. "What do you want?" he asked. "We're talking out here—I don't want Chay to hear us."

"Hmph! You're trying to quit because of Vegas, right? He got you to join him!" I lowered my voice, but my tone was still furious. It enraged me when I heard Porsche was quitting, and he seemed to be growing quite close to Vegas lately. Vegas was my enemy. A guy like Vegas was a wolf in sheep's clothing—my family had always known that. Not to mention that my father had accepted all of Porsche's employment demands.

I'd been trying to treat Porsche better. I hadn't meant for us to have sex; it just happened. As for what we did in that club bathroom... I just wanted to mess with him, but I got carried away. I'd tried not to let him provoke me, but every time I saw his face and the way he acted, I couldn't help it.

"What does Vegas have to do with this?!" Porsche snapped, like he didn't know what I was talking about. His brows knitted together in confusion.

I rolled my eyes. I couldn't tell if he truly wasn't getting it or if he was just pretending. After that gunfight at the range, I'd ordered Pete to follow him as closely as possible. I was worried he'd be targeted by the Minor Clan and bought off.

"If it wasn't because of Vegas, why would you quit?" I stood my ground and glared at him. He glared back. His eyes were accusatory, as if I had done something wrong; both of his hands were curled into fists. He turned his face to the side and cursed, the vein in his temple throbbing furiously.

"Then what is it?!" I yelled at him.

"It's *you*, you son of a bitch!" Porsche shoved me violently, sending me stumbling backward. He fisted a hand around my collar and yanked me back toward him.

"Me?" I asked.

Porsche punched me in the face with a heavy fist, sending my head sideways. The force of it nearly made me fall over.

"Yes, you! You made me like this, asshole!" he declared, grabbing my collar again. The emotions he'd bottled up were about to burst, and his fist flew at my face again. This time, I held him by the wrist and blocked his punch. I pushed him away and slammed his back against the wall, holding both of his hands down.

"What did I do?" I asked, even though I was pretty certain what he was getting at.

"Do you even need to ask?" Porsche shook my hands off with all his strength, managing to free himself.

"If it was that day...you know how it happened," I said, trying to grab his hands again.

"And even after that day, you still weren't done tormenting me!" he barked, dodging my grasp.

"Why are you so stuck on it? You can't change the past."

"It's *because* I can't change the past that I don't want to keep seeing your face!" Porsche's voice grew louder and louder, and I noticed the neighbors opening their doors to see what was going on. "Damn it!" Porsche cursed, shoving my chest again in frustration.

"I didn't think it would upset you that much," I admitted quietly, not wanting to draw any more attention. But it seemed Porsche was so angry that he didn't care if anyone heard. He kept yelling and shoving me again and again.

"How could you say that?! How could you?! I don't know who the *fuck* I am right now! Do you know how disgusted with myself I am?!" he roared. He glared at me like he wanted to tear me apart.

It was me. I'd been careless and inconsiderate because I was so used to having sex with men. I hadn't realized it would affect him so drastically. I could see it with my own eyes, as if I could peek inside his mind. That night must have traumatized him—he was a straight guy, and he'd been violated. I hadn't considered that aspect at all. I'd thought it was just a mistake that would blow over.

"Porsche... I didn't think you'd get this bad," I admitted.

"What happened that night haunts me constantly," Porsche said. "Every time I try to forget, it comes flooding back. I'm going fucking insane. How can you expect me to get over it, you bastard?!"

Something in his eyes had changed. I could see no trace of the Porsche I knew—only pain, sorrow, fury, and fear.

I grabbed his arms and tried to talk some sense into him. "Porsche, listen to me! I didn't mean to—"

"Like *hell* you didn't mean to! Let me go, you animal!"

"Porsche!" I raised my voice and pinned him against the wall.

"Let me go, Kinn! I can't stand you anymore, you son of a bitch!"

I held down his wrists and locked his body into place against mine until he started to give in. I was in better shape than him, so I figured he couldn't buck me off—but instead of trying to break free, he bit down on my shoulder. Hard.

I stood still and didn't utter a word, even though it hurt like a bitch. I let him take out his pain on me.

"Porsche." I called his name flatly. His teeth still sank into me, but his body started to calm down.

Porsche lifted his head up from my shoulder. "I hate you," he whispered, exhausted.

Even though my eyes were fixed on him, I could sense that something in the air was off. I badly wanted to clear things up with Porsche—I wouldn't let him quit so easily—but it would have to wait.

"You should go back inside," I said.

Porsche went still and looked at our surroundings.

"You feel it too?" I asked, just to be sure.

"It's not your men?"

"I came alone."

I let go of Porsche's hands, then glanced left and right. Blinded by my anger, I'd driven straight here without any bodyguards.

I didn't know why I'd gotten so upset when I heard that Porsche quit. Our bodyguards put in their resignations all the time. But it was Porsche... Only he could rile me up like this.

"You're still feverish. Go inside," I said. He looked tired.

Porsche's brow furrowed, his eyes no longer focused on me. He looked out to the main road as we broke away from each other.

A group of five men charged at us, all wielding knives. I put up my fists immediately, punching them in their faces as soon as they got close. Porsche kicked one of them in the face, sending him to the ground.

Bang! Thud!

Porsche and I scrambled to defend ourselves. Panicked noises erupted from the neighbors, but nobody dared to intervene because these bastards were armed. Amid the chaos, I heard the door to Porsche's house open. Porsche, who was busy breaking the guys' limbs, turned toward the sound. His eyes widened in horror.

"Hia! What's going on?!" Porchay shouted as he ran out of the house. As soon as he saw the scene in front of him, shock spread across his face.

"Get inside!" yelled Porsche.

I was bashing an attacker's head against the wall when I heard Porchay. I let go and went over to him as he darted toward his brother.

"Get inside!" I pushed Porchay away while simultaneously kicking out at the gang of attackers.

"I have to save my hia!" Porchay insisted, hesitant to leave.

"Porsche's phone is inside, right? Find Pete in his contacts and tell him to come here now! Go out the back door, Porchay. If you want Porsche to live, get out of here, quick! Go!"

Porchay didn't have time to question my command—I shoved him back into the house and locked the door from the outside. He banged on the glass and yelled but I shot him a glare, silently willing him to do as he was told. He dithered for a moment before finally going inside.

I wasn't surprised that I'd managed to order Porchay around without getting a scratch—Porsche had been fending off our attackers the entire time. He grabbed them, yanked their heads, and jabbed them with his elbows and knees. It looked like he'd taken a few hits. I had to rush in to help him.

"You think you're so tough, huh?!" one man shouted, coughing up blood. I grabbed the knife he'd dropped and lunged to stab the man currently wrestling with Porsche. But as I brought the knife close to his side, something stopped me in my tracks.

"Put it down!"

One of the men had a pistol pressed against the back of Porsche's head. Porsche's fists stilled. He cautiously straightened himself up.

I felt cold metal against the back of my head as well.

"Knife. Down."

I did as he said, slowly placing the knife on the ground, then held both of my hands up.

"That's a good boy," the man chuckled darkly. Suddenly, he swung at the back of my head with the butt of his pistol, knocking me to the floor. The other man did the same to Porsche. I felt something heavy repeatedly hit me in the stomach and the back of my neck. Dazed with pain and unable to fight back, I passed out.

"What's this about? Didn't the boss just want Porsche?"

"Come on. Two birds, one stone! Boss is gonna be over the moon."

"Hmph! Disobeying orders like that? Better watch yourself."

"Trust me, Boss will be happy to get 'em both."

"And if he isn't, this is all on you. I only took Porsche—you had to fucking get Kinn, too."

I'd regained consciousness some time ago, but I pretended to still be out as I listened to the men talk. My arms were tied firmly in front of me, my mouth gagged by a cloth. My mind was still clouded by pain, but the rocking motion I felt told me we must be driving up a mountain somewhere.

The inside of the van was fitted with dark curtains, so I couldn't look outside. I prayed that my phone was still with me, so Pete or the other bodyguards could track the GPS. There was someone seated next to me—I squinted and saw it was Porsche, still unconscious. He was tied up in the same way I was.

The van went quiet. I tried to move my hands toward Porsche to wake him up. These guys were reckless—they'd put me and Porsche in the back seat together without anyone to watch us.

I gently poked Porsche's arm; he seemed to be getting his bearings back. He moved a bit, then squinted at his surroundings. I gently caught his arm, not wanting him to move around. He turned to me and frowned. I gestured with my eyes toward the bastards in the front seats, silently telling Porsche to look at them.

"Hey! Are they awake?" one of the men said.

As soon as we heard them, Porsche and I quickly pretended to be unconscious.

"Not yet," the other man said. "What if they're dead?"

"The boss wouldn't mind if Kinn dies. But if Porsche croaks, you can kiss your ass goodbye. Hah!"

"I just hope he won't be mad that we got Kinn, too."

"Man, cut it out. Boss will be pleased—and maybe we'll get some extra pay."

I squinted my eyes open slowly, making sure everyone had turned back around. Porsche raised his head and frowned, probably pondering what they'd said. I was curious as well, because this was the second time Porsche had been targeted. I needed to find out who they were and what they wanted. Stuffing the idea away for later consideration, I glanced at Porsche.

We needed to find a way out of here, and quick. It sounded like they really wanted me dead. Plus, we were outnumbered; once we reached our destination, it'd be harder to escape.

I reached to untie Porsche and he gave me his hands without protest. I managed to loosen the knot quickly even though it was tied tightly. Porsche then untied me as stealthily as he could, constantly checking our surroundings.

Once we managed to free ourselves from the rope, all we could do was wait. The car was still moving.

We communicated with our eyes—I signaled for him to wait until we had an opportunity to take them by surprise. I wanted him to prepare for a fight. He seemed to understand my message, nodding and bracing himself to attack.

The driver cursed and hit the brakes.

Screech!

"Shit! What was that?!"

I turned to Porsche and gave him a nod. He nodded back, then reached out to the guy in front of him and twisted his neck, hard. I yanked another guy's hair and bashed his head against the window. The van skidded to a halt again as chaos unfolded.

"The hell?! You little shit!"

Porsche and I didn't stop until we'd knocked two of them out, putting them in headlocks. The van was small and hard to maneuver in, making it difficult for the men to fight back.

Since we had taken them by surprise, we had the upper hand. They tried to grab their guns, but Porsche kicked them away. Once I finished beating one guy's face into a pulp, I snatched a gun off the floor and pointed it at the rest of the men. I hurriedly dragged Porsche toward the van door before opening it to our freedom.

"Stay back, or I'll shoot!" I threatened as we retreated from the van. Porsche managed to wrestle a gun from one of them as well. They all gulped and raised their hands.

As we backed further and further away from the van, I found that we were truly in the middle of nowhere: there was nothing but forest and mountains around us, with barely any cars in sight.

One of our attackers recovered from Porsche's beating and barked orders at everyone in the van. "Why the hell are you just sitting there?! After them!"

The three men who were still conscious got out of the van and ran toward us. Porsche and I fired at them.

Bang! Bang!

But they had guns, too, and they were ready to fire back. I grabbed Porsche's wrist and sprinted into the forest to find cover. The dark made it easy to hide—there was no moon in the sky tonight. I heard more gunshots on our tails. Porsche and I fired back at them from time to time as we fled deeper into the forest, away from their bullets.

"Kinn, it's too dark!" Porsche panted as he tried to keep up with me, but I didn't slow down at all. Those guys were relentless, so we needed to run as far and as fast as we possibly could.

Bang! Bang!

I kept ducking to dodge the bullets. Porsche turned to fire warning shots back at them. I could barely see anything. It was nighttime and we were surrounded by forest—we were running completely blind.

Bang! Bang!

The shots drew closer and closer. I tried to crouch as I ran, but I could only do so much—I kept getting caught up in tree branches and the underbrush, stinging my arms and legs with pain. I couldn't see the path in front of me at all. I stepped without looking and lost my balance, lurching forward.

"Shit!" I cried out. Instinctively, I pulled Porsche into my embrace to shield him as we hit the ground and rolled down a steep slope. I didn't even think about it; it just happened automatically—my subconscious told me to protect the man in my arms from all harm.

We tumbled down the hill, grazed by bullets.

Bang! Bang!

I kept my eyes tightly shut. My mind couldn't register what was happening. Then my head slammed against something rock-hard, and everything went black.

"A cliff! Oh, fuck!"

"If the bullets didn't finish them off, that sure as hell did!"

"Shit, Boss is gonna *kill* me!"

Bright light hit my eyes as I struggled back to consciousness. Pain shot through my entire body, the worst of it in my head. Confused, I opened my eyes with difficulty; my vision was somewhat blurry.

Something heavy was pressing down on my body. I lifted my head to look around. From what I could remember, we'd been chased last night until we stumbled and fell down a steep hill or some sort of ravine.

I didn't know how we'd managed to survive. We'd fallen quite a long way down. I must have hit my head against one of the rocks nearby, which would explain why it ached so badly. I hugged the body in my arms tightly before I realized it was Porsche, still out cold.

"Porsche!"

I gently shook his arm and held my finger under his nose. I sighed in relief when I felt him still breathing, but his breath was burning hot. I shook him again.

"Porsche!"

He groaned, his brow furrowing. Then, he slowly started to move. "Ouch," he croaked, cracking his eyes open.

"You okay?" I asked quietly.

"Last night, we were..." he muttered, eyes widening as he lifted his head to scan his surroundings.

"Yeah. We're being hunted." I nudged him to get off of me. "Are you okay?" I asked him again, propping myself up into a sitting position.

Porsche didn't reply, grimacing as he sluggishly tried to move. He was wearing only a t-shirt, so his skin had been unprotected when we tumbled down the cliff—his arms were badly scratched.

Crunch, crunch.

The sound of footsteps on dry leaves made me freeze for a moment. I hastily grabbed the gun that had fallen next to me and hauled Porsche upright. He couldn't really stand up, but I dragged him into the bushes anyway.

"Get some ropes and climb down to see if you can find their bodies," one man's voice echoed through the forest.

"Can you walk?" I whispered to Porsche. He looked completely drained, but he still managed a small nod.

"Over there," I said, grabbing his wrist and leading the way as carefully as I could.

Clack!

"I can't find anything."

"Then they're not dead yet. Split up and find them!"

As soon as I heard the distant voice shouting orders, I tried to pick up the pace, pulling Porsche into a run. More of them were coming, and I was afraid we'd get caught if we waited around any longer.

"You... I can't," Porsche wheezed, looking weaker than I'd ever seen him. He tugged at my wrist to get me to slow down.

"Hey! Over there!" a voice called.

"Tough it out!" I told Porsche, moving my hand from his wrist to his torso, dragging him along with all the strength I had left.

I kept running. By now it was light enough to see the way in front of me, allowing me to dodge the tangle of branches and underbrush. I didn't know where we were going, only that I had to put some distance between us and our pursuers. I supported Porsche's body the entire way, holding him up when he threatened to keel over. I felt so sorry for him—he was deathly pale and panting heavily.

The further we ran, the darker and cloudier the sky became. I slowed down a little when I felt we were far enough away. I turned to look at Porsche and pressed my hand to his face.

"Is your fever back?" I asked.

"It never...went...away," Porsche said as he gasped for air. "I can't keep going!"

Just like that, Porsche collapsed. It shocked me—I wasn't used to seeing him so weak. I walked over to stand in front of him, my eyes still darting around, afraid our pursuers were going to catch up to us.

"Porsche, you have to hold on a little longer," I said. He shook his head as he sat there panting.

As if nature was taunting us, rain began to pour down. Our situation just kept getting worse. Now that I was done running for my life, I had to find shelter.

"Get up! Or else you'll get malaria," I said, standing with my hands on my hips as I stared at Porsche. He sat there in silence, looking like death.

The rain fell even harder. *Just my fucking luck! Fucking hell!*

It was really coming down now, but the guy in front of me refused to budge. What the hell was I supposed to do?

I turned my back to Porsche and crouched down, patting my shoulders.

"Whatcha doing?" he asked, his voice hoarse.

"Get on. We need to find shelter."

Porsche hesitated, not responding. With the rain beating down on us, I didn't want to wait. I reached behind me and pulled his arms over my shoulders before hooking my arms under his legs and standing up. After adjusting my grip, I walked forward.

Porsche wasn't exactly light, and my arms still hurt from the fall. How was I supposed to manage this? *Fuck!*

I walked for some time before I felt the weight of Porsche's head burrow into my shoulder. His arms lay haphazardly over my shoulders, but now they hugged me tight as the heat emanating from his body warmed my back.

The rain was starting to obscure my vision. I kept walking until I found a large hollow, almost like a small cave. I quickened my pace and ducked inside.

"Porsche?"

I crouched down so he could hop off my back.

"Mmph," he groaned, pulling away from me and leaning back onto the rocks. His eyes remained closed; he didn't bother to look

where I'd brought him. It was like he was completely cut off from the outside world.

I unbuttoned my rain-soaked shirt, making sure to take off Porsche's shirt, too—I didn't want him to get a cold on top of his fever.

"What do I do now...?" I asked myself aloud. I thought hard as I wrung out our shirts.

The wind hit my bare skin and sent a chill through my body. I quickly turned to look at Porsche, who was hugging himself tightly from the cold. Shit, this was bad. I hadn't paid any attention when I was a boy scout. I hadn't even gone on the camping trips! I had absolutely no survival skills...but I *had* played survival games online before. How different could it be?

I tried to recall what I did in that game. First, I needed to start a fire. Luckily, there were some twigs and dried leaves in the hollow, so I gathered them into a pile. I'd seen in documentaries that you needed to rub twigs against a rock and turn toward the sun in order to start a fire, but it was raining. How could I make a fire with no sunlight? I bit my lip as I pondered the question. I couldn't wake Porsche up to ask for help; he was shivering so hard I was afraid he might die right then and there.

It dawned on me that Porsche must have a lighter with him—he was a smoker, after all. I fished through the pocket of his sweatpants and found it.

I spent a long time trying to get the lighter to ignite because it was so damp, but eventually it worked. The first fire I'd ever made crackled into existence. Deep down, I was kind of proud of myself. I really could do anything if I set my mind to it.

I sat there with my knees up, watching the flames flicker, when I heard a trembling voice.

"M'cold," Porsche rasped out.

I moved toward him and pressed the back of my hand to his forehead. He was still burning hot. Normally, a sick person should be wiped down and covered in thick blankets when they slept. Right now, his clothes were soaked, so I draped them over some rocks to dry out. What was I supposed to do now?

"I started a fire," I said, glancing at his face. His brow was furrowed and his eyes were tightly shut.

"Cold..." Porsche's lips quivered so badly that I couldn't make out the rest of his words. Both of his arms were wrapped closely around his torso.

"Damn it! Don't be like this, Porsche. I don't know what to do either," I exclaimed in frustration. It irritated me when things were out of my control.

I looked at Porsche's bare upper body, at his tattoo and defined muscles. A tough guy like him really shouldn't be in this position—the sight was a little jarring. The Porsche I knew was strong, proud, and unyielding. But instead of getting up to yell at me like usual, he lay there sick and shivering. He looked like he was at death's door. My heart sank as I watched him. He was only in this situation because of me.

I scooted closer to him, lifting his back away from the rock he was leaning against and carefully inching myself into the space behind him. I embraced his damp, feverish body, letting him lean on my chest instead.

"Better?" I asked quietly.

His head rested on my shoulder. He was still shivering, I realized. I tightened my embrace.

"Mmm," he groaned, turning his face to burrow into my neck. I smiled and rested my cheek against his head.

I thought about everything that had happened these past few days. I never thought I could hurt Porsche so deeply. It shocked me to see the light in his eyes change so drastically, but I understood why. He was probably finding it difficult to accept what had happened between us, probably feeling that his pride had been ripped from him and trampled on—something like that, anyway—and I was the one responsible. I hadn't meant for it to turn out like this! The blame didn't rest solely on me!

Having sex with him that night had felt new and exciting. I'd never done it with a man who was the same height and build as me. It felt like a fun challenge, and it was so much better than I'd imagined it would be.

As for what happened in the club bathroom... I only meant to tease him, but I got carried away. It was just too thrilling, and it felt amazing. I hadn't realized how my actions could hurt a straight guy like him. I was gay, and hooking up with a guy in a bathroom was a normal situation for me.

I had to admit that I was really into Porsche. Every time I was with him, I couldn't hold myself back. He angered and annoyed me so much that I constantly fought him. And today, I had won—but I didn't feel proud of this victory at all.

"Dad... Mom...help me, please," Porsche said. I tilted my head, watching him as he called for his parents in his sleep. "Mom... hold me."

Porsche's trembling voice made me hug him even tighter. He snuggled closer to me, burrowing his head into my chest. As I studied him closely, I began to wonder... Could it be that his strength was only a façade? A shield to protect him from his innermost feelings? He put up a good front, but he was more sensitive and fragile than he seemed.

"Heh... I like you when you're asleep like this," I said with a smile. "You're just like a kitten." The more I watched him, the more interesting he became. I could hardly believe it. He was just as big as I was, with those fearsome tattoos—why couldn't I look away from him? Something about him compelled me to lean down and press a featherlight kiss to his forehead. I pulled back to look at Porsche's face one more time and saw his lips curl up into a small smile.

Sweet dreams, Porsche. I hope you get better soon.

PORSCHE

I WOKE UP CONFUSED. I scanned my surroundings, finding myself in some sort of cave. It wasn't big, but it wasn't small, either. A small fire was dying out next to me. The sky outside was completely dark, and it was pouring rain.

Feeling something warm behind me, I frowned. I tried to get up but to my surprise I found my body held in a tight embrace. Someone's legs were stretched out and lined up against mine. I cringed and quickly pulled myself away.

"Kinn!" I called out to the man behind me, eyeing him warily. We were both shirtless—completely forgetting where I was, I could only come to one conclusion: *You and me? Again?!*

"You're awake...? Ngh... Has the rain stopped yet?" Kinn pushed himself up from the rocks and blearily rubbed his eyes before looking at the smoldering fire. He got up and went to grab some twigs and leaves to throw on it.

"I could tell it was getting cold," he said, squatting down next to the fire and trying to relight it. I watched him warily. When had that lunatic stolen my lighter?

"Where's my shirt?" I asked. Kinn pointed to a big rock on the other side of the cave, where both our shirts were laid out to dry.

"It's still soaked. Don't bother putting it on," he said, yawning.

"What did you do to me?" I demanded, glaring at his back.

"What *could* I do to you?" Kinn asked, tilting his head as he turned to look at me.

"Well, my clothes are...and you were holding me!" I growled.

"You don't remember a thing, do you? It was raining. You said you were cold. I didn't know how to help with that, so I hugged you. Was it warm?" he asked with a shit-eating grin. I wanted to kick his smug face right into the fire pit, but I wasn't strong enough right then. My head was spinning.

"And who said you could do that?!" Shit, it wasn't like I'd forgotten *everything*. I knew we were chased into the middle of the woods, then it started raining, and my body ached to the point that I couldn't take it anymore. I also remembered Kinn giving me...a piggyback ride? I bit my lip hard as I felt my heart skip a beat.

"Come on, Porsche. You really think I'm in the mood for that? Read the room!" Kinn said with a laugh, but I didn't find it funny in the least.

"Who knows? A coldhearted son of a bitch like you could do it. Motherfucking scum of the earth."

Kinn sat there poking at the fire. "That sharp tongue of yours is back to normal. You must be feeling better, hmm?" he said, turning back to face me.

I ignored his remark. "Damn it! Where the hell are we?" I hugged my knees to my chest. The rain made it fucking cold and damp in here.

"I don't have my phone. And I don't know if Pete could even track us if I did," Kinn said. He walked up to the opening of the cave and held his hand out, checking the rain.

"I'm thirsty," I mumbled to myself, looking around for something to catch the rain, but it wasn't like I had a water bottle at my disposal.

"What do we do? We don't have a cup," Kinn said.

I turned to him and frowned. He'd just said the stupidest thing ever. Of course there was no cup—we were in a fucking forest!

"Go get some big leaves. We'll collect water that way," I said, annoyed.

"I can't. It's raining."

I didn't bother replying to him and kept searching, but there was absolutely fuck all in the cave apart from twigs and leaves.

"If you're that thirsty, you can take a drink from me," he joked, his gaze shifting toward his crotch.

"Fuckin' pervert!" I cursed.

Kinn just chuckled before walking out into the rain. I watched him, curious to see what he had planned. Soon after, he ran back with a few big leaves. He rolled them into cones to catch the rain.

"Here," he said, handing one to me. I hesitated briefly, but took it anyway and drank from it; Kinn followed soon after.

"What kind of leaves are these? There's no sap or anything on them, is there?" After I finished drinking, I unfolded the leaf to check.

"Dunno. But it didn't kill you. So it's safe, yeah?" Kinn remarked before raising his cone for another gulp. Had this jerk tricked me into tasting it for him? Yeah, he definitely waited for me to take a sip before he started drinking, the bastard.

I moved closer to the fire pit and held my knees. Why had life screwed me over this bad?! *Damn it!* Being hunted down was bad enough, but now I was stuck in the forest with Kinn! I was *so* fucked.

Kinn walked over and sat across from me. "You heard them talking in the van, right?" he asked.

"Mm-hm." I hummed a reply without looking at him. My eyes were fixed on the fire. I didn't know how to act around Kinn now. At least I'd gotten some of my anger out earlier when I punched him in the face. But under the current circumstances, it wasn't a good idea to start a fight.

"They were targeting you, not me," Kinn said flatly.

"I have no enemies except you!" I growled.

"Hah! Bullshit," Kinn said.

I shot him a burning glare. What made him think he could talk to me like that? That treating me like this was acceptable?! *Asshole!*

"This is the second time they've targeted you," Kinn said, concerned. "And they also know who I am. I don't know what their motive is. Who are they? What do they want?"

I was just as surprised as he was. Kinn was targeted all the time. But they'd wanted *me*. I didn't get it either.

"Let's get out of here first. Then I'll figure out who they are," Kinn said. "They wanted me dead."

I'd overheard that, too. I was the one they wanted to abduct, not Kinn. I hadn't even done anything wrong!

"Are you feeling better?" Kinn asked.

"Yeah."

"It's because you were in my arms—my healing touch worked wonders," he said with a smirk. His face was so annoying that I hurled a twig into the fire, making sparks fly up. He turned away to avoid getting burned, smiling at me with a teasing expression that I'd never seen before.

I rarely saw Kinn act so casual. It felt strange to witness, but maybe it was just this crazy situation. I was used to seeing the elegant and polished young master who was serious about everything; this

Kinn was the opposite. Everything about him was different, from his unkempt hair to his informal demeanor.

"You called for your parents in your sleep," Kinn said. I glanced up at him before averting my eyes, focusing on the fire again. I probably had called out to my parents in my sleep—I'd had a dream that they came to visit me and hugged me tightly. I hadn't felt that kind of warmth in my heart in so long. I felt safe and secure in my parents' embrace, and I was so comfortable that I didn't want to wake up.

"Mm," I hummed.

"How long have you been on your own with your brother?" Kinn asked.

"Almost ten years now," I said quietly.

"At least you got to spend time with your parents. That's good. I don't even remember what my mother looks like," Kinn said with a chuckle.

"Why?" I didn't know what compelled me to ask him.

"My parents got divorced when Kim was just a few months old. I was so little... She's nowhere in my childhood memories," Kinn said, looking into the fire pit.

"Why did they split up?" I was curious about Kinn's past—the fever had to be getting to me.

"I don't know. I've never asked him... Or maybe I did? I don't remember," Kinn said. "I'm happy living with my father, though, so I don't think about it much."

I glanced at Kinn as he spoke. Even though he seemed unaffected, his eyes went dim for a moment. He must have pondered this subject deeply, but he didn't want to reveal his emotions.

"I see."

"You're a good brother, you know? Raising Porchay to high school age. Imagine Tankhun raising me. I would have gone crazy like him by now," he said with a laugh. I cracked a smile, imagining it along with him.

Talking about Chay made me start worrying about him. After they knocked me out, did they get him, too?

"Do you think Chay's gonna be all right?" I asked.

I didn't know if it was the quiet of the forest, the rain pouring down, or my fever that compelled me to speak to Kinn like this. I was able to put aside my fear and fury toward him for a moment. Deep down, however, I was still afraid.

"I told him to sneak out the back," Kinn told me.

"Is he safe?"

"I told him to use your phone to call Pete. You have his number saved, right?"

I nodded. I was so worried for Chay's safety. What would I do if something happened to him?

"Don't worry. I'm sure your brother is safe. Those guys aren't very smart—I mean, look at how they've screwed this up," Kinn said, analyzing the situation. I agreed with him; those bastards were a bunch of reckless amateurs. They hadn't tied us up properly, and they were dumb enough to put us together in the back seat. Fucking morons.

"If he didn't call Pete, I hope he at least called Tem or Jom," I said. Kinn nodded in agreement. I didn't know when I'd let myself study his face so closely. I couldn't help but feel comforted that he was here—I didn't have to be alone in this dark forest in the middle of the night.

I'd bottled up my anger for now. Once we got out of here, I could go back to hating him.

"You want to get some sleep?" Kinn asked. "The rain should stop before tomorrow. We can figure out how to get out of here then."

I nodded slowly, starting to feel a bit dizzy. Had getting rained on made my fever worse? I shuffled back and leaned against a cold rock. Chills shot through my body, but I couldn't do anything to brace against the cold except wrap my arms around myself.

Kinn moved closer to me and I shifted away from him a little. "What?" I asked.

He nudged me off the rock, creating space for him to slide in behind me.

"Do you want to freeze to death?" he said sternly as he pulled me back toward him. He held me tightly, my back pressing against his chest.

"The fuck?! Let me go!" I tried to wrestle out of his embrace, but he held me firmly.

"Stay still! I'm not gonna do anything!" he insisted.

I calmed down a bit, but still turned my head to tell him off. "Let me go, Kinn!"

"You're burning up again... If you freeze and die here, I'm not gonna carry your corpse out of the woods," Kinn said. "Get some sleep. I mean it."

Kinn rested his head on the rock and held me securely in his arms. I couldn't have pried him off if I tried. But...sleeping against him felt better than sleeping against that rock. My whole body warmed in his embrace, and I was overcome with a strange sense of safety. Kinn's chest rising and falling in time with his breathing was a comforting feeling—it meant I wasn't alone in this creepy forest.

Sick and exhausted, I had no choice but to let myself drift off to sleep.

KINN
PORSCHE

19

Lost

THE SKY BEGAN TO BRIGHTEN. I had no idea what time it was or how long I had slept—the only thing I knew was that I felt much better compared to yesterday. My muscles still ached, but I had more energy.

"Are you awake?" a sleepy voice asked from behind me. I felt Kinn rustling around as he held me in his arms. "Did you sleep well?"

"Mmm," I hummed in reply. I didn't want to admit it, but Kinn's body was warming me up nicely.

"Get up, then! You're giving me cramps," Kinn said.

"Let go of me," I scoffed. I managed to pry his hands off, and quickly pushed myself away from him.

Kinn chuckled and sat up. After stretching for a couple of moments, he got up to retrieve his shirt and tossed mine to me. I quickly put it on even though it was still slightly damp.

Kinn turned as if to leave the cave.

"Where are you going?" I asked.

"It's still cloudy, but I'm going to look around," he replied. "You wait here. I'll be right back."

I remained silent, my eyes lingering on his broad back as he vanished from my sight. Kinn had held me the entire night as we slept, and it felt like lying on a soft bed with a warm blanket wrapped around me. It was a comforting feeling; I couldn't deny that Kinn might be the reason why my fever broke.

The fire pit had completely burned down, so I began looking for dried leaves to cover it. We needed to find a way out of this forest today. I didn't know where we were or how deep into the trees we had run. I was afraid we might be trapped. *What should I do?*

The thought should have freaked me out, but I wasn't too worried. I had Kinn with me—at least I wasn't alone.

After emerging from the cave, I tried looking for Kinn, but he was nowhere in sight. I wondered if he had run away and left me stranded in the middle of the forest. That evil bastard must've thought I was a burden because I was sick and ditched me to save his own ass. I started looking for a way out, my eyes darting left and right as I went.

Scrape, scrape.

I paused, scrunching my brow. I thought I heard the faint sound of wood scraping and water running nearby. I was reluctant to rush toward the sound, but I wanted to check if it was Kinn. Maybe he'd run into our pursuer while looking for a way out and got hurt. That man could be so damned stupid sometimes. I needed to go check on him. If he hadn't been killed already, I could at least put an end to his misery.

I found Kinn preoccupied with a tree branch. He appeared to be sharpening the end of it using a rock. Weird.

I stopped in front of him. "What the hell are you doing?"

Kinn ignored me, his attention still fixed on whittling the stick. "Hungry?" he asked.

"Yes," I replied.

"All right, give me a minute," he said. "There's a stream over there—why don't you go clean up?"

I nodded and proceeded in the direction he'd indicated. Although his actions still baffled me, I stopped myself from questioning him further. He seemed deeply concentrated on whatever he was doing, and I didn't want to interrupt.

Not only was Kinn sharpening the tip of the branch, he was also lifting and scrutinizing the stick at a variety of angles. He repeated this awkward maneuver again and again. What on earth was he doing?

Kneeling at the bank of the small stream, I splashed cold water on my face. Despite the chill, the water was refreshing.

Splash, splash!

I looked up toward the sound. Kinn was staring intently into the stream, clutching his sharpened branch as he repeatedly jabbed his makeshift spear into the water. I glared at him, my brows knitting tightly together in bewilderment.

I couldn't ignore his strange behavior any longer. "What the *hell* are you doing?"

"Catching fish," Kinn replied without looking at me. He kept his gaze fixed on the stream and stabbed his spear into the water.

"Huh?! Why do you want to catch fish?" I asked, genuinely curious.

"Because we're stranded in a forest. What will we eat if we don't catch fish? Haven't you played a survival game before?"

Kinn's answer surprised me. I bit back my laughter at how awkward he looked, coming to the realization that Kinn was just as crazy as Tankhun—only better at hiding it. I was speechless. Did their parents raise them in a glass dome or something? How did he expect to catch anything by vigorously stabbing the water like that? The fish would have to be idiots to get caught.

"At first I wanted to catch a chicken, but I searched for a while and I didn't see any. So fish will have to do. Just wait a bit."

I almost spat out the water I was drinking from the stream. Was *Angkor*[1] the last TV drama he watched? *Damn, he's testing my patience!*

I left the stream and headed to a nearby banana tree. I picked one and peeled it, observing Kinn as I ate. I had to say that I admired his dedication, but I couldn't stop laughing at his serious expression. I never expected Kinn, a meticulously dressed snob, to reveal such a crazy side to himself.

When it became apparent that Kinn would persist for quite a while, I decided to sit on a nearby rock, enjoying my banana and watching as if I were at a comedy show.

"Argh! I can't see any fish!" Kinn grumbled in frustration.

"What are you jabbing at, then?" I asked with a chuckle. Kinn looked so ridiculous. I suppressed my laughter as much as I could, but some inevitably slipped out.

"I saw some ripples in the water and thought it was a fish. Damn it!" Kinn cursed, throwing the branch into the water and giving up. He turned toward me with a sour face and asked, "What the hell are you eating?"

I sighed and pointed at the banana tree.

"Why didn't you tell me there was a banana tree?" Kinn groaned and headed in my direction.

"You said you wanted to eat fish, and I didn't want to discourage you," I said, taking another bite of my banana.

Kinn plucked a fruit from the tree and started eating it. "Why is it so easy to catch fish in games?" he mumbled.

I almost choked. *Kinn, you are absolutely Tankhun's brother!*

"Unbelievable," I muttered.

---

1   Angkor is a Thai action fantasy TV-drama. One of its memorable scenes features a character grilling chicken in a forest.

"Let's finish eating! We still need to find a way out of here. The sky is overcast. If it rains again, we're fucked," Kinn said, tossing away his banana peel. The peel nearly hit me in the head. *Jerk!*

"Do you remember the way we came?" I asked.

"Hmm..." Kinn seemed deep in thought. He looked around and counted on his fingers before finally replying, "I think?"

Don't just say, "I think," dipshit! I swore internally. I remembered warning Kinn last night before he ran that it was dark and he should be careful. He'd ignored me.

"Is your fever gone?" Kinn placed his hand against my forehead to check my temperature. I was slightly taken aback but remained still until Kinn lifted his hand away. I didn't know why his touch made my heart skip a beat, but I tried not to overthink it.

"It seems to have gone down. Shall we get going, then?" Kinn said.

We finished eating the bananas, and I waited as Kinn completed whatever calculations he was making in his head. He then began leading us down a path that he swore was the right way out. I didn't have any objections—after all, I was unconscious the night before, so I didn't remember anything.

"Are you sure this is the right way?!" I asked, standing with my hands on my hips. I was starting to doubt whether we'd make it out of here alive. Kinn wandered around aimlessly, taking three steps forward and four steps back. He kept turning left and then right, until my head spun.

"Just trust me... Ah, I recognize this tree," Kinn said, pointing at a large tree.

I frowned at him wearily. "Yeah!" I scoffed, "it's because we've walked past it three times already, dumbass!"

That asshole pretended like he knew what he was doing, but he was failing miserably. If I'd known it would turn out like this, I would have just let those guys take us. At least it might have been easier to escape and survive. Right now, it felt like we were lost in a maze.

"Well, if we keep heading north, we'll find the way out," Kinn said, and continued forward.

"Humor me—which way is north?" I asked.

"This way." Kinn pointed ahead. I let out a heavy sigh, feeling the urge to scream at him surging inside me.

"How the hell do you know?!" I yelled, stopping in my tracks. The sky was so murky that it was impossible to tell which way was north or south. I knew Kinn was just making shit up!

"Come on, let's keep moving," Kinn said, dismissing my objection.

I wondered how far we needed to keep going. I feared we would wander deeper into the forest instead of finding our way out. Kinn seemed equally frustrated that the situation had not turned out the way he planned. He was definitely the type of guy to get mad when things were out of his control.

Lost in thought, I followed Kinn without paying attention to our surroundings. When Kinn abruptly stopped, I walked right into his broad back and almost fell backward. Fortunately, Kinn managed to grab my wrist and keep me upright.

"Shit! Why didn't you tell me you were going to stop?" I grumbled at him. I was frustrated and exhausted; it was hot outside and we'd been walking all day with no progress at all.

"Why should I? You're the one not watching where you're going."

Disgruntled by his harsh reply, I tried to pull my wrist away from his grasp. "Let me go," I said, but Kinn tightened his grip.

"Let me hold your hand—it might jog my memory. Hurry up!" Kinn held my wrist and dragged me behind him. I tried to free myself several times to no avail; eventually I grew tired of fighting him and decided to save my energy for walking.

"Shall we try running?" Kinn turned to ask me. "It might help me remember."

I huffed, annoyed. He didn't remember the way after all!

"I'm not gonna run! I'm exhausted!"

Kinn chuckled at my answer and continued to irritate me. "I'm going to turn right," he announced before taking a right turn.

"Turning left," he said before turning left. "Now I'm going straight."

"Why are you telling me?!" I yelled in exasperation.

"Aww... I didn't want you to complain that I didn't tell you where I was going," he replied cheerfully. I started to wonder if he really wanted to find a way out of here or if he just wanted to piss me off.

We continued on our journey, my legs growing tired and my throat drying up. I was worn out. I kept focusing on the path ahead, helping Kinn look where to go. I didn't notice when Kinn let go of my wrist and firmly took my hand instead. I unconsciously tightened my grip, not resisting him. Having your hand held when you were nervous was comforting. It calmed me down and assuaged my fears.

"Argh, Kinn! Just admit it if you don't know where we're going!" I finally snapped, pulling him to a stop.

"You're such a crybaby," Kinn said, his lips curving into a smirk. In my entire life, I'd never whined at anyone as much as I did at Kinn. He constantly annoyed the shit out of me. *Asshole!*

"Do you remember the way?" I asked sharply.

"Come on, just keep walking," Kinn dismissed me. However, he seemed to have accepted the fact that we were lost.

"Where are you trying to go? Don't you see we've looped back to where we started—*twice*?!" I groused.

We walked all day only to end up right back where we started. The stream in front of us was the same one I'd used to wash my face that morning. The forest was growing dark; I was astounded at our ability to walk all day and yet get absolutely nowhere.

"Fine. We'll rest here one more night and try again tomorrow," Kinn said. I swore *I* would be the one to look for a way out tomorrow—I wasn't going to let Kinn lead again!

"Let me go!" I said, yanking my hand from his.

Kinn smiled at me. "I thought you would never let me go," he teased.

This derelict, lost-in-the-forest Kinn was utterly different from the snobbish Kinn I knew. I could see the difference in his actions and expressions. This version of Kinn seemed more playful, although he still managed to get on my nerves.

"I'm starving!" I exclaimed, plucking a banana from the same tree as before. If banana trees could talk, it would have asked why I came back to eat from it again. Damn it, this was all Kinn's fault. What an idiot!

"I'm hungry," Kinn said, rubbing his belly and coming to stand next to me.

"Then eat," I replied, irritated.

"I'm tired of bananas. I want to eat something else," Kinn said, looking around.

"Picky!" I muttered. We were barely surviving in this forest, and Kinn dared to be finicky about food? It was unbelievable!

"I get bored easily. I don't like eating the same thing twice in a row," Kinn replied, nonchalant. It was true, though—judging from his previous behavior, he was precisely the kind of guy who got bored quickly.

"What are you going to eat, then? Fish? Chicken?" I asked wearily, not knowing what Kinn was thinking.

"Nah, I'm going to eat that," Kinn said, pointing at a tall tree with dense leaves and red fruit.

I squinted at it, wondering what kind of tree it was. But before I could say anything, Kinn kicked off his shoes and awkwardly began to climb the tree. I couldn't believe my eyes! Kinn really was as crazy as Tankhun, just more pretentious. I only hoped that Kim, the youngest of the family, was not as screwy as his two older brothers.

Kinn grabbed at the branches and flung himself up into the tree. He was so ungainly that I couldn't hold back my laughter. All this time his serious and stern demeanor must've been an act he put on to earn people's respect—this awkward weirdo was likely his true self. His men would be horrified to see their boss making a total ass of himself like this.

"Pfft!" I bit my lip and stifled another laugh. I followed Kinn closely with my eyes: his face was so earnest, but his climbing was utterly graceless.

Thud!

Kinn jumped down and offered me the fruits in his hand. I immediately shook my head.

"No way!" I didn't know if they were edible or poisonous. We could die from eating them! "What even are they?"

"Some kind of wild cherry?"

I smiled at Kinn's naivete. They *looked* like cherries, but I was sure they weren't. There wouldn't be any cherry trees growing in this forest. When Kinn saw my disinterest, he popped one of the fruits into his mouth.

Ptui! He immediately spat it out. I roared with laughter as his face scrunched up in disgust.

Kinn dashed to the stream to rinse his mouth. I felt bad for him—he'd tried so hard to climb that tree only to discover the fruit was inedible. "What the hell is this? It's full of sap," he grumbled.

If we had gotten lost separately, I was confident I would've been the only one who survived. I'd looked after myself for most of my life; I was pretty confident in my survival skills. Meanwhile, Kinn would probably get himself killed the first day on his own. He acted like he knew what he was doing, like he was someone you could rely on, but in reality he had no survival skills whatsoever. What made him think he could just eat any random thing he found in the forest?

Kinn glared at me. "The hell are you laughing at?"

"Pfft! Why aren't you eating them? We wouldn't want all that effort to go to waste," I joked.

"Well...it was kind of worth it. I got to see you smile," Kinn replied. He spoke so quietly I could barely make out his words.

I didn't really care, though, so I continued chowing down on the banana in my hand.

"You really like bananas, huh," Kinn said lightly, shuffling his feet closer to me.

"I'm eating what's available. There's no need to be fussy." It was the truth. We could die at any moment; how could we afford to be picky eaters?

"I've got a *banana* too, you know. It tastes better than the one you're holding."

Kinn loved making sexual innuendos around me, the damned pervert. I threw the banana peel at his face.

"Ow!"

"Screw you!" I shouted.

"Cut it out, Porsche! I'm still your boss!" Kinn hissed.

"Boss, my ass!" I snapped, turning away. I couldn't stand seeing his annoying face any longer.

Kinn then stood behind me and leaned in close to whisper coldly into my ear: "Call me *boss*."

I shivered before shoving hard at his chest, making him stagger backward. "You're not my boss, you're my *burden*! Fuck off!"

Kinn just chuckled at me as I stormed away to the stream. I splashed cool water over my face and drank several gulps to clear my head.

"It's already getting dark. Do you want to wash up?" Kinn asked.

I felt sweaty from walking all over the forest, so I glanced at Kinn and pondered if I should do as he suggested. The forest was dark at night, and I was afraid to dip into the stream by myself. Even though Kinn was here, I didn't really trust him.

"Well, do as you please. I'm going to start a fire," Kinn said, as if he read my mind. He was about to leave and give me my privacy, but I didn't need it right now. The sky was darkening even further, and the eerie atmosphere creeped me out. I could admit I was afraid of ghosts!

"Wait!" I called out to him. Kinn turned around, lifting a brow.

"Just stay here...and...we can leave together," I stammered. I was reluctant to ask for his help, but I had no other choice.

"Hmm..." Kinn looked around curiously at our surroundings. "Ah! Are you scaaared?" he teased, drawing out his words.

"I'm not scared!" I said sharply.

"Can I leave, then?" Kinn asked jokingly, turning and pretending to walk away.

"Wait!" I called to him again. Kinn turned back around and flashed me a shit-eating grin. I still wasn't sure whether I should wash up or not and became annoyed at my own indecisiveness.

"Hah! Are you afraid of ghosts?" Kinn asked between giggles.

I frowned. "I just don't want to be alone. What if some animal attacks me?" I lied. I didn't want him to know about my fear of ghosts—it was embarrassing.

"Someone like you shouldn't be afraid of anything!" Kinn said, laughing again. "Fine, I'll stay with you. I don't want a tiger to come get you when you can't call me for help." He sat down on a rock near the stream.

A tiger? Why did he have to jinx it? And if a tiger showed up, what could a guy like Kinn even do? The man was fucking useless!

"Turn around! Don't look at me!" I commanded. Right now, I wasn't sure what was worse: ghosts, or Kinn.

"Such a pain in the ass," Kinn complained lightheartedly, but he did as he was told. I glanced at him one more time to ensure he wasn't looking, then stripped off everything but my boxers. I swore under my breath, wondering why I was acting like some kind of blushing virgin around Kinn—we were both men, for fuck's sake!

"*Brrr!*" I shivered as I waded into the stream. The water was freezing cold, but it felt refreshing.

"Don't stay in there for too long, or you might get sick again," Kinn cautioned me. We both had our backs to each other.

I walked a bit further into the stream, but didn't dare turn around to look at him. I was afraid those horrible memories would flood back, especially since I was half naked around him. It would just disgust me.

I continued to cross the stream until I reached the bank on the other side, where I placed my palms together in a wai gesture to the tree before relieving myself there.[2]

The forest was unsettlingly quiet and dark. If I'd been alone, I'd have lost my mind with fear. I hurriedly dipped my body in the stream to wash myself, thinking how lucky I was that the moon in the sky provided a bit of visibility.

2   In Thailand it's customary to apologize or ask permission from the spirit of a tree before doing something that might be disrespectful—like peeing on it.

"Kinn?" I called out. He was so quiet—I wanted to check he was still there.

"Hmm... What?" he replied, still with me. That was a relief.

"Nothing," I said, continuing to wash up.

Five minutes later, a sense of unease crept up on me again.

"Hey, Kinn."

"Yes? I'm still here."

I smiled slightly at his reply and heard him make swatting sounds, probably trying to shoo the mosquitoes away. I was thankful he had patiently waited for me instead of doing something to provoke me like usual.

I was almost done cleaning myself when I realized I hadn't heard a sound from Kinn in a while. I began to tremble, freaking out again.

"Kinn!" I called out. I waited for his reply, but none came.

"Hey, Kinn!" I shouted louder, unease twisting my stomach. My body grew tense with fear, and I hesitated to turn around...

"Kinn! This isn't funny!"

I was so petrified that my legs shook. It was already difficult to see in the dark forest, but the creepy vibes and the cold water made it feel like ghosts could appear at any second.

Splash!

Suddenly, someone—or some*thing*—emerged from the water and wrapped their arms tightly around me from behind.

"Fuuuuck!" I screamed at the top of my lungs, terrified.

"Ha ha ha, you're afraid of ghosts!" Kinn said, cackling. I shakily took a deep breath to calm myself before turning around to shove him with all my strength.

"Son of a bitch! You almost gave me a heart attack, you asshole!" I kept pushing him away, but his arms held firm around my waist.

Finally, I gave him a hard shove that sent him tumbling backward into the water—and he pulled me down with him, the fucker.

I made a gurgling sound, swallowing water. Kinn tried to stand and pulled me up with him. Then his arm returned to wrap tightly around my torso.

"Let go of me!" I barked at him as soon as we regained our balance. Kinn ignored my words. His gaze was fixed on me, and I unconsciously stared back into those dark eyes. Our faces were so close that it made my heart race uncontrollably.

"Nope!" Kinn stubbornly replied. He leaned his face even closer to mine, forcing me to jerk my head back.

"Kinn, let go of me. Please. I don't want to think of that night ever again!" I pleaded, trying to pry off his hands. I meant what I said—after spending the day with him, I'd almost forgotten about those painful memories. However, with his arms around me, images from that night threatened to come flooding back.

"Porsche, listen to me..." Kinn sighed, his tone serious. His arms stayed tightly wrapped around me, reminding me vividly of that fateful night. I felt the hurt and horror slowly creep back into me.

I remained silent, unable to tear my eyes away from him. I was captivated every time I looked at him, like some kind of wicked magic in his eyes compelled me. Everything went still save for my heart, which fluttered frantically in my chest.

"I didn't mean it," Kinn said with regret. "I didn't know it would cause you so much pain." His words were much softer than usual; he must have seen how shaken I was.

When I didn't respond, Kinn continued: "I forgot to take your feelings into account... I know what I did was horrible, but I didn't mean for it to turn out that way."

His firm yet gentle words echoed in my ears. The sincerity I saw on his face in the darkness made me believe he genuinely regretted what he did to me.

"I know you might not have a shred of sympathy for me anymore, but I can't change the past. I wish I could turn back time—I don't want you to hate me. At least let me say one thing... Don't leave me, please."

I frowned. He didn't want me to leave, but why?

"Please don't quit being my bodyguard," Kinn whispered.

I wanted to ask him why he was so fixated on me, on just one person. He *did* turn over every rock to find me and make me his bodyguard, so I guessed he didn't want me to quit after all the effort he'd spent on me.

"Don't go unless I tell you. Can you do that?" Kinn's plea sounded vaguely like a command, but it hit me hard. I didn't notice him leaning in closer until I felt his lips brush mine. Unsure of what to do, I stood motionless as a whirlwind of feelings tumbled through my head.

"I'm sorry," Kinn said, evoking a warm sensation in my heart. He gently pressed his lips against mine once more, confusing me further. A part of me wanted to hate him and reject his apology, but another part told me to accept it.

I slowly closed my eyes, finally accepting his gentle kiss. Kinn nibbled lightly at my lower lip before delicately slipping his tongue inside, exploring my mouth and igniting a spark that spread through my entire body. This kiss was unlike any other we had shared before; there was no sense of force or coercion. It felt like a promise, an assurance that Kinn's words were true. Without thinking, I let my emotions take control once again.

I remained still and let Kinn declare his feelings through his kiss. I didn't reciprocate his actions, but I didn't reject him, either. My heart went into overdrive, like it might burst out of my chest.

Kinn eventually pulled his lips away, but he stayed close, his forehead touching mine. "Are you cold?" he asked. At some point, he'd released me from his arms in order to gently hold my face between his palms, brushing away the hair that fell over my forehead with his thumb.

"Mm-hmm," I hummed softly.

"Get to the riverbank and wait for me. I'll wash up quickly," Kinn instructed before moving away.

"Okay," I replied, emerging from the stream. Confusion and disbelief swirled inside my mind—why had I let Kinn kiss me without protest? Why hadn't I pushed him away? *Why? Why? Why?!* My thoughts infuriated me. Why was I so conflicted? What had happened to make me feel this way? Damn it, I should hate him! Fear him! Be disgusted by him! *He did horrible things to you, Porsche!*

"Turn around," I told him. "I'm gonna get dressed."

Kinn looked amused but did as he was told. I swiftly removed my wet boxers and pulled on my sweatpants and t-shirt.

"Why are you so quiet?" Kinn asked.

"How loud do you want me to be? We're in a forest, not a Thonglor dance club," I quipped, wringing the water out of my boxers.

"It still shouldn't be this quiet," he insisted. I didn't understand Kinn's logic. Did he think he was at The International Horticultural Exposition, where ambient music played everywhere you went?

"Why don't you sing a song if you think it's too quiet?" I remarked. Bantering with him like this made the atmosphere of the dark forest a bit less creepy.

"Are you sure you want me to sing?" Kinn joked.

"Mm-hmm," I confirmed, thinking it would be better than sitting in silence. I wasn't particularly concerned with what Kinn did as long as there was some kind of background noise. I was still scared as I waited alone on the shore—ghosts could show up at any time!

"All right, how about this? *Oh-la-hey, oh-la-heuk. I'm mourning for you, my beloved phi-Mak!*" Kinn sang.

I nearly grabbed my shoe to hurl it at his head. Fucking idiot! He was singing a lullaby from *Nang Nak*[3] in a solemn and haunting tone, obviously trying to freak me out!

"Kinn, you jackass! Can't you sing something else?!"

Kinn laughed. "Forget ghosts, you should be scared of these damned mosquitoes. There're so many of them, I wouldn't be surprised if we get malaria," he complained before falling silent again. I heard the sound of water sloshing. I assumed he'd gone to take a piss at the same place I did earlier.

This entire situation fucking sucked. I would much rather be back at home in my soft bed. Could we get out of this forest? Did Kinn's family know where their young master was? It was all stressing me out. *Argh!*

My mind wandered as the silence continued to envelop us. Abruptly, Kinn started singing again:

"When I see your face, I lose control.
When you smile back, I'm shaken up.
It happens every day—I have to hold myself back!"

I felt better hearing Kinn's voice cut through the quiet of the dark forest. His singing was all right—not great, but not bad, either. It was better than nothing.

"When I see your face, I lose control.

---

3   Nang Nak (1999) is a supernatural horror film based on Mae Nak Phra Khanong, a well-known Thai ghost story.

Would it be wrong to catch your eye by chance?
I dream about you every single night.
Tell me, please—what should I do next?"[4]

This Kinn was way more cheerful than the Kinn I knew, but I was starting to get used to this version of him. I was seeing sides of him I didn't even know existed; he was sillier than I thought.

"Did I sing well?" Kinn asked.

"You listen to Thai rock?" I asked, surprised. I assumed that someone with his lifestyle would prefer jazz or sappy ballads.

"I do, but I usually listen to Western pop music. I stuck to Thai because I was afraid you wouldn't understand English lyrics."

I frowned, trying to figure out if he was calling me stupid.

"Jerk!" I retorted when I heard him snicker. I organized his English report in the wrong order *one* time, and he was never going to let me live it down!

Kinn finally returned to dry land and immediately began to put on his clothes. The weather had cooled as night fell, prompting us to return to the cave where we had slept the previous night.

Kinn gathered some dried leaves and twigs into a pile and set them aflame with the lighter, boasting that this was his first time in a forest and he could already start a fire by himself. I wasn't sure if that was really something you should be proud of—he was a grown man! He should know basic survival skills!

"What the hell is Pete doing?" Kinn grumbled as he lowered himself to sit in front of the fire.

"In case you forgot, Pete works for Tankhun. Why don't you ask about Big?" I asked, curious. I was the current leader of Kinn's bodyguards, and Pete wasn't on my team anymore. Kinn should have asked where Big was.

---

4   The song's name is Wan Wai (Shaken) by Bodyslam, a famous Thai rock band.

Kinn seemed slightly taken aback. "Well...whatever. Someone should come get me out of here already!"

"I've never seen you act like this," I said, not looking at him. I pretended to focus on finding more leaves to add to the fire.

"Act like what?" he asked, chuckling.

"Like *this*!"

"What do you expect me to act like, then?" Kinn asked, arching his eyebrows.

"I don't expect you to do anything," I replied. Kinn seemed satisfied with my answer.

I honestly hadn't expected anything from him. I was genuinely surprised to see his goofy behavior, though, considering he acted so mature all the time.

"That's good," Kinn said, leaning back against a rock and sighing contentedly. "I want to relax sometimes. I'm in my twenties—I'm only one year older than you. What do people expect of me?"

"But you look way older than that," I joked. It was true; everything Kinn did in the forest conflicted with his mature appearance.

"Hmph. Watch your mouth! Sometimes, everyone's expectations just exhaust me," Kinn said. "I wanted to live my life like other kids... but look at my brothers! Tankhun is a flake, and Kim barely comes home. Don't you think they give my father enough headaches on their own? I didn't need him to worry about me as well."

I was stunned to hear Kinn vent his feelings to me. It was probably the longest string of words I'd ever heard him speak. He seemed frustrated from striving to be the perfect son, especially considering he was the son of a mafia boss. He was forced to shoulder a multitude of responsibilities and live up to many expectations—I sometimes forgot he was only a year older than me.

Kinn's life was far from carefree. After classes, he had to do paperwork and attend business meetings as his father's representative. Of the three sons, Kinn was the only one I ever saw taking the family business seriously.

"Mmm..." I hummed in response.

"I'm fed up with trying to act stern and put on a front to make people respect me. But if I don't maintain the façade, all hell will break loose," Kinn went on.

"But Tankhun acts however he wants," I pointed out.

"I can't be like him, either. Look at him. Do you see anyone who respects him, fears him? People only fear his tantrums," Kinn said with a hint of amusement. "I don't want our business's reputation to worsen. I want our competitors and partners to continue to fear and respect us."

I nodded, agreeing with everything Kinn said. I knew that respect was essential in this business. I had to admit that Kinn's thoughts on the matter were rather mature.

"Aren't you frustrated? You say you have to pretend... So everything you do is just a front?" I asked curiously.

"Yes. That's just how it has to be. At least I can be myself when I'm alone or with my friends...or like right now," Kinn said, briefly glancing at me before returning his gaze to the cave around us.

I didn't understand what he meant, but I didn't object to him letting his guard down around me. I was glad he didn't have to pretend to be someone he wasn't.

"All right," I said.

"What about you? Do you realize you've been smiling and laughing more than usual?" Kinn asked, still unusually talkative.

"I'm laughing at your stupidity," I replied truthfully.

"Yeah? That's good."

I frowned. What was good about that? Kinn just kept irritating me.

"Should we move to the forest? I'm starting to like it here," Kinn joked.

"Knock yourself out," I replied before lying down with my back against a rock on the opposite side of the cave. I was beginning to feel drowsy.

"Why don't you lie down here?" Kinn said, patting his chest.

I flipped him off. "Like hell!" I growled.

"If you say so..." Kinn started singing that haunting tune again. *"Oh-la-hey. Oh-oh-la-heuk..."*

I covered my ears. Kinn just laughed.

"You piece of shit!" I shouted.

"Hurry up and come here before the ghosts get you," Kinn beckoned.

I turned my back to him. I kept my hands pressed against my ears, but I could still hear him singing.

"Oh-la-hey, oh-la-heuk. I'm mourning for you, my beloved phi-Mak..."

I squeezed my eyes shut and tried to drown out as much of his voice as I could. I rolled over to scold him, but was surprised to find he had scooted over to me. My face squashed against his chest.

"What the hell?! Get off of me!" I yelled, shoving at him.

*"Oh-la-hey, oh-la-*oof?!"

I swiftly covered Kinn's mouth with my hands to shut him up, and he took the opportunity to pull me in by the nape of my neck and press my head against his chest.

"Let me go, damn it!" I yelped, trying to wrestle my way out of his embrace. He kept his arms locked around me, leaning leisurely against a rock with his eyes closed.

I noticed the hollow sound of wind outside the cave, and it freaked me out. My eyes darted nervously to the darkness outside as I lay still against Kinn's chest.

"Hey! Open your eyes!" I commanded while shaking his body.

"Why?" Kinn asked, opening his eyes and smiling languidly.

"Don't fall asleep before I do," I said. It was Kinn's fault for singing that creepy song. I'd always been scared of ghosts. One time I saw something lurking in the shadows at home, and I had to sleep in Chay's bed with him for several days until I could go back to my own room. I was not easily fazed, and I was ready to face anything head-on—anything except ghosts. I'd have a heart attack if I ever encountered one.

"Shall I sing you a lullaby? *Oh-la*-mmph!"

Kinn began singing, and I quickly slapped my hand over his mouth again. He chuckled in amusement. I kept my hands over his mouth as I lay my head on his chest once more. I would have been mortified if someone happened to see us right then—two fully grown men cuddling each other.

I wasn't sure if it was a good idea to sleep in Kinn's arms. But he was keeping me warm, so I eventually let it go and slept soundly. I decided to stop hating Kinn, at least for right now. After we got out of this forest, it'd be a different story.

I was happy to see him be himself, though. It was reassuring to have the real Kinn around.

KINN
PORSCHE

20

Worried

TODAY MARKED OUR THIRD DAY of being lost in the forest. Luckily, there was some sun out this morning compared to how overcast the last two days had been. I kept walking ahead, ignoring Kinn's protests from behind me. *I told you I'm not going to listen to you today!* I wasn't stupid enough to let him get us lost again. If I let him lead the way, we weren't gonna make it out of here alive.

"I say we go left," Kinn said, pointing. I nodded and immediately turned right. *I'm telling you, I'm through with your bullshit guesses. I'm not going to follow you like a fool!*

"Why don't you believe me, huh?" he asked, sounding a bit annoyed. Despite his protests, he kept following me.

"The sun's so fucking hot!" Kinn complained. Even though we were in a forest full of oxygen, walking all day made us work up quite a sweat.

"Can we rest for a bit?" Kinn asked. He slowed down and tugged at the hem of my shirt before collapsing on a log under a few large trees. I sighed, stopped walking, and stared at him in silence. I was tired, too, but if Kinn kept wimping out, we weren't going to make it out of here before dark.

"Come sit," Kinn patted at his thighs, inviting me to sit on his lap.

I quickly lifted up my foot. "Sit on this!" I shouted.

"Heh, it's just sitting on my lap... That's nothing compared to cuddling me all night," he said with a smirk.

I gave him the middle finger. *Motherfucker! If it weren't for the cold and my fear of ghosts, I would never have done that!*

"Come here!" Kinn insisted. He refused to give up, tugging at my wrist to force me into his lap. I fell back onto him and he wrapped his arms around my waist, nuzzling his face into my back. I tried to get up, but the more I struggled, the tighter he held me.

"Let me go!" I shouted.

"Sit still. Let me recharge," Kinn said. *What the fuck is he talking about?*

"Let me go, you shithead!" I yelled.

"Ow!" Kinn cried. I must have struggled a bit too hard—we both went rolling backward off the log.

I landed on top of Kinn but hurriedly stood up. "What the hell are you playing at?!" I shouted at him.

Kinn lay on the ground, holding his arm and writhing around in pain. "My arm hurts!" he wailed.

I could only laugh. *Serves him right.* I stood there with my hands loosely on my hips, guffawing as he threw a pitiful tantrum.

"It hurts! My arm got scratched by the branches," he said, making a face like he was mortally wounded. I sighed and bent down to take a look.

"Where?!" I snapped. I turned his arm over and found a long cut on his wrist slowly oozing blood.

"Serves you right, annoying me like that!" I scolded him with a spiteful little laugh, then used the hem of my shirt to carefully dab at his arm. He pushed himself up from the ground as I tended to his wound.

"Am I going to die?" he asked.

"You better die!" I snapped.

"Nooo, do I have to die in the forest?" he whined as he leaned onto my shoulder. He was exaggerating for sure; his pained expression looked fake as hell.

"You'll die because I'll beat you to death!" I replied darkly, glaring at his wound. He was totally overreacting—it was just a surface-level scratch. I shook his head off of my shoulder.

He sat up straight and looked at me. "Can you kiss it better?" he asked with a smile.

I stared at him, irritated, and his smile instantly disappeared. *I knew you were fucking with me.* I shoved his arm away and stood up.

"Cut the bullshit," I demanded. "Let's go."

Kinn grimaced as if he was dying again. "My arm hurts. I can't walk! Carry me," he whined.

What is wrong with him today? He's so fucking immature. The bastard deserves a swift kick in the ass.

"Why would I carry you? There's nothing wrong with your legs," I said.

"Yesterday *I* carried *you*," Kinn said. I snorted. I got so annoyed when Kinn acted like this—it was like the more frustrated I was, the happier he became.

"Let me break your legs, then I'll carry you," I said, deadpan.

"Pull me up first," he said, laughing and holding out his hand. I resigned myself to helping him up.

"You can let go now," I told him, shaking off his hand.

"Let me hold onto you! My arms are weak," Kinn said. He spoke in his normal voice, but his words just got brattier and brattier, the impudent little shit.

"Such a pain!" I sighed and carried on walking ahead, Kinn still holding my hand tightly.

"Admit it," he whispered, so softly I could barely hear it, "you're worried about me, too..." I did my best to ignore it—to pretend it was the birds or the wind. Kinn clearly just wanted to rile me up more.

"This way," he said, quickening his pace to push past me.

"No! We're going that way," I said. I no longer trusted his sense of direction. I pushed past his shoulder to go the other way, his hand still in mine.

"No! I remember where we came from. It's this way!" He sped up, trying to take the lead again.

"Ugh! Kinn, just stay still, you idiot!" I snapped.

He turned to shout at me. "I'm the leader; you have to listen to me!"

"Who made you the leader?!"

"My dad!" he proclaimed, smug. I was completely fed up with him. In the end, I managed to pull him by the hand in the direction I wanted. After a bit of huffing and puffing, he followed.

Maybe he was afraid I'd disappear and get lost or whatever, but he was still holding my hand like he had yesterday—the only difference being I was not reciprocating the gesture. We kept walking along the path, bickering and shouting. Honestly, all this walking wasn't nearly as tiring as having to deal with a pain in the ass like Kinn. He just sucked all the energy right out of me!

"Well, you know what they say," Kinn began out of nowhere.

I furrowed my brow but kept walking. "What?"

"That if you feel like you're getting more lost the further you go, it's because there's something blocking your sight," Kinn said. I flinched but tried not to think about it.

I stayed silent, but Kinn continued. "You know, forests like this are usually home to supernatural beings and wandering spirits,"[5]

---

5   สัมภเวสี (Sampawesi): wandering spirits who haven't yet entered the cycle of rebirth.

he said, lowering his voice, and I reflexively squeezed his hand before turning around to scold him.

"Why the fuck would you say that?!" *Who says shit like that alone in the woods?*

"I'm serious! Have you never read up on this kind of stuff? On what happens when you wander around and circle back to where you started?" he said evenly, face deadly serious.

"Motherfucker! Why are you saying that shit out loud?!" I snarled back angrily. *Of course I've heard about wandering spirits, but can you take a look at where we are? Is this really the time to talk about it?!*

"Yesterday, we ended up back where we started... So, do you think...?" he trailed off with a wary expression. I was really starting to freak out. Chills crept down my spine and I shifted a little closer to Kinn, not letting go of his hand.

"Think what...?" I asked quietly.

"That we might have accidentally offended the guardians of the forest?"[6]

"Well, *I* didn't offend any spirits," I said, tense. "Did you? A guy like you, I bet even your thoughts are offensive."

Kinn quickly shook his head. "No. I gave a wai this morning. Since you've been here, have you paid any respects?" he asked as he stared at me, like I was the one in the wrong. When Kinn put it that way... Other than giving a wai gesture to the tree before taking a piss, I hadn't given it much thought.

"I also gave a wai," I said, then whispered, "when I went to pee."

"There it is, I knew it! That's not enough... You have to take things seriously, otherwise we're gonna be stuck here. We've been walking for so long, it feels like we're never gonna get out of here—you feel it too, right?" Kinn asked soberly.

---

6 เจ้าป่าเจ้าเขา (Chao pa chao khao): *guardian spirits believed to reside in nature.*

"So what should I do?" I asked. I was actually getting scared now. I did believe in the supernatural, even if I'd never experienced it firsthand. My mom had told me that I'd been afraid of ghosts since I was a little kid, but I had no idea what happened to make me so afraid of them.

"Come here! Face that way, and put your hands together." Kinn ordered me into position.

"I have to do it now?" I asked him, confused.

"Yes! Quickly, so we can get the hell out of here," he insisted.

"What about you?" I asked.

"I did it this morning... Just do it," he insisted when he saw me hesitate. "We can have some peace of mind that way at least."

"What do I have to say?" I asked. The fear made me do exactly as Kinn said.

"There's a prayer. Ready?"

I nodded at Kinn, palms pressed together.

"*A... nan... ta... pad...* You have to say it louder," Kinn urged. I repeated after him, word by word.

"*...Cha... ye... A... pad... ti... de... de... na...*"

"*...Na...* Wait, this prayer sounds familiar," I said, looking at his face. I thought I caught him smirking, but maybe I was overthinking things.

"You've probably heard it before—it's famous. Come on, keep going: *A... pad... ti... ya... A...pad... di... de... de... tue,*" he continued.

Yeah, right. I glared at Kinn. He laughed and tapped out a rhythm on a tree, singing, "*Anantapad chaye Apadti dedena!*[7] Ha ha ha!" He cackled at me again. I marched over to smack his chest in frustration as he laughed himself to tears.

"You believe in this stuff? Hah! You're hilarious."

---

7   *Referencing a fake chant/song from the comedy movie Luang Phi Theng 3.*

"Fucking waste of my time! Bastard! If you've got the balls to joke about this shit, you're gonna run into the real thing!" I shouted and punched his arm.

"Ouch! I don't believe in ghosts, Porsche. I've never seen one with my own eyes. I didn't think you really believed in them!" He kept on laughing.

"I hope you get haunted by one, you shithead!" I yelled. *This motherfucker!*

We ended up chasing each other around for a long while. When we got back to civilization, would Kinn still let himself act silly like this? Right now, alone with me, he wasn't putting on airs. He was acting like a total fucking moron and annoying the shit out of me, but at least he wasn't the regular stuck-up, serious Kinn.

"Aww, you're stressed out. Your eyebrows are so knotted up they've tied themselves into a bow," Kinn said. He threw his arm over my shoulder and massaged between my eyebrows.

"This isn't funny, Kinn!" I angled myself away, fuming, but he pulled my head down onto his shoulders.

"I'm just trying to lighten the mood. Don't be like that..." He was still trying to annoy me. *Lighten the mood, my ass!* My mood was actively getting worse as he played around and disrespected whatever spirits might be out here.

Rustle!

I jumped at the sound of a bush shaking. I grabbed Kinn's shirt at his waist and held on tightly, burying my face in his shoulder. My heart thumped wildly against my chest as I thought about all the freaky shit Kinn had just been talking about.

"What is that?!" Kinn yelled, his arms around me.

Rustle! Swish!

Kinn let out a relieved laugh. "Ah, it's just a hare. Are you scared of bunnies? Hah!" He rubbed my back soothingly as I lifted my head and smacked his chest.

"Aww, it's okay," he cooed, lifting his hand to pat my head. I glared at him. *Damn it, my tough image is totally destroyed! Now I look like a weak little bitch!*

"You motherfucking bastard!" I cussed Kinn out, irritated, then spun around to stride away without listening to any more of his laughter or teasing. *The nerve of this asshole! I should just leave him out here!*

"Wait for me!" Kinn called, jogging over until he caught up. I kept walking, vowing not to waste any more time putting up with Kinn's nonsense.

"I think this is the right way," I said. We'd been walking for a while, and the path was becoming more familiar by the minute. Kinn and I started half walking, half jogging until we reached the cliff face we originally fell from.

"This is it! We just have to find a way to get up there." Kinn looked upward, thoughtful.

"Find them! Don't stop until you do!" a harsh voice resonated through the forest. Kinn and I immediately ducked behind a tree.

"Shit! They haven't stopped searching?" Kinn cursed. He pulled out his gun, ready to fight.

"What do we do?" I asked him. We only had the one gun between us—I'd lost mine when we fell.

"I see footprints over here!" another man shouted. I held my breath, glancing over at Kinn. He cocked his gun and reached over to hold my wrist.

"Give me the gun, Kinn. I'll deal with them," I said, but he wasn't listening to me. His eyes scanned our surroundings.

"We'll have to fight, or it won't end here," he said.

"They're over here!"

Bang! Bang!

Kinn fired as soon as he heard the men shout, and two bodies fell to the ground in a heap.

"Shit!" I exclaimed. Kinn still wouldn't hand me the gun. He pulled at my hand, weaving between the trees as gunshots rang out.

Bang! Bang!

"We're running out of bullets," Kinn said as he checked the gun's magazine before sliding it back in and shooting another man until he, too, fell to the ground. Things weren't looking good, so I shook off Kinn's hand and dove out from behind the tree, grabbing a gun from one of the bodies.

"Porsche! What the hell are you doing?" Kinn yelled, his face drawn tight. He ran after me, still firing.

Click! I cocked the gun and took aim. There were nearly ten of them circling us. Kinn pulled me behind a tree again to take cover.

Bang! Bang!

"What the fuck do you think you're doing? You're gonna get yourself killed!" Kinn scolded me before twisting out from behind the tree to fire another shot.

"Fuck! There's too many of them. We have to make a decisive attack, or we're not gonna make it!" I told Kinn. I didn't know if I was oversimplifying, but if we went back into the woods it was going to be the same shit all over again. *Might as well go all out. Give them a taste of their own medicine.*

"Porsche! Don't you dare!"

Ignoring Kinn's demand, I sprang out from behind the tree, firing madly into the crowd.

"Kinn, you go that way! I'll go the other way," I told him, and ran off, not really caring if he followed my command or not. I took cover and fired back.

Bang! Bang!

We were still outnumbered. Our attackers circled us, drawing closer and closer. I panted heavily as I checked the pistol's magazine. My eyes locked with Kinn's worried ones as he looked out from behind a different tree. I didn't know what else we could do. If we went after them head-on again, I was going to run out of bullets. I tried to gather my wits, but before I could, the muzzle of a gun pressed against my forehead.

"Give up! You can't win," the man said. Three of them surrounded me. I closed my eyes. I hadn't expected to fuck up so quickly. I aimed my gun at one of them, but I was cornered.

Thwack! Kinn threw himself over, kicking at the man's wrist and making his gun misfire into a tree trunk. To do something so brazen, Kinn was probably out of bullets himself. I tried to find an opening, kicking and punching and knocking another gun from their hands. Weakened as I was, I stumbled and took a couple of punches to the face. I could usually down someone in a single hit, but in my weakened state, my hands and feet were only half as powerful.

Bang!

The men kept firing. I tried to duck, grabbing one of them to shield myself. Another one managed to knock the gun from my hand as I took hit after hit, but I kept fighting back. Kinn was no different, putting up his best fight but getting his ass kicked, too. Someone grappled me into a full-body lock as another kicked me straight in the chest, the pain momentarily stunning me. Kinn's voice rang out:

"Shit! Porsche!"

My eyes widened in surprise as Kinn's body crashed into mine, his arms wrapping around me.

Bang! Bang!

I froze when one guy pointed a gun at me, but I couldn't feel anything as Kinn's body shielded mine. My heart sank with fear when I felt wetness seep onto my body. Kinn went completely still. I saw the men take aim for a second shot, so I grabbed a fallen gun and returned fire, holding Kinn up with my other arm.

Bang! Bang!

"Over there!" came another shout as the men switched targets from us to a band of newcomers. Blood rushed in my ears. It felt like my mind was short-circuiting. I fell to my knees, trying to hold up Kinn. His eyes were closed and he was bleeding from his abdomen. I didn't know what to do—my heart trembled and my mouth could only shout his name.

"Kinn! Kinn! Shit! Stay awake!" I yelled at him. The image of Kinn bleeding out in front of me was terrifying. I slapped his face and shook his body. I didn't care what was happening around me— I was scared for Kinn's life.

Pete's blurry face appeared above me. He took Kinn's weight off of me as Arm ran over to support me, calling out to me.

"Porsche! Porsche!"

The pain and exhaustion made my vision go dark...

[HOSPITAL]

I didn't know how much time had passed, but I could feel comfortable softness at my back and a familiar warmth, similar to Kinn's embrace in the forest. I felt so relieved and secure. *Am I still in the forest, leaning on Kinn?*

"Kinn..." I whispered in a raspy voice, throat parched, before slowly opening my eyes to an unfamiliar ceiling.

"Hia! Hia's awake! P'Tem, P'Jom!" my brother's voice happily shouted. "How are you feeling?" he asked me.

I pushed myself up slowly and pain shot through my body. My eyes scanned the room—my hand was hooked up to an IV drip and I was wearing a hospital gown.

"Hey, how are you doing? You slept for two days straight." Tem and Jom beamed at me from beside my bed.

"Chay!" I pulled my brother into a hug. I'd been so worried about him.

"Are you thirsty? Have some water." Chay pulled away to pour me a glass before bringing the straw to my lips. I drank my fill and tried to make sense of what had happened, when I suddenly remembered...

"What about Kinn?" I asked. The only thing I remembered before everything went black was Kinn getting shot as we fought those guys.

They all went still and silent. I began to feel anxious. I wasn't sure why, but my heart sank with dread.

"How is he?" I asked, my voice tense.

The three of them looked at each other silently.

"Shit! He's dead?" I asked, biting my lip. My heart ached. No matter how much I hated him, I still didn't want him to die like that. Besides, I felt guilty—I was his bodyguard. I was supposed to be protecting him, but he'd been the one to protect me. I was responsible for his death. I felt despair creeping in.

"No..." Tem tried to tell me something, but my mind was spinning in circles. I just wanted to see Kinn one last time.

"What temple[8] is he in? Take me there," I said, trying to get down from the bed. Tem and Jom quickly grabbed me.

"Porsche, listen to me!"

My friends were trying to tell me something but I refused to listen. I tugged at the IV line in my hand.

"Let me go. Take me there. At least let me pay my respects," I said. My voice trembled with grief and fear, even though I should be happy a bastard like him was gone.

"Porsche! Stop that, Porsche!" my brother and my friends yelled as they all tried to push me back onto the bed.

"No! I'm going to the temple! Take me there!" I shouted.

Click! The door opened to reveal a smiling face. We all froze.

It was Pete, wearing casual clothes. "You're awake? What are you all doing?" he asked. He walked over to us, looking confused.

"Pete! Take me to the temple," I cried out, trying to push my brother and my friends away as they held me down.

"Why? If you wanna pray away your misfortune,[9] you can wait until you're better. Luang Por[10] isn't going anywhere," Pete said. His brow was furrowed, but he was still smiling. I didn't understand why he wasn't wearing black to properly mourn his boss.

"Take me there, please. I want to ask for forgiveness from Kinn one last time. Let me go see him," I pleaded with Pete, but I just seemed to confuse him further.

"Wait, wait, I think you're misunderstanding." Pete came to a stop in front of me and nodded at my brother and my friends to let me go.

"Kinn is dead because of me! *Fuck!*" I cried, slamming my hand on the bed.

8   Thai funerals are usually held in Buddhist temples.
9   สะเดาะเคราะห์ (Sa dor Kror): a ceremony believed to alleviate misfortune resulting from bad karma
10   หลวงพ่อ (Luang Por): a way to refer to an older male monk around the age of one's parents

"Porsche, wait! Listen to me!" Pete laughed. "Mr. Kinn is in the room next door!"

I gaped at him. "What did you just say?" I asked, just to make sure.

"Mr. Kinn isn't dead, dumbass!" Pete said, shaking his head and laughing. "He just hasn't woken up yet."

"Oh!" I fell silent for a bit, glaring at my friends. "Then why were you all making such sad faces?" I groused, but I felt the weight in my heart lifting.

"We were trying to tell you that, but you weren't listening at all. Mr. Kinn's still unconscious," Jom told me with a small smile.

"Motherfucker! You all looked so serious it made me panic," I complained, settling back into the bed.

"You can go visit him if you don't believe me," Pete said.

I hesitated. "Are you telling the truth? That he's not dead." I needed to be sure.

"Yes! Look! If you listen carefully, you can hear Khun singing his face off," Pete said. It was true—I could hear faint singing emanating from next door.

"Damn! Making a scene so early in the day—what's your boss's problem?" Jom asked Pete.

"Well, he read somewhere that music soothes the patient and promotes healing," Pete said, resigned.

"I think Mr. Kinn isn't waking up because he doesn't want to deal with all that noise!" said Tem. We all nodded in agreement.

"You wanna go take a look?" Pete asked me with a smirk, his eyebrows raised. The fucker was teasing me.

"Nah, I'm too tired to deal with Tankhun. He'll just give me a headache. Wait for him to leave first, then I'll get Chay to take me over," I said quietly. I wanted to see with my own eyes that Kinn was safe, but right then I'd rather not go. Tankhun's raucous voice echoing through the walls was already making my head hurt.

"I'd rather not. I don't want to see Kim," Chay said, scowling. I was surprised Chay even knew who Kim was.

"Do you know him?" I looked at Chay questioningly.

"I don't want to know him," Chay muttered.

What the hell does that mean, Chay?

"Yeah, forget about him. Are you hungry?" Pete cut in. I nodded in reply.

"You three go down and get him something to eat... I'll watch him," Pete told Tem, Jom, and Chay, and they complied. I knew he wanted to talk to me alone—probably about what had happened in the woods.

Click!

Once the door closed, Pete dragged a chair over.

"Do you know anything?" I asked immediately.

"No. We didn't recognize the dead bodies, and the rest of them got away from us. We were too shocked to go after them, seeing you pass out and Mr. Kinn get shot," Pete said, voice somber.

"I don't even have any enemies," I told him, serious. Pete frowned and asked me to recount everything.

I started with the day Kinn showed up at my place. I didn't go into too much detail, just focused on anything that might be useful information to Pete, especially what the men were talking about in the van: how they planned to capture me alive but kill Kinn. The more I talked, the more Pete's face fell.

"Damn! This isn't just a nuisance anymore! This involves both you and Mr. Kinn," he said, analyzing the situation. "Fuck, I'm drawing a blank here. Ever since the incident at the hotel, they've been targeting you, and Mr. Kinn is affected, too." I didn't understand how Kinn was affected—they only wanted me. Kinn was just unlucky enough to be in the wrong place at the wrong time.

"But I don't know who would want to target me," I said, trying to think about everything that had happened recently. "Maybe the guys that attacked us at the shooting range want to get revenge on me for killing their men?"

"I thought of that at first, but what happened when you got, uh... drugged... It's all too strange. I don't know how everything connects." Pete stumbled over his words, like he was trying to be considerate of my feelings. I turned away, thinking about what happened to me that day.

"Hmm... And why did it take you guys so long to find us?" I jokingly scolded him.

"You bastard, do you know where I found you and Mr. Kinn?!" he exclaimed. I shook my head. *How would I know? I was unconscious the entire time—both ways!*

"In the forest near Khao Yai!"[11] Pete said. "When your brother called me, I went to your house right away. He was sitting there out back shaking and crying, the poor thing." My heart sank when I thought of how scared Porchay must've been.

"I tracked Mr. Kinn's phone signal all the way to the outskirts of the city and it just fucking disappeared," Pete went on, explaining further. "So I had to get all the traffic cam footage and piece it together until I could get a rough idea of where you were! We got there a day before they found you two, and we had to spread out to search. Then we heard gunshots and our hearts dropped into our boots! Fuck!"

It sounded like a lot of work—there was barely information on our whereabouts to work with.

---

11   Khao Yai National Park, one of Thailand's largest national parks.

"So what now?" I asked him.

"Mr. Korn's not going to leave it like this," Pete said. "Right now, we're looking into why they took you and Mr. Kinn up that mountain. Someone's safehouse might be hidden nearby."

I nodded. The whole situation baffled me. I'd somehow gotten involved in something much bigger than myself, but I couldn't figure it out—and neither could Pete.

"And how is he?" I asked quietly, nodding toward the room next door.

Pete broke into a wicked smile. "If you're so worried, go take a look for yourself," he teased, giggling at me. I flipped him off.

"Be serious," I said.

Pete chuckled again. "He got lucky. The bullet didn't hit anything vital—he lost a lot of blood though. He got emergency surgery at the local hospital, but then Mr. Korn had you and Mr. Kinn immediately transferred to Bangkok."

I nodded as I listened to Pete, looking around the room. It had to be the fanciest hospital room I'd ever seen. It looked super expensive, so it made sense for Kinn to be here, but for me? A regular room would've been plenty.

"Why did I get put in a room like this?" I asked, curious.

"You're a VIP. Mr. Korn's orders," Pete answered casually, turning around to grab a snack. There was a fruit basket and a plate of snacks on top of the bedside table.

"They treat us well, huh," I said.

"Ha, maybe *you*. When we get shot half to death, we only get a regular room." Pete smiled. The more he talked like this, the more confused I became. Mr. Korn had been nothing but generous to me—unusually generous, in fact.

Creak! The door opened once again. I thought it was my brother and my friends, but I froze in surprise when the man I'd just been thinking about entered the room, with his secretary in tow.

"How are you?" Mr. Korn asked evenly.

"Hello, Mr. Korn." Pete and I both made a wai. Pete stood up and quickly arranged a seat for Mr. Korn and Chan.

"Take it easy," Mr. Korn said.

"He just woke up, sir," Pete reported.

"If you're still in pain anywhere, tell the doctor... It's good to see that you're okay. You and Kinn nearly gave me an aneurysm, you hear?" Mr. Korn's deep voice said gently. I could only smile awkwardly at his serious demeanor.

"Were you stuck in the forest the entire time?" Mr. Korn asked.

"Yes. At first they were going to take us somewhere, but me and that bast—and Kinn escaped and they chased us into the forest," I said cautiously, trying not to curse. "We were lost in there for three days."

"It's good that you both made it out of there... I don't know who your attackers are, but once I do, rest assured that I'll do to them exactly what they did to my sons." I furrowed my brow—*sons*? Surely he meant just Kinn.

Chan had been silent this entire time, but now he spoke up. "And Pete, you've asked Porsche for the details, yes?"

"Yes," Pete answered. "They were targeting Porsche, not Mr. Kinn. They wanted to capture Porsche alive and shoot Kinn dead."

"This has escalated into quite a serious matter," said Mr. Korn. "For now, you and Porchay will stay at my house. You must be careful—don't go back to your home. They won't stop coming for you. Pete, you'll stay with him, won't you?"

"I..." I trailed off. My unease at not being able to go home must have shown on my face.

"When you disappeared, Mr. Korn had Porchay move into your room on his property," Pete said, "in case they came back to your place for him. But don't worry, I'll look after your brother." I frowned even more. *What the hell is going on?!*

"I promised to look after your brother, didn't I? I will do exactly as I promised. So that's settled—stay at my house until we can catch the perpetrator," Mr. Korn said, lightly patting my shoulder.

"Yes, sir," I agreed, if only for my brother's safety. If they knew where I lived, it wouldn't be hard for them to try and kidnap me again. And if anything happened to Chay, I'd take the guilt with me to the grave.

"Hmm, good. And don't think about resigning your position with our family. Without our protection, those men won't let you go so easily," Mr. Korn said. "But don't worry, I won't let that happen. And if there's anything you're unsatisfied with regarding your employment, you can come to me. I do recall telling you that I see you as one of my own. Let me take care of you and your brother."

I looked up at Mr. Korn in surprise, but nodded my assent. Since it had come to this, I needed to put my thoughts about quitting on hold—for now, safety was much more important.

Bang! The door slammed open and a tall figure burst through. Everyone turned to look in surprise.

"*Sounds of gunshots at the sky!* Bang![12]" Tankhun sang as he pulled out a toy gun to shoot at the ceiling. I covered my ears. At the sound of the toy gun, Pol, Arm, and P'Jess dropped to the floor.

We all heaved a sigh at Tankhun's antics.

"What are you doing? And the three of you—why are you rolling around on the floor?" Mr. Korn asked.

---

12 Lyrics to ผัวมา (Pua Ma) by Kung Supaporn.

Tankhun beamed and walked over to my bed, toy gun in hand.

"Mr. Tankhun told us that we have to fall to the ground when he says the word 'bang!'" Arm admitted hesitantly.

"And he said if we didn't, he'd get a real gun," Pol said, taking his chance to complain about Tankhun to Mr. Korn. Tankhun glared at him.

"Jess! Why are you playing along? Why didn't you stop him?" Mr. Korn scolded Jess, exasperated. P'Jess slowly pushed himself up, holding his waist. Tankhun's bodyguards looked pitiful.

"I couldn't stop him," P'Jess replied.

Tankhun sniggered and started to sing again. "*Sounds of gun-shots at—*"

"Sir, please, that's enough. We're going to pass out if you keep making us drop to the floor." P'Jess tried to stop Tankhun, who made a face and turned to me, eyes sparkling.

"How was it?! Were there tiger demons[13] in the forest?" he asked, laughing. I leaned back against the headboard and rolled my eyes.

"Don't bother him. You've been causing quite a stir at this hospital since yesterday—what do you want?!" Mr. Korn scolded his son, but Tankhun paid him no heed.

"I'm here to say that Kinn's awake!"

As soon as the words left Tankhun's mouth, I whipped my head around to look at him.

"Well, how is he?" Mr. Korn asked Tankhun.

"He says he wants to go back into the forest for a couple more days," Tankhun cheerfully announced with a gleeful giggle. Mr. Korn sighed. It looked like he wasn't going to get a useful answer out of his eldest son.

---

13   เสือสมิง (Suea Saming): an evil spirit in Thai folklore that takes the form of a large tiger, but can transform into a human to trick and eat people.

"All right. Porsche, I'm going to go see Kinn. I'll be back later," Mr. Korn announced. I gave a wai to Mr. Korn in farewell, watching him go.

Tankhun stayed behind, sitting stupidly by my bed.

"How are you? Does it hurt?" he asked me. I nodded.

"You're okay now." Arm came over to pat my shoulder, and I smiled at him.

"I have a way to help you recover faster. Pol, give me the mic!" Tankhun shouted. I slid back down onto the bed. Pol looked like he wanted to die, but still handed the microphone to Tankhun. I soon realized what was about to happen. *Fuck!*

"This song is dedicated to Porsche! May he get well soon. *Ahem.*" He checked the microphone as Tem, Jom, and Chay came walking in with meatballs on skewers. All three of them glanced nervously at Tankhun.

"Calm down. Mama said you should calm down. Girl, don't make the first move. Calm down—"[14]

I turned away and covered my ears with a pillow. *Motherfucker! I can see why Kinn wanted to go back into the forest! Fuck! Tankhun's giving me a goddamned migraine!*

"Just bear with it, man," Pol said as he squeezed my hand, hard.

"Chase him into the room next door for me. I want to sleep," I grumbled to Pol.

"Bastard! Kinn already chased him into your room!" Arm cried, shaking his head.

"Fuckin' Kinn!" I groaned. *That evil bastard! How can you throw the problem to me, you sneaky little shit?!*

"Wait, wait, wait, can't you just calm down? Don't be like that, chat, chat, don't slide into his DMs—"

14 Lyrics to พักก่อน (Stop!) by MILLI.

"Can't you take him back?" I asked Pete and the others. "I've seriously got a headache."

"Can't you see he's not going to leave?" P'Jess tried to tell me, his eyes sympathetic.

"Then take him to the next building over," I said.

"Why?" Arm asked.

"It's where the psych ward is!" I shouted and pulled the blanket over my head. I could still hear them laughing. *Fuck!*

"Khun! Shut up!" a new voice shouted through the door. I peeked out from under my blanket.

"What is it, Kim?!" Khun stopped singing to glare at his youngest brother. "I'm singing Porsche to sleep."

"Father says you need to get your brain checked out," Kim smirked.

"Bitch!" Tankhun threw a bunch of grapes at his brother, who caught it and began to eat one.

"Father wants us to go home. You too, Chay—Father says we should all go back together."

Chay dawdled, like he didn't want to leave with Kim. My eyes flickered between them, confused. Chay had seemed irritated the moment Kim walked in.

"You're not staying?" I asked.

"Your brother has missed school for several days now. Let him get some sleep and go to school in the morning," Pete told me. I glanced over at Chay, who was tightly holding onto the bedrail, not wanting to leave.

"Let me stay here. Please, hia," he begged.

"Let's go! And take your microphone with you, or else I'll throw it away—just you wait," Kim announced, grabbing Tankhun by the neck and pushing him toward the bodyguards.

"Try it and I'll smash all your videogames," Tankhun shot back, shaking Kim off and sashaying out of the room. *Finally, some fucking peace and quiet.*

"You can go back. I'll be fine," I told Chay as I patted his head.

"Come on! Behave yourself!" Kim chided Chay. I whipped around to stare at Kim as soon as he said that to my brother. *When did they get close enough to speak to each other so familiarly?*

"Let's go, Chay. I'll take you to school in the morning," Pete said and began to help my brother gather his things. I looked at the situation unfolding before me, perplexed. *How long was I lost in that forest? Why does nothing make sense?*

"Hia—" Chay called for me again, but no matter how curious I was, I wanted him to go back and rest.

"Go on. You can come visit me after school tomorrow," I told him. Chay frowned before trailing after a whistling Kim. When the door closed, I quickly asked Pete, "What's up with my brother and Kim?"

"I dunno," Pete answered. "I think they've met before. Being in the house with them these last three or four days has been a total headache. They won't stop bickering." He smiled.

How did Chay get to know Kim? I've barely ever seen his face!

"It's nothing," Pete assured me. "Your brother talks back just as good as you do—don't worry about it."

"Arm's watching over you tonight. Tem and I are going back to finish our reports. We'll drop by tomorrow," Jom said, and started gathering his things.

"Thank you. All of you," I said. "But you don't have to visit so often. I'll be fine."

"How can we abandon you?! We'll be back once classes are over. And don't worry, we already notified the professors and kept copies of the assignments for you," Tem reassured me. He moved the overbed table into place in front of me. "You should eat. Pete, I'll leave him to you."

They all filed out, leaving me and Pete together.

"When you finish eating, take your medicine and get some sleep," Pete said, plating up my food. "I'll go back and swap with Arm so he can watch you."

"You don't have to do this, you know," I said. "I don't want to bother you guys."

"Hey, isn't this what friends are for?" Pete said with a smile. Even though we hadn't known each other for long, I sensed his sincerity—Pol's and Arm's, too. I had good people around me.

"Who's watching Kinn?" I asked absentmindedly. I was still his bodyguard, after all. Naturally, I was curious who was assigned to him.

Pete huffed a laugh. "That room's got a fierce protector spirit[15] keeping watch all day and all night, refusing to share the duty with anyone," he teased.

I frowned as I shoveled food into my mouth. "Who?" I asked, listening to Pete while I chewed.

"Big, of course. Guarding Kinn like a mother hen. So dramatic," Pete muttered in irritation.

I relaxed, still eating. "Isn't that good? Your boss will get better faster."

"It's good. But you're gonna have to call dibs as soon as you can, or that bastard will snatch Kinn right up."

I glared at Pete's smirking face. "What do you mean, *dibs*?!" I shouted at him.

"Heh, dibs as head bodyguard, of course! What did you think I was talking about?" I glowered and turned my focus back to eating.

---

15   เจ้าที่ (Chao ti): Protector spirits in Thai folklore, believed to watch over specific places.

"Finish eating, take your meds, and go straight to sleep," Pete instructed. I nodded in reply, finishing my plate and taking my medicine. Pete helped me over to the bathroom so I could do my business, then took his leave, promising to quickly fetch Arm to keep me company. I lay there and channel-surfed the hospital TV until early evening, when a nurse came in to remove my IV line.

"We're taking your IV out, but the doctor would like to keep you under observation for two more days," the nurse told me as she checked my wounds. "You still have cuts and bruising... If you have a headache or any other pain, you can press the call button at any time." She got everything in order before leaving my room. In truth, my whole body still ached, but it was a lot better than those last few days in the forest. I had bits of gauze and bandages all over me, but it wasn't too bad.

Before long, Arm showed up in casual clothes and sprawled across the sofa by my bed.

"Have you eaten yet?" I asked him.

"I have. Go to sleep, Porsche. Call for me if you need to go to the bathroom," he said, tapping away at a game on his phone. I lay down and he reached to turn off the overhead lights, leaving only the bathroom light on.

I tossed and turned, unable to get to sleep. The nurse brought me another pill and told me it'd help me sleep, but I was more awake than ever...

"You think he's asleep?" I finally decided to ask Arm, who raised his eyebrows and looked at me before going back to his phone.

"Who?" he asked.

"Kinn. You think he's asleep yet?" I wasn't sure why Kinn occupied my thoughts.

Arm smiled slightly and looked at the clock. "It's nine o'clock. He's probably asleep. Big and the others got chased out of his room already."

"Oh, good. Can you bring me over to take a look at him?" I asked, springing up from the bed.

Arm eyed me skeptically. "I said he's asleep. Why don't you wait to see him after he wakes up tomorrow morning? You're being weird."

"Well, I don't want to go when he's awake. He's too much of a headache." I decided to tell Arm the truth: if Kinn were awake, he'd be sure to find some way to annoy me. I just wanted to make sure he was okay—partly because he saved me. I still felt guilty that he got shot because of me.

Arm pondered this. "Hmm... Sure, if Big lets us in," he said.

I grew irritated at the thought of Big. "Why wouldn't he? I'm Kinn's head bodyguard!"

"Ugh, fine. I'm bored, anyway. Let's go make some trouble for Big," Arm said.

He helped me down from the bed. Although my legs felt a little heavy, I was still able to find my balance. I opened the door to the hallway to find Big and his gang all crowding around Kinn's door.

"You're surprisingly hard to kill," one of Big's men taunted me. I didn't pay attention; instead, I returned Big's furious glare.

"Where are you going?!" Big barked as soon as Arm's hand reached for the door handle.

"To the fucking market!" Arm sneered. "We're going into Mr. Kinn's room, obviously."

"Who gave you permission to enter?!" Big yelled again. I looked at him dubiously. *I barely have anything to do with him anymore. Why is he always acting like he's ready to fight me? And even though I'm the head bodyguard, I never interfere or order the other guys around.*

"And what right do you have to stop us? Are you his wife or something?" Arm put his hands in his pockets and turned to stare at Big. Big frowned and strode up to us.

"Don't do it, bro... Mr. Kinn's asleep. Go back to your room," one of his lackeys said as he pulled Big back.

"We're just going in to take a look," Arm said. "Porsche is Mr. Kinn's head bodyguard—can't he check that everything is in order?"

I stayed silent, watching Arm and Big argue. I couldn't be bothered to say anything, and Big would start a fistfight if I did.

"No! I won't let you in!" Big yelled, causing the nurse on duty to come over and check what was going on. She left when one of Big's lackeys talked her down.

"You're like a dog guarding a bone," Arm said. "But the bone isn't yours, huh?"

"Arm!" Big growled, gritting his teeth. He lunged to grab Arm by the collar. I hurriedly pushed his shoulders away and put my body between them.

"Don't touch him!" I snapped. "And don't make me tell you again." I pointed my finger in Big's face as Arm tried to maneuver me to the side.

Big looked askance at me. "You got beaten up like a stray dog, but you still have the guts to pick a fight with me?"

"You want to try?" I goaded, readying to launch myself at him. I couldn't take it anymore. My body wasn't fully recovered, but if he started shit and hurt me or Arm, he was going to answer for it.

"Porsche! Let me!" Arm pulled at my shirt to jump at Big himself, but they were quickly separated, me holding Arm back and Big's lackeys holding onto him.

"What are you all doing?!" a stern voice shouted from the elevators. We all looked over and stood to attention, heads bowed.

"P'Chan!" Big's voice trembled.

P'Chan surveyed the scene. "If you're going to fight, take it outside," he said evenly. "This is a hospital. Learn some manners." He looked at me. "Porsche, why are you here?"

"Porsche is just here to visit Mr. Kinn, but these guys won't let him in," Arm took the opportunity to complain first. Big and his gang all glared at him. P'Chan glanced at Big out of the corner of his eye, then opened the door.

"Go on," P'Chan said, angling his body to let me in first, then Arm, before he closed the door. The room was completely dark; Kinn must have been asleep.

"P'Chan, why are you here?" Arm whispered.

"To bring Mr. Kinn his new phone." P'Chan walked over to place a black box beside Kinn's bed. "Don't disturb him too much," he said, and left the room.

When the door closed, Arm headed over to sit on the sofa as I approached Kinn's bedside. The light from outside filtered through the curtains, allowing me to see his face clearly. His face was bruised, but that didn't take away from his striking features. He lay there utterly motionless, his steady breathing the only sign that he was still alive.

Kinn was hooked up to an IV drip, a blood bag, a heart rate monitor, and who knew what else. That was bad, wasn't it?

I studied his face for a long while and unconsciously reached out to put my hand over the left side of his stomach. Through the blanket, I gently ran my hands over his gunshot wound, worried it'd feel painful. My lips pressed into a thin line. *Fuckin' show-off! Did he think he was a hero, throwing himself in front of the bullet like that? What a drama queen!* I smiled to myself, startling in surprise when the hands folded at his chest suddenly slid over and grasped my wrist.

"Did I wake you up?" I whispered. Kinn smiled a little before looking over at Arm.

"Go do whatever you have to do," he ordered, his hard voice making Arm jump up from the sofa.

"Where are you going?" I tried to call Arm back before he reached the door.

"I'll go wait in your room!" he replied, flashing me a smile before closing the door behind him. I turned back to Kinn, but before I could say anything, he scooted over and turned onto his side, pulling me to sit next to him on the bed.

"What are you doing?!" I exclaimed. How could a gunshot victim have this much energy? He gave one firm tug and I braced myself on the bed. He beamed up at me.

"I can sit over there," I said, pointing to the chair next to the bed.

"No, I'd rather you sit here," Kinn said. He squeezed my wrist, as if afraid I'd escape.

"Let me go!" I tried to gently yank my hand back, mindful of his wounds.

"Don't fight me. If you bump into my wound, I'll have to punish you!" Kinn said, letting go of my wrist to circle my waist with both arms. I pushed at his chest, but his clingy hands weren't letting go.

Click! The door opened.

"Porsche..." Big stopped short.

I pushed harder at Kinn, but he held onto me even tighter.

"What?" he snapped, irritated.

"Let go!" I yelled, trying to get his hands off of me.

Big was so shocked at the sight of us that it looked like his soul had left his body. He stood as still as a statue, watching me and Kinn in stunned silence.

"What do you want?!" Kinn repeated, more irritated than before.

"I... I thought you were asleep, Mr. Kinn, so I was going to...to..." Big looked at me, disapproval clear in his eyes.

"Get out!" Kinn ordered him. "If I don't call for you, don't come in." Big looked away, almost as if he was trying to hide his expression. In the end, he bowed his head and exited the room.

"The hell are you doing?!" I snapped at Kinn. That fucker Big was gonna get the wrong idea! "Let me go, Kinn! Or I'll kick you in your gunshot wound!" I threatened. He slid his hand off my waist, but just when I thought he was done, he grabbed my neck and pulled me to lie down next to him. I resisted with all my might.

"What are you doing? Let go," I protested, but he maneuvered my head down onto his pillow.

"Don't struggle so hard! Ow!" he yelped, and I froze. He let go of me and held his wounded abdomen.

"Serves you right," I told him and straightened up, looking at him wailing in pain. *Motherfucker! Did I seriously hurt him or is he just being a crybaby?*

"Where does it hurt?" I pulled his hands off his body, pushing the blanket back and pulling up his shirt. I could faintly see blood seeping through the gauze. "Should we call the doctor?" I asked, worried. The surgical site didn't look that big, but seeing it bleed freaked me out.

"Nah," Kinn said as he flipped over to lie down on his back, staring at the ceiling and bracing himself against the pain.

"Let's call the doctor. You could die, and I'm not gonna take responsibility for that!" I reached over to press the call button, but Kinn caught hold of my arm first.

"Then take responsibility," he said, tugging at me to lie down on his other arm. "Don't struggle again, or next time my wound will really get inflamed." He pulled the blanket over my body. He positioned me to face him and I stayed still, not knowing what to do. A part of me wanted to struggle, but another part was afraid of bumping into his wound.

"What do you think you're doing?!" I demanded.

He hugged me tight. "I can't sleep... Maybe I've gotten used to you sleeping on top of me," he murmured, cradling my head against his chest.

"Let me go, you bastard!" I yelled. I shouldn't have come here! Fuck! If I punched his wound and it got infected and he died, would his father blame me?

"Shush! Go to sleep. Comfort me—I took a bullet for you," Kinn murmured, laughing.

"I didn't ask you to do that," I said.

"So ungrateful," he replied, hugging me. I moved around a bit and settled down, resigned to my fate. I wanted to push him away, but he just had to point out that he took a damn bullet for me. *Bastard! Fine, I'll sleep.* I started to feel drowsy, drifting off to Kinn's familiar scent.

Just you wait! Once you're all healed up, I'll get my revenge for every damned thing you did to me!

21

Waver

CLICK!
I heard a noise and started to move, but I still couldn't pry my eyelids open. I snuggled my face into the comforting warmth beside me, the scent and softness lulling me back to sleep.

"Porsche... Porsche," a soft voice called as a finger poked at my arm, the sensation forcing me to open my eyes. Annoyed, I glanced up at whoever it was who dared to disturb my sleep.

"What?" I asked quietly. Everything started to come into focus. Even though I could remember what happened the night before, my drowsiness was making me fall back asleep.

Kinn didn't say anything, but he nodded at the door expressionlessly before loosening his hold on me. He shifted over to pillow his own head instead.

"Shit!" I practically jumped off the bed. Kinn shook the arm I'd slept on like he was trying to get rid of the stiffness.

"If... If you're not ready, we can come back later," Tay said with a shocked expression. He, Time, Mew, and Pete were at the door, along with Tem and Jom, who looked even more stunned than Kinn's friends did.

I didn't say anything, just got off the bed. Kinn laughed, but I didn't dare lift my head to look anyone in the eye. My face was burning with embarrassment. I walked quickly past the group as they looked between me and Kinn, not caring if I was being rude. I wanted to hit my head against the damn wall! Fuck, they were gonna get the wrong idea!

I made it back to my room. I washed my face and took a piss before trying to decide what I was going to say to my friends. Motherfucker! What they just saw would make their imaginations run wild—seeing me cuddled up to Kinn like that?! Fuck! What should I do? I leaned against the sink as I tried to come up with some kind of explanation. This never would have happened if Kinn hadn't forced me to. I shouldn't have given in! I was fucked!

"Eat your food," my friends told me when I finally got my shit together and tried to act normal, walking out to sit on my bed. I dealt with the food on the overbed table, pretending to be nonchalant even though my heart was pounding wildly in my chest. I shoveled food into my mouth, trying to act like nothing had happened. Tem, Jom, and Pete all crowded around my bed, staring like they were trying to catch me out. The atmosphere was stifling.

"Oh!" Pete suddenly burst out amid the silence, startling me. "So that's what Arm meant when he said he left you alone all night? Heh."

I continued to eat like I couldn't hear him chuckling.

"How... How did you wind up sleeping in Mr. Kinn's room?" Jom asked, crossing his arms. I glanced over and looked back down.

"Well?" Tem asked.

The air conditioning is fucking freezing, why am I sweating so much? "You all...finished classes pretty early." I tried to change the subject. Looking at the clock, I saw it was eleven in the morning.

"We only had to turn in our reports today, and we ran into P'Time. He invited us to come over together," Tem told me. He squinted in suspicion. "You still have to answer us."

I gulped, grabbed my glass of water, and downed the entire thing.

Pete smiled and casually pulled his chair over. "We came into your room and didn't see you. We thought the nurses must have taken you somewhere, so we decided to go see Kinn, only to find you guys...hugging..."

"What?! What are you getting at? We're both men!" I snapped before Pete could finish his sentence.

"Really? That's it? We're just surprised, Porsche... Don't you have something to tell us?" Tem asked seriously.

"No! Why? I went to visit him late last night and I was sleepy. My feet hurt and I was too lazy to walk back to my room, so I asked to stay over and didn't think much of it," I said, passing my glass to Pete so he could refill it. Why was my throat so dry?

"Heh," Pete chuckled.

"What are you laughing for?! I'll kick your ass!" I lifted my foot to kick at Pete. This fucker! He kept looking at my face and giggling like a fool!

"Are you done eating?" Jom asked. I nodded, and Tem pulled the table away from the bed. I was relieved that they'd stopped giving me the third degree. I leaned back against the headboard and turned on the TV, trying to find something to distract myself from it all.

"What the hell are you doing?!" I yelled at Jom as he climbed up onto my bed. Luckily, I was in a VIP room, so the bed was quite large—but what the hell was he getting up there for?

"What?! You said it yourself that it means nothing. We're both men," Jom retorted. I felt my face tighten. Pete and Tem looked on, smiling.

"Kinn's still recovering from his surgery, but he let you sleep with him with no problem," Jom told me as he straightened up. "I'm your friend—why did you make such a fuss when I did it?"

"You can go lie down on the sofa over there," I told him, irritated. I knew he was teasing me.

"But your bed is so much softer! I just want to lie down for a bit. Or, when you went to sleep next to Mr. Kinn, was it because..."

"Fine, fine, if you want to sleep in my bed then sleep in my bed, you bastard!" I cut Jom off before he could continue. I frowned, crossed my arms, and stared at the TV.

"So comfy," Jom said as he rolled around, pulling at my blanket. It was practically suffocating, having two guys as big as water buffaloes squeeze onto the same bed. It felt completely cramped. We were in each other's way, and he kept rolling around and bumping into me. I tried to ignore my discomfort for a while but eventually I couldn't take it anymore.

Thwack!

"Ow!" Jom yelped, and rolled off the bed. I kicked at his hip as hard as I could, wanting him out of my sight. Pete and Tem howled with laughter.

"What'd you kick me off for?! That hurt like hell!" Jom turned his head to yell at me from the floor, painfully holding onto his butt.

"You're annoying me!" I shouted back.

Jom pointed at me and grinned. "You didn't seem to mind when it was Kinn! Is it because—"

"Bastard! Get out! I'm trying to sleep!" I quickly burrowed into my blanket, but he wouldn't stop making fun of me. *Kinn annoyed me, too, but he's not as annoying as Jom! Shit!* I didn't know why, but when Jom lay down next to me, it felt utterly unbearable—but with Kinn, I hadn't felt the same discomfort. It was kind of nice, actually.

Click! I heard the door open, pissing me off further. *Who the hell are all these people visiting me?!*

"P'Time, you come in first," Tem called. P'Time was Kinn's friend—what the hell was he doing here?!

"Kinn told me to bring these desserts over for Porsche...here." I heard P'Time set a plate on the bedside table, but I didn't bother emerging from my blanket to look.

"Say thank you," Pete told me, nudging at my back.

"I don't want it!" I said harshly.

"Oh, P'Time, did you ask P'Kinn why my friend here was in his room?" Tem chuckled. *That insolent little shit!*

"Why do you want to know?!" I flipped the blanket over and turned to aim my foot at Tem's face until he moved away. P'Time glanced at me out of the corner of his eye and smirked.

"I didn't ask, but I have an idea," he said.

"Get out! I'm going back to sleep!" I burrowed back under the blanket. Fuck! What did they think they saw between me and Kinn?! It was like the more I talked, the more they teased me. *And Tem, why are you acting all friendly with Time, talking like you're so fucking close—it's annoying to look at!*

"Don't forget to eat your dessert, or else my friend will be disappointed in you," P'Time said cheerfully.

I heard the door close, so I got up and out from under the blanket again. "Why are you being so friendly to him?" I asked Tem.

"What? We keep bumping into each other. Plus, I have way better social skills than you," Tem said. He walked over to look at the desserts on the plate, his eyes shining. "Those look amazing."

I looked over at the desserts. There were choux cream puffs along with a large slice of cheesecake arranged neatly on the plate.

"You want some? I'll get you a spoon," Jom said, coming over to look at the desserts in Tem's hand.

"No!" I shouted.

"Then we'll eat it. Come on, Pete." They passed out the spoons and dug in with gusto, especially Tem, who looked almost euphoric. I couldn't help but wonder if Kinn was really the one who'd sent us these desserts. He wasn't usually this generous—when had he ever shared anything with me? He'd reprimand me just for moving a little, so why would he suddenly send all this over? Or was the Kinn I saw in the forest still there and the normal Kinn had yet to return?

"Give me one," I said hesitantly. Pete looked up with a smile and carefully placed a piece of cheesecake and a cream puff onto a plate. He moved the overbed table over and put the plate in front of me.

"With love and care, from Mr. Kinn," Pete said, smiling. I flipped him off before picking up a spoon and eating. It was tasty. I was one of those guys that liked dessert—any dessert, even if it wasn't necessarily my favorite, like those chocolates in Kinn's room. At first they tasted kind of strange, but after a while, I'd developed a taste for them. Plus, I'd been sneaking them quite often. If Kinn found out, he'd chew my head off.

"Eating and smiling to yourself... Are you in love?" Tem asked, spoon still in his mouth. I frowned. What was I even smiling about? *What's wrong with you, Porsche?!*

"The dessert and the man who gifted it—which is sweeter?" Pete asked. I threw the TV remote at his head. "Ow! Don't be so violent, I'm just teasing you!"

"Bastard! Give me my medicine, I'm going to sleep." I ate the last of my cake and took a sip of water. Pete passed me the medicine, which I quickly knocked back before reclining on the bed. I didn't lie flat, though, or else I'd get heartburn. No matter how much I wanted to burrow completely into my blankets and hide from their prying stares, I couldn't.

I sat there unhappily, watching the TV and trying to make sense of it, but my mind kept coming back to what happened this morning. I ended up just staring blankly ahead while everyone whispered and laughed at my bedside. I tried to not pay attention, attempting to understand the show on the screen—it was some kind of rap contest.

Click! The door opened again.

Oh, come on! Who were all these people visiting me?! Did they want me to get better or worse?

Truly, I was grateful that they all came to visit, but I was so annoyed today that I wanted to be left alone.

"Hellooo," came a voice. I closed my eyes and sighed, fed up.

"Hello, Mr. Tankhun," everyone greeted. I turned to give him a casual wai. *Is there any poison in this hospital? Even formaldehyde will do—just come end my misery!*

"Ah, so you're eating and slacking off over here, Pete," Tankhun scolded him, hands on his hips. Pete looked perfectly placid, like he didn't give a damn about what Tankhun thought.

"Mr. Korn told me to come help watch over Porsche and Mr. Kinn," he said evenly, still shoveling cake into his mouth.

Pol walked over. "I'll come by tonight to keep you company," he said. Arm came over, too, throwing his arm over Pol's shoulder and smiling that stupid smirk of his.

"You don't have to come keep him company; he's got someone to sleep with him already."

Kill me now! I hate you all! What is wrong with everyone today?! Everyone was looking at me differently because of Kinn!

"What are you talking about? Let me join you!" Tankhun chimed in, stopping the conversation short. I sighed once again as he reached out to massage my arm. "How are you feeling? Does it hurt anywhere?" he asked. I looked at where he was massaging; he was squeezing over a piece of gauze. *What do you think, moron?!*

"It hurts here," I said and pointed at his hand. He quickly removed his hand and smiled viciously.

"I brought you something," he said with a giggle. I looked over to see P'Jess carrying some sort of gift basket into the room. I frowned.

"Tada!" Tankhun exclaimed. I straightened up to take the gift basket from his hands. The huge basket was stuffed to the brim with the familiar-looking chocolates that were scattered in various corners of the house.

"With love and care from Mr. TK! Arm, take a picture so we can upload it to the page!"

I was a little confused, but I looked at the camera anyway, posing with my arms held up to receive the gift basket from Tankhun.

"One, two, three... All done, sir," Arm said, handing the camera back to Tankhun to check the photo.

"Didn't put in much effort, huh?" Pete whispered. I grabbed one of the chocolates, tore it open, and took a big bite. I kind of missed them after not having one in so long.

"Do you like it? I arranged the basket myself!" Pete said. He walked over to grab one for himself. *Hey!* Wasn't that for me?

"I'm going over to the other room, or else Kinn will miss me," Tankhun announced as he left with his entourage. Pete, Tem, Jom, and I all sighed with relief. I'd been afraid he was going to stay to stir up trouble.

"Gimme some," Jom said, coming to grab one of the strange-looking chocolates. He made a disgusted face. "Ugh, these are gross."

The first time I had them, I felt the same way—but after eating them for a while, I'd developed a taste for them. I grabbed another piece, chewing as I leaned against the headboard.

"You like them?" Pete asked.

"They're edible," I said and looked at the wrapping. I was still hung up on these three cartoon characters—they looked so fucking stupid!

"Oh! Good! That's perfect if you're—"

"By the way, why do you have these chocolates all over the damn place?" I asked, not letting Pete finish his sentence.

"What, you didn't know? The family owns the chocolate company that makes these—of course they're going to be everywhere," Pete told me. I frowned, surprised. Huh. I'd been wondering why they were everywhere. It was kinda ridiculous that these big, tough mafiosos were making chocolates.

"Look, this face is young master Tankhun," Pete said, pointing to the boy in the middle of the logo, who sported a wide grin. "And this is Mr. Kim," he said, noting the boy with his tongue sticking out.

"And this is Kinn?" I pointed to the boy on the left who had an indifferent frown. I unintentionally barked out a laugh. He looked so fucking dumb!

"Hmm," Pete looked at me suspiciously.

"I knew it! That's why they taste so disgusting," I declared as I took another bite. The only thing the chocolate was any good for was staving off hunger.

"Umm, you say it's disgusting, but you're still eating it... So your mouth is saying no, but your heart is telling you yes," Pete said, smirking.

"The hell are you talking about?" I leveled him with a stare. This motherfucker got more annoying by the day.

"Nothing! Finish eating, then go to sleep." Pete shrugged and went to sit with the rest of my friends. I looked at him, puzzled, then drank some water to wash everything down and got ready to sleep.

I napped on and off the entire day, with Tem and Jom helping take care of my every need. Pete flitted back and forth between Kinn's room and mine, randomly coming over to annoy me before going back to Kinn's room. After he got out of school, Chay came to sit and chat with me too.

Once it started to get dark, everyone went their separate ways. Kim came to collect my little brother like before, causing Chay to linger, dragging his feet until I managed to chase him away. I sat by myself for a bit until Pol came by to keep me company. Not long after, a nurse came in with my medicine and checked on me. Then, I fell asleep.

Hmm...

I woke up in what felt like the middle of the night to find the room dark; only the bathroom light was on. I looked drowsily at the clock—it was ten o'clock. Had I only slept for two hours?

I got up from the bed and saw Pol fast asleep on the sofa. I grabbed my phone, which Chay had brought me, and scrolled for a while.

Waking up this late... How was I supposed to go back to sleep? Fuck! Why did I even wake up in the first place?

Suddenly, I felt wide awake. The medicine the nurse said would help me sleep wasn't working at all.

Click! The door opened and I turned to look. Who was visiting me at this hour?

"Are you asleep?" a familiar voice asked. He came in dragging an IV stand, heading straight for the bed. I glowered at him before pushing myself up to sit.

"Why are you here?" I asked, watching Kinn's every move. He slowly padded over and sat on the edge of my bed. I quickly scooted over to the other side.

"Pol is keeping you company?" Kinn didn't answer my question, looking over to Pol where he lay dead asleep on the sofa.

"Hmm," I hummed in reply.

"Pol...hey!" Kinn hissed at Pol, who sleepily rubbed at his eyes. "Pol!" Kinn said, louder this time. Pol opened his eyes, blinking rapidly, before jumping up from the sofa as fast as he could.

"M-Mr. Kinn," he sputtered, startled.

"Go sleep in my room," Kinn ordered him.

"What! Why?" I hurriedly cut Kinn off. Why was he chasing Pol away?

Kinn turned to whisper to me. "I'll let him stay...if you can stand him seeing me sleeping cuddled up to you."

I glared at him. "Who's letting you sleep here?!" I was worried about Pol as he dragged his pillow and blanket away, getting ready to leave the room. I quickly tried to call him back. "Don't go!"

Pol turned back to smile awkwardly at me, and hastened out of the room.

Kinn chuckled and went to recline on my pillow.

"Get out!" I used my arms and feet to push Kinn away, preventing him from lying down like he wanted.

"Don't kick me! You're hitting me right on my injury!" he scolded me. His voice was even, but his brow was furrowed.

"Then get out." I stopped moving my arms and feet and turned to stare at him in silence.

"I know you're having trouble sleeping. Go to sleep, it's late," Kinn said and grabbed hold of me, using his weight to pull me down onto the bed, hugging me tightly.

"Kinn, you bastard!" I shouted at him, but he was utterly shameless. He lay down on his side while cradling my head to his chest, his other arm sliding under my neck as a pillow. I could smell that familiar scent and feel his comforting warmth. I froze for a moment, my heart beating rapidly.

"Don't move around," he warned me. "If you hit my wound, I'll hit you back!"

I didn't listen, writhing around in his arms. He had so much strength—hadn't he just had surgery? And did he not need that blood bag and heart monitor anymore? Was that why he could come annoy me now?

"Let me go!" I kept shouting, but then he quickly lowered his face to mine and pressed his lips to my cheek. *Why the fuck did he do that?!* I bit my lip as a shiver ran through my body, momentarily stunned into silence. My face flushed so hot, I didn't know what else to do but bury it into his chest to hide from his laughter.

"Heh heh," he snickered.

"The hell are you doing?!" I exclaimed, smacking his chest. I wasn't sure why I was hiding from the shame by burrowing further into his chest, but it wasn't like I had anywhere else to hide. *Porsche, you idiot!*

"Stop snuggling me and go to sleep," Kinn said. I reared back, trying to get away from him, but he held onto my head. *Where else am I supposed to go, Kinn?! You're holding onto me so tightly!*

"Let go!" I wailed.

"Your heart's beating so fast—should we call for the doctor?" Kinn laughed. "Maybe you've got a heart condition."

I felt like I was losing a lot of face right now. My body was such a damn traitor, reacting like this when I was around Kinn! Fuck! What was wrong with me?!

"Bastard! If you want to sleep, then sleep. But *actually* go the fuck to sleep, please!" I bargained with him.

"Shush! Sleep, sleep," he said, obviously not listening to me. He never fucking listened to me.

Kinn rubbed at my back gently, as if he was trying to soothe me, until I stopped struggling. He withdrew the hand that was holding me to touch his flank with a grimace. I looked up at his sudden movement.

"Does it hurt? Do you want to call the doctor?" I asked as I leaned over to inspect his wound.

"Don't. It only hurts because I overextended myself. Go to sleep." Kinn pulled me down to lie on his arm like before and hugged me back into place.

Fine, I'd sleep. I'd *better* sleep—if Kinn died, his father would blame me! Fuck.

I didn't know when Kinn's unique scent had started comforting me so much. I felt safe and secure in his arms. His embrace made my heart hammer; even as I dozed off, almost asleep, my heart kept racing...

No, no, no, I couldn't think about it! I wasn't gay! How could I think about another guy like that?!

And this guy was so fucked up, too. *How many times has he made you angry, Porsche? How many times has he made you hate him?! Motherfucker!*

[MORNING]

"Mr. Kinn, sir...um...that is..."

I heard Pete's voice as I woke up, but I didn't dare to lift my head, afraid for a repeat of yesterday. *Shit!*

"What do you want, Pete?" Kinn loosened his hold on me but stayed where he was.

"Sorry, sir, but in ten minutes, the doctor will be here for Mr. Kinn's checkup," Pete said remorsefully.

"Hmm. Go wait for me in my room. I'll be there in a minute," Kinn told Pete evenly, before turning to hold me again.

"Get up!" I hissed, twisting away from his embrace.

"I can't get up yet," he said, holding me tighter. I felt something hard poke at my thigh.

"What are you kneeing me for?!" I complained.

"Heh heh, that's not my knee..." Kinn chuckled before proudly declaring in my ear, "I'm standing for the flag and anthem in the morning."[16]

I shuddered, understanding his insinuation.

"Perv!" I used my leg to push away from him. Kinn loosened his hold and lay flat on his back. I sat up, my traitorous gaze accidentally focusing on the part of his body making a bump in the blankets. "Ugh. Go take care of that!" I yelled at him, looking away.

"What's the big deal? It's a natural phenomenon!" he yelled back.

Whoosh! Kinn lifted the blanket just like that. I bit my lip, my heart racing. The same heat from last night flared up inside me.

"Kinn, you bastard!"

"Wanna raise the flag with me?" he laughed, smiling wickedly. I bunched up the blankets into a ball and threw them at his face and then scrambled off the bed, half walking and half running to the bathroom to hide from him. *Motherfucking evil pervert!*

I stayed in the bathroom for a long time, not wanting to leave. Kinn was so damned diligent about annoying me.

Knock, knock.

The sound of knocking on the bathroom door startled me.

---

16 Every morning at 8 A.M., the Thai flag is raised, accompanied by the national anthem. It is customary to stop and stand at attention for this.

"There's no need for anyone to watch you tonight—I'll come sleep in your bed!" Kinn yelled through the door. I threw a toothpaste tube at the door in anger.

"Motherfucker!" I shouted. *Just you wait—tonight I'll bring all my friends and relatives to stay with me!*

I heard the door to the room close, signaling Kinn's exit. I finally emerged from the bathroom and collapsed angrily on the bed, still mentally cursing at Kinn.

Soon the door opened once more, and I saw Pete enter with a wide grin. I pulled my blanket over my head and pretended to be asleep.

"Hey, what are you acting so embarrassed for?! Wake up and get your medicine and food!" he said with a laugh. *What do you mean, embarrassed? Pete, you bastard, I'll kick you in the mouth one of these days!* "Come on, quickly. You'll suffocate sleeping like that," he continued, pulling my blanket off. I surrendered to my fate and sat up.

Pete pulled the overbed table over for me, along with food and medicine. I kept my head down as I ate, not looking at my friend at all. I didn't know what sort of stupid faces he was making, but I could hear him laugh periodically. *Motherfucker!*

I leaned against the headboard with my knees up. I'd been glancing at the door repeatedly since early evening. I frowned, feeling paranoid. *What am I so stressed out for?* My finger pressed the buttons on the TV remote, changing the channels while I barely paid any attention to what was onscreen.

Porsche! What the hell is wrong with you?! Every time a shadow passed by the door my heart lurched. I was getting frustrated with myself. Fuck! Why did I have to be the one waiting for *him*? Why should *I* have to wait for that door to open? This was crazy. I was going crazy. I should have been hoping he wouldn't come back! That they'd pump him so full of sedatives tonight that he'd sleep until he was dead!

There was another knock at the door. As soon as I heard the door creak open, I sat up with both legs crossed. I stared at the door, heart beating in anticipation.

"Oh..." I sighed at the man entering with a giant basket of fruit. Beaming, he headed straight for the bed.

"Why do you look so disappointed, hmm?" Vegas asked with a smile. *I'm making a disappointed face? When did I do that?!*

"Hi," I greeted him evenly.

Vegas carefully arranged the basket on the bedside table and pulled a chair over to sit next to my bed. I was a little surprised that he'd come to visit me.

"Sorry for disturbing you so late," he said. "I only just heard from P'Beam at dinner that you were in hospital."

I nodded and glanced at the clock. It was nearly nine in the evening—it was true, he was bothering me quite late.

"It's fine... Thank you," I told him.

"Have you taken your medicine yet, Porsche?" he asked, as cheerful as always. I nodded. "You're not upset at me for visiting like this, right?" he asked.

"Uh...no." I wasn't upset at him. I could say we were friends, even if we weren't close enough to meet up that often.

"Are you feeling better?" Vegas was determined to continue asking me questions, apparently. His eyes roamed over my body.

"Much better, but it still hurts a little," I said truthfully.

"Please, let me see." Vegas abruptly reached out to gently take hold of my arm, slowly rubbing at my bruises. I froze at his touch. He leaned his face toward my injury and gently blew on my arm.

"Phew! Get better soon," he said, looking up at me and smiling. I quickly pulled back my arm, skin crawling. What the fuck?! None of my friends would do that! It was the same shit as with Kinn all over again. But if I looked at it another way, it might not mean anything—just part of his caring nature.

"Thank you," I answered, voice flat.

"Would you like some fruit? I'll peel it for you," he said with a smirk, turning to the fruit basket he'd brought.

"You don't need to, it's fine," I replied quickly when he started looking around for a plate.

"Porsche, are you tired already?" he said. "Your eyes are still bright, you should have some fruit while you watch TV... Relax, I'll take care of it."

When he said it like that, how was I supposed to decline? I sat and watched him peel some fruit and arrange it on a plate. He went into the bathroom to wash more fruit, clumsy in that spoiled young master way—exactly like Kinn in the forest. Speaking of Kinn, when was he coming over? I'd been glancing at the door every now and then, but there was no sign of him.

"I'll peel that," I said, grabbing the knife from Vegas's hand along with the green apple he was about to peel. Seeing how oddly Vegas was holding the knife scared me. He was acting like he didn't know how to use it but was going to try his damnedest anyway. I could see the knife barely missing his hand and it frustrated me. If Vegas and Kinn went out in the real world with no one to serve them, they'd be dead in no time.

"Heh. All right, I'll listen to you." Vegas pulled the overbed table to me and silently watched me peel the apple as he grabbed some grapes to eat himself. I should've guessed it—urging me to eat, but he was the hungry one.

"Be careful of your hand... Is there someone at the door?" Vegas asked me. I looked away from the door and focused on peeling the apple. My eyes had a mind of their own, wandering back to the door constantly.

"No," I muttered.

"Ah, eat this while you're waiting for the apple," Vegas said, holding a grape to my lips. I went still before opening my mouth to eat it. Yeah, this was weird, but Tem also liked to feed me things sometimes. It wasn't a big deal.

I glanced at the clock, my mind wandering as I absentmindedly peeled the large apple. It was past nine o'clock and I was peeling a fucking apple—this was stupid.

Click!

I startled at the sound of the door opening. The knife in my hand slipped, cutting my finger. "Ow!"

"Hey!" Vegas quickly grabbed my hand.

"Vegas, what are you doing here?" came Kinn's icy voice as he walked in with his IV stand. Vegas and I looked up at him at the same time. His expression was stern, his brow furrowed.

"Ah, big brother, I was about to visit you," Vegas said with a bright smile, his hand not letting go of mine.

"What happened?" Kinn asked, getting closer. He looked questioningly at my hand in Vegas's.

"Just a little accident," Vegas said, turning back to stare at my bleeding finger again. Both he and I made the same shocked expression when Kinn yanked my hand out of Vegas's grip.

"What's wrong?" Kinn asked, irritated, before looking at Vegas.

"Just a cut, big brother," Vegas grinned.

"I see. You won't die, then," Kinn said. He let go of my hand like he didn't care. It was his fault—he was the one who'd come in and surprised me!

"I'll take Porsche to the bathroom to clean it up." Vegas began to help me stand, but Kinn stopped him with a hand on his shoulder.

"I'm going to trouble you to go ask for a bandage from the nurses' station out front," he said expressionlessly. Vegas looked at Kinn for a while before nodding with a smile and leaving the room.

"What's he doing here?!" Kinn barked as soon as the door closed.

"Attending the monkey banquet,[17] I guess." What a stupid question! He was here to visit, obviously.

"Don't piss me off!" he yelled. What the hell was he so angry for?

Kinn breathed in deeply in an attempt to calm himself down before drawing my hand over to the fruit plate. He took a glass and poured water over my finger to wash off the blood. He wasn't gentle at all, gripping my finger tightly until I cried out.

"Fuck you, Kinn, that hurts!" I tried to pull back, but he held on and continued washing the cut.

"When did you become such a whiner?" he asked, staring at my finger.

"How about I hit you where it hurts?" I said, annoyed. Kinn looked at my face and loosened his grip.

"Why is he here so late?" he continued, still preoccupied with Vegas.

"How am I supposed to know? Go ask him!" I pulled my hand back when I saw that he was done.

"The fuck is he here for?" Kinn cursed as he nudged me to the other side of the bed and sat down next to me.

"How would I know?! He's your cousin, not mine!"

Kinn sighed and shook his head, seeming lost in thought.

---

17   Monkey Banquet: An annual festival in the Lopburi province where locals leave out a banquet of fruit for wild monkeys to eat.

Vegas returned. "Here we are," he said, handing me the bandage.

Kinn intercepted it. "If there's nothing else, you can go, Vegas. Let Porsche get some rest." He glared at Vegas silently.

Vegas paused and nodded. "Of course. Will you be going back to your room? I can accompany you there." His expression was as friendly as usual.

"It's fine," Kinn said. "You can go."

Vegas smiled in answer and gave Kinn a wai. From their conversation, it sounded like Vegas hadn't even gone to visit Kinn. Why had he visited me first and not his cousin?

"Get well soon, Porsche," Vegas said. "You too, big brother." Kinn sat still and stared at him, not taking his eyes away until he left the room.

Then Kinn sighed and turned to me. "What did he say to you?"

"He was just visiting. He asked how I was feeling," I answered truthfully. Kinn must have still been concerned about Vegas inviting me to work for him. That would explain why he blew up like that.

"Just that?" Kinn asked, raising one eyebrow.

"Mm-hm," I hummed in reply.

"Was he here long?" he asked.

I looked up at the clock and shook my head.

Kinn sighed. "I don't like him sticking his nose where it doesn't belong," he said. He went still for a while, seeming to be pondering something. I looked away. I didn't know where all this anger had come from, why Kinn was so bent out of shape like this. I knew his whole damn family hated Vegas, but what did I have to do with it? Besides, Vegas had been nice to me. We were all adults here—expecting me to hate him just because everyone else did was incredibly childish.

I stayed silent until Kinn's hand slid over and caught my wrist, pulling me toward him. I jerked backward, afraid his hand would brush against my cut again. It didn't really hurt *that* much, but I'd rather avoid any further pain.

"Stay still!" he snapped. He tore the bandage packaging open with his teeth, then gently applied it over my cut. I stopped resisting when I saw how carefully he was tending to it.

Kinn lifted his head. "Does it hurt?"

"It hurt when you cleaned it," I answered, irritated.

He smiled slightly and lightly kissed the bandage. "Feel better soon."

I bit my lip, not knowing what to do. What was he doing? Was he trying to piss me off? But my heart was beating so fast, completely different from when Vegas blew on it.

I didn't speak.

"Go turn off the lights, I'm sleepy," Kinn said. What the fuck was his problem?

Kinn took off his shoes and collapsed onto the bed. I looked at him in confusion until he had to repeat himself: "Go turn off the lights! Do I have to drag my saline with me to turn it off?" *Motherfucker, you managed to haul it down the hallway to my room by yourself. Are you gonna die dragging it to the light switch?!*

"What the hell is wrong with you? You've got your own room; can't you sleep in it?" I asked, not lifting a finger to follow his order.

"I'm lonely!" Kinn enunciated each syllable, smiling. "Hurry up and turn off the lights!" He tried to push me to get off the bed.

"Go sleep in your own room!" I yelled back. *Coming to my room and forcing me to wait on you? Bastard!* I got off the bed, hands on my hips, and looked at Kinn. He was spread out on the bed like a starfish, as if he owned the damned thing.

"Go on. And don't even think about sleeping on the sofa," he said when my eyes slid over to the couch. *If I have to turn off the lights, I might as well sleep over here, motherfucker!*

"I hope your wound gets infected!" I huffed and turned off the lights and the TV. I sure as hell wasn't going to get into the bed with Kinn. I sank onto the sofa with a resigned face.

Kinn raised his head to look and chuckled. I lay back on the sofa, even though I had no pillow or blanket.

Silence enveloped the room. Kinn seemed to let the matter go quite easily. I was relieved, thinking he wouldn't bother me any longer, but then...

"Hey... Do you know how many years this hospital has been in operation?" he asked. I frowned at him.

"Who wants to know?" I said, irritated.

"This is an old hospital... You know that people die in hospitals, right? And this building... They say that this building..."

"Fuck off, Kinn! Stop that! I don't believe you," I said with a nervous gulp. I knew he was spouting nonsense to try and scare me like he did in the forest, but I couldn't help but think that the hospital at night was creepy as hell.

"It's up to you if you believe it or not," Kinn said, "but did you know...?"

"I don't know, and I don't *want* to know," I said, using my hands to block my ears. I could still faintly hear his laughter. *Fucking bastard!*

"Why don't you try looking under the bed?" I heard Kinn say. I slowly looked toward the space under the bed, which was directly in my line of sight from the sofa. I started to feel lightheaded, my heart beating erratically even though there was nothing there. *Why did I have to look?!*

"You stop that!" I lambasted him.

"Sounds echo underneath the bed at night...*thump, thump, thump,* like someone knocking," Kinn kept going. I felt cold sweat form on my body and fear build in my heart.

"You evil bastard!" I yelled.

"Ah, I'll go back to my room, now, so it'll be more comfortable for you on the bed," Kinn said, sitting up. He slipped his feet into his shoes, acting like he was about to get up and leave. I jumped off the sofa and lurched toward the bed, grabbing onto Kinn's arm.

"Fine, you can stay, asshole!" I snapped, clinging tightly onto him. Fuck, this was embarrassing! I knew Kinn was probably making shit up, but I was too creeped out to care.

"Hah, that wasn't so hard, was it?" Kinn leaned back down, laying his arm across the bed and pulling my head down to rest on it.

"You better sleep properly. And don't hug me, I'm gonna suffocate!" I declared, scooting away from him. That fucker didn't listen, of course—he moved onto his side and used his free arm to pull me to face him. I struggled, but he wouldn't let go of me.

"Shh! Do you hear that?" he said as he poked at my back. I looked up from his chest.

"Hear what?" I whispered, my mind going to all sorts of terrible places. *Is it the ghost under the bed?*

"Like a *thud, thud, thud* sound. Can you hear it?" he asked me, his voice grave. At this point I was more scared of ghosts than worried about maintaining my tough guy image. I burrowed into his chest, not wanting to hear anything. It was too fucking creepy.

"It's getting louder," he said. I held tightly onto the hem of his shirt. He leaned down to whisper in my ear. "Do you want to know what it is?"

I shook my head. *Stop asking if I want to know! I don't want to know anything!*

"It's the sound...of..." he trailed off ominously, "your heartbeat! Hah!"

Kinn's head dropped onto the pillow as he howled with laughter. I slapped at his arm with all my strength before his hands and feet all locked onto mine, not letting me move.

Kinn, you asshole! I'm like this because of you!

I woke up in the morning without Kinn beside me. The doctor was there to give me a checkup. The night before, I'd struggled against Kinn until I was so exhausted I fell asleep.

As for Chay, Tem, and Jom, they helped pack everything up to get me ready to leave. Unlike my first day there, my body had now fully recovered and I had plenty of energy.

"Hia, I'll go with the others and wait for you downstairs. We'll put everything in P'Pete's car," Chay told me. I nodded in reply, and they all filed out as Pete entered.

"Mr. Kinn requested you see him before you leave," Pete said. He checked that everything was in order, then sat down on the sofa.

"Do I have to?" I asked, irritated.

Kinn needed to be monitored for a few more days before he could be discharged. Honestly, I'd have preferred it if he got stuck here for a month just so I wouldn't have to see his face. Kinn was so fucking annoying.

"Just go with it. You're still his head bodyguard—he might want to assign you some work," Pete said.

Shit, I forgot I had to work. I wasn't even out of the hospital yet and I already had duties. Fucking hell.

"Fine! I'll go," I grumbled, deciding I might as well just in case it was his dying wish or whatever.

"Oh, Porsche?" Pete's voice suddenly turned serious. I turned to face him. "I'm not teasing you, but what's going on between you and Mr. Kinn?"

It was true, he didn't have his usual teasing expression and playful tone—he looked deadly serious as he stared at me.

"...Nothing, why?" I mumbled.

"I don't want to pry, it's just... I was just teasing you before, but lately I've noticed this thing between you and Mr. Kinn..."

I was quiet as I listened intently. He sighed before he continued. "You don't actually have feelings for him, do you?" he asked, looking at me in concern.

"No!" I exclaimed, swallowing thickly.

"That's good... I'm sorry for teasing you this whole time. I figured a guy like you wouldn't feel anything for him anyway."

I looked away and began to pack a charger cable into my bag. "Hmm," I hummed instead of replying to Pete.

"And this whole sleeping together thing," Pete pressed. "You're just sleeping together, right, not *sleeping* together?"

"What do you mean?" I tried to act normal, looking everywhere but at Pete.

"I see you as a friend, Porsche. I hoped when the both of you disappeared together—in that hotel room and in the forest—that you would get out okay. You wouldn't have done anything untoward with Mr. Kinn, right?"

I bit my lip hard, feeling strangely hot as sweat formed on my skin. "Just say what you want to say," I told Pete.

Pete looked unsure. I doubted he actually knew anything that was going on between me and his boss—he was just teasing me.

"I'm warning you, Porsche," he said, "if you climb up to such high places, it hurts when you fall..."

I stared at him, trying to understand. Did he mean his boss was far too high up for someone like me? That he was out of my league?

"Don't worry, your boss is just trying to annoy me," I said.

"I'm warning you because I know Mr. Kinn very well... I don't want to see you get hurt," Pete said somberly. "But I know you're totally straight, so you can't be too far gone." He looked at me with uncertainty.

"I'm fine! You can go. The fuck are you going on about, anyway?" I said, hauling my backpack onto my shoulder. I heard Pete sigh as I walked out of my room and headed toward Kinn's. I knew Pete was warning me out of the goodness of his heart, but it was kind of too little, too late...

Bang! I slammed open the door, then stopped in my tracks when I saw someone unfamiliar in the room with Kinn.

"Sorry, I didn't know you had a guest," I said evenly as I looked at Kinn. He was sitting up against the headboard.

"Come see me tomorrow evening," he told me.

I looked at the stranger. He had opened the door to the balcony and was leaning against the doorframe, blowing cigarette smoke outside. Wait, why had no one told me smoking was allowed in here?! I wanted a cigarette! I'd been so fucking stressed out!

"What did you call me here for?" I turned to ask Kinn, frowning.

"You still work for me. I have an assignment for you," he said calmly.

I sighed in frustration. "Uh-huh," I answered with a weary expression on my face.

"Mek, are you going to leave now?" Kinn asked the stranger—Mek, apparently. "I can have Pete drive you."

I turned to look at Mek. He was tall, with darkly handsome features and a slightly stubbled face. His gaze was trained on the cigarette smoke billowing in the air in front of him. I stared at him, feeling my hair stand on end. He was good-looking, but also oddly off-putting.

"I'll go back by myself," Mek's deep voice answered.

"Didn't you say your underlings already left?" Kinn asked.

"I happen to have some business to take of nearby," Mek said. He eyed me from head to toe, sending a shiver up my spine.

"If that's all, I'm leaving," I said. Kinn nodded at me in acknowledgment, so I turned and immediately left the room.

I came downstairs to find that Chay, Tem, and Jom had already dealt with my things, and Mr. Korn had taken care of the hospital bill. Pete had brought a fancy-looking car around and parked it out front. I waved goodbye to Tem and Jom, who were going back to their separate homes, before I got into the car. I sat shotgun and Chay sat in the back seat.

"So who's that Mek guy?" I asked Pete as we pulled away.

"Mr. Kinn's friend," Pete replied.

"I've never seen him before."

"They don't really hang out. Something happened, so they've been distant for a while. Today is the first time I've seen him," Pete said in a worried tone. Pete seemed strangely out of sorts today, so I dropped the subject, letting him drive us back to the compound without any further questions.

"You'll be staying in the main house, Porsche. On the first floor beside the stairs, next to P'Chan's room. Arm and the rest moved your stuff out of your old room," Pete told me as he led me to my new room.

"What, why?" I asked. Why did I have to change rooms?

"Your brother's going to be living here, and your old room wouldn't be big enough," he said as he headed inside, leaving our stuff on the bed. "So, Mr. Korn is having you two brothers move into this room instead."

I looked around the room curiously. It was larger than my room in the bodyguards' quarters, with a queen-sized bed, some furniture, and an ensuite bathroom. It wasn't the fanciest, but it was so much roomier. It would have been cramped squeezing Chay into my old room.

"You get some rest first. I'll go watch the boss," Pete said and left the room. Pete was currently working practically two jobs, looking after both Kinn and Tankhun. I wondered what his salary was for toiling away this much. Kinn himself was using Pete to do his bidding and entertain his every whim—he was no better than Tankhun. Pete must be so tired from all that work.

"Hia, can we really not go home?" Chay asked as he arranged our things.

"Hmm... I don't want to risk you going back there right now," I said.

"I told you to quit from the start," Chay complained. "Now it's too late."

I was too lazy to listen, so I collapsed onto the bed and played on my phone until I fell asleep.

I woke up again at some point in the evening to find Arm, Pol, and Chay loudly playing games, their shouts filling the room. I sat up blearily and saw them sprawled out on the floor with their phones before they looked up to wave at me guiltily.

"You're awake? Let's get dinner," Arm said. I nodded and got up to wash my face in the bathroom, then came back to wait for them to finish their game so we could head out together as a group.

"Porsche... You're feeling better now, yes?" It was Mr. Korn.

I hurriedly turned to greet him with a wai gesture. "Yes, I'm much better now, sir," I replied.

"Remember to rest up. Porchay, do look after your brother," Mr. Korn said as he fondly ruffled my little brother's hair.

"What's for dinner, Father?" came a loud voice from the front door. We all turned to look at the newcomer.

"You've been coming home so often these days. Has hell frozen over...?" Mr. Korn teased Kim, who had just come in with a confused look on his face. Then he turned to greet the man following behind Kim. "Oh, Mek, where did you come from?"

I furrowed my brow when I saw Mek again, feeling a strange aversion to him that I couldn't explain.

"Hello, Uncle. I ran into Kim, so I asked to come with him to visit you," Mek said politely, his face revealing nothing.

"Good, good, we can all eat together," Mr. Korn said. "There's extra dinner these days, since Kim has been home so often."

"Isn't that a good thing?" Kim said. "If you lose your senses and let Khun inherit everything, our family will fall to ruin." He laughed and headed straight for the kitchen.

"Come join us for dinner, Mek," said Mr. Korn.

"I'll be right there." Mek stepped aside for Mr. Korn to lead the way. His eyes followed the older man before moving over to me.

"Yes?" I raised my brows in question. Mek was acting like he had a problem with me or something. His smile twitched a little before he offered a hand in greeting.

"I'm Mek," he said. I looked at him, confused, before offering my hand for him to shake.

"Porsche," I said calmly. He stared at me for a moment before walking away toward the kitchen.

"What was that?" Pol asked, curious. Everyone watched Mek's retreating back with the same expression. We stood there in confusion before making our way to the staff cafeteria.

"Why did Mr. Mek try to talk to you?" Arm asked as we ate.

"I don't know," I said. "It's weird. Do you guys know him?"

"I just know he's called Mek and he's Mr. Kinn's friend, but that's about it," Arm replied. "We haven't seen him around for quite a while."

I sat there and pondered Mek's actions, but I couldn't figure anything out. So I let the subject drop and finished eating before returning to my room to shower, take my medicine, and collapse on the bed. I was alone in the room because Chay had gone to play games with the others—he said he didn't want to disturb me with all the shouting. I let him go, knowing I could trust Pol and Arm with him.

I tossed and turned in the dark for almost an hour. Why wasn't I tired? I'd tried scrolling on my phone and playing some songs, but still couldn't fall asleep. *Fuck!*

Counting the nights in the forest, I'd gotten used to Kinn sleeping next to me for practically the entire week. I could admit that his scent and his touch helped me sleep... *No, no, no!* Now was the time to harness the hate I'd been holding onto. I needed to remember how much I despised him, how mistrustful I was of him. I was disgusted with myself for letting another guy do those things to me. But at some point, that feeling of hatred and fear had disappeared. So much had happened in such a short time—how could I have forgotten how much I abhorred the bastard?!

My paranoia had turned into a racing heartbeat whenever Kinn came near. Images would come flooding back into my head, but they didn't make me feel as bad as before. Disgust had been replaced with uncertainty in my heart. How quickly could hate be erased? Would I still feel the same a week from now?

Had I never even hated him to begin with?

Argh! What was wrong with me?!

KINN
PORSCHE

22

Bewildered

HOW LONG DID IT TAKE to fall in love? How many years... No, how many months? How many days—how many minutes?

No, no, no, I wasn't feeling anything.

What should I do?! I couldn't feel something for him! How could I face everyone if I did?!

"I emailed you the slides," Tem said over the phone. "Just do the report like I told you. You were away for a while, so there's a lot of homework."

"Fuck, there's so much," I complained.

"I'll help you! Just share the slides with me."

"Thanks, man," I said, hanging up the phone and turning to look at the schoolwork on my laptop. It was a good thing Chay remembered to grab it for me, otherwise I'd be done for; I had a mountain of work piled up. I didn't know how many years it'd take to get through all of this, but the professor had set deadlines for Monday and Tuesday. I was going to die!

"Hia, I'm going out with Tee and the rest," Chay said. I nodded. It was the weekend, so I should have been working, but Mr. Korn was letting me take a break. It was probably out of sympathy—both for my battered body and the unimaginable amount of university work hanging over my head.

I opened the slides and slowly read through each unit. Honestly, my major was more focused on practical work, but I'd disappeared for so many days that I had to make up for it in other ways. What I hated the most was all the busywork—especially analyzing data.

Fuck! I'm so fucking stressed out!

[LINE GROUP CHAT]

TEM: I shared all the info with you.

PORSCHE: Got it, I'm stressed just seeing it!

TEM: Just keep at it, you'll be done in no time.

PORSCHE: Jom, you better come help me.

TEM: Do you want to just pass, or do you want a good score?

PORSCHE: I'm so fucking stressed! As long as it gets done, I'll take whatever help I can get!

JOM: Sure! I'll help you, my friend :) *video file attached*

TEM: Bastard, what did you send?! I'm at a food stall! The moaning is so loud, you fucker!

JOM: I'm helping Porsche relax. One round to clear his head :) then everything will go smoothly. lol

I frowned before pressing play on Jom's video, but when it loaded the image on the phone screen made me smirk. *Now that's what I'm talking about!* I pushed myself away from my laptop, glanced at the door to make sure it was locked, then sat down. I leaned back against the headboard and watched the video intently. Fuck homework!

Now that I thought about it, I hadn't jerked off in ages. Maybe that's why my thoughts had been so strange, all that crazy shit about Kinn. Now I could finally relax and get some sense back!

"Ah... Ah... Mmm!"

I smiled at the image of the porn star masturbating onscreen. I licked my lips and reached down into my sweatpants, taking myself in hand and slowly stroking.

I focused on the screen in front of me. The video kept playing as my hand tried to get my cock interested. My mind clearly comprehended the images in front of me, but I just wasn't feeling excited by the sexy chick in the video at all. I bit my lower lip, moving my wrist in a rhythm that I'd always liked...

"Argh!" I snarled in frustration. My body wouldn't fucking cooperate! No matter how hot the woman in front of me was, I wasn't feeling anything. Maybe I was too stressed out about my report.

I closed my eyes to try once again. This time, I tugged my sweatpants down past my dick and increased the pace.

I furrowed my brow, looking at the actress with no results. Starting to feel suspicious, I closed out of Jom's video. It could be I just didn't like her moves. I'd fucking change the channel, then! I went to my usual website, clicking on a video I knew I would enjoy.

This time I'd watch something with both partners right in the middle of it. I'd get in the mood faster that way. I skipped to the middle, watching the actor snap his hips into the actress's body. I felt my blood begin to pump, arousal building up inside me. I started to move my wrist again.

The woman moaned wantonly underneath the man. My eyes strayed from her to the guy: muscular, good-looking, sweat glistening on his skin. Suddenly my heart skipped a beat. The man's body and his passionate movements called to mind the image of a certain someone... That bastard Kinn!

I swallowed hard and shook my head to chase away the thought, but I couldn't look away from those fit abs and his blissed-out face.

I was absorbed in the scene onscreen, watching the guy fuck, and the image started to overlap with Kinn's face in my mind. I began to pant, my heart beating erratically, and just like that—my dick woke up.

I slowly loosened my grip, not wanting to accept the state I was in. But fuck—if I didn't get some release, I'd just be uncomfortable, right?

I took a deep breath and resigned myself to my fate, pumping my cock fast and letting my mind fill with images of Kinn. I couldn't stop myself.

Fuck! What am I doing?! I bit my lip hard. The closer I got to coming, the more I thought of his face, and the more I remembered his scent and his touch. I gripped my phone tightly. The images on the screen were no longer important to me. My focus drifted away from the video, toward the images in my mind...

Just a bit more...

I felt a throb low in my gut and my ass. I didn't know when I'd begun to feel such intense sensations.

I'm so close... Hnng...

Rrrrrrr! My phone buzzed.

"Fuck!" I swore. My hand stopped abruptly as I came back to my senses, mentally cursing at myself. *What the fuck are you doing, Porsche?!*

I gulped again, not wanting to believe what I had just done, and angrily picked up my phone. My eyes widened in surprise as I recognized each digit of the number, a chill spreading through my body. I wanted to hit my head against the wall—it was like the universe knew Kinn would torment me with what I had just done.

I pressed the answer button, sweat starting to form on my skin despite the chill from the air conditioning.

"What took you so long?"

I almost stopped breathing as soon as I heard the voice on the other end. "What do you want?" I asked, barely managing to stop my voice from trembling.

"What are you doing?" Kinn asked. His question made me look down to my still-hard cock. Mortified, I covered it up with a blanket.

"My report," I answered brusquely, my heart hammering nonstop.

"Hmm... Ah..."

I froze as Kinn groaned at the other end of the call. I bit my lip hard and tried to control my breathing.

"What the hell are you moaning for, Kinn?!" I snapped, remembering the pile of reports next to me to distract myself from him.

"I'm just adjusting my posture—why?" Kinn answered flatly.

"What do you want?" I asked, googling scary pictures to get myself out of the mood.

"Come see me tonight."

"No! Your father said I could have today off," I replied.

"I gave you my orders yesterday," Kinn insisted stubbornly.

"I'm off duty today! I'm not even done with my schoolwork, you bastard!" I stared at some scenes from a horror movie until my strange feelings began to die down.

"Then bring your reports here," Kinn said.

"What?! No! I'm not going! Bye!"

I hung up the phone and heaved a sigh. That was fucking awful—how could I have done that? I couldn't ever do it again! If Kinn's image popped up in my head like that again, I'd die!

I got up from the bed to wash my face, the cold water bringing me back to my senses.

There was a knock at the door. I pulled at my hair in frustration. What was it with today? I calmed down and went to open the door.

"There's...someone here to see you," Pol said, glancing backward. I looked behind him and smiled awkwardly at my visitor.

"Hello. I'm not disturbing you, am I?" Vegas smiled broadly as he came to a stop in front of me. Pol veered back and gestured that he was going to go upstairs, so I gave him a nod in acknowledgment.

"Not at all," I answered Vegas politely.

"I'm here to visit. You're feeling better now, right, Porsche?" Vegas smiled as he held up his hands. Both held bags of snacks.

"Thank you." I scratched the back of my head, resigned to the situation.

"Why the frown...? I'm disturbing you, aren't I? Ah, I'm sorry," Vegas said guiltily, visibly wilting.

"No, no, I'm just a little stressed about my school reports." I pointed toward my room and Vegas's gaze followed.

"Oh... Is there something I could help with, then? Excuse me," he said, brazenly walking straight into my bedroom. I sighed inwardly and followed him.

Vegas set the snacks on the floor and started clicking away at the slides on my laptop screen. "General education requirements? My university has them too. I'll help you, yes?" He looked at me expectantly. I slumped to the floor and nodded, giving him permission to help. *Fine! If he's volunteering and my work gets done, I'll take it.*

Vegas sank down next to me and brought the laptop to the edge of the bed, typing away. I watched him work for a bit, then opened a textbook to try and help. A strange nagging feeling still tugged at my mind. The report was partially why I was so stressed out, but a much bigger part was coming from the lingering sexual frustration. I shook my head to chase away those thoughts and tried to focus on the work in front of me.

Vegas turned to look at my face and scooted closer. "Are you still not feeling well?" he asked, placing his hand on my forehead. I backed away a little but allowed him to check my temperature.

"No, just a bit dizzy," I said.

He smiled and pulled the bags of snacks over to me. "Eat something! Get your blood sugar up. This store sells some pretty good desserts," he said, holding up a cream-filled pancake. He'd wrapped it in a napkin so I could hold it without smearing my hand. I took it from him with a small smile.

I wasn't actually hungry, but it would be impolite to refuse. I didn't want to look down on his kindness.

He turned back and continued working quietly, studiously helping me research and adding relevant information to the slides. His university was no less reputable than mine, so the content shouldn't have been too different. Plus, this general education requirement included English—for someone terrible at languages like me, having someone to help was a huge relief.

"Are you thirsty? I brought boba as well. I didn't know what kind you liked, so I got all four flavors..." Vegas pushed himself away from the laptop and handed me the boba. The cup had an open top because of the cheese foam topping. I slowly sipped the milk tea, my eyes on Vegas's face. He really was a decent guy—helping me with my schoolwork and even bringing me a bunch of snacks.

"Oh! I almost forgot, Porsche, you're still not well... You shouldn't be having cold drinks." Vegas took the cup from me. I looked at him in confusion before taking the cup back.

"It's fine. I'm better now," I said.

"No, you shouldn't. If you catch another fever, I'd feel guilty." Vegas tried to take the cup again, but this time I didn't let go.

"There's really no problem." I wasn't trying to be difficult, but I was feeling much better now. I wanted to go back to normal—I wasn't that weak. I tried to pull the cup back, but Vegas held tight. Our tug-of-war caused the liquid inside to slosh and spill on his shirt.

"Ah!"

"Shit!" I exclaimed and let go of the cup. I quickly went to grab a towel while Vegas set the cup on the floor and looked down at his shirt, a little stunned.

"Sorry," I apologized, sitting in front of him and trying to blot the foam out of his shirt. Vegas glanced at me and smiled, but I couldn't pay attention to anything other than the mess on his clothing. Shit! He was wearing such an expensive shirt, too!

"You should change. You're a mess," I told him. Vegas nodded in answer, and took his shirt off right then and there. *Shit!* I hurriedly looked the other way. I wasn't embarrassed or anything, but I was afraid what happened earlier when I was watching the porno would repeat itself. I didn't want to start thinking of Kinn again.

"Err... Can I borrow a shirt, Porsche? I'll return it after a wash."

I nodded and got up to open the wardrobe, looking for a t-shirt for him. *Shit! It's just a guy's chest. What is going on with me?! Fuck!* Whenever I looked at Vegas, the image of him shirtless was superimposed with Kinn's body. I was going insane. Did I need to see a psychiatrist?

"Here." I shoved a shirt at Vegas and quickly turned away, picking up things in the room and setting them down aimlessly.

"Are you nervous, Porsche?" Vegas asked with a quiet chuckle. *I'm not nervous about you! I just don't want to see Kinn in my head anymore!* It was like I was hallucinating!

"No, I'm just not used to it," I answered.

"Not used to it? We're both men! There's nothing to worry about."

I'm not worried about other men, I'm worried about Kinn! "I'm not worried about anything," I told him evenly.

"Then turn around," he said. I took a deep breath and turned around, then stopped short. Vegas had moved to stand directly in front of me, still shirtless, mere inches away.

"Uh... What is it?" I took a step back, looking at his face in puzzlement. Vegas was about the same size as Kinn, but Kinn was slightly more muscular. *No, no, no, stop thinking about Kinn!* I shook my head to chase the thoughts away.

"Porsche, is something wrong? You're looking a bit flushed. Let me see..." Vegas used the opportunity to press up close and take hold of my waist. I froze, a shiver running through my body. *Motherfucker!* This was exactly like when Kinn was chasing me around! What was wrong with these guys?! Why did I always end up the victim?!

"You don't have a fever... I think."

Slap! I swatted Vegas's hand away from my face and stepped back in surprise. In my hurry, I tripped over my own feet and tumbled backward onto the floor.

"Hey! Porsche!" Vegas immediately caught my arm, looking concerned. I winced; my tailbone had hit the floor with a lot of force. It hurt like a motherfucker! *What were you even panicking about, Porsche?*

"I'm fine, I'm fine." I waved Vegas away, but he came over to help support me, looking over my body with concern.

"You're hurt, aren't you? Be careful when you get up," he said.

The door swung open with a bang. Vegas and I looked up at the sound as we awkwardly tried to get up off the floor.

"Vegas!" Tankhun roared, standing in the doorway with his hands on his hips.

"Big brother?" Vegas called, surprised.

"What are you two doing?!" Tankhun strode over and pushed Vegas's shoulder until he staggered and fell away from me. Since I hadn't regained my balance yet, I stumbled as well, hitting my tail-bone in the same exact place as before. *Ow! Just my fucking luck!*

"Brother, please calm down." Vegas held up his hand at Tankhun, who kept closing in on him.

Tankhun looked back and forth between Vegas and me. "You! Porsche! You and *Porsche*?! You're shirtless! Hmph! This isn't a whorehouse, y'know! What are you trying to do to my employee, you freak?!" he shouted as Pol hurried over to help me up.

Vegas backed away, one eyebrow raised. "At first I thought there was nothing between those ears of yours, but your head is clearly full of dirty thoughts."

"Vegas, I'll fucking kill you!" Tankhun yelled. Chaos erupted in my room as Tankhun chased Vegas, kicking the snacks and drinks on the floor and spilling them all over the place.

"Hey! Stop! Mr. Tankhun... I told you to stop!" I called. Pol and Arm stood outside the room, looking uncertain. It seemed they wanted to stop their boss from attacking Vegas but weren't sure how to do it. I tugged at my hair in frustration. My room was a mess! It looked like a goddamned warzone in here!

"Porsche! Don't be scared, I'll protect you! Pol, go get the mat!"[18] Tankhun shouted as he ran. I picked up my laptop and papers, hugging them tightly–I was terrified they'd get stomped on.

"Brother! Stop!" Vegas shouted, running away.

"I'm going to destroy you, Vegas!"

"Stop!" I yelled, but they showed no signs of relenting.

At last, Pol brought in a long mat and laid it down at the front of the room. Tankhun caught Vegas and flipped him down onto the

---

18   *Referring to a traditional Thai woven mat, often made with rattan reed.*

mat, but Vegas quickly got the upper hand. He pulled and kicked Tankhun as Tankhun was rolled up into the mat, with only his head poking out.

"Vegas, you bastard! Let me go!" Tankhun shrieked. Vegas wouldn't back down, rolling Tankhun further into the mat and cursing. As for Pol and Arm, they tried to hold in their laughter before stepping in to help.

"Argh!" I wanted to hit my head against a wall once I saw the mess they'd made of my room. Their cursing and squabbling still hadn't stopped. I couldn't take it anymore! I wasn't staying to watch this fucking shitshow!

I stomped angrily out of the house with my laptop and papers in hand. I could faintly hear Vegas calling after me, but I didn't want to listen anymore. I'd forgotten to grab my motorcycle keys, so I figured I could just get a taxi to Tem's place. If I had to endure the clusterfuck back there any longer, the stress was going to give me an aneurysm.

"Where are you going?" Pete rolled down his window as he drove past the gates. I used the opportunity to jump into his car.

"Drop me off at Tem's place," I told him, still annoyed.

"What happened?" he asked.

"Motherfucking Vegas and Tankhun got into a fight," I said as I leaned against the car window, defeated. "They're making a racket all over the house. It's so fucking annoying! I can't focus on my work."

"Oh, good, Mr. Kinn wanted me to come pick you up anyway," Pete said while backing up the car. He then turned to exit down the driveway.

"I'm not going to see Kinn. I'm going to Tem's dorm," I said, meaning it.

"Just go. Do you want to disobey a direct order?" Pete asked, turning to look at me before focusing on the road again.

"I'm not working today. I don't have to listen to anyone's orders."

"Hah. Just go, Porsche. Mr. Kinn's already in a bad mood today, and I don't want to get in trouble."

"Fucking hell! What the fuck does he want from me?!" I yelled, fed up.

"Just go with the flow," Pete said casually.

"What do you mean, go with the flow?!"

"Spoiled people like Kinn... If you go along with them for a while, they'll get bored and stop. If you keep resisting, it'll only rile them up," Pete said. He sounded exhausted.

I furrowed my brow and humored his line of thought. It was true—every time I resisted Kinn's orders, he looked like he was in such a good mood. If I went along with what he wanted, he might actually stop trying to get on my nerves. Those spoiled young masters were all sick in the head! The harder something was to obtain, the more they wanted it. But if they got bored, they'd stop.

Pete ended up driving us to the hospital. I walked behind him, huffing and stomping the entire way to Kinn's room.

"Didn't you say you weren't coming?" Kinn asked, looking up from his phone as soon as he noticed me enter. I didn't answer, making a face as I sat down on the sofa.

"Ow!" I cried out. I'd forgotten I'd hurt my tailbone. Both Kinn and Pete turned to look at me.

"What's wrong?" Kinn asked, brow furrowed in curiosity. I didn't want to answer him, so I turned on my laptop to continue working.

"Do your wounds hurt?" Pete asked me in concern. I shook my head.

"What are you doing?" Kinn asked sternly before he got up from the bed and slowly made his way over to me. I noticed that his IV drip had been removed.

"School report," I said, scooting away from him. He sat down next to me and stared at my laptop.

"You can do it," he said, looking at the slides.

"Yes! Ve..." I was about to say Vegas helped me and that was why it was almost done, but I had to quickly swallow my words. If I told Kinn that, he'd fly off the handle and interrogate me for sure.

"'Ve'? What do you mean?" Kinn looked up at me questioningly.

"Ve... Very important to get things done! When you gotta do it, you gotta do it," I said, averting my eyes. I could see Pete smirking, but Kinn didn't seem too intent on the matter. Instead, he kept staring at my slides.

"There's not much left—go ahead," I said, glancing up at him. I thought Kinn was going to help me finish the work, but he let go of my laptop and went back to his bed.

"What?! You're not going to help me?" I asked, a little irritated. Even Vegas helped me until the work was almost finished. Plus, this was in English! Sure, I only had three more pages to get through, but those three pages were full of text.

"It's your work. You do it," Kinn replied breezily. He put on his headphones and reclined, tapping his feet. I huffed and looked at him in annoyance. Tankhun shouldn't have come in when he did. If he'd waited just a little longer, Vegas would've finished the entire thing!

"Then you come and help me," I told Pete, who had been standing to the side and watching silently.

"Ha! I only graduated high school, Porsche—how would I help you? I'm going to go find something to eat." Pete left me and walked straight out of the room. I watched him go and turned back to my laptop screen.

"What's your LINE ID?" Kinn asked suddenly.

"Why?" I snapped back at him.

"I can search for it with your number," Kinn muttered to himself before my phone dinged with a notification sound. "Use this website as a reference; it'll be easier."

I looked down to see a new account had added me. I accepted the request. Kinn's message included several articles from a website that confused me even more. *Motherfucker! It's all in English, you bastard!*

"Send it to me to check when you're done," he said.

"Ugh!" I exclaimed, tired of Kinn's shit. I slowly worked my way through with the information Vegas had left behind.

Kinn didn't disturb me any further; he alternated between listening to music and playing games on his phone. I concentrated on my work, trying to get it done as quickly as possible.

Hmm... I stretched out, chasing away my fatigue. I looked up at the balcony to see that the sky had begun to darken. I'd spent quite some time working on this.

"If you're done, send it to me," Kinn said, pulling himself up to lean on the headboard. I couldn't be bothered to argue with him, so I picked up my laptop and walked over. His face darkened as he looked through the slides.

"What are you doing, Porsche?" he asked sternly. I raised my brows at him.

"What?"

"Why is your grammar all over the place?" Kinn pointed at the screen, staring at me fiercely.

"You fix it, then," I answered him nonchalantly.

"And why were the first few slides all correct...?" Kinn's voice suddenly took on an edge. "Who did them for you?!"

"What, it's just... Fuck it! I can only do so much. If it's wrong, it's wrong." I slammed my laptop shut and picked it up from his lap.

Kinn looked at me skeptically. Before he could find out who worked on the slides and go berserk, the nurse interrupted us.

"Time for your sponge bath, Mr. Kinn," she said with a smile, blushing a little. I frowned.

"Oh..." Kinn sat up and moved to sit on the edge of the bed. I sat down on the sofa, arms crossed, silently glaring at him.

"We'll have to remove your shirt first," the nurse said. I immediately looked the other way. I let out a huff at the nurse's bashful manner—her eyes had been sparkling when she looked at Kinn.

"You can just prepare everything and leave. I'll have him do it instead," Kinn said, pointing to me.

The nurse looked over to me. I made a bewildered face and pointed at myself. "Me?"

"Ah... Of course." The nurse seemed disappointed, but she brought the bath stuff over and set it next to the bed. "Please be careful not to get the wound wet," she instructed, and left.

I sat still, too afraid to move. Kinn stripped until he was bare from the waist up. I hesitantly glanced at him and felt my heart beat faster. Shit! I'd had all those fucking filthy thoughts about him when I was touching myself, too—what should I do now?!

"Make it quick," Kinn demanded with a smirk. "I'm cold."

"I... I don't know how. You better call the nurse back to do it," I replied, restless.

"Come here!" Kinn started to raise his voice. "I said come over here! Now!"

I scowled and walked straight over to him. "I'm afraid I'll agitate your wound," I told him, reluctant.

"It's fine. Just do it," he said.

I crossed my arms until Kinn pulled at my hand and held it against his chest. Touching his bare torso almost made me stop breathing. A heady rush surged inside me and threatened to burst. Sweat began to form on my face and my hands got colder. *Ah! Get a hold of yourself, Porsche!*

"What's wrong? Your hand is shaking," Kinn teased.

I took a deep breath and pulled my hand back. "Bastard!" *Fine! I'll just get it over with! Fuck!* I wrung out the towel from the water basin and hastily wiped at his muscular chest.

"Heh," Kinn chuckled and caught my wrist, stopping me. He forced my hand to move in a slow, careful motion. "Be gentle... Careful, now," he whispered.

I looked away, feeling my heart beat erratically. His hand moved mine in slow circles against his chest before sliding down to his stomach, back and forth, again and again. My breath stuttered for a moment; I didn't dare to meet his gaze or look at his body.

Thump! Kinn abruptly grabbed me by the waist and pulled me to stand closer to the bed.

"How can you be comfortable standing so far away?" he said. "Help me take my pants off."

I stood still as Pete's advice came rushing back to me: go with the flow. If I went along with what Kinn said, he'd get bored and stop provoking me. I bit my lip and threw the towel across the edge of the basin, giving him a long-suffering stare. I yanked his pants down, leaving him naked save for his black boxers.

Kinn stared at me in surprise, probably wondering why I was following his orders so easily. I picked up the towel, wrung it out once more, and cleaned his body attentively.

"That's strange. What happened to you?" Kinn asked with a laugh. I paid no attention to him, trying to keep my emotions from exploding. I just wanted to get this over with as quickly as I could. I slid the towel to his shin and wiped gently.

"Mmm…" Kinn let out a satisfied groan, making my heart stutter. He put his hand on mine and forced it up to his boxers.

"Shit!" I cried out when the back of my hand brushed against his hardening length. I immediately pulled away.

"Why are you so surprised?" he rasped.

"What are you doing?" I asked with a scowl.

"You have to clean me *everywhere*." He smirked.

I furrowed my brow and threw the towel at his face. "You bastard!" I shouted. Kinn didn't wait for me to keep cursing; he grabbed my waist with one arm and pulled me down onto the bed. He flipped us over, settling on top of me to prevent me from escaping.

"Ah!" I quietly yelped when his weight pressed into my hip, crushing my bruised tailbone against the mattress.

Kinn frowned when he saw my face contort in pain. "What's wrong?"

"Let me go!" I yelled, using both hands to push against Kinn's chest.

"Shh! Do you want people to hear you?" Kinn said. He grabbed hold of my arms and pressed them against the bed.

"Kinn! Let me go!" I thrashed against his hold. Kinn lowered his face and pressed his lips against my cheek. I startled and went still, face flushing as a strange feeling rushed through my body.

"I missed you so much," Kinn told me, smiling, his nose still rubbing against my cheek before he moved down to nuzzle at my neck.

My lips pressed together in a thin line. No matter how much I wanted to resist, my traitorous heart was telling me to accept his touch. I stopped squirming, warily watching him from the corner of my eye. I was starting to feel excited. His sweet words may have been brief, but they made me lose myself to the warmth surging inside my heart.

"Hmm..." Kinn pulled away from my neck and kissed his way up to my face.

The tip of Kinn's nose brushed against mine before he pressed a tender kiss to my lips. I closed my eyes and accepted his touch, the heat in my chest burning like a flame. He deepened the kiss, languidly nibbling at my lips before his scorching-hot tongue tangled with mine.

I responded instinctively, not wanting him to have the upper hand. Kinn licked and sucked at my tongue demandingly, searching. I felt the edge of his teeth nip gently at my lower lip before his tongue twined with mine once more. Lost in my desire, I didn't notice Kinn had released my hands. When my awareness came back, I found my arms looped loosely around his neck.

"*Oh...*" I groaned, showing how much Kinn's actions affected me. His hands were just as busy as his mouth, reaching into my shirt and fondling my chest. The sensation was hard to describe, but it wasn't unpleasant. I felt a swooping sensation low in my belly, the ache I had been holding back since the afternoon steadily building. Kinn's hand slid from my chest to softly caress my body. Then he pulled me up by the waist and reached down to give my ass a firm squeeze...

"Ow!" I pulled sharply back from Kinn's lips and pushed his face away.

"What's wrong?" Kinn asked, voice tense. Both his lips and mine were wet with saliva.

"That hurts!" I cried, my face twisting in pain. Kinn stroked my ass gently before squeezing even harder.

"Ow! Kinn, you bastard!" I yelled, shoving him off of me. Kinn swayed a bit, but soon righted himself and sat up straight.

"What did you do?" he asked icily, glaring at me. I squinted at him as I lay there, then propped myself up on my elbows and swallowed thickly.

"I-I slipped and fell," I stammered. I didn't want Kinn to lose his shit again, so I didn't dare mention that Vegas had visited me at the house—but it seemed it was too late. Kinn sat there and silently looked me up and down with an accusatory stare.

"Don't look at me like that!" I shouted, my voice trembling with the effort of not exploding in frustration. I sat up to face him.

"Who did you fool around with?!" Kinn snarled, his eyes lit up with rage.

I glared at him. "What do you mean, *fool around*? I slipped and fell!" I snapped back. I fucking hated every word out of his mouth!

"*Who?!*" Kinn growled.

I met his eyes with an equally furious glare of my own, unafraid. "I'm not some slut screwing every guy in sight like you! Don't you *dare* look down on me, asking me who I fucked!" I retorted, jumping down from the bed. Everything I felt during the kiss vanished into thin air, leaving only fury.

Kinn stared at me disdainfully. "You had no problem getting fucked by me!" he shouted as he flung the basin onto the floor, water splashing everywhere. I hurriedly turned away to avoid getting soaked.

"You only think that because you're a fucking pervert!" I shouted, tugging my hair back in frustration. "You scumbag!"

Kinn gritted his teeth and continued to curse at me. "I only fucked you once! Did you like it so much that you had to find someone else to scratch the itch for you? Hah! Get lost! I won't have anyone else's sloppy seconds!"

Kinn's words enraged me so much that I clenched my fists and started shaking. "That one time with you will haunt me for the rest of my life, you bastard!" I kicked the hospital bed with all my might, making it lurch forward.

"Hey!"

I didn't pay attention to Kinn's shouts as I stormed away, shoving the door open with a loud bang. All the bodyguards outside turned to look at me at once. I rushed past Pete, who looked like he was about to call out to me. I didn't give a damn about anything anymore. I rushed out of the hospital as quickly as I could.

I took a taxi straight to Tem's dorm. He'd been a little reluctant when I called him, but still came down to the first floor to pick me up in the end.

"Have some water," Tem said, pouring a glass and handing it to me.

"Am I troubling you?" I asked Tem as he sat uncomfortably on the sofa.

"No, it's fine. What happened to you, though?" he asked.

"Nothing. Can I sleep here tonight?" I asked, hesitant. Tem immediately nodded in reply. I didn't want to face anyone associated with Kinn right then.

I didn't really want to admit it, but I felt practically heartbroken. Heartbroken about everything—both Kinn's words and his actions. I didn't want to believe he could make me this upset.

"You can go wash up. Just borrow some of my clothes for now," Tem said, throwing a towel at me and looking for some pajamas I could wear. I took a shower, washing myself distractedly.

Once I'd sorted myself out, I went out onto the balcony, lighting a cigarette and letting the smoke fill my lungs. I used the time to call Chay and tell him I wasn't coming back tonight, and asked Arm to take care of my brother while I was gone. Then I remembered that I forgot all my stuff—including my laptop—in Kinn's hospital room, so I had to call Pete and ask him to bring my belongings to the university tomorrow. Everyone sounded concerned as they agreed to my requests, but I didn't want to hear or explain anything else. I left it at that and turned off my phone.

"Tem, it's going to rain." I poked my head back in. "Aren't you going to bring your clothes in?"

Tem had just emerged from the bathroom, still toweling his hair. He startled at my sudden reappearance but nodded. I looked at the drying rack and gathered the clothes on it, cigarette still in my mouth. I held up a t-shirt, puzzled—it looked way too big for Tem, and not his style, either.

"Thanks," Tem said as he took the pile of clothes from me and hurried inside. I decided to stop thinking about unimportant things and sighed, trying to let out my resentment. I lit my third cigarette, stressed out and at my limit.

"Get lost! I won't have anyone else's sloppy seconds!"

I was fucking devastated!

Kinn, you fucking depraved bastard! Damn you all the way to hell and back! Since when did he have such an effect on my feelings? That motherfucker!

"Porsche! What the hell are you doing?! You're going to break my washing machine!" Tem burst through the balcony door to shout at me. I'd kicked the appliance so hard it let out a loud bang.

"Sorry!" I hissed.

Tem called me back inside to sleep. Predictably, I couldn't fall asleep at all. I tossed and turned until eventually Tem got me some allergy medicine, which made me drowsy enough to settle down and finally rest.

The next morning, Pete came by to drop off my laptop and papers in front of the Sports Science building. He didn't look so good—he seemed exhausted and stressed out.

"Porsche, you should go see Mr. Kinn tonight," he told me.

I sat there silently, going through the slides I had to submit today.

Pete tilted his head. "If there's a problem, why don't you just talk to Mr. Kinn about it?"

"He chased me out himself," I replied sharply.

"Hah... None of us could get any sleep last night. Mr. Kinn went on such a rampage that we all nearly burst a blood vessel," Pete sighed, looking pitiful.

"Why don't you give him a fucking sedative, then?" I snapped, then squinted my eyes at my slides as I saw the content of the last three had been changed completely. Tem leaned over to look at my laptop screen. Although he seemed interested in whatever was going on between me and Pete, he kept his eyes on the work.

"Hey, you're better than I thought," he told me. "Your summary's pretty good."

I went still before letting out a long sigh. "You can go back. I'm not working today—don't order me around," I said harshly. Pete looked reluctant, but I stalked off into the building, no longer paying attention to him. Tem and Jom awkwardly smiled and waved goodbye to him.

By the third day of staying with Tem, I started thinking less about what happened with Kinn and more about school—I had multiple reports to submit by eight P.M. that evening. Tem, Jom, and I, along with Ice and Teen from our major, were all piled up on the floor of Tem's room, rushing to finish at the last minute.

"I can't take it anymore! After we send this in, let's go out for drinks," Jom said, and everyone nodded in unison. I wanted to get shitfaced too—wanted to forget everything about my fucked-up life right now. Speaking of which, I had to go back to work tomorrow... Should I ask for another week off?

"Let's invite Pete, too," Tem begged me. I rolled my eyes. Pete had been coming by every day and looking around, trying to persuade me to go back to the house. He was in the dorm building right now, sitting downstairs. I didn't care if it seemed heartless; I was too tired to listen to his same plea over and over.

"Damn it!" I cursed, frustrated, and continued to work on my report.

When it was eight o'clock, we submitted our reports. The day's work was done, and we all collapsed on the floor for a while before getting up to get dressed to go out like we agreed earlier.

"Porsche... You..." Pete trailed off.

"If you want to stop, you can go back. Don't kill the mood," I said, pointing at Pete. We'd arrived at the bar, Pete having volunteered to drive the three of us, with my other two friends from Sports Science following on their motorcycles.

"What do you want, Pete? I'll mix it for you," Tem said, trying to defuse the situation.

"Just soda water," Pete replied.

Once we were handed our glasses, we knocked back drink after drink, enjoying ourselves. Pete began to relax, swaying along with the music. He kept stealing glances at me, and I glared back at him fiercely every time.

"Porsche, what a coincidence!" It was Vegas. He walked over with a wide smile to clink his glass with mine. I grabbed my glass and chugged the entire thing.

"Vegas, come sit. How'd you get here?" Jom said, nudging our friends to scoot over and make some space for Vegas.

"I came with P'Beam and the rest." Vegas pointed to the table full of my upperclassmen. I gave them a weak smile. I had left P'Beam hanging. I felt a little guilty, to be honest.

"Hey, you! Ghosting me like that! If I was a girl, I'd be dead from a broken heart by now!" P'Beam came over and looped his arm over my shoulder, spouting nonsense.

"I've been really busy," I said, sipping my drink.

"Hah! Sports day is next week—why don't you come?" P'Beam asked beseechingly.

"If I'm free," I replied. He nodded like that was the answer he was expecting.

"Porsche, if you're competing, can I come watch?" Vegas piped up.

"Yeah, come! If Porsche is competing, you'll be lucky to watch him. He always has girls screaming for him, and his skills are unmatched," P'Beam said. He'd praised me so much that I had to gingerly shake my head.

"Can I come?" Vegas asked with a smile.

"Mm-hm." I hummed my agreement before excusing myself to the bathroom. Tem and Jom followed behind me.

"Vegas was watching you without even blinking, you dog!" Jom smirked. I furrowed my brow. It's not like I hadn't noticed. Sometimes someone just stared at you for a while, and I didn't think Vegas's tastes were...

"How bad is his eyesight?" Tem interjected, chatting as we stood in a row at the urinals. "Porsche is so manly!"

"Why? If it's *you* it's a different story, right?" Jom raised a brow and stared at Tem's face.

"Hah! If a guy's going to have a crush on Porsche, it's gotta be a cute little twink, right?" Tem continued. "Not a burly buffalo like Vegas."

I started to hyperventilate at what my friends were implying.

"True... A guy who looks like Porsche *has* to be the top. It'd be weird if he was the bottom!" Jom laughed. My expression was definitely awkward. *Fuck!*

"Tops, bottoms, the fuck are you talking about?" I said as I zipped up my fly, heading straight to the sink to wash my hands.

"Hah, I just want to give Vegas a piece of my mind. Hitting on my friend... Can't that motherfucker see your badass tattoos?!" Jom kept spouting stupid shit. Vegas did give me the creeps sometimes, sure, but I didn't think he was hitting on me—it had to be in their heads.

"Aww! He can keep flirting, but Porsche won't give him the time of day! This handsome bastard only has eyes for the ladies, yeah?" Tem turned to smile cutely at me and went to wash his hands.

I gulped nervously when I saw how confident my friends were about who I was. To be honest, I did not have that same confidence.

"Err... If... If I liked dudes... What would you guys say?" I mumbled, not knowing what compelled me to ask it out loud.

Tem and Jom immediately whipped around to look at me.

"No, no, I'm just asking hypothetically!" I quickly waved my hands, trying to cut off that train of thought, but it was too late. Tem squinted at me suspiciously before I averted my eyes, looking down at the sink instead.

"Hmm... Kinn?" he asked.

I stopped breathing for a moment before lifting my head to look at my friend. I quickly bent down to splash water from the faucet onto my face. What the hell had I just said?! I'd only tried to test them like that because my heart was in turmoil. If I really *was* attracted to a man, would everyone around me be able to accept it?

I certainly didn't want to accept myself just yet, although some things were clear. That clarity scared me even further. It wasn't like I didn't know what I was feeling, but I was going to resist it—I wanted Kinn as far away from me as possible.

"What is it? Tell us." Tem leaned in, like he was trying to get me to slip up.

"I'm just asking! I didn't mean anything by it," I insisted.

"Hah! You can do whatever you want—I won't say anything. Just don't keep secrets from us. We'll definitely accept you! We're just surprised, that's all," Jom said. He really did look shocked.

"I'm just asking! I didn't say I liked men!" I insisted, trying to make them believe me. Tem and Jom just looked at each other and sighed.

"Uh-huh, you're just asking. But is there anything you need to tell us? I'm worried about you," Tem said, concerned.

"Fuck off! I'm just joking!" I shouted, storming out of the bathroom. I didn't know if they believed me, but I really was trying to feel out their opinions. Although they said they could accept it, I didn't believe them!

Who could? I couldn't wrap my head around it, either.

Tem and Jom's voices echoed behind me from inside the bathroom, but I wasn't in the mood to pay attention to them anymore.

"My plan to trick him into confessing worked pretty well."

"I don't want to believe it! Shit! It can't be true, can it, Tem?"

"Wait and see. The world's not gonna end—you don't have to look so surprised, asshat!"

I went out to have a smoke in front of the bar. The more I thought about what happened in the bathroom, the more restless I became. If I accepted what I was feeling, how could I face my friends? Damn it! Jom said he'd accept me, but his face had looked so pale... I had to be drunk—nothing more.

"Is something bothering you? Why do you look so upset?" Vegas walked up to me, still smiling, and lit a cigarette. I glanced at him out of the corner of my eye, watching him smoke as Jom's words replayed in my mind.

"Nothing," I said.

"Ah... Is it really nothing?" Vegas asked. "Porsche, if anything's bothering you, you can talk to me. I'd be happy to lend an ear." He was still grinning, smiling at me so much that I couldn't help but give a small smile back.

"Mm-hm," I hummed.

"But if I had to guess, it must be work-related. Did the eldest one bully you?" Vegas asked, his voice turning stern.

I shook my head.

"The second brother, then. He's really something," Vegas remarked. I watched as he blew out smoke and talked about his cousins with a troubled expression.

"It's not that," I said, rushing to make excuses. Why was this crazy fucker throwing out so many guesses?

"Heh. It's good that it wasn't Kinn. Leave him to his boytoys— they fight over him at every event he attends. I'll admit that even I'm jealous."

A chill ran through my body, my heart dropping strangely for a beat.

I stayed silent.

"Those boys should know better... Kinn is never serious with anyone, but his playthings still find trouble for themselves," Vegas said. "Porsche, you need to be careful, too. Brother doesn't pick and choose. Anyone near him ends up the same..."

That manwhore! I wanted to put a fucking bullet in his brain.

"Hey, did that stress you out? I was just joking," Vegas added, laughing. "You're not his type, Porsche. There's nothing to worry about."

That only pissed me off more. I breathed in and out, trying to chase away the thoughts from my mind. Wasn't it a good thing that I wasn't his type?

"Hmm. I'm gonna head back in," I said sullenly, turning to go back.

"Porsche! Watch out!"

Bang!

A gunshot echoed through the air. Instinctively I dropped to the ground, Vegas shielding me from behind.

"Shit!" I cursed, looking up to assess the situation. Vegas surveyed our surroundings as well. The clubgoers were panicking, and the music had come to an abrupt stop. I got up and looked left and right, trying to find the source of the gunshot.

"Are you all right?" Vegas asked me, concerned.

"Ow!"

Out of nowhere, someone kicked me in the back, hard. I stumbled forward into Vegas, who was looking at the newcomers in surprise.

The crowd ran erratically, darting past us to the side of the bar. I quickly got my bearings and jumped at the tall figure who attacked me, throwing a punch at his face. Several men dressed in black grabbed at me, but Vegas came to help, kicking at each of them. I kept punching. Where the hell was Pete?

My heart dropped to my stomach when I saw one of them pull out a knife. A couple of Vegas's lackeys ran over to us, trying to see what was going on and to help their boss.

"Run!" Vegas grabbed my wrist, pulling me along as chaos erupted in front of the bar. I managed to land a few more kicks, but Vegas eventually dragged me to the parking lot.

"Porsche, get in the car!" his harsh voice shouted. I jumped in when I saw the men still chasing after us. Vegas started the car and stepped on the gas, speeding out into the main road.

"Are you hurt?" he asked, worried.

"No..." I sat there catching my breath before sighing in relief.

"Who were they, Porsche?" Vegas asked as he sped down the road.

"I don't know," I answered truthfully. I had no idea who they were, let alone what they wanted from me. I didn't know who was behind all this.

Vegas turned to look at me. "Ah, Porsche, your eyebrow's split open."

He quickly parked by the side of the road. I'd only just begun to notice the pain; I rubbed the area with my finger to find it stained with blood. I was about to ask for a tissue, but Vegas leaned toward me. I startled back, but he quickly grabbed the back of my neck to lock my head in place.

"Stay still. I'll wipe the blood off for you," he said as he gently dabbed a tissue at the edge of my eyebrow.

"I can do it myself," I said, twisting away.

"Don't be so stubborn."

I stopped resisting and let him dab the blood away like he wanted. The more I struggled, the closer Vegas leaned in—he was now practically on top of me.

"Do you have bad blood with anyone? Why would you get targeted like this?" he asked. I turned away when I felt his warm breath on my face. I didn't like how close he was getting.

I remained silent.

"Can't believe this is how the Major Clan treats their employees—putting them in danger like this," he muttered.

I immediately frowned. "In this circle, how safe can it be?" I said. Just stepping into this line of work automatically put a target on your back.

"They shouldn't let their people get injured. It's the least they can do." I knew what Vegas was going to say next—his words had been oddly persuasive thus far. "Do you want to come work for me? I promise to take better care of you, Porsche."

My frown deepened. I was just a bodyguard, and I wasn't here to take someone else's job. What did being taken care of have to do with it?

I felt goosebumps all over, becoming wary of Vegas. His words seemed well-intentioned, but it was getting fucking weird.

"Porsche, you don't look happy at all. Every time I see you, you look troubled," Vegas said, still leaning in close. Although I wanted to pull back, his arm was blocking the way.

"Come work for me, please... Please?" he softly rasped, hand grasping my neck so I couldn't pull away. Vegas's face came closer, so close that the tip of his nose gently brushed against my cheek.

"Let me go!"

A vehicle screeched to a halt in front of Vegas's car. He quickly turned and scowled as I tried to pry his hands off.

"Let me go, Vegas!" I yelled, successfully shoving his hands off my neck. I turned to look to the other car and saw Kinn step out, absolutely fuming with rage. Strangely, I felt relieved to see him.

"Come out!" Kinn shouted angrily while banging on the car window closest to me. I saw Vegas smirk before he unlocked the car.

"What the hell are you two doing?!" Kinn barked, dragging me out so forcefully that I stumbled.

"Brother! How did you get here?"

"What about you, Vegas?! Why are you taking my men, huh?" Kinn's shouting made me flinch. I'd never seen him explode at Vegas like this—usually he was perfectly civil to his cousin.

Vegas frowned as he got out of the car. "Porsche was attacked. I was helping him escape," he explained anxiously.

Kinn snorted in derision. "Get in the car," he said, pulling me along and stuffing me into his car. *Ow! What the hell?!*

"Brother, please calm down. I was just trying to help Porsche," Vegas said. He walked over to stand next to Kinn, who had his hands on his hips.

Kinn pointed an accusatory finger at Vegas. "Don't interfere! I won't warn you again!"

Kinn checked his shoulder against Vegas's before getting into the driver's seat and speeding away. I turned to stare at Kinn silently before turning away to look outside.

"It's a good thing Vegas helped me. What if I'd died?" I said calmly. Why was Kinn so pissed? Was he crazy? I was getting beaten up—if Vegas hadn't stepped in, I'd understand why Kinn would be angry, but Vegas had *helped* me...if you didn't count whatever the fuck he was doing in the car just now.

"What were you doing with him?!" Kinn asked harshly. I immediately turned to glare at him. "Answer me!" he yelled and slammed on the gas pedal, making me career forward and almost hit the dashboard.

"He was wiping blood off my face!" I said, feeling my voice tremble as dread settled in my heart. The more I witnessed Kinn's wrath, the more afraid I became.

"What do you mean, wiping blood?! More like you were about to fuck Vegas in his car!" Kinn continued to berate me in a harsh voice.

"The fuck are you talking about?!" I shouted back.

"What, was fucking him at the house not enough for you?" Kinn asked.

I looked at him in confusion, my brows knitting together. "What?!"

"Khun told me everything—how you were messing around with Vegas in your room!" he shouted.

I bit my lip and glared at Kinn. "You think everyone's a fucking whore like you?!" I exploded at him, all my bottled-up anger finally bursting. I could barely contain myself. How dare he look down on me!

"So you've chosen Vegas, huh?" Kinn said.

"Kinn, you motherfucker! I fucking hate you!" I punched the dashboard hard enough for Kinn to turn to look at me resentfully. I slumped forward against the dashboard, my head aching from Kinn's presence and the fact that he was swerving the car enough to make me want to puke.

"Sit properly! I can't see the side view mirror!" Kinn exclaimed, pulling my shoulder to make me sit upright.

"Then die!" I snapped, shaking his arm off. He left me slumped forward like that the rest of the drive.

When we got back to the house, he dragged me out of the car, not caring whether anyone might see us. Arm and Pol ran over but were driven back by Kinn's shouting. Even Big was pushed to the side.

In the end, Kinn flung me onto his bed, momentarily knocking the air out of my lungs.

"The fuck are you doing?!" I demanded, glaring at him.

"So you fucked him, huh?!" Kinn stood there with his hands on his hips, his expression that of barely controlled fury.

"I didn't fuck him! And I don't *want* to fuck him!" I snarled, shaking with anger.

"Then answer me—why did your ass hurt the other day? And why did Khun see Vegas shirtless in your room with you?!" Kinn interrogated me, then rubbed his face and loudly huffed.

"I told you, I fell! And I spilled boba on his shirt, you bastard! Why do I have to explain everything to you?! I didn't do anything wrong, you asshole!" I threw pillows and blankets at Kinn, but he deftly dodged them.

"My brother saw it! Why the hell was Vegas in your room?!" Kinn's expression had begun to ease up, but his voice was still strained.

"You seriously believe your lunatic brother? Vegas was just here to visit! Fuck!" I snapped, clenching the bed sheets in a tight grip. I didn't understand why Kinn was so furious.

I didn't understand anything at all right now.

"Hah!" Kinn smirked as he looked at me incredulously.

When I saw his expression, I got up and yanked his shirt collar. "I hate you, you bastard!"

"Porsche! Stop it! What was I supposed to think? You and Vegas were acting so friendly!"

I hit and pushed at Kinn until he caught hold of my wrists, making us both tumble back onto the bed. I refused to let go of his collar, shouting at him indignantly.

"I've had enough of this! You'd better stop talking to me. Stop looking at me. Stop *everything*! Don't make me feel more disgusted than I already am!" I let out all of the emotions that were suffocating my heart. Kinn's gaze started to soften.

"Porsche! Stop!"

Kinn squeezed my wrists until it started to hurt. I turned away from him, and both of us fell silent. The tension in the air was stifling enough to drown us. Neither of us wanted to say what we were feeling; the only sound in the long silence was our gradually slowing breaths.

"Come here!" Kinn seized my shoulders and moved me to face him, before sitting down on the bed beside me. "Were you hurt anywhere?" he demanded, annoying me even more.

"Why don't you ask me tomorrow?!" I snapped back, but I stayed still and allowed Kinn to gently brush his finger against my brow.

"When Pete called to say that Vegas was with you, I drove out there as fast as I could." Kinn's voice had softened a bit, but he was clearly still irritated.

"Vegas came to help me! I was targeted again," I explained.

Kinn frowned, then slowly sighed. I grabbed his hand to stop it from roaming over my face. "I'm asking you seriously, Kinn: why did you get so angry at Vegas?"

Kinn's steely gaze began to tremble. I could see the confusion in his eyes, as well as a feeling that I didn't quite recognize. I didn't know what he was thinking. Was he angry because Vegas was from the Minor Clan and trying to recruit me?

Or was he angry...because Vegas had gotten too close?

"You really didn't do anything with him?" Kinn asked me again, adjusting his expression. I felt a heaviness in my heart. I was numb all over, confused.

All sorts of emotions churned inside of me. I slumped my head onto his shoulder before I admitted in a trembling voice:

"I can't get it up with anyone else..."

KINN
PORSCHE

23

Erase

I LIFTED MY FACE to look into Kinn's eyes. He looked back, something wavering in his gaze before a warm hand came up to touch my face.

"I kept seeing images of you, images of what happened that day coming back," I said, my voice shaking. "I tried to forget, tried with other women, but I couldn't..." I stared ahead blankly, unfocused, my mind overwhelmed with emotion.

Kinn didn't speak.

"It's like...what happened that day stayed with me. It followed me everywhere, all the time," I continued. "Fuck, Kinn! I knew I hated you, but I hated myself. I couldn't accept myself... Why do I keep seeing you in here?!" I pointed at my head, my lips trembling. My words and my actions made it seem like I expected an answer from Kinn, but what kind of answer did I even want?

"...Porsche." Kinn softly called my name.

"The more I saw you, the more those feelings kept coming back. I don't understand—why did I let you hurt me? You've cursed me, insulted me, so *why*? Why do I feel like this?! How long will you keep hurting me... Is it not enough for you?" My voice hardened, not because I was still angry with him, but because I was so lost. How could one person be the cause of so much pain in my heart?

No matter how much I tried to tell myself that Kinn had done unforgivable things to me, I kept yearning for him, losing myself to his words. It scared me—I was afraid for my heart. I was terrified that I was in too deep, that from now on I would only desire his touch...

"Porsche... I understand that you must hate how you feel right now," Kinn said. I allowed his warm hand to gently stroke my face.

"Why did I let it get to me?! I've never felt so pathetic in my life!" I burst out, feeling helpless. I was disgusted by myself, but if I kept resisting my attraction, I'd continue to be tormented. I couldn't get rid of how I felt that day at all; instead, it intensified with every passing hour. Behind my self-hatred was a longing for Kinn that was stronger than ever...

Why am I like this?

"What happened that day... It was terrible, wasn't it?" Kinn said, leaning in closer. His hand grasped the nape of my neck. Our foreheads were touching.

"It was terrible...but those feelings? They never left." I avoided his gaze and looked down as the tip of his nose brushed against mine. I searched for the answers within myself.

Kinn's warm breath ghosting over my skin made me waver. No matter how terrible that experience had been for me, I couldn't forget it. It was hard to accept, but those feelings of warmth, excitement, and confusion refused to leave me.

"I'm the cause of all your distress," Kinn said. "Can we start over? Could you give me the chance to fix those terrible feelings?"

"I already feel terrible."

"It can't be... The fact that you're suffering because of those memories... I feel awful. Can I...?" Kinn paused for a moment. I didn't say anything. "I... I'm asking to be the one to erase those terrible memories, Porsche. Please...let me?" he whispered softly, asking for permission.

I didn't answer him verbally, but I closed my eyes and accepted the gentle press of his lips against my own. I wasn't sure why, but I wanted to believe him—that he could erase all those awful images from my head.

Kinn kissed and sucked at my lips, nibbling until I felt an intoxicating rush of pleasure spread through my body. He positioned himself over me, holding me tightly as he settled himself above me. Our lips never parted. We kissed until I was gasping for breath. He took the opportunity to dip his hot tongue into my mouth. I let go of control, yielding to the feeling that Kinn told me he could erase.

It seemed Kinn was trying his hardest to create new memories for me, better ones than before. When his tongue flicked playfully inside my mouth, my heart began to beat erratically. He sucked and nudged at my tongue with his, making my entire body flush hot; he slid his tongue all throughout my mouth until I melted with desire.

Click! Kinn reached over to the air conditioning remote and turned off the AC, even though our lips were still pressed together. I furrowed my brow. Although I wanted to ask what he was doing, there was no opportunity to speak. Kinn was a good kisser, alternating between sucking and biting my lips and sucking at my tongue like a starving man. His demanding kisses made my stomach swoop.

"Mmm..." I moaned quietly.

Kinn smiled, satisfied, before moving his mouth down to my jaw and nipping at the skin there. After a while, he nuzzled his face into the slope of my neck and shoulder, his hot tongue licking all the way up to my ear. It felt practically ticklish. He began to gently bite my neck, wet and dizzying.

"Don't... Don't leave a mark...*oh*," I gasped, turning my face away to give Kinn better access to my neck. I didn't know if he heard me or not, but he kept going, his hand sliding under my shirt. I flinched when his fingers brushed against my nipple and gave it a firm pinch.

"Mmm..." I bit my lip to stop myself from making embarrassing noises. My hands wandered all over Kinn's back, trying to find purchase.

Kinn's hand pulled away from my chest and yanked my shirt up and off. I breathed in heavily, looking up at him through half-lidded eyes. He bent down to lick my nipple, sucking and biting it until I felt a tingling sensation spread through my entire body.

"Ah!" I tensed up when I felt the scrape of his teeth, but I didn't want him to stop—I just let my feelings take control. Kinn's hand groped and squeezed the other side of my chest, pausing to pinch my nipple until I squirmed. His tongue teased my nipple once more before he dragged his hot tongue down to my belly.

I clung onto his shoulders, harshly digging my nails into his back as he nipped and sucked hickeys into my skin wherever he went. My feelings were a tangled mess, but I had no thought of stopping; I only felt a thrilling rush in my body as my heart pounded in excitement.

"Ah... Mmm ...*Ah!*"

Kinn's other hand slipped inside my pants, stroking me to hardness through the fabric of my boxers and turning me on even more. I wanted Kinn to get his hand around my cock *now*, but he had other plans, lazily drawing circles over the fabric instead.

"K-Kinn...touch me!" I gasped out, looking at him with bleary eyes. His face was still flush with my abdomen as he licked it enthusiastically.

Kinn smiled before pulling my pants and underwear down to my knees. I threw my head back and moaned helplessly when he finally took my dick in a loose grip and slowly stroked up and down the shaft, his thumb lazily circling the leaking tip. My pulse raced as arousal simmered inside me.

"*Ah*... Hmm... Ah!"

Kinn leaned down to kiss me once more. I responded, kissing him back as his hand pumped faster. My body twisted and curled with need.

"Do you know how fucking sexy you are...?" Kinn whispered against my lips. I felt like I was floating, warmth spreading in my chest. Kinn's hand sped up until I couldn't take it any longer.

Kinn pulled away to lie down on his side next to me, his eyes fixed on my cock in his fist. I glanced up at his face and his clouded eyes, thinking how sexy he looked. He bit his lip, hand still deftly pumping my dick. He licked his lips before locking eyes with me, my face twisting in pleasure.

"Are you close?" Kinn asked, leaning in to inhale deeply at my cheek and my neck, his sweet voice making my heart stutter.

I nodded. "M'close... *Mmm*... A bit more... *Ah!*" I moaned with abandon.

I had to admit he was good at this—thumbing hard at the head of my cock again and again, alternating with frantic strokes. My whole body tensed up as I came, white fluid shooting out of my dick. My vision blanked out for a moment, the tension I'd been bottling up for so long finally finding its release.

"My turn..." Kinn whispered in my ear. I lay there panting as he took hold of my body and flipped me over. I heard him swiftly remove his shirt and trousers. I turned my face to look at Kinn. His cock was rock hard and standing tall. He gave it a few unhurried strokes before sliding over to the bedside table to bring out a box of condoms and some lube.

I swallowed thickly, watching as Kinn stood there stroking his cock. My face flushed with heat and my heart pounded against my ribcage as Kinn leaned down to press tender kisses to my back.

He settled his weight on top of me again, nuzzling the crook of my neck, then licking and nipping his way to my lips.

"Mhmm..."

Kinn's body glistened with sweat, his musky scent growing stronger. The more I inhaled it, the hotter I felt, my burning desire almost reducing me to ashes. Kinn licked a hot stripe all the way down my back to my asscheek, one hand kneading at it incessantly. I felt a dull ache around my tailbone where I'd fallen, but Kinn's ministrations only aroused me more. His teeth scraped against my ass before he bit down harshly.

"Ah... Ahh, that hurts!" I yelled at him, but it felt so different from that first time. It had been so careless then; now, he was trying to make our time together memorable. It was exhilarating, yet laced with a hidden fierceness and tenacity.

"Ah... I can't hold back any longer," Kinn rasped as he dragged my hips up in the air, my torso still pressed against the bed. He then spanked me with a hard slap.

"Ah!" I yelped, twitching. Kinn laughed before mouthing at the swell of my ass, his hand dragging down the cleft. My entire body shivered.

"I won't hurt you too much," he said. "I promise."

Kinn's warm tongue licked down the seam of my ass as his hands pushed my legs apart. As soon as his tongue touched my entrance, I squeezed my eyes shut, tightly gripping the bedsheets. The burning desire in my chest and the wetness from Kinn's saliva smearing all over my hole made my cock throb.

"Mhmm... Y-you... *Ah*... I need..." I could barely speak as the new sensations threatened to overwhelm my body. I'd never felt this turned on in my life. The tip of his tongue teased and circled my hole with no hesitation, his fingers holding my cheeks apart until he pulled away to open the tube of lubricant. He squeezed it onto his fingers before pressing them against the tight furl of my asshole.

"Ahh... It's c-cold," I said, feeling the chill of the lube along with a hard finger nudging its way inside.

"Mm, don't tense up," Kinn whispered in my ear, trying with difficulty to insert his finger into my body. His voice trembled. "If you're tense...it'll hurt."

I panted, bracing myself for the pain. Kinn captured my lips in another kiss.

"Ah... Only one finger, and you're so tight," Kinn whispered against my lips before pressing kisses to my face, distracting me from the painful intrusion.

"Ah! It h-hurts," I cried out, grimacing when he pushed his finger in nearly halfway. I turned my head away from his kisses, burrowing my face into the bed. Kinn quickly placated me by nuzzling into my neck, and my pain was subsumed by the tingling thrill of his touch.

"Ah...ahh..." I groaned as he pushed all the way in. I collapsed on the bed, as if drained of all energy. Kinn had to hold me up by the hip with his free hand.

"Relax, Porsche," he said as he slowly moved his finger in and out.

"Easy for you to say," I muttered, frustrated.

Kinn kept pressing comforting kisses to my face. He started moving his finger in circles, repeating the action until I got used to it.

"You're already taking me so well," Kinn praised. Before I could prepare myself, he slipped a second finger inside.

"Agh... Ah... K-Kinn!" I clawed at the sheets, my body glistening with sweat. The heat in the room made me even more aroused.

Kinn pumped his fingers slowly and deliberately in and out of me as he pulled away to roll on a condom, smearing lube all over his length before positioning his cock against my hole.

"Ahhh!" I squeezed my eyes shut as pain shot through me.

"Shh, relax... Easy, now," Kinn murmured.

Why did this feel so different from that first time? The contrast was like heaven and earth. Kinn really did help ease my worries, one hand supporting my hip as he slowly pushed inside.

"Ah!" I startled a little as the head of Kinn's dick pushed past my rim.

"Just a little more...relax," he rasped. Kinn seemed just as overwhelmed as I was. I bit down on the sheets as Kinn pushed in further. It felt like my body was on fire. It was almost too much to bear.

"Don't clench down so soon, I won't last...*ah*," he groaned.

I tried to get my breathing under control, but I felt my stomach do somersaults as Kinn pushed his length inside of me almost to the hilt.

"*Ah!* Ow, it hurts," I hissed out. Kinn let out a sigh before stilling his movements, bending down to press kisses to my back.

"You're so fucking tight! Mmm... You're driving me crazy," he groaned, pausing for a moment before whispering in my ear: "I'm going to move now. If I wait any longer, I'll come."

Kinn began to slowly thrust his hips, sending a shiver through my body. My stomach flipped again, and I was starting to feel a tightening in my cock. The scent of Kinn's sweat made me delirious with arousal.

I noticed a small bandage on his abdomen. He was thrusting so vigorously—didn't it hurt where he was shot?

"So good! *Fuck*, it feels so good to be inside of you."

Kinn increased his pace, his knees preventing my legs from closing. Both his hands supported my hips as he pounded into me. My entire ass felt tight; I was so full and nearly numb, but it felt so good.

"Ah! Th-there!" I cried out. Kinn seemed to understand, because he hit the same spot over and over, the sensation driving me wild.

He didn't speed up; instead, he slowed the rhythm of his hips, sliding deliberately against that spot again and again until I bit down on my lip.

"Ah...I can't... Mmph..."

When Kinn saw that my legs could barely hold my body up, he slammed inside once, twice, before speeding up again, thrusting hard and fast until I was rocking along with the bed.

"Ah... Ah... *Ah*..."

Our moans filled the room as Kinn kept driving in, not letting up for a second. My mind short-circuited and my body went taut as I orgasmed again, come shooting out of my cock.

"Ah... I'm close... Nngh," Kinn warned me. I gasped. He gritted his teeth and fucked into me even faster. Then, I felt his cock twitch inside me as he followed me over the edge.

"Ah!" Kinn shouted as he came. He let go of my hip and lowered me to lie flat on the bed, his body plastered against mine.

For several minutes, Kinn and I lay there heaving for air. He eventually pulled out of me and took the condom off.

Kinn flipped me onto my back, and I went with him easily. Then, he did something that made my breath catch—he brought out a new condom and rolled it down his still-hard length, smiling at me as I squinted up at him in apprehension.

"One more round," he said. "I want to see your face."

I was sure he wouldn't listen to any protest from me, but I didn't have the energy to voice any objections in the first place. He lifted my hips and slid his knees under my thighs, getting me into position before smearing more lube onto his dick and thrusting inside.

"Ah! Shit, Kinn, it hurts!" I exclaimed, my face twisting in pain. Though he did slide in easier than the first time, I wasn't prepared; Kinn took the breath right out of my lungs. He stayed still for a while before he leaned down to kiss my face, his hips starting up a rhythm once again.

"Ah... Ah..."

Kinn began with a lazy pace, aiming his thrusts at my prostate until I felt my entire body tingle.

"I'm sorry... Mhmm," Kinn said as he moved inside me, whispering softly in my ear.

"Ah... *Oh*... A-about what?" I asked with a trembling voice, my arms wrapped around his body.

"Mmm... I believe you... You really weren't messing around with Vegas..."

I frowned. Why did he have to bring that up now?

My heart began to race again at a particularly hard thrust of his hips. "Ah... I-I'm close, Kinn," I told him, biting my lip. He kept aiming for that spot, making my cock feel tight with need.

"Careful, calling my name like that...you'll get another round," Kinn moaned.

I pursed my lips and squeezed my eyes tightly shut, shaking my head. I writhed with pleasure at the feeling of fullness in my ass. Kinn sped up his pace, fucking me rapidly until I shook with the force of it.

"Ah... T-turn on the AC, please..." I asked Kinn shakily. My body burned with heat and exertion, sweat soaking into the sheets.

"Shh... I like the smell of your sweat... Y-you like it too, right?" he said.

It was true—Kinn's own musky scent was making me ache, and whatever was building up inside me was threatening to overflow. My body shivered with the force of his thrusts, and in no time at all, my cock was stirring again. My mind began to blur...until...I came again.

"Ahh!" I arched my back, Kinn still driving his hips into me. I thrashed underneath him, the strength and speed of his thrusts building minute after minute until finally he pulled out of me. He ripped the condom off and aimed his dick right at my face.

"So fucking sexy... *Ah!*" he gasped. He licked his lips and gazed down at me through half-lidded eyes. I looked up at him through my eyelashes, watching as he stroked himself twice and came all over my face. I turned away to avoid it, my cheeks flushing at the sight of his cock so close to my face.

"Pervert... You watch too much porn," I panted as I used my hand to wipe his semen off.

"I love seeing you like this." Kinn smiled and stared at my face hungrily. "The more I look at you, the hornier I get..."

I could tell things weren't heading in a good direction, so I turned to flee, but Kinn quickly pounced on me. I sighed in exhaustion as he whispered into my ear: "Seeing your face dripping with my come... You're so sexy right now."

That was the last coherent sentence either of us said that night. The rest of the evening dissolved into moans.

Tonight's sex with Kinn was completely different from last time, borne from affection rather than provocation or pure lust. Kinn had made me feel good, so good that I practically drowned in pleasure. Although the pain was just as intense as before—and so was Kinn's demanding nature—the warmth in my heart overshadowed it all. It was sex with real feelings, not just getting it over with or satisfying a need like before.

Whether it was right or wrong, I didn't care—I buried that all deep down. Maybe that first time scratched an itch, but this time there was enjoyment and pleasure.

I might've always had a taste for it, but I'd only recently begun to realize it. It was like eating something I'd never had before and getting addicted to it. Having it the first time was rather unappealing, but the taste wasn't bad. I kind of enjoyed it, even if I felt really confused. I wanted to go back to my usual favorites, but the more time passed, the more I thought of that new dish. I hadn't realized it, but I'd liked it so much that I forgot what my usual favorites tasted like...

I woke up with a shooting pain in my backside, along with full-body aches and bone-deep exhaustion. I'd fallen asleep after the fourth round, vaguely hearing Kinn's voice calling for me, but I only had so much stamina.

I put on a clean robe, watching Kinn bustle about between his bedroom and his office. He was already dressed in his university uniform.

"How are you feeling, Porsche? Do you want to take the day off from school?" Kinn walked over with a glass of water and some medicine.

"Mm...I can handle it." I obediently took the medicine from his hand.

Kinn smiled and gently stroked my head. "Have you stopped being angry with me?" he asked in a gentle tone, his gaze filled with so much warmth that I turned my face away from him.

"Mm-hmm..." I hummed my answer and drank the entire glass of water.

"Get dressed. You can catch a ride to university with me," Kinn said, putting on his watch in front of the mirror.

"I can drive there myself," I answered evenly.

"Like you can drive in your condition! Don't be stubborn. And go take a shower!" Kinn's voice grew irritated.

I scoffed before getting off the bed, grabbing my carefully folded shirt and heading to the bathroom. My legs still trembled, and I was walking kind of funny, but it didn't hurt as badly as that first time.

"I'll give you twenty minutes," Kinn said. "Go wait out front when you're done."

I nodded and opened his door, looking left and right to check that no one was there before I hurried downstairs to my room.

Phew... Why was I sneaking around?

There was no one in my room. Chay probably went to school earlier in the morning. I felt a little guilty that I barely got to see my brother.

I quickly showered and got dressed, then headed over to wait for Kinn in front of the house. I saw a black luxury sedan already running and waiting for us, along with various bodyguards milling around.

Arm walked over and slung his elbow over my shoulder. "Are you okay?" he asked, worried. He'd probably seen me get attacked last night.

"I'm fine," I said, standing there with my arms crossed. "What about my brother? Did you guys take good care of him?"

Arm nodded vigorously. "Your brother is the young master's new favorite. They get along like a house on fire."

I frowned, feeling sorry for my little brother. "Do they?! And Chay is *happy*?" I asked nervously. Tankhun was batshit insane! If Chay hung around him too long, he might go crazy or get depressed!

"Hmm...maybe. Hah! Don't worry, we're keeping an eye on them," Arm said. "By the way, are you going to university with Mr. Kinn today?"

I nodded. He looked a little surprised, but he didn't ask any further questions because Big was standing pretty close to us. Suddenly, Big walked straight toward me, clearly looking for trouble. At the last second, he walked past me and knocked into my shoulder, making me stumble.

"Heh," he snorted.

"Hold up!" I shouted. I wasn't going to let him off so easily. I turned back to look at him—he'd stopped walking, facing away from me. I shook Arm's hands away and shoved Big from behind so hard that he fell forward onto the ground.

"Fuck you, Porsche!" Big said, glaring at me as his lackeys crowded around us.

Meanwhile, Arm had to hold his hand over his mouth to stifle his laughter. "Hey, you bumped into him first," he pointed out.

Big shook with anger and surged forward to grab my uniform collar. I gave him a small smile and grabbed his collar in return.

"What?" I demanded.

"You want some of this?!" Big yelled back, his entire face red.

"Try me!" I shouted, slamming him into a pillar with all my might.

"Augh!" Big cried out, grimacing. He loosened his grip on my collar and tried to pry me off of him. But as my body recovered, so had my strength. I was still exhausted, but if I had to fight this stupid goon and his buddies, it wouldn't be a problem.

"Let go!" Big yelled. I lifted him up by the collar until his feet no longer touched the ground. I hadn't planned on messing with him, but he kept getting on my nerves.

Arm laughed. "Stay in your lane, Big, and don't go looking for trouble with my friend anymore," he said as he blocked Big's lackeys from coming to help him.

"You're just some rich boy's pet!" Big snarled. I frowned, yanking his shirt and hurling him into the pillar again.

"What did you just say?!" I growled. I wasn't letting this shit slide today. I wanted to pummel him into the ground. His words were getting on my fucking nerves! *Don't think you'll escape my foot, you bastard!*

"What is going on?" Kinn asked, emerging from the house. Everyone quieted down at once.

"Porsche..." Kinn called my name. I loosened my hold on Big and huffed. I was a little irritated that Kinn had interrupted me.

Big's lackeys helped him up and he immediately opened his mouth to complain. "Mr. Kinn, he started it!" he said, coughing. I rolled my eyes and looked at Kinn.

"Get in the car, or we'll be late for class," Kinn told me. I smirked when I noticed that Kinn didn't even glance at Big, who stared at me silently before he went to open the driver's door for Kinn. I couldn't figure out what expression Big was making, but I knew Arm looked extremely satisfied when I got in the passenger seat next to Kinn.

I fastened my seatbelt and looked at Kinn out of the corner of my eye as we sped away from the house.

"Did you want me to drive?" I asked. I'd forgotten that I should be the one driving him. He shook his head and smiled.

"I don't want to work you too hard. I worked you hard enough last night."

"The hell are you talking about?" I grumbled. I quickly looked out the window, resting my elbow against the edge.

"What happened back there?" Kinn asked, his eyes still on the road.

"Big shoulder-checked me, that fucker! He's obsessed with fighting me," I said and cursed softly. Kinn didn't reply, which pissed me off further. "You think I started it?" I asked indignantly. *Every time some shit goes down, Kinn loves to blame me.*

"Nonsense," he said as he stopped the car at a red light. He reached over to wrap his arm around my neck and pull me in, pressing a quick kiss to my forehead.

"The hell are you doing?!" I jerked my head back and pushed lightly at his shoulder.

Kinn chuckled. "I'll pick you up this evening," he said with a smile. "Wait for me at your college building."

"No! I'll go back myself," I replied stubbornly.

Snap! Kinn flicked my forehead.

"Shit!" I swore under my breath, rubbing at it. *I shouldn't have slicked my hair back today!*

"Don't be so pigheaded, Porsche," he said as we got moving again.

I kept arguing about him coming to pick me up at the Sports Science building, but Kinn eventually won, insisting he'd pick me up. I was too tired to continue trying to convince someone like him. I knew how spoiled he was—I was still crazy enough to argue with him, though.

"Ooh, someone got dropped off in a BMW," Tem teased. He was sitting on the wooden bench outside our building. I quickly changed the subject.

"Where's Jom?"

"In the cafeteria. I'm waiting for my photocopies to finish printing out, then I'm gonna go eat," he answered. I nodded and slumped down next to him. When he was done with photocopying, we headed to the cafeteria together.

"I was so worried about you last night. After we heard the gunshot, we looked for you everywhere." Jom was talking with his mouth full, and Tem made a sound of disgust.

"And are you guys okay?" I asked, concerned.

"Of course. Pete ran over to us and sent us back to our dorms," said Tem. "At first, we wouldn't let him, but he said you'd already gone home so we didn't worry too much."

"It's good that no one got hurt." I was relieved. I didn't want my friends to get caught up in this shit, too.

"So, were these the same people that were hunting you down in the forest?" Jom asked.

"I don't know. I don't know anything about it at all," I admitted.

"Just be careful when you go out," Tem said, still looking fretful. I nodded.

I was beginning to worry—I didn't know who was after me or what they wanted. Why were they coming after me so relentlessly?

I ate my food and chatted with my friends for a while.

Ding! A LINE notification rang out, so I quickly pulled out my phone.

KINN: What are you doing?

My eyebrows rose when I saw Kinn's name. What was he messaging me for?

PORSCHE: I'm eating.
KINN: Do you want to go out for Japanese food tonight?
PORSCHE: Are you paying?
KINN: No, we'll split the bill.
PORSCHE: Then I'm not going!
KINN: I'm kidding! Of course I'll pay. I really worked you to the bone last night, so you can eat as much as you want. My treat!
PORSCHE: Bastard!

"Porsche! Porsche... Porsche!" Jom's voice made me jump. I quickly looked up from my phone and raised my eyebrows at him.

"What?"

"Who are you talking to? I called your name like, a million times."

Tem and Jom looked at me without blinking, their eyes curious.

"No one." I shoved my phone back into my pocket and carried on eating.

"Are you...in *love*?" Tem lowered his voice. Both my friends were still staring at me questioningly.

"What do you mean, in love?!" I snapped, grabbing a cup of soda to drink.

"Well, you kept staring at your phone and smiling... Who are you talking to?" Jom put his spoon down and pointed at me with a calculating look. *Was I smiling? When did I smile?!*

"Mind your own business!" I barked, and turned my attention back to my plate.

"You've got a different vibe... And your skin is practically glowing. Y'know, like a girl who just did it for the first time!"

That made me choke. I pounded my chest, coughing. Tem hurriedly passed me some water.

"What, did you lose your virginity? How? *Who?*" Jom started yelling. *The hell is he talking about, losing my virginity?*

"Stop talking!" I said between fits of coughing. "We have to get to class, bastard!"

Having changed the subject, I got up to put away my plate. Tem and Jom didn't give up, though—they kept trying to get an answer out of me all day. I kept evading their questions, acting irritated and snapping at them until they eventually stopped.

"Wait, should we go to the gym for a bit?" Jom asked as we walked out of the classroom.

"I can't," I said. "Maybe next week."

"Just ten minutes. They're busy selecting athletes. If you don't show up, people will say you're not pulling your weight," Tem said. *If you put it like that...* So much had happened lately that I could barely pay attention to college activities.

"Ugh... Fine, I can do ten minutes," I conceded.

I picked up my phone and opened LINE to send Kinn a message.

PORSCHE: Tell me when you get here. I'm going to the
    gym to watch them select athletes.
KINN: As you wish.

I looked at his answer and pursed my lips. *What the hell is going on with Kinn? He's never this polite...except when he was telling me not to tense up when we... Shit, what am I thinking about?!*

"You're smiling again, you motherfucker!" said Tem. "You're keeping secrets from us now."

"The fuck are you talking about?" I grumbled. "Are we going to the gym or not?"

I walked ahead of them into the gym. Everyone seemed surprised that I showed up. I greeted the seniors with wais and received greetings from the juniors. They all looked a bit amazed and alarmed at my presence. What, was it really *that* rare for me to make an appearance?

"It must be raining," joked P'Beam. "I should take a photo... You made it all the way here!"

I stood there with my arms crossed, watching the juniors take turns grappling and throwing each other onto training mats.

"We're competing next week," P'Beam said with hope in his voice, coming to throw his arm around my shoulder.

"Let me check if I'm free. If I am, I'll sign up," I said. P'Beam sighed but left me to continue watching the juniors practice their judo skills.

"Oh, Vegas! You're here early again," P'Beam called out. I immediately spun around to look.

"I finished up early. Didn't know where else to go," Vegas said to P'Beam, then saw me. "Hey, Porsche!" he said, walking straight over to me. I backed away. Didn't he have his own university to go to? Why did he keep showing up here?

"How are you, Porsche?" Vegas asked, concerned. I frowned when I thought about what happened in the car last night. "Ah...are you afraid of me? I'm sorry about last night. I really didn't mean to do anything to you, Porsche."

I wasn't afraid, honestly. Just nervous. I had no idea what Vegas was really thinking.

Tem and Jom saw my displeased expression and immediately came over to stand by me.

"What do you want, Vegas?" Jom asked.

"Porsche, I'm sorry if I made you uncomfortable. I only meant well," Vegas said, frowning. I'd never seen him frown before—he usually had a cheerful smile plastered on his face.

Tem lifted his chin. "What's this about, Porsche?"

"You can say anything—yell at me, please, but please don't hate me," Vegas said, coming closer. I backed away even more, sighing wearily. *Why don't you try having someone grab your neck and try to kiss* you, *motherfucker!*

"Vegas..." A familiar voice called from the door. I turned toward the sound to see Kinn walking in with three of his friends.

"Brother..." Vegas mumbled, shrinking in on himself. As Kinn walked over to me, the whole gym went silent; it was like they were astonished at the sight of Kinn and his entourage.

"What are you doing here?" Kinn demanded. His voice was steely, but hushed, like he was trying to be mindful of all the people in the gym.

"What are you all looking at? Get back to practice!" P'Beam shouted at the entire gym, making all the athletes get back to what they were doing.

Vegas walked over and held onto his cousin's arm. "I'm here to see the seniors. Brother...please don't be angry with me. I just wanted to help him," he insisted, his voice pitiful.

Kinn let out a huff, his expression still stormy. "Don't come near my people again!" he warned Vegas, pointing at his face. "And be careful that your meddling doesn't go too far." Vegas frowned, looking pensive for a moment, but then he nodded.

"Let's go, Porsche," Kinn said, his tone back to normal. I nodded and went to say my goodbyes to the seniors before following Kinn outside.

"Tem, Jom, do you want to come eat with us?" Tay invited my friends, who had come to see me off.

"Is it free?" Jom asked, cracking a shameless smile.

"Of course it's free! Kinn will pay for everything," Tay said cheerfully as he looked at Kinn.

"They're coming with us," Kinn told me. I didn't really get why he felt the need to tell me, but I nodded.

We all went as a group—Kinn's friends in one car and my friends in another. I tried to get into Tem's car, but Kinn was having none of it, stuffing me into his own car instead.

We arrived at a Japanese restaurant on a side street in the middle of the city. It looked kind of shady, but Kinn said it was good enough to earn a Michelin star and was incredibly exclusive. It seemed he'd already arranged everything in advance, because when we walked in, the chef and staff came out to greet Kinn and his friends.

"Welcome, Mr. Kinn, Mr. Tay, Mr. Time, Mr. Mew. The food you ordered is ready in your room. Please let us know if you need anything else."

Tem, Jom, and I stood there awkwardly. The staff here seemed to hold Kinn and his friends in high esteem; they were practically rolling out the red carpet for them. I felt a little uncomfortable having people bring me my drink and utensils and constantly ask if I wanted anything else. Tem and Jom seemed uneasy as well, not daring to move.

"Go on, eat," Kinn said. I was sat next to him, with Mew on his other side and Time at the head of the table. Everyone else sat on the opposite side. Kinn saw my hesitation and placed a piece of sushi on my plate. From what I'd seen online, I'd guess it was foie gras. I'd eaten Japanese food before, but only at those buffets you saw in shopping malls. This restaurant was so damned fancy that I was freezing up.

"Do you like it?" Kinn asked when I finished chewing. I nodded. He poured soy sauce for me and everything—I didn't have to lift a finger. He kept putting various things on my plate, expensive food that I'd only seen on the internet and never thought I'd get the chance to try.

"Can I order more foie gras? You gave it all to Porsche," Tay whined. Tem and Jom looked at me before looking down at their own plates.

"If you want to order more, get your dear husband to pay for it," Kinn said, pointing his chopsticks at Tay. I looked between Tay and Time, only now realizing that they were boyfriends. Time often pampered Tay, but at times he seemed to barely pay any attention to him.

"What? That's so unfair!" Tay exclaimed, and called a server over.

"Do you want anything else?" Kinn turned to ask me. I looked at the food on the table before turning to my friends.

"Do you guys want anything?" I asked. My friends shook their heads. "Nah," I said to Kinn, who nodded and turned to the server to order more food for himself.

Shit, I had so many different foods on my plate. It was a good thing I'd watched so many restaurant review videos online, otherwise I wouldn't know what half this crap was.

"Make sure to eat and get your strength up," Kinn leaned in to whisper softly, smirking. "The night is young."

I elbowed his side, hard, until he made a face. I scooted away from Kinn and looked up to see the whole table staring at me. My two friends sat in stunned silence. I glared at them, and everyone looked away to continue eating. *The hell are you guys looking at?!*

"Hey, isn't that Mek?" Time asked, pointing outside. The restaurant was sectioned off into private rooms, but there were no doors; we could see people as they walked by.

"Ah," Mek said, seeing us and walking over. I noticed Kinn and his friends acting awkwardly, like they were caught up in some kind of predicament.

"Why did you have to point him out?" Tay quietly scolded Time, who looked guilty.

"You guys came here and didn't invite me?" Mek said, propping his elbows on the table and eyeing everyone.

"I thought you already went back to the UK," Mew said, looking at Mek apprehensively.

"My business here isn't done," Mek said. He glanced at me before turning to greet Kinn. "How are you doing, Kinn? Feeling better now?"

"Mm-hm. Much better," Kinn answered evenly.

"That's good." Mek turned to me. "Is the food to your liking?"

I didn't know what to say. "It's...good." Whenever I saw Mek, I got the same nervous feeling in my gut as I did around Vegas.

"I didn't think you'd bring him here," Mek said with a chuckle. "Do you still like this place? Doesn't look like anything here has changed at all. Same atmosphere, same vibe. I haven't been back in so many years, but I still think about the past."

Mek looked around the restaurant. I noticed Tay furrowing his brow, looking displeased. He opened his mouth like he was about to say something, but Kinn raised a hand to stop him.

"Did you just arrive, or have you finished? Do you want to sit with us?" Kinn asked him. I could see he was sighing to himself but trying to act normally. I remembered Pete had told me that Kinn and Mek didn't get along.

"No thanks, I'm meeting someone. You all go ahead," Mek said, straightening up and putting his hands in his pockets. He turned to smile disdainfully at me before walking away.

"Shit! What's he playing at?" Tay grumbled. He thwacked Time on the head—it was his fault that Mek had come in, after all.

"So, who is this Mek guy?" I turned to ask Kinn, who had put his chopsticks down and was sitting there in contemplative silence.

"No one important. Let's continue eating," Kinn replied. I saw Mew rub Kinn's arm, as if trying to comfort him. The whole situation baffled me. Mek didn't seem to be Kinn's friend, with his sarcastic comments and mocking words. But I didn't want to pry, so I continued eating.

"Excuse me, uni sushi for Mr. Kinn," a server announced, placing a plate in front of him.

Kinn went still. "...I didn't order this."

"Mr. Mek said to give this to you," the server said.

Kinn huffed and pushed the plate away from himself.

If I remembered correctly, uni was sea urchin. Damn! I'd always wanted to try some. "Are you full already?" I asked Kinn.

"Mm," he hummed in answer.

"Then I'll eat it." I gestured at the uni with my chopsticks. Kinn looked between me and the uni with a blank expression. I frowned, then ate one without waiting for his permission.

"Hey! This is good," I said. Why did it taste so buttery and mellow? Damn, this was awesome. Why didn't Kinn order any?

Out of everything I'd eaten today, this was the best. I happily grabbed another one. With the exception of Tem and Jom, the entire table eyed me strangely. What the hell was their problem? Kinn was full already, so it wasn't that rude for me to eat it!

"The bill, please!" Kinn shouted to the staff. Everyone quickly put down their chopsticks. What the hell was wrong with him? I wasn't done eating yet...

I felt the atmosphere grow more oppressive by the second. Nobody uttered another word.

Kinn took his credit card from the server and led me to his car, turning around to say goodbye to our friends and driving away. He was completely silent during the drive. I turned to look out the window. The mood felt so off—what was Kinn's deal? He drove with a grave expression, not saying anything until I sighed loudly, making him turn to look at me with his eyebrows raised.

"Are you still hungry? Do you want anything else?" Kinn asked, breaking the silence. I looked at him and decided I should keep the conversation going.

"I'm full...but that last plate was especially nice," I said. I pressed my lips into a thin line when Kinn's face darkened even further.

What did I do? Was he allergic to uni? Was that why he was angry? He couldn't eat it, so Mek purposefully ordered it to taunt him?

Kinn fell silent for a moment. "It's good that you liked it," he said at last. I hadn't seen him like this in a long time—this sort of quiet, brooding Kinn.

"Did I do something to make you angry?" I asked him directly. He turned to smile softly at me and gently grasped my head, rocking it back and forth. "Hey, you'll fuck up my hair, bastard!"

The mood lightened immediately, and Kinn turned on the music to chase away the last of the tension. I adjusted my seat to lean back and dozed off. With traffic like this, it'd be an hour at least before we got home...

I felt pressure on my cheek, along with the sound of someone taking a deep breath. I squinted drowsily at the sight of Kinn's face brushing against my cheek. My heart skipped a beat before I pushed his face away and pulled myself upright.

"We're home," he said.

"Hmm." I stretched and brought my hand up to cover a yawn. Was it dark already? Damn, just how bad had the traffic been?

I got out of the car and separated from Kinn to go shower and change into casual clothes, taking the time to talk with my brother. He was lying down and playing games on the bed. Damn, why did it feel like I hadn't seen Chay's face in forever?

I sat around in the room for a while until Chay got called over to play games with Tankhun. He pouted, but immediately agreed to go. Had I brought my brother here just to torture him? It was like Chay was Tankhun's shiny new toy.

I walked up to Kinn's room. He'd sent a LINE message to me half an hour ago, but I dithered around, holding off until I realized

I couldn't escape my fate. When I walked in, he immediately pulled me into a hug from behind.

"Have you showered already? You smell so nice," he said, nuzzling into my neck and breathing in deeply.

"The hell are you doing?! Let me go!" I scolded him, pulling away from the circle of his arms.

"You still need to pay me back for dinner," he rasped in my ear.

"Didn't you say you'd pay for it? I don't have the money!" I raised my voice. That dinner cost six figures, you bastard! How the hell was I going to pay for it?!

"I wasn't talking about money..." Kinn bent down to nibble my neck. I shivered all over, my breath stuttering when I realized exactly what he meant.

"No!"

"I haven't washed up yet... Will you help me?" Kinn asked. I gulped as his hand began to roam all over my body.

"You can't bathe by yourself? Wh-what are you, a fucking child?" I stuttered, my heart beating erratically.

"Heh... I promise to be a good boy," Kinn said.

Kinn pulled me into his bathroom, and there was no need to guess what he had in mind. I wanted to curse at him, but I could only moan as I received his touch. *Like he said, the night is young, and we've got a long way to go...*

My feelings for Kinn had deepened considerably. Soon, there would be no turning back. I knew that the higher I climbed, the more dangerous it would be if I fell.

Even if I fall, I'm not afraid anymore... I want to see how far I can fly.

KINN
PORSCHE

24

Overthinking

"DAMN IT, TIME! Watch my back! They're attacking our tower!" Kinn shouted from across the room. I paused from organizing documents and looked up at the sound.

Kinn was shouting and clicking his mouse furiously, eyes focused on his computer game. He only let himself act silly when the two of us were alone in his room. When other people were around, he'd go back to acting serious. Now I'd spent time with him and really got to know him, I could see that he was good at putting up a front.

There was a knock on the door before someone slowly opened it. It was one of Kinn's men. I glanced at Kinn—he straightened his back and quietly sipped his water. I pursed my lips slightly at his sudden change in demeanor.

"Mr. Kinn, your father has asked you to check on the company's account at the office two days from now, sir," said the newcomer. Kinn just nodded, not paying any attention. The guy gave me a hostile look before he left.

I raised my eyebrows at the closed door, confused. I knew people were getting curious these days—I'd been spending most of my time in Kinn's room, even when I was off duty. I tried to show my face in the mess hall and find the time to sleep in the room I shared with Chay, but Kinn was always messaging me and asking me to come to his room. He even came to fetch me when I refused. That man didn't give a damn what his other employees thought of him.

The days went by like usual. I still worked for Kinn like I always had...but it would be a lie to say *everything* was the same. Whenever he saw me now, he pushed me onto his bed and had his way with me. It happened at least twice a day. I wasn't sure if agreeing to let him replace those terrible memories of him with these new ones had been the right decision. It was like he used a permanent marker to rewrite new memories in my head every day. I hadn't expected his sex drive to be this high!

"Argh! Don't just stay in the middle, Tay. Join the gang, asshole!" Kinn resumed shouting at his game. I sighed and looked at him again. He could be really fucking crazy sometimes.

I returned my focus to the documents in my hand. These days, Kinn didn't make me work as hard as he had before. He only asked me to check the status of the orders, the stock, the account—shit like that. I wasn't that good at paperwork and I screwed it up sometimes, but Kinn didn't seem to mind. Maybe he'd given up on nagging me.

"Mew, you cover the jungle! Fuck, he's stealing your buff! Are you fucking blind or what?!"

Ugh! You're so annoying, Kinn! I was trying to check these calculations and he kept screaming his head off. It was so damned difficult to concentrate!

"Can you quiet down?!" I barked. Kinn glanced at me, frowned slightly, and returned to his monitor.

"Hungry?" he suddenly asked, not looking at me.

I glanced at the clock on the wall. It was already three. "Nah," I said. "By the way, I'm staying with Chay tonight."

It was Saturday, and I thought I should spend time with my brother. Kinn rarely let me have any free time, so I only saw my brother during meals or when we walked past each other in the house. I felt like I was neglecting him. My brother and my friends wondered why they rarely saw me. I told them I was studying with Kinn for the upcoming final exams, but I was ashamed of myself for making up excuses.

"Sure," Kinn replied. I was surprised that he agreed, but I was also relieved that he didn't throw a fit over it.

"And don't keep texting me, either! Or I'll turn off my phone," I warned him. Kinn just snickered and continued playing his game in silence.

I continued organizing the documents and calculating revenue. The room was quiet for several minutes, and I began to feel uneasy. When Kinn was calm and peaceful like this, he was usually planning something vicious.

Kinn turned off the microphone, shut down his PC, and abruptly stood up. He took off his watch and put it on the desk. I wondered why he even put that thing on when he was home. He unbuttoned the top two buttons of his black shirt, revealing his pecs. My heart fluttered at the sight, and I quickly averted my gaze.

A chill crept down my spine as Kinn approached me. I was so nervous that I moved off the sofa before he could reach me.

"I'm hungry. I'm going to grab something to eat," I said, piling the documents on the coffee table. I started heading for the door, but Kinn held me tightly from behind before I could take a single step.

"Let me go!" I yelled, trying to squirm out of his hold. I didn't know why, but lately, I couldn't fight him; I just felt so weak whenever he came close to me.

"Why are you resisting?" Kinn whispered, pressing his nose into the nape of my neck and inhaling deeply.

"Damn it, Kinn! Not in broad daylight!" I yelped, trying to pry his hands off of me to no avail.

"Why not? You aren't sleeping with me tonight, so I've got to do it now while I have the chance," he said, lightly nipping my shoulder.

"What, will you die if you don't come every day, you asshole?" I cursed. Kinn just chuckled and continued nibbling along the column of my neck until he bit my earlobe. My body shuddered with a sudden tingling sensation.

"I'll let you go...after one round," he whispered against my ear. I tried moving away, but that only gave him the opportunity to press his face against my neck.

"N-no! Get off me!" I yelled and grunted. Kinn made me feel so powerless. Just a second ago I'd been trying to push him off, but now I let him plant soft, wet kisses all over my face.

"I've been so nice to you. Why can't you be nice to me?" Kinn asked, pushing my arm so I'd turn to face him. I frowned at his actions. Kinn kept leaning closer until he stole a kiss from my cheek and then my lips. Then, he backed away slightly, still maintaining eye contact. "Pretty please?"

His voice was tender, and his eyes were filled with desire. I could never deny him when he looked at me like that. I couldn't deny him when he looked at me when he was calm or angry, either. I hadn't been able to resist those eyes since the day we met.

"Fine! Just don't forget to lock the door!" I snapped, pushing his chest slightly. Kinn's lips spread into a broad smile, and he pushed me back onto the sofa. I was stunned that he didn't take me to his bedroom.

"Wait a second," he said, straddling my lap. He gave me a quick peck on the lips before he went to lock the door. "Just wait there."

"Huh?" I looked between him and his bedroom door in confusion.

"Love isn't just in the bedroom," Kinn teased, before turning off the air conditioning.

"I'm not getting fucked on a balcony!" I warned him.

"We can also do it on the sofa," he chuckled, and disappeared into his bedroom. Soon after, he returned with a box of condoms and a tube of lube; my face heated as my heart pounded frantically.

Kinn gently pushed at my head. His affection made me feel awkward, and I wondered why I'd waited for him on the sofa instead of making a run for it. He pushed me until I lay flat on my back on the couch. I gulped nervously as I watched him crawl over me. He pressed his body against mine, took my face between his hands, and kissed me hard.

As our bodies rubbed against each another, I could feel how aroused he was. His skin was flushed and his breathing was ragged as he bent his head to deepen the kiss.

"Mmm," I moaned.

Kinn barely lifted his lips away from mine. He continued nibbling and licking, coaxing my lips open so our tongues could twine together. A wave of pleasure rippled through my body as Kinn touched me everywhere he could reach. Then, he snaked his hand down and stroked his finger along the length of my hardening cock.

"D-don't leave a mark," I told him when his lips moved to kiss my jaw and my neck. I got worried when he started to suck the skin there. He sometimes left hickeys where they could be seen, but I knew he'd try to hold back if I asked.

He moved to kiss my collarbone, pushing the hem of my shirt up. As soon as my chest was exposed, he attacked my nipple with his tongue and teeth as if he couldn't resist. When it came to anything that could be covered by clothing, Kinn never listened to my request for no hickeys—he left a multitude of marks all over my chest and my inner thighs.

"Ow, that hurts!" I cried when he bit my nipple harshly. Kinn ignored my complaint, continuing to suck on the bruised nub and swirling his tongue around it before attacking my other nipple.

He stopped stroking my dick and moved his hand to graze the skin just above the waistband of my jeans. When he showed no more sign of touching me where I wanted it, I started to get frustrated.

"Stop teasing me!" I snapped, glaring at him. I grabbed his hand and shoved it into my underwear so he could finally touch my painfully hard cock.

"You've gotten better at this," Kinn teased before bending to nip my chest, kissing down the length of my torso. I let go of his hand so I could grab his shoulder instead. He started to rub and stroke my dick, making me shudder as arousal shot through me. I let go of him to brush away the hair that had fallen over my face.

"Ah... Kinn," I moaned, trying to open my eyes to look at him as he devoured me with his lips. Finally, he pulled my pants down and started pumping my cock, *fast*.

"Mmm! S-slow down!" I cried, tossing my head back and arching my torso as he licked all over my stomach. Kinn's hand kept up its brutal pace, unrelenting from the start. My face and body contorted in pleasure.

Kinn continued kissing downward to my thigh—then I felt a sharp jolt of pain. The bastard bit me!

"Fuck! That fucking hurt!" I yelled. It only seemed to spur him on—he stroked me harder, clearly taking pleasure in taunting me. He continued to kiss my inner thigh before he pushed my legs up by the knees and spread them wide.

Kinn grunted in his throat, the sound keying me up even more. Then, he lifted my hips slightly and licked along the cleft of my ass. His eager licks and bites made my hole so wet and numb. My body spasmed and I bit my lip as another wave of arousal hit me. The feeling was so overwhelming that I had to bite hard on a nearby throw pillow to keep my cool.

His hand on my dick matched the rhythm of his tongue as he rimmed me without a trace of disgust. Kinn used his shoulder to keep me from closing my legs and continued lapping at my asshole until it was almost too much. I groaned, panting hard. My legs shook and my stomach tensed from my rapidly approaching orgasm.

My dick was so hard it hurt, and I felt like I could come at any second. "K-Kinn!" I cried as I reached down to stroke myself, increasing my pace to match the rhythm of his tongue.

Kinn lifted his face away to kiss my thigh again. His other hand grabbed the lube and squirted it on his finger, and I shuddered when I felt the cold gel around my rim.

"Ugh, Kinn! I...I c-can't," I stuttered. My body immediately stiffened up, my toes curling tightly as he pushed a finger inside of me. I almost came at the slightest intrusion. It hurt, but the pain quickly subsided. Kinn continued pushing until his finger went in to the knuckle.

I tried to control my breathing, willing my body to relax so I wouldn't be so tight around him. Kinn bent down to nuzzle my leg again and started deftly moving his finger. My body jerked when his finger brushed something inside of me; Kinn smirked and took the chance to repeatedly attack my prostate. I squeezed the pillow I was holding as I enthusiastically stroked myself with my other hand. My mind started to go blank as a tingling sensation settled in my groin.

"Nnngh...K-Kinn," I moaned his name.

"Yes? What is it, hmm?" he asked, his voice breathy and gentle in my ear. He added a second finger and continued massaging my prostate until I spasmed and spilled all over my stomach with a loud moan.

Kinn looked quite pleased with himself as he withdrew his fingers. I was still panting when he moved to lie down behind me against the back of the couch. He straightened his body and swiftly pushed his pants down to his knees.

"Put it on for me?" he asked, shoving a condom in my hand. My head was still hazy, but I took the offered wrapper and tore it open with my teeth before rolling the condom onto Kinn's hard cock.

Kinn moaned at my touch. He quickly pulled his shirt off before grabbing the lube and slicking his dick. Then he turned me on my side, lifted one of my legs, and pressed himself against me. I shuddered, but I felt too weak to resist him.

Kinn nuzzled his nose at the nape of my neck and whispered, "Can you turn around?"

I did as he asked and received another passionate kiss; then I felt him slowly push into me. I frowned when the head of his dick breached my tight hole, but he kept kissing me as if it would take away the pain.

Kinn groaned in his throat and started to shallowly thrust until he could finally bury himself to the hilt. I yelped and tried to pull away, but he swallowed my cry with another kiss. My face contorted in pain from being stuffed full. His cock throbbed inside me, the sensation so much more intense than the first time we had sex. He started thrusting his hips again, leaning back to look at my ass.

"Mmm, feels so fucking good," Kinn moaned, his voice thick with arousal. He finally let go of my leg to grab hold of my hips, forcing them to move up and down on his dick as he pleased. His other hand pushed into the sofa, lifting him up to look down at himself as he fucked me. I wasn't sure why, but watching him watch me was really hot—I had to hide my face and dig my nails into the cushions to relieve some of the tension. I moaned and cried out his name.

"*Fuck*, you're so fucking tight!" Kinn moaned, closing his eyes in an expression of pure bliss. He snapped his hips a few more times before slowing down and fucking me deeper. I stopped breathing whenever he hit that spot inside of me, sending me into full-body shivers. I bit my lip as he kept hitting my prostate and snaked my hand down to stroke myself.

"I can't hold on anymore," Kinn hissed, his breathing ragged. He pulled out and pushed me flat on my back, hovering above me and repositioning my hips. He stroked his cock again, making sure that the condom was still in place. Then, he pushed one of my legs wide open and abruptly shoved his cock back inside.

My face screwed up in pain at the unexpectedly brutal thrust. Kinn bent forward to bracket me between his arms, rocking his hips without waiting for me to adjust. I grabbed the throw pillow again and hugged it tightly to ground myself.

"Ow! You're going too hard. Damn it, Kinn!" I cried, my voice shaking. His frantic pace rocked my body back and forth uncontrollably.

I squeezed my eyes shut as pleasure washed over me; the way Kinn was fucking me now was so damned sexy that I couldn't stop myself. My mind whited out again as my orgasm approached.

"Fuck, this feels so good," Kinn moaned, his brows knitted from the overwhelming sensations. I was right there with him; this round was pretty fucking phenomenal. It felt way better than any other time we'd fucked before—and it somehow felt more intimate. I was more sensitive to Kinn's dick this time, almost like I could feel it throbbing as he thrusted into me. It was incredible!

"Did...did you change the brand of condoms you're using?" I asked, biting my lip again when Kinn's thrusts grew even more frantic. I threw my hand above my head and clutched the backrest to steady myself.

"Nope, I didn't. You like this, don't you?" he replied.

Our bodies were covered in sweat, my heart racing every time I breathed in his musky scent. I glimpsed his body—Kinn was tall and built, with just the right amount of lean muscle. His naked body was covered in beads of sweat, and he was looking at me intensely with eyes full of desire. I fucking loved the way he looked when he was about to come.

"I'm...I'm close," I warned him. I was about to come again, even though I'd barely touched myself. Kinn quickened his pace, pushing me closer to the edge with each forceful thrust. Suddenly, my body tensed, and I came all over myself.

"This feels fucking amazing," Kinn breathed.

He could say that again. This was incredible, and way more intense than usual. My ass was still pulsing and I was starting to get hard again. I glanced at his face as he kept on pounding into me, watching the vein on his forehead throb from the exertion.

Kinn's body stiffened and his rhythm started to slow down. I was surprised when I felt my ass flood with warmth. I propped myself up on my elbows and looked at where our bodies were joined, deeply furrowing my brow. Although the new sensation was exhilarating, I wasn't sure if it was a good thing.

Kinn let out a few husky moans, thrusting his hips a couple more times before slowly pulling out. He looked down and startled at whatever it was he saw.

"Wh-what?!" I asked, my voice shaking. For a moment, the only sound that could be heard was our panting.

Kinn widened his eyes and swore. "Damn..."

"What is it?!" I repeated. I couldn't see what he was looking at from this angle, and I became more anxious. Kinn remained silent as he continued scrutinizing my ass and his dick. After a while, he sighed, pulled the condom off, and wearily sat on the sofa.

"The condom broke," he said with a chuckle.

I was speechless. *What the fuck did he just say?!*

"Well...I guess it should be okay," Kinn continued, leisurely resting his head on the sofa.

"It's not fucking okay, damn it!" I yelled, finally grasping what had happened. I sat up and glared at him angrily when he showed me the torn rubber.

"Don't worry. I'll take responsibility if you get knocked up," Kinn joked, but I didn't find it funny. I kicked at him. He just smirked at me and wrapped the used condom in a tissue.

"This isn't funny!" I insisted.

"Come on! I'm clean," he said. He raised his eyebrows. "Wait, do you have any STDs?"

I threw a pillow at his annoying face with all my strength. "You're the one sleeping around, *you* could have STDs!"

I grabbed some tissues to clean the spunk off my stomach and pulled my shirt down. There was another place in my body that felt sticky with come... *How the fuck do I get come out of my ass?!*

"Get it out properly in the bathroom. You're going to stain my sofa," Kinn said, grabbing a towel for me. After I wrapped the towel around my waist, I tossed the used tissue at his face and went to the bathroom.

I cursed at him internally. I'd always been concerned about getting STDs and made sure to use a condom every time I slept with a woman. I never had any mishaps, so I was confident I was clean. But I'd seen Kinn sleep with a ton of guys before we started fucking. How could I be sure that he hadn't accidentally picked up something? I had a right to freak out!

"If the condom breaks during sex, you should get tested for sexually transmitted infections, even if you have sex exclusively with one partner. You should get tested immediately if you have a one-night stand or have sex with non-monogamous partners.

"If you and your partner want to have unprotected sex, both you and your partner should get tested every three months just to be safe. You shouldn't have unprotected sex with people who are not your exclusive partner."

I swore at my phone and took a moment to think. What was I to Kinn? His fuckbuddy? Just another hookup? My heart sank when I realized I had no idea. But it didn't matter—I still needed to get tested!

There was a knock on the door, and I heard Kinn yell, "Is everything okay, Porsche?!"

I quickly put my clothes back on, opened the door, and yelled back at him. "Take me to a hospital, now!"

"All right, if it'll make you feel better," Kinn replied casually, which pissed me off even more.

"Asshole! Now I gotta waste more of my time in a goddamned hospital!" I grumbled as I emerged from the bathroom. I went to sit on the edge of the bed, sulking and bumping my shoulder against his on the way.

"Huh? It takes two to have sex. Why pin all the blame on me? Or are you just unsure if *you're* clean?" Kinn asked, leaning leisurely against the door with his arms crossed over his chest.

"Bastard! You're the one who sleeps around!" I replied, getting angrier. I still couldn't believe how I'd gotten into this mess. *A bastard like you should rot in hell, Kinn!*

While it was Kinn's turn to clean himself up in the bathroom, I silently berated myself. I couldn't believe that I'd been so careless, letting my infatuation with Kinn get the better of me. I had to admit it—I was addicted. All it took was one touch from him, and I lost all my control in a heartbeat.

"You don't have to look so stressed out," Kinn said. We were on our way to a hospital, him driving and me riding shotgun. As his bodyguard, I wanted to drive, but he didn't let me—which made people in the house even more suspicious of us.

"Can I ask why you're so damned calm about this? Or do you usually fuck guys without protection?" I was pissed at how calm he was. I wondered if he'd still be smiling like this if he found out he had an STD.

"It's not that I'm not worried. This has never happened to me either," he said, shaking his head slightly. Somehow, his answer just made me angrier.

"How many guys have you fucked, anyway? Have you ever gotten tested at all?" I asked, exasperated.

"Hmm...four...five, six. No, it's ten, twelve, or thirteen," he said, counting on his fingers. He kept on counting, and I felt the temperature rise in my body as I boiled with anger.

"Fucking lech!" I barked.

"Don't worry. I have them tested every time," he said, looking at me in amusement before returning his attention to the road. I wanted to kick that smug fucker out of the car. I scowled the entire way to the hospital.

I got kind of embarrassed when we told the nurse why we were there. The nurses gave us both knowing smiles, and I couldn't bring myself to look any of them in the eye.

"What brings you here?" the doctor asked calmly when it was our turn to see him.

I looked down, not knowing what to tell the doctor.

"Our condom broke."

I turned sharply to look at Kinn. He'd spoken to the doctor completely casually, sitting with his legs crossed. Meanwhile, I was so mortified that I wanted to crawl into a hole and never emerge.

"There's no need to be embarrassed," the doctor told me. He probably saw how flustered I was. "When was the last time you had sexual intercourse?"

I was shocked by the doctor's question—it was like he'd just thrown ice water in my face.

"Just an hour ago," Kinn replied.

"All right. Let's get your blood tested, then," the doctor said.

Kinn and I let the doctor draw our blood. Kinn was annoyingly relaxed about the whole thing. I couldn't help but think that if he ended up with STDs, it would serve him right. But if he had STDs... would I get them too?

While we waited for our test results, Kinn asked me if I wanted to find something to eat with him. However, I was too nervous to do anything just yet. I forced him to remain at the hospital until our results came back.

Kinn connected his headphones to his cell and started playing games with his friends while I texted Tem and Jom about our schoolwork to distract myself.

"Hey... Hey!" I tried calling to Kinn, but he didn't seem to hear me. I pulled his headphones out of his ears. He looked at me, raising his eyebrows in question. "I'm taking a day off tomorrow," I told him. "I need to work on a group project at Tem's place."

"Denied," Kinn replied flatly.

I closed my eyes and sighed wearily. "You can't do this. It's my project, too, and I need to help my friends work on it." I tried reasoning with him, wondering why he had to be so annoying all the time.

"Then they can do it at my house," he said.

"Why?"

"Just tell them to work on the project there. It's best if you don't go out. What if something happens to you again?"

"It should be all right," I replied. "I went to classes for a week, and nothing happened."

It was still unclear who was behind all of this since we couldn't catch the culprit. But Kinn couldn't just force me to go to university and come straight home.

"The university campus is safe. Anyway, tell your friends to come here," Kinn said, his voice stern and final. He looked at me sharply, silently warning me not to say no.

"Fuck you!" I swore and kicked him in the shin. Kinn just smiled and tried to ruffle my hair. I had to dodge his hand.

"It's settled, then," he said cheerfully. "Who's coming over tomorrow, anyway?"

"Tem and Jom," I replied, disgruntled that I had to follow orders. I couldn't just leave, since I was on the clock tomorrow—Kinn could have used the excuse to deduct my wages.

"Jom and N'Tem?" Kinn repeated.

I glared at him through narrowed eyes, wondering why he'd referred to my friends so differently. "Yeah."

"Tell them to come here. They know me already, and..." He smiled. "N'Tem is pretty cute."

I immediately frowned at him. Unpleasant feelings popped into my head, and I remembered what Vegas had told me—*you're not*

P'Kinn's type. The men Kinn slept with were usually petite and cute; I could hardly be called either.

Perhaps Kinn was into Tem. I guess you could call him a cute guy. Tem was tall and fit, but he was slender and sweet, too. He had also been crowned the College Prince.[19] It wouldn't be that surprising if Kinn was interested in him.

"Do you like him?" I asked before I could stop myself.

Kinn's smile widened. "He's cute." He leaned closer with a smirk. "Don't you think he's cute?"

I sprang up from the bench and stomped off to the bathroom. I didn't know why I was so easily agitated, but I blamed Kinn for being so aggravating. I was usually an expert at hiding my feelings, but when it came to Kinn, I wanted to let everything out—including my anger and frustration. I wanted him to know how I felt, and that wasn't like me at all. I'd practically laid my soul bare to Kinn when I'd never let anyone see it before.

Damn you, Kinn!

I returned to sit with him, crossing my arms over my chest and frowning from the stress. Kinn smiled at me occasionally until it was time to get our test results. My pulse raced as we walked over to receive them.

I looked at Kinn in anticipation as he read the report. Then, he said, "It's negative."

I frowned. "What does that mean?" I asked. I honestly had no clue how this worked. I'd never gotten tested before.

"You got infected!" Kinn announced. I broke out in a cold sweat. *It's not true, right? Right?!*

---

19 The Prince (or Duen in Thai, which means the moon) and the Princess (or Dao in Thai, which means the star) are similar to the Homecoming King and Queen in US college and high school.

"I'm just fucking with you," Kinn said between laughs. "Negative means you're clean." He draped his arm around my neck and pulled me closer. Meanwhile, I was still in shock. When I realized he was messing with me, I nudged him sharply in the gut with my elbow.

"Asshole! Don't scare me like that!" I yelled. The nurses smiled at us. I lowered my head slightly, embarrassed.

"Come on, you should be glad! And it was a good thing that we got tested, because it means…" He trailed off, grinning suspiciously.

"Means what?!" I demanded.

"I can fuck you raw," he whispered against my ear. I whipped my head to glare at him and kicked his shin—hard.

"In your dreams, you bastard!" I yelled, shoving him off me and walking away. This pervert and his one-track mind!

I was still pissed at Kinn for being so annoying, but I was also relieved at the results. When we returned to the car, I got in and didn't say anything.

"What's wrong?" he asked, his eyes flickering between me and the road. "I was only joking with you."

"It wasn't funny!" I snapped. He probably thought I was angry at him for joking about the test results. I was angry at him about *everything*!

"I didn't know you could pout so much," he chuckled.

"I'm not pouting!" I yelled back. I *wasn't* pouting—I was furious, and Kinn's stupid teasing smile pissed me off even more.

"Whatever you say. Anyway, are you hungry yet?" he asked. "What should we eat? You can pick the place."

I pondered over it for a moment. It was dinnertime—maybe the reason I was so angry was because I was hungry. We'd also worked up quite a sweat earlier. I chuckled to myself. *Do you want me to choose? I'll pick the most expensive place, and you're paying!*

"I want to go to that Japanese restaurant," I said. Kinn's smile immediately faltered. So, that place was expensive as hell, huh? He probably paid more than ten thousand baht last time. This time, I intended to break the record and order whatever I wanted!

"Can we go to another place?" he asked, his voice sincere.

"I want to eat uni sushi," I declared, turning to glare at him.

"We can go to a different restaurant. It's just as good."

I wondered if there was something about that place—his demeanor had changed the moment I mentioned it. But he was the one who took me there first!

"No! I want to go to the same place," I insisted. I wasn't going to let him be the only annoying one. It was my turn to piss him off, and I wanted to know why that restaurant made him so nervous!

"Come on, let's go to a different place," he said.

"No. If you don't want to go, we can go home. I won't eat anywhere else!" I insisted, smirking at how irritated Kinn had become.

"Fine! Fuck it," he agreed reluctantly, turning the car into the alley that led to the restaurant.

Riling him up delighted me. He was the one who introduced me to this place, so he didn't have the right to get mad.

The car stopped in front of the traditional Japanese restaurant. Like last time, everyone greeted Kinn very politely when we entered. They were so eager to serve us that they'd probably spoon-feed us if we asked.

"Ten uni sushi, please," I said. Kinn glanced at me, but he sat sulking at our table for a while without saying anything. I didn't care, though; I intended to drain him dry today. I was so mad about the broken condom and the way he messed with me at the hospital. Now it was my turn to fuck with him!

"Yes, sir," the waitress said. I didn't hold back, ordering almost every dish on the menu—even the ones I didn't know.

Then, the waitress turned to Kinn and asked, "Would you like your usual order, Mr. Kinn?"

"Yes," Kinn replied before turning to me. "Order only what you can eat, will you?" he warned me when I didn't stop ordering.

I glared at him, knowing I wouldn't be nervous like the last time I was here. Now I knew exactly what to do!

"You're paying, right?" I asked.

"Yes! Are you planning to bankrupt me or what?"

I grinned in satisfaction. Once our food was served, I started shoveling it in. Kinn also ate, complaining that I'd ordered too much food. I feigned ignorance and continued enjoying my meal.

"Try this," I said, sliding over one of the ten plates of uni sushi. There were two pieces per plate. He silently stared at it and shook his head.

"You don't like it?" I asked curiously. "Or are you allergic to it?"

"No..." He looked contemplative for a moment before letting out a sigh. His strange behavior baffled me, but the fancy food in front of me was far more interesting.

I'd ordered a cook-your-own-takoyaki dish, because it reminded me of an old computer game where you owned a takoyaki shop and had to cook before a timer ran out. I thought it'd be fun, and I wanted to try something new.

"Fuck!" I swore after I fumbled adding the batter to the mold. Had I gotten myself into trouble? This was supposed to be fun, but I'd screwed up big time.

I kept cooking, but nothing seemed to be edible. Kinn chuckled and tried to help me shape the batter into a ball with skewers, but he didn't have any success either.

"I should have ordered the ready-to-eat ones," I grumbled.

"This one is almost ready," he said.

"Which one?" I asked, and he pointed at one of the strange-looking pieces of takoyaki. I frowned at the ridiculous ball and flipped it several times until I figured it was fully cooked. I poked it with my skewer, took it out of the pan, and blew on it. When it seemed cool enough, I held it in front of Kinn's mouth. "Here."

"You want me to be your guinea pig?" he chuckled, opening his mouth to take a bite.

"How is it?" I asked expectantly. He was right that I was making him my guinea pig. Although I wasn't afraid it'd taste bad, its peculiar shape weirded me out.

"It's all right," he said, sipping his tea.

"This one is about to burn," the waitress pointed out pleasantly. "Please let me help cook the rest." She expertly used the skewers to flip the batter into a nicely shaped ball.

"Thank you," I said politely, relieved to finally have some normal-looking takoyaki.

"I remember when Mr. Kinn ordered this takoyaki set for Mr. Tawan to try, and he couldn't do it either," the waitress remarked.

Kinn tensed up, his smile disappearing. I looked between him and the waitress, wondering what was going on.

"Ah, I'm so sorry! I shouldn't have said that," apologized the waitress profusely. She quickly finished cooking the rest of the takoyaki batter before she left.

Kinn straightened up and didn't speak. His face looked so grave that I didn't dare ask who Mr. Tawan was.

Kinn put down his chopsticks and got out his phone. The atmosphere had turned sour, and Kinn's serious persona was back. He no longer showed any sign of the cheerful personality that emerged when we were alone.

"Umm...I'm going to the restroom," I said, getting no response from him. I just went to splash some water on my face, then went outside to light a cigarette. There was a small smoking area out back, decorated in a way that mimicked the restaurant's interior. I took a long drag from my cigarette and looked at the array of flowers and Japanese-style flags adorning the area.

A brown corkboard hung on the wall outside, with photos tastefully pinned all over it. It caught my attention, so I checked it out, wondering who was meant to see these pictures.

My eyes swept over each photo; they were mainly shots of restaurant customers. One photo in particular stood out to me.

It was a picture of Kinn, Time, Tay, and Mew smiling cheerfully at the camera. I pursed my lips slightly, annoyed that he looked so happy eating with his friends but scowled when he was with me. Then I saw the photo next to it and frowned.

It was another photo of Kinn, but this time he was with Mek and another man. The other man was more cute than handsome—not just cute, but beautiful. He sat next to Kinn with their bodies leaning into each other, Kinn's arm around his shoulders. They weren't looking at the camera; instead, they were gazing at each other with broad smiles.

Something was written on the white border of the photograph. The ink had faded, but I could clearly read "Mek, Kinn, and Tawan." There was also a drawing of a heart. I looked at the heart curiously and felt empty all of a sudden. The server had mentioned Mr. Tawan—who was he? And what was he to Kinn?

"Mr. Porsche?" One of the waitresses interrupted my thoughts. "Mr. Kinn is asking for you."

I nodded at her, stubbed out my cigarette in the ashtray, and went back inside. I kept thinking about that picture, wondering who Tawan was.

When I reached our table, Kinn looked just as annoyed as when I'd left. "What took you so long?" he asked.

"I went out for a smoke."

"Hurry up and finish eating. I want to leave soon," he groused. His attitude was frustrating—judging by that photo, he was obviously capable of smiling.

"I'm full," I replied brusquely, crossing my arms. The whole Tawan thing was getting to me. I wanted to ask about him, but I didn't understand why I was so curious about the guy.

Kinn looked at the leftover food on the table, shook his head slightly, and called to the waitress, "Check, please."

There wasn't much food left, but it was still a shame that I no longer had the appetite to finish it.

As I expected, the bill came close to ten thousand baht. After Kinn paid with his credit card, we drove straight home in complete silence. Kinn didn't even turn on the radio. The tension only made me more anxious, but if he wanted to give me the silent treatment, I could give it right back.

"Hey, what's wrong?" Kinn asked after pulling up at a red light. He sighed and pulled my head over to rest on his chest.

"Argh! Get off me!" I yelped, pushing him off and sitting up rigidly in my seat.

"What's wrong?" he repeated. This time, he patted my head.

I jerked away from his touch. "What's wrong with *you*?!" I yelled, fed up with his shit.

His demeanor turned as icy-cold as it had been in the restaurant. "I was...thinking about something," he replied flatly.

I turned away from him and looked out the window. "Next time, don't take me to a restaurant if you don't want to go," I said. Everything about him annoyed me—he always pissed me off.

Kinn sighed again and turned on the car's audio. It connected to his phone and a song began to play. The intro was lively, and Kinn instantly hummed along to the tune. But it did nothing to improve my mood.

The car started moving again. I kept looking ahead at the road in front of me until I felt that the tense atmosphere had dissipated somewhat. Then, Kinn burst out singing the chorus of the song:

"I just have you, and that's it. I don't need anyone new. You've got me falling forever. Only you can make my life all right. You came in and brightened up my world. It's better than I could have imagined... I can't believe it!"[20]

I glanced over at Kinn. He alternated between looking at me and the road, and I smiled despite myself when his voice went out of tune at the last part of the chorus.

"Your voice is way off-key," I ribbed him. Kinn just shrugged and started dancing to the *"do do doo doo"* part of the song.

"It got your attention, though," he replied flirtatiously. I quickly looked away, blushing slightly. What the hell did he just say?

"Shut the fuck up!" I said, turning off the audio. I lowered my seat and pretended to be asleep. I never knew what to do when he flirted with me.

I heard Kinn chuckle quietly. I tried to control my breathing so I wouldn't get more anxious, and eventually fell asleep for real.

When we arrived home, Kinn woke me up with a big kiss on my cheek—he loved doing that. I insisted on sleeping in my room tonight. There was no way he could convince me to sleep in his room. He merely smiled back at me, which made me suspicious. I wondered if he had any more dirty plans up his sleeve.

---

20 The song's name is ดีดี (UNEXPECTED) by JAYLERRxPARIS.

After I showered, I went looking for Chay. He said that he'd be in Tankhun's room. I ran into Pete on the way, and he asked me to smoke with him in the garden instead.

"I'm telling you, your younger brother has become everyone's favorite," Pete said, taking a long drag of his cigarette and smiling at me.

I usually met up with Pete during our mealtimes or my smoke breaks, but we didn't usually get the chance to talk much.

"Do you think all this is stressing him out?" I asked. "I'm afraid he might be depressed." I knew how demoralizing it was to spend time with Tankhun.

"It's better than him spending time with Mr. Kim," Pete replied. "You don't need to worry."

"Should I rent an apartment for my brother? I don't want him to grow up to be like Tankhun," I said wearily, blowing cigarette smoke in his direction. Pete almost choked.

"What about you? I haven't seen you around lately," he said.

I gulped nervously. "Well, finals are coming up. I gotta study," I mumbled.

Pete gave me a knowing smile. "Really?"

"Yeah, really! Anyway," I quickly changed the subject, "I wanted to ask you something."

"What about?"

"Who are Mek and Tawan? I mean, I know Mek was Kinn's friend at some point. But what about Tawan? Is he his friend, too? I haven't heard Kinn talk about him before."

Pete's cheerfulness disappeared. "Why do you want to know?"

"I just do," I said.

Pete sighed. He looked very reluctant to answer. "What got you interested in them?"

"It's just... I've been bumping into Mek a lot lately."

"Mmm...how do I put this? Promise me that you won't overthink it," Pete said in a serious tone.

I frowned at him. "Why would I?"

"Well...you'll find out eventually. Mr. Mek is Mr. Kinn's friend. He's also Mr. Tawan's younger brother. And Mr. Tawan is..." Pete paused for a moment. I patiently waited for him to continue. "Mr. Tawan is Mr. Kinn's ex-boyfriend."

I was stunned.

"I don't know why they broke up," Pete continued. "All I know is that it ended badly. I haven't seen Mr. Kinn enter a serious relationship with anyone since."

I threw my cigarette into the ashtray. I was utterly shocked and confused.

"Are you all right?" Pete asked when I didn't say anything.

"Yeah... Why wouldn't I be?" I replied, trying to look as normal as possible.

"That's good—"

Bzzzzzzt! The walkie-talkie cut Pete off before he could finish. He huffed and cursed. "That fucker! It hasn't even been ten minutes!"

"Pete!" Tankhun's voice came from the radio. "Where the hell are you? I went for a quick shower, and you disappeared. Didn't I tell you to keep an eye on Porchay? Where is he? Find him for me, *now*!"

"I gotta go. My shithead boss is calling me," Pete said, giving me a pat on my shoulder before running back into the house.

I stayed in the garden and thought about what Pete had just told me. I didn't know what worried me more: that Kinn had an ex-boyfriend, or that Kinn hadn't been in a serious relationship since.

25

Unstoppable

I OPENED MY EYES, my face nuzzling into a strong chest. Like always, Kinn was lying on his side with his arm pillowing my head. I burrowed into his familiar warmth and inhaled his scent. He tightened his embrace, his arms encircling me. I'd gotten used to it—I was too lazy to complain when sleeping like this was actually kinda nice.

Yesterday, I'd told Kinn I was going back to sleep in my room, but in the end he'd come knocking on my door at two in the morning, saying he couldn't sleep. I couldn't sleep, either, and I didn't want him to pitch a fit and wake everyone else in the house, so I obediently followed him back to his room. I'd been too easygoing with him lately—but to be fair, we hadn't done anything except sleep all night.

I slowly moved to get off the bed, walking to the bathroom to do my business and brush my teeth. Kinn had even procured me my own toothbrush in his bathroom now. I was drowsily brushing my teeth when the bathroom door opened and Kinn rushed inside. I blearily looked at him in the mirror, confused, as he took off his trousers and peed into the toilet.

"The hell are you doing?" I mumbled, toothbrush still in my mouth.

He turned to look at me. "Pissing." He still looked handsome despite his hair sticking up everywhere, disheveled from sleep.

"Have some manners, you bastard!" I scolded him, rinsing my mouth with water. What kind of person was this shameless? I avoided his gaze and focused on washing my face.

"Why? Are you embarrassed? Isn't this something you're already familiar with?" Kinn said without shame.

"Familiar, my ass."

"Yes, your ass, my house. I can do whatever I want. Look!" I turned away from the sink to see him shaking left and right, still peeing.

"Bastard! So fuckin' gross. You're getting it all over the seat, asshole!" I shouted at him. Kinn laughed but grabbed the bidet hose[21] to spray the toilet clean. I straightened up and wiped my face with a towel, not wanting to witness Kinn's terrible personal hygiene any longer. After a while, he walked up behind me and pulled me into a kiss.

"Jerk!" I grumbled, stumbling but quickly righting myself.

"There's your good morning kiss," he said before exiting the bathroom. I clicked my tongue, but found myself smiling a little despite myself.

I went downstairs to shower and get dressed. I was starting to get used to the dirty looks everyone sent in my direction. I didn't pay attention to them, acting like everything was normal.

After getting ready, I went to eat with my friends, who were waiting at the staff cafeteria. I greeted Pete, Arm, Pol, and my little brother. Chay just sat there with a petulant look on his face.

"What's wrong?" I asked as I sat next to him. He turned to glare at me.

"You left me again last night," he said. The whole table turned to stare at me. I felt so awkward I could barely sit still, looking left and right like I didn't notice what Chay just said. Fuck! Why did he have to say that in front of everyone?!

---

21 People in Thailand use bidets. The most common type is a hose and nozzle, as depicted here.

"That bastard! I hate Kim, I hate Kim, I hate Kim!" Chay exclaimed, stabbing his spoon into his omelet again and again. He looked super pissed.

"What did he do to you?" I asked, my voice dark. Chay turned to meet my gaze for a moment before sighing.

"I just hate him! No reason." He got up to put his plate away before stomping out of the mess hall.

"The hell is wrong with Chay?" I asked as my friends and I watched him leave.

"Porsche, go get something to eat. It's all stuff your stomach can handle," Pol told me. I turned to look at the food. Pol was right—it looked like I really could eat all of this. Where did all those vegetable dishes go?

"My...it must be nice to be the favorite," someone remarked. "If you can't eat our food, everyone in the entire house has to change for you."

I squinted at the opposite table, suddenly realizing something: I had complained to Kinn that the food at his house was shit. I didn't like spicy food or vegetables, so I'd only been eating omelets. I'd had so many at this point that it felt like I was turning into one. But these past few days, there were dishes that I could eat more easily, and a greater variety. *Don't tell me Kinn told the cooks!*

"Barking so early in the morning, doesn't your throat hurt?!" Arm shouted.

"Heh, what did you do that has the boss so messed up?!" one of them howled.

"Must have been put in a lot of...positions," another one offered.

Bang! A hand slammed down onto the table. It didn't come from me, but from Pete, who stood up to glare at them. Pol and Arm stood up, too. I sighed, sitting there with my arms crossed as

I watched the situation unfold. I was fed up with the whole thing.

The opposite table quickly shoveled food into their mouths and went to put their plates away. We stared at them until they walked out of the kitchen and disappeared from sight.

"Bastards! Not so brave now, are they?!" Pol spat, kicking a chair.

"You don't have to worry about it—they're all talk. Go get something to eat," Pete told me.

"I'm not hungry anymore. I'll go wait for Tem and Jom outside." I grabbed a bottle of water and some of those stupid chocolates. I headed straight to the garden, lighting a cigarette and biting into a chocolate. By the time I finished smoking, Tem called me to say they were here.

I led Tem and Jom to the garage, then we brought what we needed for our report to the garden. Pete, Arm, and Pol came to greet my friends and sat with us for a while.

"You guys have to be productive, too." We'd all gotten close because we'd met up together and grabbed drinks pretty often. Since Pete, Arm, and Pol weren't on duty yet, they'd come over to help. Although they were a little older, I could talk to them comfortably as friends.

The other bodyguards in the house might stare at us disapprovingly because I'd brought my friends over, but what could I do? The boss forbade me from leaving.

As soon as I thought of Kinn, he appeared. Speak of the fucking devil!

"What are you doing?" he asked.

Pete quickly got up from his chair and stood at attention, Pol and Arm following suit.

"Mr. Kinn, have you finished eating?" Pete asked.

Kinn had to wave his hand and tell them all to relax.

"Hello," Tem and Jom greeted Kinn, their wai gestures stiff.

"Make yourselves at home. Oh, Arm, go get some water and snacks for them," Kinn said. I squinted at him as he slid a chair over to sit next to me. *They're my friends, not yours. You don't have to provide such good hospitality.*

"Of course." Arm went to do as Kinn ordered.

"You don't have to," Tem said quickly. "It's... We'll finish up and go. We won't bother you for long." I saw Kinn smile, his eyes staring past me. I scooted over a little, blocking his view. I still remembered that he called Tem cute.

"It's fine, you can stay however long you want. My friends are coming over, too," Kinn replied. His friends, really? And why was he being so creepily polite? How come he was never this nice to me? He was always shouting his head off when it was just us. What a fucking hypocrite!

"Y-yes," Tem said, looking at Kinn and freezing up for a moment before turning back to keep cutting paper.

"If you want to check him out so bad, why don't you jump over my head?" I grumbled. Kinn glanced at me out of the corner of his eye and smiled even wider.

"What's the big deal? He's cute," Kinn said, half joking. I felt weirdly irritated. I wanted to stab his head with those scissors. I huffed at Kinn without reason until he let out a laugh.

He leaned over to me. "Have you eaten yet?" I leaned away, glaring at him in silence.

"Come on, don't give me the silent treatment," he said. I tried to ignore him, but he reached over with his finger to poke playfully at my mouth.

"Fuck off, Kinn!" I smacked his hand away. He quickly reached over with his other hand, placing it on my head and ruffling my hair.

"You've really learned to pout lately," he quipped. I twisted away, pushing at his shin with my foot.

"I'm not pouting!" It was like the more I scolded Kinn, the happier he became. He reached over to squeeze my cheeks until my mouth puckered up. I swatted his hand away again, so focused on his nonsense that I forgot about the group project...

"*Ahem...* Where should we stick this?" Jom cut in. Kinn and I jumped away from each other. I looked around to see my friends staring at me in stunned silence for a moment—then they turned away and acted busy. *Fuck!*

Kinn chuckled and leaned back contentedly in his chair, crossing his arms. I turned to silently mouth "asshole" at him, then went back to work. Not long after, Arm came by with a large tray of snacks, but who had time to eat except Kinn? He sat there enjoying his food, still doing his best to provoke me. He kept trying to touch my waist, my neck, my arms, and my legs, whatever he could do to get a rise out of me. And he kept grinning so cheerfully, the psycho!

Eventually I couldn't take it anymore. I turned to him. "Don't you have anything else to do?"

Kinn brushed crumbs onto me. "I'm waiting for my friends, can't you see?" he said, holding up a cookie to my lips.

"Then go wait somewhere else! What the hell are you bothering me for?" I asked. I couldn't work in peace. I wasn't putting up with his bullshit any longer!

"It's my house. I can wait wherever I want," he said with a straight face. Bastard! If he wouldn't go, then I would! I dragged my chair to sit between Pete and Pol.

"Scoot over and let me sit," I said. My friends quickly made space to let me sit between them. I turned to glare at Kinn, but he only laughed, then made an expression like he just thought of something.

He scooted closer to Tem, picking up a plate of snacks and offering it to him.

"N'Tem, would you like some?" he asked. Tem looked a little confused, but he picked up a cookie out of courtesy, glancing at me in confusion.

"Oh! The gang's all here. Hey, guys," Tay remarked brightly as he walked over. The whole table greeted Tay, Time, and Mew with wais. I sat there motionless, not really wanting to pay my respects—not that Kinn's friends treated me badly or anything, but I was annoyed.

"Hello."

"We're working here?" Mew asked, pulling his laptop out. I figured they were here to do their schoolwork, too.

"Right here," Kinn answered. Arm and the rest had to bring another table and some chairs over for Kinn's friends.

"So, are you guys here to work on your reports too?" Tay asked. He always acted way too familiarly with my friends. They all nodded in reply.

"Good! When we're finished today, let's go out for dinner, yeah?" Tay continued, turning to his friends for approval.

"Sure. But before you think about anything else, you've gotta finish this first!" Mew declared, holding Tay in a headlock and forcing him to look at his laptop. I just sat there looking at my report, but I was barely able to concentrate because Kinn kept staring at me.

"The fuck are you looking at?" I mouthed to Kinn, as slowly and clearly as possible so he could read my lips. He shrugged before trying to provoke me again.

"Are you almost done with your report?" he asked Tem, who flinched a little and turned to answer him awkwardly.

"Uh... We're nearly done," he said. "We'll hurry up so we can leave soon." I looked between Tem and Kinn in irritation, a strange itch tugging at my heart.

"Hey, no, I'm not chasing you away, I'm just asking," said Kinn. "When you're done tonight, do you want to go for a drink?"

Tem glanced at me, then at Kinn, looking pretty uncomfortable. He seemed even more tense than when he first arrived.

"Er...Porsche, what do you think?" Tem asked me.

I said nothing, staring at Kinn in silence. He looked back, smiling mischievously. He was clearly trying to piss me off.

"So, what do you think, N'Tem, do you want to go?" Kinn pressed.

Tem looked even more sheepish; he shrank back in his seat and turned to Jom for help. "What the hell is Kinn pressuring me for?" he whispered.

"Oh! Kinn!" Time suddenly shouted, looking up from his phone. Everyone turned to look at him. "Did you watch N'March's new show?"

I furrowed my brow at the question. Kinn made a puzzled face, looking at Time like he didn't understand what he was saying. "What are you talking about?" he asked cautiously.

"N'March! He's in a new drama and he's the second male lead. Look, he's so cute!" Time shoved his phone screen at Kinn's face, which made his expression darken further.

Tay elbowed Time and looked between Kinn and me. "Shit, Time, what are you saying?"

"Ow! I'm talking about N'March! Kinn said he was the best out of all his boytoys!"

I froze at Time's words. My heart lurched, and a strange feeling welled up within me.

"The fuck, Time?! Stop spouting bullshit and be quiet!" Tay hissed, holding his boyfriend in a headlock and giving him a firm knock on the head.

"Shit, ow! What, I was just scrolling my Facebook feed and saw it!" Time protested loudly.

Kinn took a sip of his drink, acting indifferent. Meanwhile, my mood plummeted. What was wrong with me? Why did I feel so bad? That Tawan guy was still stuck in my thoughts, and now there was March, who was apparently best out of all Kinn's hookups. *Why does it feel like the more I get to know Kinn, the more I get hurt?* Pain and tightness twisted together in my chest.

"I'm going to the bathroom," I said to Tem and Jom, who were eyeing me in concern. I had to get my emotions under control. I didn't want to accept what I was feeling right now—but deep down, I knew.

I went into the house and headed to my room, making a beeline for the sink to splash water on my face. I couldn't get Tawan and March out of my head. I was struggling to accept that right now, I liked Kinn. I liked him so much that I was worried I might be in too deep. I'd started to care less about everything else around me and focus more and more on him. The hurt and confusion had begun to fade, replaced with something akin to infatuation. Maybe I was just getting carried away. I didn't like myself like this—catching feelings for him.

I shouldn't feel like this, right? How was I supposed to face myself?

"What's wrong...?"

As soon as I stepped out of my room, I was met with the sound of Kinn's voice. He'd been waiting for me outside my door, standing with his arms crossed.

"What?" I asked curtly, not meeting his eyes.

"When you're done in there, I'll take you out for dinner." He reached over to hold my head, rocking it from side to side.

"I'm not going." I twisted away and stared at him unhappily out of the corner of my eye.

"Don't tell me you're overthinking what Time said," Kinn remarked as he tried to put his arms around my neck. I resisted, shaking my head. Kinn was getting more and more brazen with his affection these days. Wasn't he ashamed to be seen by everyone else in this house?

"I'm not overthinking it. Let go of me," I said, pushing him off. He pushed back, then bent down and...

Mwah! He kissed my cheek and quickly pulled away. I pushed at his chest and frowned, even though my heart was pounding and my face was heating up. I was surprised he'd dared to do something like that out in the middle of his house. *You're lucky there's no one around, you jerk!*

"The hell are you doing?!" I snapped.

"Apologizing," he said, grinning.

"The fuck are you apologizing for?!"

"For making you jealous."

I closed my eyes and sighed, forcing myself to voice my thoughts out loud. "...What are you to me—why would I have any right to be jealous?" Although I knew I felt jealous, how could I admit it? His actions were so obvious. I didn't know if his apology made me feel any better.

Kinn raised his eyebrows like he hadn't expected me to say that. Irritated, I purposely bumped into his shoulder as I headed back out into the garden. If he couldn't say it, then I didn't want to let him keep playing with my heart anymore.

I went back to my work without saying a word to anyone else, and nobody dared to ask me anything. A while later, Kinn came back to sit in his chair. I wasn't paying attention to how often he looked at me or what expressions he was making; instead, I kept my head down and focused on getting my work done.

Almost the entire day passed like that, with people making small talk at the table and Pete, Arm, and Pol taking turns coming and going. They alternated between checking in on Tankhun and messing around with us, but I wasn't in the mood to joke with anyone.

Do you ever feel uncertain like I do, Kinn? Or are you just teasing me, making a fool of me for your own twisted amusement? Fuck!

By the time evening rolled around we'd finished our reports, and Tay invited us all out for dinner. Although Tem whined about not wanting to go, all three of us got dragged along in the end. More importantly, we planned to go drinking after dinner—we all wanted to let loose after all that work.

Of course, when news of our outing reached Tankhun's ears, he tagged along and brought his gaggle of guards with him. Porchay made a bit of a fuss about wanting to go with us, but he wasn't old enough to drink, so he got dragged back into the house by Kim.

I'd been seeing Kim a lot recently. I heard him tell my brother that he got a new game, and they both went up to his room to play. While I looked at Kim suspiciously, it was good that the people here were looking out for my brother. I shouldn't worry so much...

After dinner—paid for by Tankhun—we headed to Madam Yok's club. There was a bit of a commotion when Tay wanted to go chill at a fancier bar, but Tankhun wanted somewhere he could dance—and who could win an argument against Tankhun? No matter how good you were at making your point, you couldn't win against his brand of crazy. Plus, we weren't dressed up—if we went to a bougie bar, they probably wouldn't even let us in. So we ended up at the same old place Tankhun loved so much: Madam Yok's.

"Hello, boys!" Madam Yok said. "Make yourselves at home. I've got your table and drinks all ready for you. Welcome, welcome." I'd called ahead to get us a VIP table.

The club was currently pretty empty. The live band hadn't started yet, and soft music was coming from the speakers. I let the others head over to their seats while I went to greet the people I knew—both my old coworkers and our regulars. Of course, when they saw me, they all offered me drinks without me having to ask.

"You disappeared for ages! I've been coming here every day to catch a glimpse of you," a familiar customer said, though I couldn't quite recall their name. I smiled, knocking back a glass and chatting for a bit before a member of staff dragged me over to the bar.

"Hey, you! What's the great job you snagged? Tell us!"

My old coworkers crowded around me and handed me more drinks, talking in the way people who haven't seen each other in a while do.

"Has the bar been busy these days?" I asked.

"Same as always," the bartender on duty said, and handed me a drink. "Here, try this—I just came up with it."

I didn't know how many drinks I'd already had, but I was drinking whatever anyone handed to me. Fuck, why did everyone keep passing me drinks?

"Why the fuck are you trying to get me drunk so early?" I asked as I drank.

"You look happier. What happened? Are you making good money? Take me with you!"

I went still at their words. They weren't the first people to say shit like that to me. Tem and Jom had also said I looked happy, even though I had a lot on my mind. Did I really look happier? How?

"What are you all gossiping about over here? Get to work! The customers are waiting!" Madam Yok's voice broke our little circle apart. Everyone quickly scattered in different directions and got back to work. I smiled at them and sat there at the bar, sipping my drink.

"Hey, you." Tem and Jom came over with their drinks and sat next to me. I quirked my brows at them, but my eyes inadvertently looked past them to see Kinn staring at me. I quickly looked away.

"Did you get in a fight with Kinn?" Tem asked. He threw an arm over my shoulders and greeted the staff members he knew.

"No..." I answered him.

"No? You and Kinn haven't spoken to each other all day. You're avoiding him," Jom added.

"Am I really that obvious?" I asked, heaving a long sigh. My worry about what my friends thought of me came back. If they knew how far I'd gone with Kinn... Would they still accept me?

I didn't want to keep it a secret from my friends, but everyone around us seemed to notice. If it was that blatant, then I probably couldn't avoid the subject any longer.

"...I'm your friend," Jom said, taking a drink. I glanced at him. He made an awkward face. "I'll admit it's a little hard to believe, and a little confusing..."

"But you don't have to worry," Tem added. "We can accept you. Like, really accept you."

"Kinn's not my boyfriend," I murmured. Tem and Jom looked at each other.

"Then...what's going on between you two?" Jom asked.

I paused, then called the bartender I was familiar with: "Hey, can you give me another glass, please?"

"The same thing? I've got you." The bartender smiled back and quickly started on my drink.

"Okay, well, how far did you guys go?" Jom changed his question. I froze, not knowing whether I should keep hiding from my friends or just admit it.

My silence spoke multitudes. Jom continued: "Hmm...who's the top and who's the bottom?"

Tem shot Jom a disparaging glare. I sat there scrambling for an explanation, swallowing down a lump in my throat. I didn't want to keep secrets from my friends any longer, and I could see that they knew I was sleeping with Kinn, but to tell them the actual positions? Hell no. Plus, those two were so sure that I topped...

"I'm the top," I said, secretly wincing at the lie. I knew my friends could accept me, but I didn't want them to look at me any differently!

"Shit, really?" Tem was shocked. "Kinn's the *bottom*? Shit, shit, I'm seeing Kinn in a new light! I can't see him the same way anymore."

I nodded a little to convince my friends that what I said was the truth.

"Damn, I wasn't sure who'd be the top or the bottom. I guessed right. See, Tem! I told you Porsche was the top!" Jom crowed, though he had an equally shocked expression.

It seemed like they'd known for some time now—they'd made guesses and everything.

"What do I do? I can't see Kinn the same way!" Tem looked like he wanted to cry, occasionally stealing glances at Kinn sitting at the table. I lifted the glass the bartender handed to me, secretly pleased with myself. I'd been kind of irritated before, and slandering Kinn had cheered me up considerably.

"So...you guys can accept it?" I asked them again to make sure. I'd been straight my whole life, and now I liked a guy—I knew there would be people around me who wouldn't be okay with it.

"We can more than accept it!" Tem assured me. "I'm just a little curious, that someone like you could...er...never mind. Anyway, don't overthink what P'Time said to Kinn earlier—they were probably just teasing each other." Tem was quick to try to comfort me. Fuck, everyone around me could tell.

"Is it really that noticeable?" I asked them.

"Kinda... And quit sulking like a bottom, dumbass. You're a top! You have to be more stoic," Tem said in a rush, squinting at me in suspicion. I quickly turned away, looking at anything other than my friends.

Suddenly, Madam Yok's voice interrupted us. "Who's the bottom?"

I felt a shiver run down my spine. My friends immediately shook their heads.

"N-nothing, ma'am."

"Don't play coy, I heard you! If Porsche is the top, then who's the bottom?! Don't tell me... *Naega jeil jal naga!*[22] You've switched to guys now, huh?" Madam Yok said, pressing a hand to her chest. I paled. Was this the grand opening for my sexuality or some shit? Why was everyone around me finding out?

"Nothing, ma'am, it's nothing," I said. Although I was willing to let my friends know, I wasn't prepared for anyone else to find out.

"I heard it with my own two ears," Madam Yok said, dragging a chair over.

"Ma'am, I think that table is calling for you," Tem said, trying to shift her attention elsewhere.

---

22 From the K-Pop song I Am the Best by 2NE1. Madam Yok is just using this lyric as a sassy interjection—it doesn't have much to do with what she's talking about.

"Don't try to trick me, or I'll make you my wife," she teased. Tem's face fell and he turned away to gulp down his drink.

"There's really nothing to talk about," I insisted, wanting to drop the subject.

"It's okay if you don't want to tell me, but if there's anything you want to ask about topping or bottoming, you can come to me. I'm particularly experienced when it comes to pleasing men in the bedroom," she said. Tem and Jom looked at her in disbelief until she leveled a fierce glare at them. "I'm serious! For example, I'm a bottom, but I've got my own special techniques—how else would those men fall so hard for me?"

We squinted at her.

Madam Yok might look a little stocky, but she had men lining up to serve her. Like today—I'd seen a fresh-faced man hanging around her office!

"How?" Tem asked earnestly.

"Ah, Tem, you're pinging my gaydar pretty hard too... Is Porsche the top and *you're* the bottom?" Madam Yok asked. We both hurriedly shook our heads. I'd rather have died than sleep with Tem!

"Ma'am, you started it, so you have to finish telling us," Tem protested. I turned to look at him. I was starting to suspect Tem liked guys too—he had a different vibe about him lately.

"Ah, I'll tell you," she said. For some reason, I really wanted to hear her advice.

"If you're the top, you've got to have the right moves. You need to find exciting new things for your partner to keep things interesting," she explained. "But if you're the bottom, you can't just lie there like a dead fish! The more you take the initiative, the more exciting it will be. Have an active role in bed—don't let the top dictate everything."

Tem and I went silent as we listened to Madam Yok, while Jom looked like he would rather die than be subjected to this conversation any longer.

"And then what?" I blurted, kicking myself as soon as the words were out of my mouth. Why the fuck had I said that?!

Madam Yok laughed as I took a sip of my drink to hide my embarrassment.

"Didn't you say you were the top?" she teased.

"I *am* the top! ...Why don't you keep going?!" I raised my voice. It seemed the longer I talked to Madam Yok, the more my secrets were revealed.

"I'm surprised to see I wasn't wrong when I said you'd end up with a man," Madam Yok said.

"When I say I top, I mean it. Are you going to continue?" I pressed.

"All right, fine, fine. Bottoms like us need to have our own signature style. How else are we going to get the top hooked on us, especially those playboy types? We have to make them so captivated that they can't look away! You have to control the game, let them follow you—don't let them boss you around too much. The more they feel like we're in control, the more challenged they'll feel too."

"How?" Tem asked, furrowing his brow. Madam Yok leaned down and gestured for us to come closer. Tem and I leaned in and she whispered so only the two of us could hear her. As for Jom, he was distracted by a bunch of girls who'd gotten up to dance nearby.

Tem and I were mystified by what Madam Yok said, but we quickly schooled our shocked expressions back to normal.

Pete showed up to call us back to the table. Tankhun was starting to feel lonely, apparently, and wanted me to mix some drinks for him. I looked at Tem suspiciously, and Tem looked back at me.

"I don't believe you're a top," he whispered as he sat back down in his chair.

"What about you? Whose bitch did *you* become?" I retorted. Tem acted like he hadn't heard me.

I turned my attention back to everyone else at the table. Kinn kept shooting me unhappy glares, but I didn't pay attention to him. Even though I'd calmed down considerably, his face still pissed me off.

"Let's play a game while we wait for the band," Tay suggested. It wasn't that late yet, and the music playing through the speakers was the same slow, sappy shit. We all nodded in agreement.

"I want to play!" Tankhun exclaimed as he handed me his glass to mix him another drink.

"It's called Never Have I Ever," Tay said. "I've always wanted to play it."

Everyone listened intently except for Kinn and I, who were seated opposite each other and staring each other down like we were waging psychological warfare.

"Oh, I've heard of it," said Tankhun, explaining the rules. "We each take turns. When it's your turn, you have to say 'never have I ever' and say something you've never done. If anyone else at the table has done that thing, they have to drink."

"P'Tankhun still has a brain, I see," Tay joked. Tankhun threw some ice at him.

"Let's start," Tankhun said. He ordered a round of vodka shots and lined them up in front of everyone.

"I'm not playing," Kinn said.

"Me either," Tem and I said hurriedly. I had a bad feeling about this. This stupid game didn't sound very creative, either.

"You have to! Anyone that doesn't play has to do fifty push-ups," Tankhun ordered. I rolled my eyes. Was he a Territorial Defense[23] instructor, ordering people around like that? Bastard! We all ended up agreeing to play, or Tankhun would throw a tantrum—then we'd have a real mess on our hands.

"The guys who don't want to play must have a lot of secrets," Mew said, eyeing me skeptically.

"Fine, fine, let's play." I was too tired to argue. *Let's just fucking get it over with.* Kinn smirked and gave me a wicked look.

"I'll go first," Tay said, raising his right hand and holding a shot glass in his left. "Never have I ever cheated on my significant other."

At the end of his sentence, everyone looked at each other in panic. No one dared to pick up their glass.

"This game requires honesty," Mew piped up. "Anyone who doesn't admit the truth, I curse them to—"

"Be haunted by a ghost!" Kinn offered with a laugh.

"Such a light punishment? Fuck, I wanna curse them with erectile dysfunction!" Tay snapped, turning to stare at his boyfriend.

Time sighed. "I'll drink. But it's in the past, so don't bring it up!" he said, pointing his finger at Tay and knocking back his shot. No one else dared to pick up theirs, so the game continued.

"My turn," said Mew. We all looked at him in anticipation. "Never have I ever...had a *boy*friend." The whole table got anxious. Tankhun started to frown, like he wasn't pleased with the subject. The people who ended up drinking were Tay, Time, and Kinn. I felt a twinge in my heart as I thought of Tawan... He really was Kinn's ex-boyfriend, then.

---

23   Territorial Defense (Ror Dor) is a program for all eligible Thai males, usually completed during high school, as an alternative to military service conscription. They act as a reserve for the military in times of war or crisis.

"My turn." Jom raised his hand. Tem and I looked away, knowing from his expression that we'd be targeted. "Never have I ever...slept with another man."

Everyone started to fidget. I looked at Tem with a pale face, but he wasn't looking any better. We both nodded at each other's glasses, as if daring the other to go first.

"Haunted by a ghoooost..." Kinn piped up. I snuck a glance at him and saw that he had already finished his shot, same as Tay and Time. I straightened up and sat back casually, refusing to pick up my glass. I'd pretend I hadn't heard it.

"Cursed with impotence!" Jom said with a cackle. I acted even more indifferent.

"Hey! The things you guys are saying are fucked up!" Tankhun complained, but now it was Pol's turn. He pointed at himself, looking confused.

"We have to play?" the bodyguards hiding in the corner asked.

"Of course you have to play!" Tankhun insisted. "Don't tell me you didn't think you were playing this whole time."

"Even if we *were* playing, there was nothing we could drink to," Pol answered cautiously.

"Play!" Tankhun shouted.

"Yes, yes, never have I ever..." Pol stilled, thinking, before he continued, "crushed on anyone at this table."

I closed my eyes and sighed before looking up to see Kinn going still for a moment and picking up his glass. I smiled, but I was torn about whether I should drink or not. The question wasn't too explicit—should I drink? There was nothing to gain if I acted like I didn't hear, but I didn't want to get haunted.

I swiftly knocked back my shot. I knew everyone was staring at me, but I acted like nothing was wrong. Of course, Tay and Time had to drink, but why was Tem looking awkward? He leaned back in his chair like he'd made his peace with it. Did Tem have a crush on someone at this table? Who? Was it Kinn?

"I'll continue from Pol," Arm said. "Never have I ever slept with anyone at this table!"

I froze, my breath hitching. I turned to glare at Arm as he laughed hysterically. If I wasn't wrong...I was the target of this game. Kinn let out a satisfied noise before taking a shot as well, but what shocked and drew everyone's attention was Tankhun, who also took a shot without a care in the world.

"Wait, Khun! Y-you...with *who*? When? How?" Kinn stuttered out as the rest of the table sat in silent shock. I took the opportunity to drink my shot while everyone was distracted.

"I didn't sleep with anyone! But with the stuff you guys are saying, I can't drink at all. I'm dying to drink my vodka! I don't fucking care!"

We all sighed in relief. I doubted anyone at the table would be fucked up enough in the head to sleep with Tankhun, anyway. Kinn turned away from Tankhun to look at me, smiling as his gaze slid down to my empty shot glass.

"Ah, it's your turn, sir," Pete said, sliding a glass in front of Tankhun.

"Yay! My turn. Never have I ever...eaten dog food," Tankhun declared as he downed his shot. We all looked at him wearily, no one picking up their glasses. Who would be crazy enough to eat dog food? *You're insane, Tankhun!*

"Let's stop. The band is here," Time said, exhausted. The entire table nodded in agreement. We finished off the leftover vodka and swayed to the music.

"I'm going out for a smoke," I told Tem, who nodded in acknowledgment. I glanced at Kinn, but he wasn't paying attention to me.

He had his hands full trying to hold back a tipsy Tankhun from dancing and knocking over the bottles on the table.

I lit up my cigarette at my usual spot: the alley behind the bar, where I'd met Kinn for the first time. Thinking of that day made me want to laugh. How had I ended up here? I should've let those guys beat him to death so I didn't have to feel all these confusing emotions. But if I could go back in time, I would probably make the same choice all over again. Although I was still resisting my feelings, I could at least admit that I...

I liked him. For real.

I exhaled, smoke trailing from my mouth as I leaned against the wall. I tried not to think. In my mind, there was no one else but Kinn. He had so much sway over my feelings—*too* much. He could make me feel so many things at once. I'd been so pissed off this afternoon, but my heart was utterly relieved tonight when he drank to 'liking anyone at this table' with his eyes staring into mine. It was probably biased of me to think he meant me and not anyone else.

It was hard to accept that I had fallen for another man, but what could I do? I didn't want to lie to myself. Kinn was the only person who could send my heart into a frenzy every time I looked at him. He had slowly broken down my walls and infiltrated my heart. Before I knew it, he'd made himself at home in there, and I couldn't get him to leave.

I tried not to overthink it...but how could I not? The more time we spent together and the closer we became, the harder it was to control my feelings. And what about Kinn? The confusion, the vulnerability, the joy—did he feel the same way I did?

Did he feel anything for me at all?

The door behind me opened and Kinn emerged, coming to a stop in front of me. "You're drunk already?"

"I'm not," I lied, rubbing my tired eyes. I was starting to feel a bit dizzy. People had kept handing me glass after glass of alcohol from the moment I stepped foot in the bar. I'd had too many drinks to count.

"I kept seeing tables sending you drinks," Kinn said, putting his hands in his pockets and sighing. "You're quite popular."

"...Not as popular as you," I said, looking up at him. I'd noticed a lot of girls checking him out.

"Hey, I didn't flirt back with anyone." Kinn raised his eyebrows and glared at me. "You kept smiling at everybody."

"Just my old regular customers... Hell, why would you want to flirt, anyway? You've already got March, your best lay," I said, not knowing what compelled me to bring it up.

"Don't talk nonsense." Kinn reached over to stroke my hair, smiling. "My best lay...isn't March at all." I squinted at him and he gave me a salacious smile. "Don't you want to know who it is?"

My heart thumped erratically in my chest. I secretly hoped for a certain answer. I remained still until Kinn leaned down to whisper in my ear.

"It's you," he murmured. I smiled, but quickly schooled my features back to normal. I put my hands on Kinn's chest and pushed him away from me. Even though there was no one out here, I still didn't know what to do.

"...Pervert," I scolded him. *Don't you dare fall for his playboy bullshit, Porsche!*

Kinn chuckled. "What about you? You lied quite a lot during that game," he said as he pulled the pack of cigarettes from my hands and lit one for himself. Kinn smoked sometimes, but not often. Sometimes after we, uh... He'd go out for a smoke on the balcony.

"I didn't even want to play," I muttered. Why did seeing Kinn smoke turn me on?!

"Aren't you afraid of being haunted...?" Kinn teased. Strangely enough, my heart swelled. The anger I felt before had all but disappeared, leaving only one feeling. Not to mention the fact that I was drunk—I wasn't overthinking things like before.

"What do you mean, *haunted*?" I asked Kinn.

"Liars will be haunted by ghosts," he said. I smiled at him.

Here goes nothing...

"If I sleep with you, what ghost would dare to haunt me?" I said, gently lowering my head to lean it against his shoulder. Kinn froze. My heart pounded wildly. The alcohol was giving me courage, and Madam Yok's words came back to me:

"You have to learn to act spoiled... All of them will lose to someone who knows how to beg."

"Why are you acting like this...? Do you want a house or a car?" Kinn took the cigarette out of his mouth and bent down to kiss the top of my head. I grabbed his waist in a loose hug and bit my lip as I figured out what I was going to say next.

"...I want you," I whispered.

Kinn stiffened for a moment, and my head slid down from his shoulder to his chest. I heard Kinn's heart beating wildly—just as frantically as mine—and I felt a little better. At least I was starting to get a handle on his feelings.

I looked up at Kinn through my eyelashes. "Kinn...let's go home."

He smiled, then stubbed out his cigarette and pulled away from my embrace.

"I'm not in the mood for partying anymore, either...but I *am* in the mood for something else." Kinn bent down to give me a chaste kiss. I nodded, my face flushing with heat as I watched Kinn go back inside the bar.

I rubbed at my face, not wanting to believe what I'd just done. That was mortifying! Why the fuck did I do that?! Fucking hell, Madam Yok!

I followed Kinn inside and said goodbye to my friends, who were having a blast dancing to the music. Before we left, Kinn entreated Pete to look after Tankhun. No one dared to ask why we were excusing ourselves early.

It was good that Kinn had driven his own car here, so no one had to drive us back. Madam Yok's words kept circling through my mind the entire way to the house. How shameless was I to have done something like that? Argh!

The closer we got to the house, the more anxious I became. Kinn made small talk, but I only had the presence of mind to answer part of the time. Thankfully, Kinn didn't pry.

"You're drunk, huh?" Kinn asked with a chuckle. When we got to his room, he went to pour me a glass of water. I stood there in the middle of the room for a while, my mind somewhat fuzzy. The next thing I knew, Kinn was holding up a glass in front of me.

"Mm-hmm... I'm dizzy," I said, looking at the water. I deliberated, then steeled myself and walked right up to Kinn. I leaned my head against his chest.

"What's up with you today?" Kinn asked, twisting around to put the water down on the table before encircling me in his arms.

"Why, don't you like it?" I asked, my voice muffled against his chest.

"I like it," Kinn rasped. "I like it so much my heart is racing."

I pulled away to loop my arms around his neck.

"Hmm...if you keep this up, you won't get to sleep tonight," said Kinn, kissing my cheek.

I let him do as he pleased as I tried to get my shit together. Was I really doing this? I looked up at him through my lashes and asked for something that I knew would surprise even him...

"Sing me a song," I said.

In truth, I wanted to buy some time to gather my courage. I'd heard Kinn's off-key singing a couple of times before, and it would probably help calm me down.

"If the top has a wandering eye, you must have him wrapped around your little finger—he needs to know he can't get what you have anywhere else."

Madam Yok's words kept coming back, echoing in my mind again and again. I'd already fallen for him—should I grow a pair and follow Madam Yok's advice...? What the fuck should I do?!

"What kind of mood are you in now?" Kinn asked, smiling.

"Please...please," I said, using my eyes to compel him.

"Mm... What song do you want me to sing?" Kinn laughed, and I smiled at him. *"Do you know that you're cute when you're drunk, Pachara? But I won't fall for a drunk, I don't want..."* [24]

His song made me laugh. I wasn't sure when he'd walked me to his bedroom, but the next thing I knew, we were standing at the foot of his bed. I leaned in to whisper softly in his ear, "You really don't want..."

As my voice faded away, Kinn pushed me down onto the bed, his body crashing into mine. He kissed me unrelentingly, his breath tinged with alcohol and cigarettes. A heady rush of arousal washed over me as I parted my lips for him, letting his hot tongue sweep into

---

24 Lyrics to ธารารัตน์ (Thararat) by Youngohm, with the name changed to Pachara (Porsche's given name).

my mouth. I nudged my tongue against his, our tongues twining together in turn.

I slowly unbuttoned Kinn's shirt before tugging it off, my hands wandering all over his body with passionate caresses.

"Mm!" I cried in protest when Kinn's teeth gently nipped at my tongue, but the pain mixed with pleasure felt amazing. He stripped off my shirt and trousers, baring me to him. His mouth didn't stop, licking and biting at my lips before he carefully nosed his way down to my jaw and the crook of my neck, breathing in deeply.

"K-Kinn," I called. His hands traveled from my sides down to my thighs, making me writhe in pleasure; I was worked up and sensitive from the alcohol.

Kinn moved his face from my neck to my chest, his hot tongue licking each nipple before his teeth scraped at my skin. He bit down hard, making my body jerk.

"*Ah!* Mmm..." I didn't even think about stopping him. I already had so many bite marks from Kinn all over my body—where they could be hidden by my clothes, of course. He sucked on my skin until I tingled all over. Then his hand moved to squeeze my cock in his fist.

I felt feverish, my entire body sweltering hot. Just the warmth from his hand was enough to make my heart skip a beat.

"Ah...*ah!*"

Kinn's lips moved lower until he reached my belly. He bit and licked hungrily at my abdomen, but before I lost myself to the pleasure, I remembered what Madam Yok had told me:

"You have to be the one taking action. Your best strategy is to use your mouth—if you use your mouth on him, I guarantee he'll become obsessed with you."

I looked at Kinn with half-lidded eyes as he lost himself in exploring my body. I swallowed nervously, then grabbed his shoulders and pulled him up for a kiss.

"Hmm..." Kinn hummed, his brow furrowing.

I licked into his mouth as I pushed myself up from the bed to flip us over, putting Kinn on his back.

"Wh-what are you—?" Kinn asked hoarsely when I pulled away from his mouth. I slowly began to lick and nip at his face.

"Mmm..." Kinn closed his eyes, receiving the touches I gave him. Although he still looked confused, he let me do as I pleased. I kissed my way downward to his nipple and did the same to him as he had done to me, sucking as hard as I could. Kinn lifted his head up to look at me and smiled, satisfied, before resting his head back on the bed. "Ah..."

I gathered my courage one last time, my tongue circling his stomach, before slowly moving down to the base of his cock. Kinn lifted his head up again before calling out my name in a trembling voice. "P-Porsche...nngh..."

I didn't wait for him to say anything else, running my tongue along the length of his shaft. Although my face burned and my heart raced, when I looked up to see Kinn biting his lip hard and throwing his head back in pleasure, I felt proud—and emboldened.

I used one hand to stroke Kinn's cock as I licked him from root to tip, circling the head until clear fluid leaked out. I sucked at the head of his dick with my lips, eliciting a groan from Kinn. As a man, I knew which spots to focus on. I'd never done this before, but I knew what *I* liked, so I focused on those parts. I knew sucking hard on the tip would drive him wild.

Kinn lifted his head up to look at me. "Oh, shit, I... I'm close... Wh-where did you learn this?" He stumbled over his words as he twisted and writhed. I hadn't thought I'd ever give someone a blow-job, but now I wanted to do it for Kinn—and only Kinn.

I pulled my mouth off his cock. "Do you like it?" I asked, pumping him with my hand.

"So much... It's so fucking good..."

I smiled, satisfied with his answer. I bent down to envelop him with my lips again. Although I couldn't take his entire length, I tried to move and bobbed up and down in a familiar motion.

"Ahhh, I'm not gonna last...*ah*," Kinn gasped. I pumped faster and sucked harder at the head, looking up into his eyes. He looked back at me and groaned.

"So sexy... Your rhythm... Ahh..." Kinn reached over to stroke my hair before gently gripping it and moving my head at his pace. I followed him easily, but Kinn kept bucking his hips up, forcing me to pull my mouth back quickly—otherwise I'd gag.

I coughed and spluttered. "Kinn!" I scolded him.

"Sorry, sorry!" he said with a smile.

I carefully moved back down to suck his cock. He tugged at my hair and moved me like before.

"Ah... Ohh... I can't... M'so close, my love," Kinn murmured, his sweet words making me feel warm all over. I kept moving my mouth as my cock throbbed with need. It felt so good, pleasing him like this.

Kinn sped up, making my mouth slide up and down his length, before his body tensed. I tried to back away, but his grip kept my head locked in place as tangy fluid filled my mouth. I swallowed in surprise before I pulled free from his hold and backed away, spitting out his come.

Kinn laughed at me. I smacked his abdomen as hard as I could. "You fucking bastard!" I yelped, wiping the mess away from the corner of my lips. It was so bitter!

It wasn't really *that* bad, almost pleasant, really, but it was completely unexpected! Shit! Why did that have to happen to me?

"Come here, then." Kinn pushed himself up to lean against the headboard and motioned for me to sit beside him. I glared at him but eventually relented, scooting close.

"Fucking asshole," I grumbled, still irritated.

Kinn gathered me in his arms and nuzzled my neck. "Hmm... you're good at that... How did you get that good?"

"...Never done it before," I muttered.

"Really? I loved it," he said, nudging me down onto the bed and crawling on top of me once more, a signal that it was now Kinn's turn to be in control of the game.

"K-Kinn... Hurry up, I'm uncomfortable," I breathed, my cock aching with want.

"You're driving me crazy... I'm already afraid for my heart, you know," Kinn mumbled. Although I could make out what he said, I wasn't in the right headspace to figure out what he meant.

I arched up into Kinn's touch, moaning without caring how loud I was. Kinn teased various parts of my body before he settled between my legs, spreading them apart as I canted my hips upward. Cold lube smeared against my hole as Kinn entered me with a skilled finger. Although I felt a little pain, it was soon replaced by pleasure.

"Can I fuck you raw...?" he asked. Kinn pushed his dick into my body, nudging the head inside little by little and thrusting shallowly. I frowned at the fullness in my ass.

"Ugh... Ah... K-Kinn," I moaned, biting my lip. I was already so full of his cock, but I wanted him to fuck me deeper, faster. Halfway inside, Kinn stopped moving, wiping the sweat off his face.

"Shit... Feels so fucking good to be inside you," Kinn gasped out, trying to steady his breathing. Without a condom, I could only imagine how hard it must be for him to restrain himself. I felt the intimate closeness of his cock pulsing inside of me and I almost came. It felt so different from the times we used a condom; every throbbing ache was amplified.

"K-Kinn, ah, *faster*," I begged him. I was afraid if we waited any longer, I wouldn't be able to bear it. Kinn pushed all the way in and set my body ablaze, hot and burning.

"Ah... If you can't hold on for long, I want more rounds tonight..." Kinn smiled before moving in and out, his hips setting a slow rhythm. He hit that spot inside of me until I trembled at the sensation.

"Kinn, I c-can't," I gasped. Kinn was acting differently this time, thrusting his hips while grasping my cock in his fist. He sped up until I writhed in pleasure that spread through every molecule of my body.

Kinn hissed in pleasure. "Inside...you... Mmm... I can't," he said, stumbling over his words. He pounded into me frantically until I swayed with the force of his thrusts. In mere moments, my body tensed and I came all over my stomach. Kinn kept thrusting for a few minutes longer before he, too, stiffened and came inside of me. I felt a warm, wet sensation in my ass.

"Ah... I...I'll help clean you up," Kinn rasped. My face heated up immediately. He plastered himself to my body and kissed my face as I lay there panting from exertion.

Kinn didn't let me rest for long. He flipped me over and started fucking me again. I didn't know how long this night would last, but I knew I was falling for him more each day.

What was I doing? Had I given my heart away too easily? Did Kinn feel the same way as me?

I really couldn't stop myself anymore.

"You're the one who sent those pictures to my brother, weren't you?!" Angry shouts echoed through a rental home in the suburbs.

"Please calm down, Mr. Mek."

"You're a pain in the ass, Big! Don't you know how painful it was for him? You should have let my brother forget!"

The shouting didn't stop. Mek was in a rage after finding out exactly who had been sending Tawan the pictures of his ex-lover's movements. Although over a year had passed since they broke up, the wound in his brother's heart had never healed. It pained him every time to see Tawan cry over Kinn, Mek's childhood friend and Tawan's first love.

"Mr. Mek... If you really want to help Mr. Tawan, shouldn't you help him get Mr. Kinn back?"

Mek didn't reply for a moment. "I know you like Kinn as well, Big. Why are you bringing my brother into this?"

"Please calm down, P'Mek. We can talk this through," said a new voice, addressing Mek. Mek turned to look at the tall figure, who was calmly smoking a cigarette.

"You're sick in the head," Mek snapped, with no care for the men standing in a line behind the taller man.

"I'm no different from your brother. Heh." His smirk enraged Mek even more.

"I'm telling you now, don't bring my brother into this!"

"Shouldn't you ask P'Tawan first, P'Mek? P'Tawan wants P'Kinn back...and I want Porsche. Isn't that a fair exchange?" the tall figure said, shrugging his shoulders.

Mek looked between the two men and cursed internally. One was the trusted subordinate of his friend, the other a slithering snake ready to strike at any moment. He'd known all along that these two were keeping secrets, but he didn't know how to warn his friend...

"Mr. Mek should go back and think on it."

Mek kicked the couch, knocking it over. The homeowner's men tried to hold him back but were stopped by their boss. Mek marched out of the house with a scowl, getting into his car and punching the steering wheel in frustration.

Soon, his phone rang.

"Yes, Phi?" Mek said, forcing his voice to return to normal.

"Did you go and meet them?"

"I just got out of there," Mek said.

"You have to help me, Mek."

"This should've ended a long time ago."

"It won't end easily," the voice on the other line pointed out.

"Phi... I don't want you in these troubled waters anymore," Mek said.

"You have to help me. If you don't, I'll have to deal with it myself."

"And when are you coming back to Thailand?" Mek asked.

"Now."

KinnPorsche 1

"**K**INN... KINN! KINN!" I called Kinn for the millionth time since he'd brought me here. We were going to get something to eat at the mall, but as soon as he parked his car, he just sat there staring blankly ahead for some reason. *If you didn't want to go out, then why did you agree to it?!*

"What is it?" Kinn turned to ask me, unbuckling his seatbelt.

"What's wrong with you?" I muttered. Kinn just sat there watching me, motionless. "Fine, what do you want to eat?" I changed the subject. I didn't want to bother him too much; these days, his awareness seemed to constantly drift in and out until he'd practically become a second Tankhun. Well, they *were* brothers, after all.

"What about you—what do you want to eat? You're the one who invited me out," Kinn said.

"Oh, uh, one second." I took out my phone and quickly opened LINE, texting the person responsible for encouraging me to do so many strange, confusing things.

PORSCHE: We're at the mall. What do I do next?
YOK: Go one round in the parking lot
PORSCHE: Are you crazy?! Give me actual suggestions
YOK: Ugh! Eat something, watch a movie, do karaoke
PORSCHE: Eat what?

YOK: Go to a restaurant. Whatever you want to eat, just
    take him there! Argh! Is he your top or mine?
PORSCHE: I told you, he's my bottom!
YOK: Hee hee

"So fucking annoying," I muttered quietly.

"Who are you talking to?" Kinn leaned over to look.

I quickly twisted my phone away from him. "Don't be nosy!"

"Hah..." Kinn raised his eyebrows. "When you invited me out, what did you want to eat?"

"I don't know. Let's just go in and see."

"Oh," Kinn said. I opened the car door and got out, irritated. I didn't know what I was unhappy about. What was I even doing?

Fuck! Everything Madam Yok told me to do was bullshit! If only I could go back in time to this morning and not read her LINE message...

[LINE, EARLIER THAT MORNING]

YOK: Oh! One more tip to hook your top. If you want him
    to really fall in love, you have to add sweetness to your
    life together.
PORSCHE: He's my bottom! Not my top!
YOK: Fine, fine. Do you still want to know?
PORSCHE: Yeah
YOK: lolololol you have to bring excitement into his daily
    life. Go to places he hasn't gone so he feels excited
    and challenged, like you've got depths for him to
    discover. Think "you make me feel like when I was

fourteen, when I had my first love"[25] or something
like that

PORSCHE: And why do I have to do that?

YOK: You looked stressed out. What, are you afraid he
won't love you or something?

PORSCHE: No. I don't feel anything

YOK: Yes, then whatever

PORSCHE: Wait, what you just said...explain

YOK: Hee hee ^_^

PORSCHE: I'm just asking for Tem, he seems worried

YOK: I know, but fine, I'll tell you. What's daily life like for
the two of you?

PORSCHE: He works all day

YOK: Where?

PORSCHE: In his room

YOK: So stuffy! Why don't you try taking him out. Go eat,
watch a movie, listen to music. Flirt like a Siam boy![26]

[PRESENT TIME]

"How the hell do you flirt like a Siam boy?" I muttered to myself,
pondering Madam Yok's advice as we walked. "And who the hell is
flirting? I'm not flirting!" I scratched my head so hard that Kinn,
who was walking beside me, had to turn to look at me in surprise.

"Are you ill?"

"No, no." I waved my hands. *Fuck! I'm not being myself at all! Shit,
Porsche, stop being weird!*

---

25 Song lyrics: 14 อีกครั้ง (14 Again) by Sek Loso.
26 Siam boy/girl: slang referring to upper middle-class teenagers and young adults who frequent
the Siam shopping district in central Bangkok.

"Fine, but you're acting a little strange." Kinn squinted at me in suspicion.

"Uh... Are you hungry?" I quickly tried to change the subject before Kinn could figure out what the hell was wrong with me.

"What about you? Do you have somewhere picked out?" Kinn asked.

"How hungry are you?"

"Not that hungry," Kinn said. "I ate this morning."

"Then let's see a movie." I pointed to the movie theater behind Kinn. He followed my finger, frowning.

"You want to watch a movie? All right." He led the way to see what movies were showing.

"Do you like going to the movies?" I asked, following him. I tilted my face to look at him, and he looked back at me with a bewildered expression.

"Are you okay, Porsche?" He brought the back of his hand up to feel my forehead.

"Mm-hm! I'm fine! So, do you go out to the movies?" I repeated my question to try and figure out whether this was going to be new and exciting for him or not.

"Not really, unless Tay drags me along," he answered.

So going to the movies was exciting and challenging for sure.

"Oh..."

"I've got a lot of work. Between classes and the business, I don't have the time. Even then, I don't like crowded places... Here, let's watch this one." Kinn pointed to a mafia movie with an average-looking leading actor. But I wasn't paying attention—my mind was trying to analyze the situation. *Is it challenging? He doesn't like movie theaters because of crowds...so...is it exciting? I'm confused!*

Kinn picked a movie with a showtime of fifteen minutes earlier, which meant we should be right on time for all the trailers to be over. We walked in without popcorn or drinks—Kinn said he was too lazy to hold them, and he wanted a lot of space—and I immediately understood what his plan was. When we got to our sofa seat, he leaned back and slowly closed his eyes, paying no attention to the sliver of the leading actor's face on the screen speaking the opening lines of the movie. Kinn was cut off from the world, with no respect for the protagonist currently running for his life in a narrow alleyway. I couldn't believe him!

"What is with you?" I grumbled quietly as Kinn softly snored. Our tickets were absurdly expensive, and we weren't making use of them at all! Kinn only came in here to nap without any distractions. Ugh...

"The main character isn't just funny-looking, he's dumb, too." I mumbled my complaints, trying to focus on the plot, but I kept getting distracted by Kinn. I stole glances at him as countless questions ran through my mind. I really tried to watch the movie for Kinn so he might get his money's worth, but before I knew it, half the movie had gone by.

As we neared the end, Kinn showed no sign of waking up. I didn't know if it was because the movie was at its climax or if I was just losing it, but I leaned in toward Kinn and cursed under my breath with all the frustration I had. "Argh! Are you excited at *all*?"

Kinn's eyes opened without warning and I immediately pushed away from him.

"Heh, do you want excitement?" he replied. I was horrified, but I tried to act casual.

"I-I was talking about the movie," I stuttered out.

"Really...? You keep looking at me. What's with you today?"

"Nothing... I'm just so invested in the story. I wanted someone to talk to, but you were asleep, so I had to talk to you while you were asleep..."

I wiped away the sweat forming on my skin. Although the theater was freezing, I could feel heat flashing through me as Kinn scooted over to hold my waist, one hand sneaking into my shirt to stroke my side.

"What are you doing?" I swatted his hand away and pushed off of him.

"Don't you want excitement?" Kinn said as he pulled me in. We hadn't put the armrest of the seat down between us when we sat down, so with one solid tug, Kinn pressed my face into his chest.

"Let go," I snapped, but Kinn didn't stop. His hand snaked up my shirt, higher and higher until he was groping and fondling my chest.

"Kinn!"

He sighed shakily and lowered his face to my neck, breathing in deeply.

"There's security cameras in here!" I said, trying to resist him—but I couldn't struggle too much.

Although there weren't many people here and there was no one else in our row of seats, what would happen if an usher came over with a flashlight?

"This is pretty exciting." Kinn chuckled and bent down to kiss my cheek, his hand still squeezing at me.

"I'm not joking, Kinn!" My voice hardened, making Kinn freeze for a moment. Motherfucker! Whoever was watching the security cameras had to be appalled to see two men shamelessly making out in the theater!

"Fine, fine, but you have to kiss me first." Kinn looked down at me and puckered his lips, hinting that I had to comply with his order.

"No!"

"Then I'm going to make you." Kinn nuzzled into my neck once more until I had to shrink back to avoid him.

"Let me go, you bastard!" I hissed. Kinn stopped, but lowered his face toward mine again.

"Kiss me first!" he said before puckering his lips ridiculously, ruining his serious, broody image. He looked so stupid like that.

He tried to lean in again, but this time, I hurriedly stopped him. "No!"

But I eventually relented. "Fine, fine, you bastard!"

Kinn stopped nosing at my neck and smiled, then puckered up again. *Fine! I'll close my eyes and get it over with. Quickly, so nobody sees. Plus, the camera might not catch us...*

I took a deep breath and gave him a peck on the lips.

"What was that? I didn't even feel it." Kinn looked dissatisfied and went in for another kiss. I didn't want to argue, so I pressed my lips to his once more. This time he grabbed the nape of my neck, pressing our lips together for a while until I started to struggle. Although he pulled away, he didn't forget to steal another kiss to my cheek before he set me free with a cheerful smile.

"Shit, Kinn!" I grumbled.

"Now *that* was exciting." Kinn laughed, then pretended to be distracted by the movie. I wanted to punch him in the face, but I was afraid that might be too much, so I settled for kicking his shin instead.

I sat there scowling at him. Although it *was* a little exciting like he said, he was being a blatant pervert. Did he not have *any* shame at all? People like him... Fuck!

It *was* kind of exciting and challenging, like Madam Yok said it would be... *Wait! Porsche, stop, what the hell are you thinking?!*

I tried to get myself under control for the remainder of the movie that I was now ignoring. After he woke up to annoy me, Kinn kept his eyes open to watch the movie for five minutes at most before going back to sleep. *I'm never going to see another movie with you, you shithead!*

When we got out of the theater, Kinn went back to putting on his aloof façade. When we were away from prying eyes—like when we were stuck in the forest—he'd show his playful side, but when people were around, he was a total dick. *Hah! I know all your tricks now, Kinn.*

"Are you hungry? You want some ice cream?" I asked, even though I didn't really like desserts that much. I only ever ate those damned chocolates at Kinn's house because I was hungry. I didn't know why I brought it up; maybe it was because I was thinking of Madam Yok's words: "add sweetness to your life together." Eating something sweet should do it.

"Sure." Kinn looked confused, but he followed my lead.

I took us into an ice cream parlor. The storefront was decorated with ponies, rainbows, and a giant teddy bear. It was so saccharine that it made me a little nervous—we didn't fit in at all. I looked like a crook, and Kinn looked like a politician on the campaign trail with his perfect posture. What a headache.

"Order whatever you want," Kinn said, crossing his legs and sliding the menu over to me like a wealthy benefactor treating his sugar baby out on the town.

"I don't know how to order something like this," I said, flicking through the menu and passing it back to Kinn.

"I'm not familiar with it either." Kinn passed the menu back to me. I went still, considering my options. *Does Kinn not like sweet stuff? What do I do now?!*

"What should we get?" I asked, opening the menu again. I randomly pointed to a sundae. "Let's order this one." It looked quite colorful, with horse-shaped cookies and sprinkles. *Fuck it, this should be sweet enough!*

"What would you like to drink?" our server asked with a smile.

"Kinn, what do you want?"

"Water."

"Just water, please," I said, handing the menu back. I sighed. *Fuck! Why did I believe every word Madam Yok said to me?*

"You like stuff like this?" Kinn asked, glancing around. I shook my head.

"No."

"What?! Then why did you invite me here?" Kinn squinted at me.

"I dunno. I saw the big teddy bear." I randomly pointed to the teddy bear outside. Our water showed up, so Kinn took a drink and smiled. *What is it, asshole? Is there something on my face?!*

Not long after, our ice cream was served. It came in a giant, gaudy-looking bowl. Why were there so many sparkly decorations? It was so fancy, I was afraid to eat it!

"Go on," Kinn said, looking just as shocked as me. The large sundae was decorated like a carousel, with horse-shaped animal crackers and cotton candy around the edges. Glittery sugar in a variety of colors sparkled in the light. The ice cream making up the base came in so many different hues that I had no idea what I was looking at.

"You have to eat with me," I said, hesitantly taking a spoonful of ice cream.

"I don't even know where to start." Kinn used his spoon to contemplatively tap at the chocolate carousel top before taking a tiny piece.

"How is it?" I asked, spoon still in my hand.

"I don't think this is my style." Kinn put down his spoon, so I tried some, too... Ugh, it wasn't my style either, because it was way too fucking sweet. It was so cloying I could barely swallow it. Shit! This place was a bust ever since we came in. I didn't know what spirit tricked me into picking out this joint! If anyone from the Major Clan saw us with this damned bowl, they probably wouldn't believe their eyes.

I didn't want it to go to waste, though. I forced myself to eat four or five more bites. And it was so fucking expensive, too. Should I bring some back to Chay? It didn't taste good, but at least it looked nice.

While I sucked on my spoon, deciding where else I should take a bite from, my gaze wandered outside and landed on a sign that read "Game Center." I saw several couples playing with claw machines, and I wondered if Kinn would think that was new and exciting. *Has someone like him ever played a claw game?*

"I'm done," I announced, putting down my spoon. Kinn looked up from his phone and nodded, calling someone over to get the bill.

"So, what's next on the program?" Kinn asked with a smile.

"What program?" I said, not understanding what he meant. "I want a stuffed animal." I pointed to the arcade machines, which made Kinn laugh, but he led the way there.

I walked down the line of machines, looking for one that I wanted to play. To be honest, I really liked these things. I'd always wanted to go to Japan someday and play crane games all over Tokyo. People said it was easier to win prizes there than in Thailand.

Kinn went to exchange his money and came back with his hands full of coins. "Which one do you want?"

"Do you know how to play?" I asked him condescendingly. He didn't look like he played these types of games. Although we were close in age, he always acted like an old man.

"I'm a master at this, didn't you know?" Kinn said. Without further preamble, he inserted a coin and prepared to show off his godly skills. When the machine started up, I couldn't help but get excited, too.

...Not only did Kinn fail to grab anything, he didn't even aim it right! This fucker!

"It's the first round! You never win the first round," Kinn said, still relaxed. He inserted another coin for a second try, but...

"What are you doing?! You have to aim right before you press the button!" I crossed my arms and circled the machine, analyzing it.

"I have to focus!" Kinn fidgeted, pushing up his sleeves and trying again.

"You can take your time before you press the button... Oh, what are you doing?!" I groused.

Kinn started to huff and puff, no longer upholding his stoic image. The game got more and more serious until ten rounds went by. Kinn scratched his head in frustration.

"Fucking hell! This machine is rigged! I was aiming perfectly!"

"Aiming perfectly, my ass! I told you to wait before pressing the button! Can't you see the claw can spin?!" I snapped.

Kinn's anger was apparent now, and he stomped off to start another claw game. I lost count of how many games we played, but Kinn took out a thousand baht note and went to get more coins. Both of us circled the machine like it was a matter of life or death.

"Move left, left. I said left!" I shouted at him, looking up and down from the other side of the machine.

"I'm moving left! If I go any further, I'll miss it!"

"Then move back! Back! You're going forward, Kinn!" I put my hands on my hips, glaring at him in exasperation.

"I'm trying to focus! If you're so good, why don't you do it yourself?!" Kinn shouted, just as heated as me.

"Fine! It's because you're dumb. I told you to move backward! Look! This is back!" I shouted. We'd been bickering for more than an hour, but Kinn wasn't giving up easily. He kept going back to exchange more money for more coins. And neither of us managed to win even one stuffed animal!

I pulled at my hair. "Argh! I can't take it anymore!" Fuck, I couldn't even get one stupid prize!

"If you're so bad at it, just *buy* one!" Kinn shouted at me.

"Someone like you has always had it easy, huh?" I shouted back. "You don't know what *trying* is!"

"If you add up all the coins we put in, you could buy a hundred of these things!"

"And if you buy them, then there's nothing to be proud of! You can drown in your defeat and keep throwing money at it—I'm not playing anymore! I'm going home!" I marched out, angrier than I'd ever been. Nothing had gone to plan today, so of course I was frustrated—plus, I had a loudmouth like Kinn ordering me around. It drove me batshit watching him try to prove that he was good at everything when he obviously wasn't! *Argh!*

If anyone knew I was getting so worked up over a claw machine, they'd probably pity me... Why did I get so frustrated over something so dumb? Kill me!

I walked ahead of Kinn all the way to the car. As soon as he unlocked my door, I slumped into the seat. It was over, it was all over!

Not only did I have no idea what I was doing, I didn't know how I wanted Kinn to feel around me. Excited, challenged, eager to discover the depths of my personality...? Right now, all I wanted was for him to be happy.

When Kinn got in, he was silent for a moment before he said, "I'm sorry."

I tried to calm down, not saying anything.

"Sorry," Kinn sighed, pulling my head toward him. "I'll do better on our next date."

My head snapped up to look at him. "What *date*?!"

"I knew you were trying to take me out on a date... I screwed up. I took it too seriously. The machine was rigged, I couldn't grab anything, and I got angry." Kinn stroked my cheek gently.

"What are you talking about? I didn't—"

Kinn pressed his lips to mine before I could finish my sentence.

"Next time, I'll take you somewhere nicer. And more fun," Kinn promised. Both of his hands stroked my cheeks as he continued to press gentle kisses to my lips.

"But I don't want claw machines or ice cream again... No movies, either," I said, frowning. Kinn laughed and pulled me in for a hug.

I didn't know why I'd done any of this today or why I listened to Madam Yok's advice in the first place, but I liked myself when I was with Kinn. I didn't have to hold back my emotions, and even if Kinn yelled back at me, he always made up for it in the end.

And I liked it when Kinn had to lower his voice with me, like he knew that he lost and I won. I felt kinda vindicated, heh.

CHARACTER
&
NAME GUIDE

Characters

The identity of certain characters may be a spoiler; use this guide with caution on your first read of the novel.

MAIN CHARACTERS

'Kinn' Anakinn Theerapanyakul

GIVEN NAME: A-na-kinn
NICKNAME: Kinn
SURNAME: Thee-ra-pan-ya-kul

The second son and de facto heir of a notorious mafia family. Has a habit of getting rough with his partners.

'Porsche' Pachara Kittisawasd

GIVEN NAME: Pa-cha-ra
NICKNAME: Porsche
SURNAME: Kit-ti-sa-wasd

A normal college student who is extremely skilled at martial arts. Since their parents died, he takes care of his younger brother.

SUPPORTING CHARACTERS

'PORCHAY' PITCHAYA KITTISAWASD: Porsche's beloved younger brother.

UNCLE THEE: The younger brother of Porsche's late father. Has a severe gambling problem.

TEM AND JOM: Porsche's best friends and fellow university students.

MADAM YOK: Porsche's former employer and owner of the Root Club.

KORN THEERAPANYAKUL: Kinn's father and the current head of the main branch of the Theerapanyakul mafia family, aka the Major Clan.

'KHUN' TANKHUN THEERAPANYAKUL: Kinn's eldest brother.

'KIM' KIMHAN THEERAPANYAKUL: Kinn's youngest brother.

'VEGAS' KORAWIT THEERAPANYAKUL: The eldest son of the Minor Clan.

'MACAU': The youngest son of the Minor Clan.

ZEK-KANT: Korn's younger brother and head of the Minor Clan.

TAY AND TIME: Kinn's friends.

'BIG': Kinn's former lead bodyguard, before Porsche took over his position.

'PETE': Tankhun's lead bodyguard, who temporarily switched positions with Porsche.

'POL', 'P'JESS' AND 'ARM': Tankhun's other bodyguards.

'NONT': Kim's lead bodyguard.

'CHAN': Korn's secretary.

TAWAN: Kinn's ex-boyfriend.

MEK: Tawan's younger brother and a friend of Kinn's from high school.

Names Guide

Thai names follow the western pattern of a given name followed by a family name. Thais are also given a nickname, which is more commonly used when Thais refer to their family, friends, and close acquaintances in their daily life. Thai nicknames can be anything the parents find appealing, a nickname their friends prefer to call them, or even nonsensical words in foreign languages.

In Thailand, it is unusual for people to use someone's surname in casual conversation, unless specifically required. To formally refer to a person, given names are preferred.

Thai honorifics

P'/PHI (IPA pronounciation: /pʰiː˩˦/): A gender-neutral honorific term used to address older siblings, friends, and acquaintances. It can be used as a prefix (P'[name]), a pronoun, or informally used to address unknown people (e.g. store clerks, or shopkeepers).

N'/NONG (IPA pronounciation: /nɔːŋ˩˦/): Used to address younger people, in the same manner as "Phi."

Teochew honorifics

The Thai Chinese are the largest minority group in Thailand, integrated through several waves of immigration. Of these, just over half are Teochew, from the Chaoshan region. Families with Teochew roots may still occasionally use the Teochew dialect, especially when referring to other family members. Some of the terms that appear in this novel are as follows:

HIA: Elder brother
BE: Older brother of one's father
ZEK: Younger brother of one's father
GOU: Older or younger sister of one's father
AGONG: Grandfather